DATE DUE

~~AP 1 6 '97~~			
~~JY 7 '97~~			
~~AG 1 '97~~			
~~SE 15 '97~~			
~~MY 4 '98~~	18		
~~NO 30 '98~~			
~~DE 1 '00~~			
~~JE 8 '05~~			

DEMCO 38-296

Two
Crowns
for
America

Two
Crowns
for
America

Katherine Kurtz

Bantam Books
NEW YORK • TORONTO • LONDON
SYDNEY • AUCKLAND

TWO CROWNS FOR AMERICA
A Bantam Spectra Book / February 1996

SPECTRA and the portrayal of a boxed "s" are trademarks of Bantam Books, a division of Bantam Doubleday Dell Publishing Group, Inc.

Library of Congress Cataloging-in-Publication Data
Kurtz, Katherine.
Two crowns for America / by Katherine Kurtz.
p.   cm.
ISBN 0-553-07562-4
1. United States—History—Revolution, 1775–1783—Fiction.
2. Washington, George, 1732–1799—Fiction.   I. Title.
PS3561.U69T87   1996
813'.54—dc20   95-32372
                                                              CIP

Published simultaneously in the United States and Canada

Bantam Books are published by Bantam Books, a division of Bantam Doubleday Dell Publishing Group, Inc. Its trademark, consisting of the words "Bantam Books" and the portrayal of a rooster, is Registered in U.S. Patent and Trademark Office and in other countries. Marca Registrada. Bantam Books, 1540 Broadway, New York, New York 10036.

PRINTED IN THE UNITED STATES OF AMERICA

BVG   10 9 8 7 6 5 4 3 2 1

Dedicated to
the Brotherhood of Freemasonry,
under the All-Seeing Eye,
whose Brethren helped shape America's destiny.
Present at the creation. . . .

Prologue

In the midnight fastness of a secluded estate in northern Germany, a solitary man sat before a blackened mirror and, by the light of a single candle, watched incense smoke roil across the surface of the polished glass. He had made his preparations, drunk the elixir that gave him the far vision; now he quested outward with mind and spirit, seeking the man whom destiny called to wear a victor's laurel, and perhaps a crown.

It was March of 1775, and Europe was in growing turmoil; but the man the Master sought had never set foot in the Master's world. Born some forty-three years before, in a land named for a virgin queen, the man had spent his life to date in preparation for a very special destiny, little though he knew it.

But the Master knew. The name of the man whose image even now was forming in the blackened mirror would soon be on the lips of thousands, both in blessing and in curse. The Master's gaze sharpened as the scene began to unfold before his dark eyes, and he leaned a little closer, setting elegant, beringed hands lightly on either side of the mirror to steady it. Two men now could be seen, one of them personally known to the Master and presently in disfavor; but it was the other on whom the Master fixed his full concentration.

Slowly the image steadied—of a tall, commanding figure in a black tricorn and a full-cut black cloak with shoulder capelets, striding across a muddy yard toward a brown-clad, slightly younger man holding a pair of horses. Behind him could be seen several other cloaked men, of whom he had just taken his leave. A black ribbon tied back unpowdered reddish hair from a noble face.

Well-muddied boots with spurs showed below fawn-colored breeches as he set one toe in the stirrup the other man held and swung up easily on a tall, rangy gray. The gloved hands that gathered up the reins were big, almost a little awkward, the thighs gripping the gray's sides thick and powerful. A silver-hilted small-sword hung at his left side, just visible beneath the cloak he settled over the horse's rump.

"Where next, Colonel?" the other man asked, mounting up on a sturdy bay. "Back to Mount Vernon, or do you wish to press on to Alexandria?"

"Mount Vernon, Doctor," the colonel replied. "The weather appears to be worsening. I intended to drill Captain Westcott's militia, but we'll make a fresh start in the morning."

The horses picked their way daintily across the muddy yard and moved out smartly as they gained the road, heading east at a ground-eating trot. Dirty snow still edged the road to either side, hard-crusted where it had thawed and refrozen repeatedly in the past week, and ice still rimmed some of the puddles pocking the road itself. The men jammed hats more closely over foreheads and hunched deeper into cloaks as they rode, for the wind was sharp, and growing colder.

As soon as a long, straight stretch presented itself, the pair exchanged confirming glances and set spurs to their mounts, anxious to reach shelter before the rain began. The horses were fresh and eager, their easy canter soon shifting to a flatter gallop—until suddenly the big gray stumbled.

So quickly was destiny set in train. Though the gray's rider tried valiantly to collect his mount, he knew from the first misstep that all his skill could not prevent the fall that was coming for them both. As if time had slowed, he felt himself catapulted from the

saddle, tumbling over the animal's shoulder, past flailing hooves, to land hard, flat on his back.

For a few breathless heartbeats, everything went utterly black. Then, through a haze of urgency that began slowly to draw him back to painful consciousness, he became aware of the dream that would haunt him for years to come.

He was standing in the doorway of a candlelit room, the apron of a Freemason girt about his waist. The place was none that he had ever seen before, but by its furnishings he could entertain no doubt that it was, indeed, intended as a Lodge of Freemasonry.

But it was no Lodge where he had ever sat. Far at the other end of the room, a black-clad man presided as Master, somehow both known and unknown; and though some of the other brethren in the room seemed vaguely familiar, the colonel could not quite seem to pin identities on any of them.

A Bible lay open on a small table before the Master's chair, as must always be present in any proper Lodge, with a square and compasses set atop it; but it was another, smaller Bible before which the colonel found himself kneeling, to lay both hands upon it in reverence. The binding was distinctive, with corners and clasps fashioned of silver gilt. The words of the obligation he swore were wholly acceptable, yet somehow beyond his present comprehension, as his stunned mind reeled from the force of his fall and a part of his body began insisting that he really ought to breathe.

There was more, all in a tangled and blurred rush of images, admonitions, instructions: a flagon of oil from which someone anointed his forehead; a wreath of laurel leaves laid upon his brow by a white-clad woman who should not have been in a Lodge of Freemasonry but somehow belonged in this one; his sword—and another sword—and something done between the two of them, so that by the time his own was laid back in his hands, he knew that it was somehow—changed.

Then he was fighting his way back to consciousness in earnest, gulping raggedly for breath and struggling to sit up as strong arms supported him behind the shoulders and a faraway voice called his name and counseled slow, deep breaths.

"Easy, Colonel. It's Ramsay. You'll be fine when you've caught your breath. You've had a nasty fall."

The face he saw, as he managed to open his eyes, belonged to the voice. It was long familiar, and he almost thought it had been in the dream.

But even as he found himself able to breathe again, and the world stopped reeling, memory of the dream began slipping away, so that by the time he could speak, he was not sure of any of it at all—except that, against all logic, one hand was clenched quite determinedly around the hilt of his sword. . . .

Smiling, the Master sat back from his mirror, watching the man named Ramsay help the other one to his feet. When they had remounted and were on their way again, he let the images fade from the mirror, drew two sheets of paper before him, and began simultaneously to write upon each.

Dear Dr. Ramsay, the first one began. And the second: *My dear Chevalier* . . .

Chapter One

An American rebellion was coming. That fact was as certain as Andrew Wallace's presence in Philadelphia's statehouse, sitting as an observer in the gallery and waiting for the Second Continental Congress to commission a Commander in Chief. It was the fourth such rebellion against Hanoverian presumption in which Andrew had been involved, and he thought it the one most likely to succeed, if only for having its roots embedded in process of law rather than military reaction.

He had been a lad of ten the first time, in 1715, when supporters of James Stuart, the de jure King James III of England and VIII of Scotland, raised the royal standard at Braemar, attempting to restore him to the throne lately occupied by his usurping half sister, Queen Anne. The Elector of Hanover was but recently come to the united Crown of England, Scotland, and Ireland, and still uncertain on his throne; but his armies were certain enough to repulse a would-be Stuart restoration. In that ill-fated conflict, Andrew had been a drummer boy, his father a piper to the Earl of Mar. An uncle had fallen at Sheriffmuir, and Andrew and his father only barely escaped with their lives.

A lesser renewal of the attempt in 1719 was no more successful. Andrew had taken a musket ball in the leg this time, running dis-

patches for the brother of the Earl Marischal at Glenshiel. He had been lucky at that, for his father was killed. King James, who had spent less than six weeks in Scotland during the Fifteen, did not even manage to set foot on Scottish soil four years later. Afterward, when the dust had settled, a cautious but still idealistic Andrew Wallace had read law at the University of Edinburgh, adopting protective coloration to survive in a political climate increasingly unacceptable to those whose loyalties remained with Scotland's rightful royal House.

Then had come the Forty-Five, with all its rekindled hopes of a Stuart restoration at last. After thirty years in exile, the hopeful young king of 1715 and 1719 was no longer young or even very hopeful, so his claim was advanced by his eldest son, the dashing Prince Charles Edward Stuart, known thereafter in romantic legend as Bonnie Prince Charlie.

That rebellion had cost Andrew two brothers and an eye and had eventually seen him transported to the Massachusetts Bay Colony with hundreds of others—and very fortunate to have escaped execution. The venture certainly had ended any further career in the law, for a man found guilty of rebellion against his "lawful" king and transported into exile could hardly expect to continue serving the laws of that king.

Nonetheless, the Forty-Five had occasioned an enduring personal acquaintance with the prince for whose line the Wallace family had sacrificed so much. Andrew had met the prince when the royal standard was raised at Glenfinnan and remained with him until Culloden, becoming one of his principal agents in the American colonies in the years to come.

He remained a key leader of the Jacobite underground in the New World—whose colonies now stood on the brink of rebellion against the same Hanoverian line that had usurped the Stuart crown more than half a century before. Many of that underground saw the coming American storm as a possible vehicle for a Stuart restoration in the New World—or at very least, a diversion of British attention and vital resources from the Old, so that a renewed attempt might be launched again in Scotland. A faction calling themselves the Bostonians were eager to entice Charles Ed-

ward Stuart to come in person to America and become the focal point for such a venture. One of those Bostonians, Dr. James Ramsay, was seated across the room beside one of the Massachusetts delegates.

But what Ramsay desired had little to do with what was unfolding here today in Philadelphia's statehouse. Forces far larger than James Ramsay were tinkering with Stuart destiny—and with the destiny of the American colonies. Andrew was an agent of those forces, as well as of Charles Edward Stuart, and believed those forces to be utterly benign; but he was not yet privy to as much of the total picture as he would have liked.

Sighing, he cast his one-eyed gaze over the assembly, only half listening as President Hancock fielded a question concerning funds that must be raised to provision the newly adopted Continental Army, formed from the Massachusetts provincial militia units now surrounding British-occupied Boston. Financing was always of critical importance in any war effort, but it was not at all what most of the men there today had come to hear about. Curbing his impatience, Andrew braced himself against his silver-headed walking stick and shifted position, stretching his left leg under the bench ahead of him to ease a stiff muscle.

In truth, his physical condition was commendable for a man of seventy. He certainly did not look his age. His old wound from the Nineteen still gave him twinges if he sat too long or walked too far, but the use of a walking stick could be as much a fashion affectation as a necessity for mobility. Andrew's stick fulfilled both functions, and several others as well, for it concealed a sword blade in its length; and the heavy silver head concealed other things, as did Andrew himself.

Not that anything in his appearance suggested concealment—rather, tasteful prosperity. As was his usual wont on important occasions, he was turned out in a mole-gray coat and waistcoat of discriminating cut, with white breeches and stockings, silver buckles on his shoes, immaculate white linen at his throat, and a black velvet patch over his bad eye. Unlike most of the gentlemen sitting in the statehouse chamber, he had no need to powder his hair, for age had done that long ago—though happily sparing the hair itself,

which was caught neatly at the nape of his neck with a ribbon of black moire silk.

In other places he might also have worn the dark-green riband of the Order of the Thistle, Scotland's highest order of chivalry, which his prince had bestowed upon him privately, years before, as a mark of his gratitude. Instead, as was his usual wont, he contented himself today with a twist of green silk ribbon in one buttonhole and a white cockade on his hat, which to most folk simply betokened an old man's romantic adherence to a long-lost cause. His Jacobite colleagues still referred to him as the Chevalier Wallace, in courteous recognition that he had personally served the prince during the Forty-Five, but only a few of them knew how fully he continued that service to this day.

But just now, the birth of the new rebellion was of far more immediate import than any long-ago accolade of a Stuart prince. What the gentlemen gathered here in Philadelphia's statehouse did not yet know was that the time for action suddenly had approached much nearer than they had thought—and Andrew dared not be the one to tell them of it.

He himself had been told in a dream, three nights before, by a beloved friend he knew he would never see again in this life. He had been dozing in front of the fire in his room at a nearby inn, digesting an indifferent meal, when suddenly the sounds around him had receded, an eerie silence pervading the room like fog wrapping itself around a sleeping town.

All at once a figure had materialized beside the fireplace, leaning one elbow on the mantel and gazing down at him a little sadly. The eyes were bright and very blue, but the handsome, aristocratic face looked ashen, the tie wig a little disheveled—not the usual fastidious appearance of the man of Andrew's acquaintance.

But his identity was unmistakable. Andrew had dined with the man before leaving Cambridge for Philadelphia. He knew the white-fringed waistcoat laced with silver, the light-blue coat with sprigged buttons, the ruffled shirt, the white satin breeches with silver loops—festive attire bought for a wedding that now would never take place. It was Joseph Warren who stood before him: physician and poet, beloved patriot leader, President of the Provin-

cial Congress and the Boston Committee of Safety, and Grand Master of the Masonic Grand Lodge of Massachusetts.

For a moment their eyes met. Andrew's tongue seemed to cleave to the roof of his mouth. But then Warren very slowly and deliberately made him the recognition sign of a Master Mason.

"Grand Master?" Andrew had murmured almost disbelievingly, struggling stiffly to rise, but then subsiding at Warren's gesture. "Grand Master, is it truly you?"

"Aye, but Grand Master no more, dear friend. Only and ever your Brother in the Craft. I have come to take my leave of you."

"Dear Joseph . . ."

"I may not tarry long," Warren interrupted, quiet but emphatic. "I have come to tell you of a great battle fought today on the Charleston peninsula, for possession of a fortified height called Breed's Hill. Twice the British advanced on our position, and twice were repelled. But for a want of powder, we might have held them a third time. Even so, it cost them dear."

"Our cost was dear as well, if *your* life was part of it," Andrew whispered, shaking his head.

Warren had laughed softly at that—a charming, gentle little chuckle that pulled at Andrew's heart.

"Dear friend, I am well content that my life should have been offered upon the altar of Liberty. British losses were nearly three times our own, even though they outnumbered us by half again. I count such outcome worth the cost. *Dulce et decorum est pro patria mori.*"

"No!" Andrew said defiantly. "I have seen too many men die for their country. What is sweet or glorious about the carnage of battle?"

"In life I would not have argued that point," Warren said quietly. "Certainly not as a physician, called upon to mend the bodies broken by war. Nonetheless, each death serves its purpose in the Plan of the Great Architect. Of that I can assure you."

"Can you?"

"I can. Today the British learned that men of the New World wage a different kind of war than the Old World knows. In the months and perhaps years to come, they will hesitate because of

what happened at Breed's Hill. And American soldiers learned today that they *can* stand against British Regulars."

"*You* were not able to stand."

"No, I fell," Warren said simply. "It was my time. And now it is
my time to go. Farewell, Brother Andrew. I leave you with my
undying affection and my fraternal blessing. Pray, remember me."

The shadowy figure was already fading, even as Andrew reached
out in wordless entreaty to bid him stay. He had come to himself in
a room suddenly gone cold, the fire spent, his hand still lifted in
the Masonic Sign of Grieving.

Nor might that grieving yet be shared beyond a scant handful of
intimates whose discretion was absolute, for express riders still had
not reached Philadelphia with news of the battle—and would not,
for several more days. Few would be surprised to learn that a battle
had taken place in Boston—indeed, any of a number of the men
sitting in the Continental Congress might have predicted it, especially after Concord and Lexington, two months before—but certain knowledge, so quickly and by such means, was another matter.

Andrew's highland ancestors might have known and honored the
gift of Second Sight in centuries now past, but the New World was
suspicious of such phenomena. The time still was not so long past
since others possessing far lesser gifts had been burned for their
differences, not so very far from his own Cambridge. Andrew himself believed that whatever powers he and his possessed came from
God, but there were those who would disagree. Indeed, some of
the men assembled here did not even believe in the traditional
Christian God, though most at least embraced a God of natural
order. His brethren in Freemasonry referred to this Supreme Being as The Great Architect of the Universe—which was as good a
name as any, Andrew supposed.

In that, at least, Andrew shared a common bond with most of the
men in the room, including the one about to be commissioned
Commander in Chief. George Washington had been a Freemason
for more than twenty years. Andrew's son Simon, sitting directly
behind the great man, had been one nearly as long—and other
things besides. The Masonic Brotherhood was well represented in
the New World.

Indeed, it largely had been Freemasons—Simon among them—
who had precipitated colonial resistance some two years before,
when Paul Revere, Junior Warden of his Lodge in Boston, had led
the Sons of Liberty in what soon became known as the Boston Tea
Party. Somewhat surprisingly at the time, the usually stolid Washington had referred to the tea coming in under heavy English tax as
"gunpowder tea." When asked why he had called it so, he had
replied that he feared it would prove inflammable and produce an
explosion that would shake both countries. In retrospect, Andrew
had to wonder whether it had been a mere turn of phrase or a flash
of prescience.

Remembering the now famous tea escapade, Andrew briefly allowed his fond gaze to rest on his son, today wearing a scarlet-
faced blue militia uniform similar to Washington's, with major's
epaulets on the shoulders. It was not only the bond of Freemasonry
that Simon and the incipient Commander in Chief shared. Like
young Colonel Washington of Virginia, an even younger Simon
Wallace had served under British officers in the French and Indian
War, gaining valuable experience for the task ahead. Neither had
practiced war in the intervening years, but both now were ready to
take up their swords again.

The two had renewed their acquaintance the previous year at the
First Continental Congress, where Washington had represented
Virginia and Simon had served as secretary to one of the members
of the Massachusetts delegation. The friendship had flourished
since then, with the result that Simon expected to be named to the
General's personal staff—which suited Andrew very well, since the
gentleman from Virginia figured in their plans.

But Washington must not know that—nor, indeed, any of the
colonial leaders save those also committed to the Vision that inspired Andrew and his kin. Patriot leaders intent on slipping the
yoke of British government would not look kindly upon other reins
of guidance already well in place in the New World, regardless of
how benign that guidance might be. Andrew's superiors did not
intend to impose their direction on the fledgling nation now
aborning in the New World, but at least the opportunity to accept
or reject must be offered. Or so Andrew had been instructed.

He returned his gaze to the podium as Hancock paused and shuffled some papers. Beside Andrew a black-haired young man in the scarlet and buff of Massachusetts's Independent Company of Cadets slipped onto the end of the bench and gave him a grin of anticipation—Justin Carmichael, the brother of Simon's wife, twenty-two years old and destined for important things. Justin's father had been a Scottish Jacobite, his mother a French one, and Justin and his sister Arabella had inherited the fire and ardent loyalties of both. Just now Justin's hero of the hour was the man about to be commissioned Commander in Chief.

An expectant hush rippled through the packed statehouse as Hancock cleared his throat importantly. The document in his hand had been unanimously approved by Congress the day before. He had sought the nomination as Commander in Chief for himself, but now he declared the appointment of another with grace and dignity.

"In Congress," he read. "The delegates of the United Colonies of New Hampshire, Massachusetts Bay, Rhode Island, Connecticut, New York, New Jersey, Pennsylvania, New Castle, Kent, and Sussex on Delaware, Maryland, Virginia, North Carolina, and South Carolina to George Washington Esquire."

Washington slowly rose as his name was read out, removing his hat and bowing slightly to Hancock as the president of Congress continued.

"We, reposing especial trust and confidence in your patriotism, conduct, and fidelity, do by these presents constitute and appoint you to be General and Commander in Chief of the army of the United Colonies and of all the forces raised or to be raised by them and of all others who shall voluntarily offer their service and join the said army for the defense of American liberty and for repelling every hostile invasion thereof. And you are hereby vested with full power and authority to act as you shall think for the good and welfare of the service.

"And we do hereby strictly charge and require all officers and soldiers under your command to be obedient to your orders and diligent in the exercise of their several duties.

"And we do also enjoin and require you to be careful in execut-

ing the great trust reposed in you by causing strict discipline and
order to be observed in the army. . . ."

As Hancock continued reading, the man who was the subject of
the document stood quietly and with head bowed as he listened to
the charge laid upon him by his associates. As had been customary
during his tenure as a delegate from his native Virginia, he wore
the uniform of his service in the French and Indian War of nearly
twenty years before: blue coat faced with red and edged with narrow gold lace—though the breeches and waistcoat, formerly of
scarlet, had been replaced by buff. He wore a black silk military
stock close round his throat, but he had set aside the gilded brass
gorget that formerly had signified his rank as a Virginia colonel.
Today he stood before them devoid of any emblem of rank save a
gentleman's silver-hilted smallsword at his left side.

Not that any further accoutrement was necessary. Even had he
not stood a solid six feet two inches, in a day when six-footers were
a rarity, by his sheer physical presence he would have dominated
any gathering of which he was a part. He was large-boned and
heavy of waist and thighs, though narrow of chest and shoulders,
with big hands and feet that, at rest, suggested the gawky. Yet in
motion, especially astride a horse, he moved with astonishing
grace. Indeed, most reckoned him the finest horseman of his age.

Today, however, he did not sit astride a horse, but stood with
buckled shoes planted firmly on the statehouse floor, big hands
fingering his black tricorn with a slightly nervous gesture, gray-
blue eyes averted beneath the tied and powdered hair.

". . . this commission to continue in force until revoked by this
or a future Congress.

"Dated Philadelphia, June 19, 1775. By Order of the Congress—John Hancock, President. Attest: Charles Thomson, Secretary." Hancock lowered the document and made a little bow.
"General Washington, may I be the first to offer you congratulations on your new command."

The eyes of his subject had lifted as Hancock finished reading,
and flinched just a little as the assembled delegates broke into
spontaneous applause and came to their feet in respect. Andrew
almost pitied the man who took the commission from Hancock's

hands, for he knew the new general's very real disquiet when nomi-
nated to the position less than a week before. Indeed, as John
Adams's intention became clear, when lodging the nomination,
Washington had slipped quietly out of the room. He had not
sought the command—indeed, had supported the nomination of
General Artemas Ward, presently commanding the forces outside
Boston.

"Mr. President," he had read to Congress in a halting, rather
high voice, in the acceptance speech that followed his unanimous
election, "though I am truly sensible of the high honor done me in
this appointment, yet I feel great distress from a consciousness that
my abilities and military experience may not be equal to the exten-
sive and important trust. However, as the Congress desires, I will
enter upon the momentous duty and exert every power I possess in
their service for the support of the glorious cause. I beg they will
accept my most cordial thanks for this distinguished testimony of
their approbation."

He had meant what he said—of both his gratitude and his distress at being handed such a responsibility. Whether most in the
chamber realized how firmly Washington meant it was another
matter. Andrew felt confident that the new general was equal to the
task—if any American was—but only time would reveal whether
that faith was justified.

Just now, however, the Congress appeared to have no doubts.
The applause and the cheering went on for long minutes as the
new Commander in Chief began shaking hands with the men who
had elected him: first Hancock, who had handed over his commission—and had wanted the position for himself; then John Adams,
who had nominated him; fellow Virginian Patrick Henry, already
notorious for his fiery and unequivocable opinions; Samuel Adams,
who had seconded the nomination; Dr. Franklin, newly returned
from England.

Andrew watched until the General had worked his way to Simon, still accepting their congratulations, then touched Justin's
sleeve and rose to leave.

"There'll be no more work here today, lad. Come."

*　　　*　　　*

Friends of the new Commander in Chief hosted him to a celebratory dinner that night, a score of them descending upon Peg Mullen's Beefsteak House, close by the bank of the Schuylkill River, to eat and drink to future glory. Most of them were fellow delegates to the Continental Congress, but a few were military colleagues or personal friends. Major Simon Wallace was among them, and also the senior Wallace. Young Justin Carmichael had retired to the inn where the three of them were staying, being too junior for inclusion in the General's circle of intimates. Dr. James Ramsay sat eating with several of the Massachusetts delegates on the other side of the room.

"Who invited *him*?" Simon said, pushing aside an empty plate as he and his father watched Ramsay through a haze of tobacco smoke, from the relative shelter of a window that looked out toward the river.

"Well, he *says* he's still employed as a secretary to the Massachusetts delegation," said the elder Wallace, "so I'd guess that's who invited him."

"I know what he says," Simon muttered. "Why is it I'm not certain I believe him? He's up to something, Andrew. I don't know what, but I do know that I'm no longer certain I trust him."

"That's a serious statement," Andrew replied, puffing on a long-stemmed clay pipe. "On what do you base it?"

Simon took a long pull at his tankard and then shook his head perplexedly. "I wish I could tell you. A gut feeling. That's hardly fair to Ramsay, I know, but—"

He shrugged and shook his head, his gaze shifting to follow Washington as the new general greeted the just-arrived Benjamin Franklin. After a moment he smiled faintly and said, "He's asked me to accompany him to Boston. I'm to be an additional aide, attached to his personal staff. The appointment carries a Continental commission as major."

"Excellent," Andrew murmured. "That appointment was vital. When does he plan to leave?"

"Probably Thursday or Friday. He'd *like* to leave tomorrow, but there are still a number of details to work out before he goes."

Andrew nodded, puffing contentedly on his pipe. "That's to be

expected. Incidentally, when the news from Boston eventually catches up with him, do what you can to ease the shock. Being in command can give such news a different potency. I don't know whether he and Warren were acquainted or not, but he may have lost personal friends."

"I'll do the best I can," Simon agreed. "Am I to mention your visitation or no?"

"Probably not—though I leave that to your good judgment at the time. If it seems appropriate, tell him. If he should find the dream disturbing, he can always dismiss it as the wishful fantasies of an addled old man. On the other hand, it could well give him comfort."

As Simon nodded grave agreement, Andrew took another puff on his pipe, his attention drawn to the flurry of laughter that welled around Franklin as he shared some snippet of homespun humor with Dr. Benjamin Rush and young Thomas Jefferson. Smiling slightly, he gestured with his pipe at the bespectacled Franklin.

"It's good he's returned for all of this. I'm informed he shall have a key part to play in the Plan."

Simon raised an eyebrow. "You've had instructions?"

"Nothing specific yet, regarding him, but *he* may have had instructions before leaving London. At very least his political role will remain important. He's well respected in Europe. I expect that Congress will send him to the French court to try to secure aid. As for other levels of involvement—we shall have to wait and see."

"Indeed." Eyes narrowed, Simon measured Franklin more carefully through the haze of smoke, then refilled his tankard from a pitcher set on the scarred table between them, emptying the pitcher in the process. "Have you any idea when we might receive more specific instructions?" he asked when he had taken a long pull.

"It still takes two to three months for a letter to cross the Atlantic," Andrew replied with a shake of his head. "If nothing is waiting when we return to Cambridge, I thought I'd send Justin with new inquiries. Besides, it's high time he met the Master in person—if he can find him."

Simon smiled. Both of them were well acquainted with the frequent and clandestine peregrinations of the man whose agents they were.

"You set him a formidable task, for his first trip abroad. I gather you're pleased with his progress, then?"

"I am. I expect I may use him as a regular courier, as the situation progresses—depending, of course, upon how the Master perceives him. Now that you have your appointment from Washington, I suggest that you arrange to make Justin your aide. That will give him the freedom to move as necessary."

Simon nodded. "I have no idea what my specific arrangements will be, but I'm sure something can be worked out. You're certain you and Arabella won't need him?"

"Oh, I'm very certain we shall—but you shall need him more," Andrew replied. "Nonetheless, we'll discuss that further once we've all gotten back to Cambridge. Do you know if the General plans any stops?"

"A few days in New York, I think, but he's eager to take up his command, now that his appointment is official. And he'll be even more eager when he gets the latest news—if 'eager' is the right word. In any case, General Gage won't stay bottled up in Boston indefinitely."

"No, he will not." Andrew cast his eye over the room. "Who else will be in his party?"

"General Lee, General Schuyler, Joseph Reed to act as his secretary, Thomas Mifflin as official aide-de-camp—and the other generals' aides, of course. He's taking a carriage, I believe, but no baggage train. He wants to move quickly. The Philadelphia Light Horse will escort us as far as New York."

"Well, he shall reach Cambridge soon enough, then, and with heavy enough heart," Andrew replied. "But look you. Here's a toast about to be made, and my tankard is empty. Is there anything in that pitcher?"

"No, but share some of mine," Simon murmured, sloshing half of his remaining ale into his father's tankard.

Across the room, and at some remove from the General as well, one of the delegates near Jefferson had gotten to his feet and set

one foot on his chair, lifting his glass, while another of his colleagues clanged a pewter spoon against a tankard of the same.

"Gentlemen, charge your glasses!" The speaker lifted his own as conversation fell off and heads were turned in his direction. "Gentlemen, I wish to propose a new loyal toast: To the Commander in Chief of the American Armies!"

The brave words brought to their feet everyone who had not already risen in anticipation of the toast, benches and chair legs scraping across wooden floor planks and voices chorusing in hearty affirmation.

"The Commander in Chief!"

Washington's craggy face had gone still and even a little pale as their intent became clear, and he did not move as they drank his health. Perhaps it had not fully occurred to him until that very moment how terrifying and awesome a responsibility they had thrust upon him, almost single-handedly to lead an endeavor that could well spell ruin for every man in the room. Almost certainly his fellow delegates had not realized the full potential.

But all of them realized it now, smiles dying and levity ceasing as they lowered their glasses, waiting for him to respond. Their new Commander in Chief rose slowly, even reluctantly. And such was the gravity of his demeanor that the moment was at once transformed from a purely social gathering into an occasion of solemnity.

"God help us, gentlemen, for I hope you know what you have done," he said softly. "Nonetheless," he went on, his voice gathering strength, "I thank you for your confidence, and I drink to your very good health—and to the health of these United Colonies. May Providence defend the right."

Not a sound could be heard as he drained his glass, but a shout went up as he finished it and set it down on the table with a hollow *thunk*, punctuated by several cries of, "Hear, hear!"

But the momentum of the evening had been lost. Very shortly the company began to disperse. Andrew watched from the window after Simon had gone to join the General, chatting briefly with several of the delegates before returning to his own inn for a good night's sleep before setting out for Boston.

Chapter Two

The General's party finally left for Boston three days hence, on Friday, the twenty-third of June. Most of Philadelphia turned out to see him off, including all of the Massachusetts delegation and many of the delegates from the other colonies, with their carriages and servants, a large number of local townspeople, and some two thousand local militia and their officers. Andrew and Justin had already set out for Cambridge two days before, but Simon waited with Generals Lee and Schuyler and their aides, mounted on a black mare and holding the General's gray.

Fifes and drums struck up a military air as the new Commander in Chief emerged from his quarters with his aides, Mifflin and Reed. A regiment of the First Troop of Philadelphia Light Horse presented arms with drawn sabers, dipping their colors in salute. In the week since Washington's appointment, someone had painted over the old British union of red, blue, and white on the regiment's distinctive yellow banner and replaced it with a canton of thirteen stripes of white and red, signifying the United Colonies.

Washington pulled up short as he noticed it, then drew himself solemnly to attention, removed his tricorn, and swept it to the side in salute before proceeding on to where his horse waited. With

Mifflin holding his stirrup, he swung up without ceremony, Lee and Schuyler falling in behind him as he moved out to review the troops.

When he had finished, the Light Horse led out, some twenty strong, harnesses jingling. The local troops accompanied him as far as the outer precincts of the city, as did some of the carriages and a few gentlemen on horseback. Following behind came the General's staff and his personal carriage—an open phaeton drawn by two white horses, with his faithful servant Will up on the driver's box.

The General set a brisk pace, even when, after the first hour or so, he retired to the carriage and invited Generals Schuyler and Lee to ride with him by turns. Simon and the other aides rotated their positions as well, one riding alongside the carriage to either side while the rest accompanied whichever general was on horseback. The spare horses followed along, tied to the back of the rig.

Nor did the passage of this cavalcade go unremarked on the long road toward Cambridge, for word of the General's appointment had gone before him, and everywhere citizens and militia turned out to cheer and watch him pass. Sometimes they accompanied him for a while. Occasionally, when the cavalcade passed through a town, flowers would be tossed into the carriage at the General's feet. Whenever the party stopped for refreshment or to rest the horses, local folk were there to offer their support, also hoping to glean some news of the intentions of the Continental Congress.

But if news of Washington's appointment had sped north, rumors of the battle at Breed's Hill also had begun to filter southward, as Simon had known was inevitable. The first intimations reached the General's party a day out of Philadelphia, when a travel-worn express rider clattered across a wooden bridge just ahead, obviously in a hurry.

As courtesy of the road demanded, the man slowed to pass the troop of horsemen leading the General's party, raising a weary hand to the brim of his tricorn in automatic acknowledgment. There was no reason he could have been expected to recognize the occupants of the phaeton they escorted—General Schuyler was riding with Washington at the time—but his sudden look of bewilderment suggested at least a vague recognition of the significance

of uniformed outriders; and Simon recognized the express. Signaling the General's driver to pull up, he gigged his black mare closer to the rider.

"Is that Phineas O'Sullivan?" he called, drawing abreast. "What news from Boston, friend?"

O'Sullivan's face lit briefly at the familiar hail, but his grave demeanor did not change. His horse was far fresher than its rider, eager to be away, and it jigged and fought the bit, rolling its eyes at Simon's black and lacing back its ears at the big gray tied to the back of the General's rig. Behind him the Philadelphia Light Horse had also reined in.

"Major Wallace," he acknowledged in a voice gritty with fatigue. "You'll not have heard the news from Boston, I suppose?"

Simon had, but he dared not let on, only matching his expression to O'Sullivan's.

"I gather that this is news I would rather not hear," he replied. "To save telling it twice, you'd best tell it to these gentlemen as well." He gestured toward the phaeton and the riders grouped around it, at the same time leading O'Sullivan closer. "This is General Washington, our new Commander in Chief. Also Generals Schuyler and Lee. General, Mr. O'Sullivan, with news from Boston."

The General acknowledged O'Sullivan's raised hat with a nod, his craggy face impassive. "Yes, Mr. O'Sullivan?"

O'Sullivan drew a deep breath, his Yankee resolve undaunted even in the presence of the Commander in Chief.

"I'm sent to inform Congress, General. There's been a terrible battle fought in Boston, now a week past. British Regulars have taken and occupied Breed's Hill, and Charleston was burning when I left."

"The devil you say!" Lee blurted, as Mifflin and Reed crowded closer, for Lee had served as a brigadier in the British army in times past.

"Did the Americans stand before the British fire?" Washington demanded.

"They did, sir."

The General closed his eyes briefly and breathed a relieved sigh.

"They stood. Then the liberties of our country are safe. Who led them?"

"General Prescott."

"And how many engaged?"

"About twelve hundred, sir. And nearly twice that many British."

"And what of our casualties?"

"Unknown when I left, sir. But I dare say it cost the British more than they'd thought to spend." A note of satisfaction crept into his voice. "They took horrific losses through their first two assaults— and we'd've made them pay a third time, if we'd had more powder! They'll not be able to afford many more such 'victories.'"

The express could give them few further details, beyond the impression that the Americans had scored a moral victory, even though they had lost the hill. And the British General Gage seemed content not to push beyond the ground he had won so dearly—or so it had appeared when the express had left the field, a week before.

More rumors concerning Breed's Hill continued to reach them as they pressed on across New Jersey, new details emerging every time they stopped at an inn to take a meal or to rest the horses. They were heading for General Schuyler's native New York, second largest of the colonies. By the following day, as they prepared to cross the Hudson just above the city, word came of the simultaneous return of the colony's royal governor, William Tryon, whose barge even now was heading up the river.

"I like not the timing of this," said General Lee as he scanned downriver with a spyglass. "Word of our coming may have preceded us. It wouldn't do for the British to capture our new Commander in Chief before he can even take up his command. . . ."

"I won't be taken," Washington said confidently. "Let us carry on, gentlemen."

Indeed, Lee's concerns proved ill founded. The crossing was made without incident. As had happened all along the new Commander in Chief's route of travel, cheering crowds greeted his landing, and uniformed horsemen were waiting to take over from the Light Horse and to escort him to the fine mansion of Colonel

Leonard Lispenard, where he was scheduled to stay. As his phaeton swept up the long, curved drive and halted before the broad front steps, uniformed volunteers were drawn up as a guard of honor and a band played a military salute.

"Welcome to New York, Your Excellency!" their host declared as he bowed them in through the front door.

At the reception which followed, the General and his party were feted in almost royal style, enthusiastically greeted by prominent members of New York's patriot community and a festive array of food. Besides the expected words of congratulation, the talk was mostly of the warships anchored in New York Harbor, and what the British might do in the aftermath of what had happened at Boston.

Of exactly what *had* happened at Boston there was little new information—until an express arrived at the mansion just after dark with a dispatch on its way from the Massachusetts Provincial Congress to Philadelphia. An aide came to fetch the generals to the front steps of the house, where a red-faced and disheveled-looking rider was guzzling a cooling tankard of ale while servants shifted his saddle onto a fresh horse in the yard below.

"Is it news of the battle in Boston?" Schuyler demanded.

As the man gulped the last swallows of his ale, he half raised his empty hand by way of affirmation and patted a dust-grimed hand against a bulge under his coat, then dragged the back of a sleeve across his mouth and his sweaty face before handing off the empty tankard to a servant.

"Aye, sir, it is," the man replied. "I don't know much myself, as I've only brought it from as far as Dobbs Ferry. But the man I took it from said I was to get it to Philadelphia as fast as I could. I only stopped here to get a fresh horse."

"Well, you can delay long enough to let the new Commander in Chief have a look at it before you go on," Schuyler said, holding out his hand and then snapping his fingers when the man did not immediately surrender it. "Come on, man. Don't let's waste time. I'm General Schuyler, as any of these gentlemen can attest, and this is General Washington, our new Commander in Chief." He indicated the General with a proud sweep of his hand. "Since he's

on his way to take up command in Boston, it would be useful if he knew what he was heading into."

Schuyler's logic could not be faulted. With a weary shrug the rider handed over the dispatch. A servant was standing by with a lighted candelabrum, and Schuyler held the dispatch briefly to the light before offering it to Washington.

"Your Excellency?"

As Washington hesitated—for the address on the outside of the dispatch clearly intended it for the Congress—Simon edged a little closer and added his encouragement.

"We already know the news from Boston will not be good, General," Simon said. "But whatever it is, you need to know about it. If anyone besides the Congress is entitled to open it, you are."

Drawing a deep breath, the General took the dispatch and broke the seal, unfolding the paper with brisk efficiency once his decision had been made.

"It's from Warren," he announced, his eyes flicking briefly to the bottom of the page and then back to the top to read down the neatly penned lines. "Yes, some of this we know already. British Regulars had to make three assaults to take Breed's Hill. . . . We did, indeed, hold them through two charges. . . . General Ward estimates that British losses may be as high as thirty to forty percent, out of more than two thousand men. . . .

"But here's more that's new. The British are contained, for the present, but Charleston has burned . . . perilous shortages of powder and supplies. If a Commander in Chief has been appointed, his immediate presence is urgently requested. . . ."

A murmur of agreement rippled among his listeners at those words, but Washington merely continued reading.

"American officer casualties, thus far known: Major Andrew Mc-Clary, Major Willard Moore of Paxton, Colonel Thomas Gardner of Cambridge, Major General Joseph Warr—but this *cannot* be correct!" Incredulity lent animation to the normally measured cadence of Washington's speech. "This cannot be correct!" he repeated. "Warren *signed*—"

He broke off as his glance darted again to the bottom of the page and then back to the fatal words.

"Dear God, this is ill news, indeed," he murmured. "Joseph Warren *has* fallen. 'Tis *James* Warren who now is President of the Provincial Congress."

To a flurry of muttered consternation around him, Washington slowly reread the dispatch from the top again, no one daring to intrude on the stunned silence that spread gradually from the front porch. Though the pockmarked face quickly regained its customary composure, Simon could see the tension in the set of the jaw and the slight tremor in the fingers that held the paper just a little too tightly.

Finally the Commander in Chief blindly handed the dispatch off to Schuyler and excused himself, heading back through the hall and the drawing room and through a door that led onto a piazza overlooking the rear gardens. Simon followed after a few seconds, shaking his head at several others who would have accompanied him. He found the General standing in the shadow of one of the square pillars of the piazza, leaning against the cool stone with his arms folded across his chest, gazing sightlessly into the shadowed depths of an ornamental fishpond.

"Pardon the intrusion, General," Simon said quietly, "but may we send the express on to Philadelphia?"

Washington looked up with a start. "What's that?"

"The express—may we send him on to Philadelphia?"

"Oh, it's you." The General sighed heavily and returned his attention to a pair of goldfish brooding almost motionless in the somewhat murky water. "Yes, go ahead and send him, Major. I—should like to be alone for a while, if you don't mind."

"Very good, sir."

Simon slipped back into the house and relayed the order, then posted a guard to be certain the General's wish for privacy was respected. After a quarter hour or so, he himself ventured onto the piazza again, circling around to approach from the garden side, so that Washington would have plenty of time to see him coming. The General had moved to a stone bench just at the edge of the torchlight, facing out over the river vista; but at the sound of Simon's approach, he turned his head and, with a sparse gesture, invited the younger man to sit.

"I fear that I was not fully prepared to read familiar names among the dead," he said quietly as Simon sank down on his left. "All at once I felt the full weight of command settling upon my shoulders."

Simon said nothing, sensing that no response was necessary save to listen. After a long moment the General spoke again, very softly.

"Do you believe in dreams, Major?"

Simon felt himself start to stiffen, only with difficulty deflecting his sharp glance to the river instead of to the man sitting beside him. In this context the question almost suggested that the General might have shared Andrew's vision of the slain Joseph Warren. But that was impossible, or the news of Warren's death should not have been so devastating. Still, for the stolid and usually private Washington, even to mention something as ephemeral as a dream betokened something extraordinary indeed.

"Do you mean—prophetic dreams, sir?" Simon murmured, trying to keep any edge from his voice as he glanced casually over his shoulder to confirm that the guard was still deflecting would-be intruders.

A grimace twitched at the General's lips as he dropped his gaze to his big hands, abstractedly intertwining the fingers between his knees.

"I—want to believe that at least part of it was prophetic," he whispered. "It—seemed to presage my appointment to the supreme command. And there was a victor's laurel wreath. . . ."

Simon said nothing, only *willing* the man not to stop there. After a long, taut silence the General shivered a little, despite the heat of the summer evening, and lifted his gaze slightly to stare into the darkness far across the river. His voice, as he began to speak, was shaky, a little flat, reflecting his tight-reined emotions; but it also sounded relieved.

"It was—three or four months ago," he said. "I recall it as a dream, but it might have been delirium, because I'd taken a hard fall and had the wind knocked out of me. My horse stumbled, and we both went down. I may even have been unconscious for a few seconds. Dr. Ramsay thought I was. He was with me that day—which is probably why he was in the dream."

He glanced suddenly at Simon, staring at him intently for several seconds while Simon dared not even breathe, then shook himself loose of whatever it was he thought he saw and looked back at the river.

"Now, that *is* odd," he murmured. "I cannot imagine why, but somehow I think *you* were in it, too."

Simon longed to pursue the point directly, also wondering what Ramsay would have had to say about the fall, but only said, "Perhaps it isn't as odd as all that, sir. We'd recently renewed our acquaintance, after all. What was I doing?"

Washington shook his head. "I cannot remember. I only know that you were there; I'm certain of it." He grimaced. "The whole thing was so very odd. It couldn't have lasted more than a few seconds—just while I was stunned by the fall—but it had that strange quality of time that dreams often have, of seeming to stand still."

"Would you care to tell me what you *can* remember?" Simon dared to ask.

To his surprise and relief, the General nodded.

"I believe I would. Perhaps you can make some sense of it. It had to do with the Craft, I think. I remember being in a room that I somehow knew was a Lodge, but there was something—different—about it. There were others present, but I could not see their faces. Nor can I tell you who the presiding Master was. A ritual was in progress, and *it* was different, even the parts that were familiar. The Volume of Sacred Law on the altar was my own Bible, but there was another Bible as well—very distinctive. I'm certain I should recognize it if I ever saw it again. But so many other things that I simply cannot remember. . . . Hands holding up a laurel wreath above my head, and—something about swords as well. . . ."

His left hand went to the silver sword hilt jutting between them, fingering it distractedly as his voice trailed off. Only after several seconds did Simon dare to press him on.

"Was it—your sword, sir?" he whispered, trying not to look at the weapon.

The General started, almost as if he had forgotten the other

man's presence, then slowly nodded as his gaze lifted off into the darkness beyond.

"I think so," he finally said, still trying to pin down the elusive memory. "But there may have been more than one. I—seem to remember surrendering my sword when I entered, and later it was put back into my hands, but—" He shook his head, obviously unable to make the memory come into focus.

"What else?" Simon asked when the General did not seem inclined to say more.

"I don't know." He shook his head again and sighed. "It's gone. I'm certain there was much, much more, if only I could remember. . . ."

As the General's voice trailed off once more and he buried his face in his hands, Simon nodded thoughtfully, wishing he dared make a closer examination of the General's sword, so close between them. The account was an odd juxtaposition of images, with just enough unusual detail that perhaps it had *not* been merely a dream. The laurel wreath and the sword seemed particularly significant, perhaps betokening some esoteric sanctioning of Washington and his mission—or a deep-seated desire on his part to be cast in the role of America's premier military leader. . . .

But Washington had not particularly *wanted* the job of Commander in Chief, and on the strength of soldiering alone, he was not even best qualified. He was not *un*qualified for the job, if any American was truly qualified, but other men with far more impressive military credentials had been passed over to give Washington the command.

It was his personal charisma that the Continental Congress had singled out, as well as his record in the French and Indian War— and his practical tenacity, and the ability to pull men together and inspire them to work as a team, regardless of regional differences— essential qualities that went beyond mere tactical ability or strategic expertise. If war came, as seemed increasingly inevitable, it was likely not to be fought according to European rules.

Which brought one to European considerations, and the tentative plan to guide the American rebellion toward a Stuart restoration. Was Washington's appointment as Commander in Chief, if

ratified at some esoteric level, to be seen as a part of this plan or in opposition to it? Simon wondered whether the Master knew of the dream.

"It's a very interesting dream," he said noncommittally.

The General sighed and raised his head, lacing his fingers together again to stare down at them, sighing as he nodded. "It was also a very frightening dream, on some levels," he said. "Words like 'destiny' and 'mission' keep coming to mind—and have, since I received the nomination as Commander in Chief. God knows, I have always been ambitious in some ways, Major, but I swear I never sought that." He snorted. "I don't even know why I'm telling you this. What must you think of me?"

"I think," Simon said carefully, "that you are a man who has been given a very difficult job to do, whether by mere men or by some Divine Providence that we are likely never to understand."

The General looked up sharply at that.

"Do you believe in Divine Providence, then?" he asked.

Simon considered carefully before venturing a reply. In Freemasonry, both he and the General were Master Masons, sharing the common terminology and symbolism of that noble fraternity, but Simon's esoteric connections went far beyond the Craft. Judging by what the General had just reported, perhaps his own inclinations ran along similar lines—or could be guided to do so.

Which raised interesting possibilities regarding the origin of Washington's dream—if dream it was. Could this be the Master's work? Neither Simon nor Andrew had received word of such an intention, but communication across the Atlantic was slow. It certainly was possible to shift the framework of conventional Freemasonry to more esoteric function; indeed, the Master's inner circle derived much of its structure from Masonic symbolism and ritual. If one wished to convey esoteric insights to a man like Washington, how better than in terms already familiar, in a context not likely to alarm? The Master was fully capable of such instruction.

Of course, there remained the possibility, even more disquieting, that the dream reflected no mortal agency at all. Simon wondered whether this latter had occurred to Washington.

"I believe," said Simon, "that the dream you have described can

certainly be interpreted in the light of Divine Providence at work. The symbolism is largely Masonic. Following that symbolism to its logical extension, we might postulate that—perhaps The Great Architect of the Universe has placed you upon His Tracing Board, for what purpose we cannot yet know. But if we have faith, we must trust that His purpose will become apparent in His time. As a Brother in the Craft, that is how *I* would interpret the dream."

Washington had turned to face him as he spoke, and even in the dim light cast by the torches nearer the house, Simon could see that the General had gone very pale.

"On—*His* Tracing Board?" the General repeated, shaken. "Are you saying that, on some level, I *have* been designated, in some way, to—"

He could not finish his sentence for the enormity of what he was suggesting, and Simon suddenly felt a great upsurge of compassion for him.

"I cannot answer that," he admitted. "I merely point out that you are the Commander in Chief of the Continental Army, and you are in a position to make a very great difference. If The Great Architect of the Universe does have a Master Plan for these American colonies—and I think, as Freemasons, we cannot doubt that there is a Divine Plan for humankind—then it seems not unlikely that you now are destined to play an important role."

He smiled in an attempt to lighten the mood.

"On the other hand, dreams sometimes mean nothing at all," he went on blandly. "Your fall could account for momentary disorientation and even hallucinations. Or perhaps only coincidence is at work. Even when you first had the dream, you had to have been aware that, if the political situation continued to deteriorate, armed rebellion might be the colonies' only recourse—and that you were likely to play an important role in such a rebellion."

"Master Plan or coincidence?" the General said quietly. "A dismaying choice, either way. I almost think I prefer the latter."

Off at the edge of torchlight nearer the house, the sentry coughed self-consciously, reminding Simon that he and the General had been here quite a long time, and that others required the great man's attention.

"Well, 'tis a question we are unlikely to resolve tonight, sir—though I do hope that, if you remember any more details, you will pass them on. I should be intrigued to know more about what *I* was doing in this rather interesting Lodge you've described. We have sat together in Lodge on occasion, but somehow I feel that this one would have had both of us wondering."

The General allowed himself as much of a smile as he ever did, tight-lipped, mostly in the eyes, sighing as he stretched his long legs out in front of him and then stretched his arms as well.

"I believe I shall be very pleased to have you on my staff, Major Wallace," he said, coming to his feet, Simon doing the same. "It will be good to have someone nearby with whom I can be entirely candid. I fear an increasing isolation as I take up my duties—necessary, perhaps, but—" He shrugged and sighed again.

"For now, however, I suppose it must be my most immediate duty to send a message on to General Ward, acknowledging that I've heard the news and am on my way." He shook his head. "I still find it hard to believe that Warren is dead."

Simon ducked his head. "The losses at Breed's Hill will have been a heavy blow to everyone in Boston, sir. Joseph Warren was particularly well loved and respected."

He had not intended to add to the General's concerns, but Washington looked at him with a start.

"I *am* sorry, Major. I had forgotten. You hail from the Grand Lodge of Massachusetts. Warren was your Grand Master."

Simon nodded, recalling his father's account of the mystic apparition seen on the very night of Warren's death, and decided that the General did not need *that* complication added to his burden.

"He was, sir. Brother Warren will be sorely missed. My father and I often sat with him in Lodge."

"I never had that honor," the General murmured, "but I certainly know of his dedication to the Craft. Despite these troubled times, I hope that he may be given a Masonic tribute at his burial. If it should not have taken place by the time we reach Boston, I hope you will inform me when it does occur. I should like very much to pay my respects."

"I shall see that the Grand Lodge of Massachusetts is informed,

sir," Simon replied with a slight bow. "It would mean a great deal to them, to have you present."

Washington gazed off into the darkness beyond the torchlight washing the piazza, the light playing eerily behind the powdered hair and the craggy profile. He was silent for so long that Simon began to wonder whether his presence had been forgotten.

"It would mean a great deal to me as well," the General finally said, very softly. "I wish I had known him. We shall not see his like again for many a year." His voice strengthened as he went on.

"But he shall be an example for other patriots who are willing to pay the ultimate price, so that these United Colonies may determine their own destiny. In his memory, and out of respect for the love he bore the Craft and this land, I intend that the comfort and solace of fellowship shall be extended to all brethren, whenever possible. You may say that for me, to the Grand Lodge of Massachusetts."

He went back inside then, to pen his message to General Ward. Simon, as he watched him go, found himself wondering how he might contrive an opportunity to examine the General's sword in private, and whether more specific attentions to the General himself might eventually be necessary, if the sword, indeed, bore evidence that the dream had not been only a dream.

In the meantime, while it was still fresh in memory, he must write up an account of what the General had told him, lest he forget some important detail. The dream demanded further investigation. He wondered what it would mean to his father, on his return to Cambridge.

Chapter Three

The Commander in Chief and his staff spent a restless night at Lispenard House, for the heat was oppressive, on top of the oppressive news. The next morning the General received an official congratulatory address from the New York Provincial Congress.

"At a time when the most loyal of His Majesty's subjects, from a regard to the laws and constitution by which he sits on the throne, feel themselves reduced to the unhappy necessity of taking up arms to defend their dearest rights and privileges," their address read, "while we deplore the calamities of this divided Empire, we rejoice in the appointment of a gentleman from whose abilities and virtue we are taught to expect both security and peace."

Washington's gracious answer only added to his popularity.

"At the same time that, with you, I deplore the unhappy necessity of such an appointment as that with which I am now honored," he said, "I cannot but feel sentiments of the highest gratitude for this affecting instance of distinction and regard. May your warmest wishes be realized in the success of America at this important and interesting period; and be assured that every exertion of my worthy colleagues and myself will be equally extended to the reestablishment of peace and harmony between the mother country and these

colonies, as to the fatal but necessary operations of war. When we assumed the soldier, we did not lay aside the citizen; and we shall most sincerely rejoice with you in that happy hour, when the establishment of American liberty, on the most firm and solid foundations, shall enable us to return to our private stations in the bosom of a free, peaceful, and happy country."

Washington spent several days in New York, first confirming General Schuyler in command of all the troops destined for the New York department and then assessing the local situation. If Tryon, the newly returned royal governor, tried anything hostile, Schuyler was to stop him. He was also cautioned to keep a watchful eye on the local Indian agent.

The new Commander in Chief and his party now pressed on toward Boston, following the usual post route northward to New Haven via King's Bridge and onward across Connecticut. Welcoming groups and entertainments accompanied him all along his route of travel. On entering Massachusetts he was met by a committee at Springfield and was feted thence all the way through Worcester and Marlboro. His last stop before Cambridge was Watertown, on the morning of July 2, where the Provincial Congress of Massachusetts gave him an official welcome.

But he did not dally at Watertown, for he was already a day behind schedule. He would learn, on arriving at his destination, that the delay had caused no little confusion. Though the fledgling American Army at Cambridge had only a few months' experience on which to draw, being formed almost exclusively from local militia and minute companies, some of the officers knew that the arrival of a new commanding officer is usually an occasion for military display and pageantry.

Accordingly, troops had been mustered to welcome him the day before, dutifully parading with as much panache as they could manage without proper uniforms and with little formal training, only to be dismissed when he did not appear. They had lined up again the next morning; but when it began to rain, and with no assurance that the new commander would make his appearance that day either, the troops again were dismissed.

As a consequence, no fanfare accompanied the new commander's actual arrival in Cambridge, just after two on the afternoon of July 2. The weather had cleared by the time the General and his escort rode into the sleepy college town, but only a few idlers were about to note the event. Washington himself was "a good deal fatigued" by the time he was directed to Wadsworth House, the home of the president of Harvard University, where quarters had been prepared for him and his staff.

Word of Washington's arrival spread quickly, however, and it was not long before the New England officers began calling to pay their respects, among them the stout, sharp-nosed Major General Artemas Ward, whom Washington would supersede. With Ward came an invitation to dine that evening at Hastings House, where Ward had his headquarters on the other side of the college yard. Once the confusion of arrival had been sorted out, with assurances that a proper military welcome and transfer of command would take place the next day, the Commander in Chief was glad for a few hours to rest before making his supper appearance. In the meantime his staff might do what they liked.

Thus released from formal duties, Major Simon Wallace availed himself of the opportunity to visit his family for a few hours, for his home was in Cambridge, not far from the Commons. He saw the parlor curtains twitch as he drew rein outside the green wrought-iron gate, but he had to duck his head to bend down and lift the latch. By the time he had ridden through and could look again, the door had been flung open and three young children were racing toward him: two boys bracketing a girl, like stair steps, all of them dark of hair and very fair of skin.

"Papa! Papa!"

The mare tossed her head in alarm and snorted, rolling her eyes and jigging to the side, causing a dismayed shriek from the little girl as flower beds were flattened under steel-shod hooves. But the shriek brought the other two into more decorous behavior as their father swung down, handing the mare's reins to the older boy and scooping the younger onto a shoulder as another figure appeared at the door.

She was wearing one of his favorite gowns: a day dress of pale green muslin sprigged with a darker emerald shade. A fichu of ivory lace covered her bosom, caught at the center with the cameo brooch that had been his grandmother's, and pearl drops bobbed

from her earlobes beneath the smooth coils of raven tresses. A little lace cap completed the ensemble, framing a pair of dancing black eyes.

"And good afternoon to you, Mistress Wallace," Simon said, smiling widely as he swept off his hat and made her a formal little bow, careful not to dislodge his younger son.

Arabella Wallace laughed delightedly and ran to him, embracing him around the boy and lifting her lips to his welcoming kiss. Behind her Justin had also appeared in the doorway and came to assist with the horse as Simon bent to give his daughter a kiss as well.

"Ah, it's good to be home, my dears, though I'm afraid it's only for a few hours. General Ward is entertaining His Excellency to supper this evening, and it will be a preliminary briefing for the new arrivals as well as a social occasion, so staff are required to attend." He glanced at his elder son. "Charles, if you ask your Uncle Justin very nicely, I expect he could be induced to give you a leg up, so you can ride Sukey back to the barn. I'm sure she'd appreciate a good feed and a rubdown."

"Can I ride her by myself?" the boy asked eagerly as Justin grinned and bent to scoop him onto the wide saddle.

"Just to the barn," Simon agreed. "She's tired enough that I don't expect she'll give you any trouble, but remember that she's a full-sized horse."

The boy's eyes were shining as Justin handed him the reins.

"Papa, thank you!" he breathed. "Giddup, Sukey," he said more forcefully as he gave the reins a shake.

When the mare stepped out toward the barn, as if aware of the tender years of her rider, Justin glanced at Simon in question. "Will you be wanting her later?"

Simon shook his head and began heading them all toward the house. "I'll walk to Hastings House this evening. I've been in the saddle enough this past week or so."

Arabella laughed delightedly and hugged her husband's arm, rubbing her cheek contentedly against the rough wool of his sleeve as they skirted the ruined flower bed.

"If that boy doesn't get a pony soon, Simon, he's going to drive me mad!" she said. "That's all he talks about. At least he can use up some of his energy taking care of Sukey, if you're going to be in Cambridge for a while. Or will you need to keep her up at Wadsworth House, so you're ready to ride off at a moment's notice on the General's errands?"

"I'll have to ask," he replied lightly. "For all I know, *I* may have to stay up at Wadsworth House."

"Oh, Simon!"

"Well, I *am* one of his aides, my dear. And there have been some rather interesting developments. Where is Andrew?"

"He's upstairs, writing some letters," Arabella said, steering him firmly into the house. "I'll fetch him after Justin and I have drawn you a bath. Why don't you visit with the children while we do that, and *then* the three of you can talk? I don't suppose you've had much opportunity for baths, on the road."

He grinned and kissed the top of her head. "I can think of several things I haven't had, but I'll settle for a bath and all the latest news for now."

Blushing prettily, she shooed him off with the children, then put a large kettle to heat over the fire in the kitchen while Justin began bringing in more water from the well. Set behind folding screens in the center of the kitchen, the tin bath was ready when Simon joined them half an hour later. He stripped off his travel-stained uniform and immersed himself gratefully while Justin straddled a ladder-back chair and gave him further details of the battle at Breed's Hill. Arabella briefly disappeared upstairs, then busied herself laying out fresh clothing and brushing up his coat and hat, listening but saying little.

"I'm sorry to hear that Warren's body has not been found yet," Simon said, sluicing water from his eyes and streaming hair. "How are the rest of our casualty figures, now that there's been time to count?"

"Something over four hundred killed or wounded," Justin replied. "It could have been far worse. It was, for the British. They lost at least twice that many. Some say the figure may exceed a thousand."

Simon shivered despite the summery warmth of the room. "We'd heard estimates of thirty to forty percent casualties."

"It may be closer to fifty percent," Justin said. "And the officer

losses were staggering: nearly one in three, when the expected ratio usually is more like one in *eight*. A very costly victory. They say that General Gage is still in shock."

"Good God, I shouldn't wonder," Simon murmured. He fell briefly silent as Arabella toweled briskly at his hair, arching with an involuntary little grunt of pleasure as she shifted her ministrations to his shoulders and back. Only reluctantly did he return his attention to the younger man, signaling Arabella to desist as he gathered himself to get out of the bath.

"So what do you suppose will be the practical effect of all this?" he asked. "It sounds like we gave Gage a good thrashing, despite the fact that he technically won, but I doubt he's going to simply pack up and go home."

"Actually, he may do precisely that," Arabella said. She offered her husband a fresh towel as he rose streaming from the bath and stepped out onto a brightly colored rag rug. "Rumor has it that his nerve is shattered."

Simon had ducked behind one of the screens, wrapping himself in the towel, but stuck out his head in astonishment.

"Where did you hear *that* rumor?"

"Oh, the wife of a British officer came to tea the other day and let it slip," she replied coyly. "Get dressed, or you'll be late for the General. Justin, please go see what's keeping Andrew. My guest said," she continued, "that her husband had been complaining that Gage is all but paralyzed by what happened at Breed's Hill. He knows it was a victory in name only. Apparently he's convinced that if he sets foot outside Boston proper, American soldiers will leap out from behind every rock and bush and tree and slaughter his men. He's never been that keen on fighting against the colonists to begin with, and this is a kind of war he simply does not understand. Parliament will replace him, of course. All the officers say so."

"Do they, indeed?"

Simon emerged in clean white breeches, raking his fingers through his wet hair, and sat on a stool so Arabella could begin combing out the snarls. Andrew had joined them during her recitation, puffing on his pipe, and nodded a greeting to his son as he pulled up a bow-backed chair.

"I was finishing some letters," he said, clasping the hand Simon extended. "Welcome home."

Nodding distractedly, Simon resumed his conversation with Arabella.

"About Gage," he said. "I think I shall pass that on to His Excellency. Speaking of whom," he added, "I'm glad you came down when you did, Andrew. I had a rather odd conversation with the General in New York, the night we received the official news of Warren's death. This is likely to sound strange, but do you know whether he has ever worked outside the structure of the Lodge?"

Arabella stopped combing his hair. Justin looked up from wiping down Simon's sword and scabbard. Andrew gazed at him placidly with his one good eye.

"By 'worked,'" the old chevalier said carefully, "I take it that you mean in some other esoteric discipline."

"Precisely," Simon replied. "And I gather, by all of your reactions, that the thought hadn't occurred to any of you, any more than it had to me." He cocked his head. "Now I'm not certain whether I should be reassured or apprehensive."

"Tell us about this conversation," Andrew said.

While Arabella continued to comb his hair dry, pulling it back in a queue to braid it, Simon told them about the dream Washington had related as they sat in the shadows of the garden at Lispenard House.

"At least I think it was a dream. *He* thought it was," he went on, when he had reviewed the basic details. "But the symbolism was more akin to a vision. Of course, that may be the way he dreams. The laurel wreath is not an unusual image for a military man who himself has admitted that he has ambitions—though he denies he ever wanted to be Commander in Chief, and I tend to believe him. Every soldier wants to be the victor. And couching the whole thing in Masonic imagery is not, in itself, out of keeping, since he *is* a Freemason."

"And you say that the sword was put back into his hands?" Andrew asked.

"That's what he said."

"A potent symbol of being given command," Andrew said thoughtfully. "And it does sound like something might have been

done to it in a ritual context. I don't suppose you've had a chance to examine it since?"

Simon shook his head. "I've watched for an opportunity, but it just hasn't been possible while we were on the road. I'll keep trying, of course. But the whole thing was odd enough that I even wrote it up, right after he told me about it."

"I'll want to read that," Andrew said neutrally.

"Of course. Remind me to fetch it before I head back to Hastings House."

As he bent to pull on clean white stockings, Justin glanced thoughtfully at Andrew, then back at Simon.

"You know, it's odd he should make such a point about the sword," he said. "I had almost forgotten the incident, but something peculiar happened the day he was nominated as Commander in Chief—which would have been not long after he had the dream, or vision, or whatever it was."

"Go on," Simon said.

"Well, do you remember when John Adams got up to make the nominating speech—and when it became apparent that he was talking about Washington, the General slipped out of the room?"

"I remember," Simon said. "In fact, he mentioned something himself, in that connection—how the sense of destiny, of mission, began about the time he received the nomination. You followed him, didn't you?"

"I did. He walked right past me. I feared he might be feeling ill. He went into the library and closed the door. I listened for a few seconds, to be sure he was alone; then I looked through the keyhole. He was standing beside one of the library tables with his head bowed and both hands clasped around the hilt of his sword. His knuckles were white, and his shoulders were shaking.

"Then he sank to his knees and bowed his forehead against the pommel of the sword. I decided he must be praying, so I posted myself outside the door to give him privacy."

"He probably *was* praying," Andrew said. "From what I've heard, he prays and reads his Bible daily."

"He does," Simon confirmed. "He gets down on his knees. The

question is, was he *just* praying that day, or was he having some kind of flashback of the dream?"

"The timing would suggest that perhaps it was a flashback," Andrew replied. "Receiving the sword in the dream was symbolic; receiving the nomination as Commander in Chief was very real and reinforced the dream. I shouldn't wonder that he might be shaken. Come to think of it, the same sort of thing could have been happening that night at Peg Mullen's. Do you remember when everyone stood up to toast him, Simon? I think it had finally dawned on him, and on everyone, just how much was being asked of him."

Simon nodded grimly, standing to pull on a fresh shirt. "Now I'm convinced it wasn't just a dream. I think a closer examination of that sword is definitely in order—and perhaps a closer examination of the man himself, if I can contrive a way without totally spooking him." He finished doing up the buttons, adjusting the ruffles at his neck. "By the way, I don't suppose you've had opportunity to talk to Ramsay since you got back? I'd like to know more about that fall that precipitated the dream, especially since Ramsay was in it."

"Ah, Ramsay," Andrew said with a sigh. "He's been a busy lad—far busier than we dreamed. No, he's said nothing about the General, but it emerges that he and some of our Jacobite brethren here in Boston have not been entirely forthcoming about their activities of late. Your instincts in Philadelphia were well founded."

Simon grimaced above the black silk military stock he had been fastening at his throat.

"What's he done now?"

"Well, let us simply say that it's a development we hadn't planned on—at least not this soon. It seems that over the past winter, while the rest of us were still doing careful groundwork, certain members of our fearless but unfortunately impetuous Bostonian Party became impatient with the slow progress toward a Stuart restoration. They decided to move things along a little. They sent a letter directly to Charles Edward Stuart. They offered him the Crown of America, if only he would come to the New World and place himself at their head."

Simon's jaw had dropped at his father's recitation, and he sank wordlessly into his chair again.

"They offered him the Crown?" he asked after a stunned silence.

At Andrew's wordless nod Simon briefly closed his eyes, breathing out with a long sigh.

"Does the Master know about this yet?"

"He does. I had his letter waiting when I returned from Philadelphia. Apparently the General's dream was a first step in damage control."

"Then he *did* cause the dream! And you let me tell you about it, when you already knew?"

"Yes on both counts, though I knew only the Master's intent, not Washington's reaction to it. And I didn't tell you immediately because I didn't want to color your account. We'll discuss that in more detail when you've returned from your supper engagement. We haven't time right now."

"Very well," Simon said, a little dazedly. "Back to this offer of the Crown—has the King replied?"

Andrew quirked a wry smile. "He has. Ramsay's coconspirators received his answer while we were all in Philadelphia. Of course he neither accepted nor declined, at this stage of negotiations. His petitioners clearly anticipated this, for they asked that, if he could not yet come in person, perhaps he might send over a personal representative—preferably a Stuart. The King graciously consented to send a cousin. You'd better finish dressing, or you'll be late."

Still shaking his head in disbelief, Simon rose to stuff his shirttails into his breeches and buckle on the sword Justin handed him.

"It was far too early to actually offer the Crown," he muttered. "God knows, we all long for the day when the King may come into his own again, but it isn't at all certain yet that this is the place from which to do that."

"Well, Ramsay thinks it is," Andrew replied. "He also pointed out—and in this, at least, he is correct—that many of the Bostonian Party think it's time they actually met a Stuart, if they're to continue working for the Stuart cause. Supporting a de jure King Over

the Water is all well and good for people like us, who have met Charles Edward Stuart; but dreams can't sustain those who have not—not indefinitely, at any rate."

Simon shrugged distractedly into the clean white waistcoat Arabella held for him and began doing up the buttons.

"I suppose there *is* a logic to that argument," he admitted. "But it was wrong of Ramsay to take such a decision on himself. And the timing could hardly be worse. Most of the colonial leaders are *not* ready to break with England, regardless of the fact that they're prepared to fight for their rights. You heard them in Congress. Whatever our personal feelings about the man who wears the English Crown, he is not yet seen as the true villain in this piece; it's Lord North and the Parliament who're to blame. What does the Master have to say about all of this?"

"Naturally, he would prefer that Ramsay had not acted prematurely. Having said that, I am given to understand that the man being sent by the King bears the Master's mandate as well. I believe he may be one of our counterparts in Europe."

"Is he to deal with Ramsay?"

Andrew shrugged, containing a faint smile. "In part, perhaps. Let us simply say that, as ever, the Master has his own approach to resolving problems, and that his perspective may take a longer view than does ours."

"Indeed." Simon ducked his head and left arm through the green riband baldric that was his insignia as a staff officer, letting Arabella adjust the ends on his left hip. "Who is this cousin the King is sending?"

"His name is Prince Lucien Rene Robert de Rohanstuart. I doubt you've heard of him. His Stuart blood is from the wrong side of the blanket, and several generations back; but blood is blood, after all. His grandfather died in the Nineteen, fighting for King James, and I knew his father at Culloden." He watched Justin wrap a crimson officer's sash twice around Simon's waist and tie it in the front. "In any case, the King was quite specific regarding who should be sent to escort the prince back. He asked for Justin. That's why Ramsay had to own up to what he'd done."

Simon heaved a heavy sigh and sat down again, enduring the

powder Arabella dusted on his hair, for the evening's dining would be formal.

"Ramsay accepted that?" he asked, suppressing a sneeze.

"Ramsay has no choice. The King requested it—though I suspect the Master's hand in the choice. After all, the King has never met Justin; he's only heard of him through us. In any event, since we were already sending Justin to Europe, it couldn't be more convenient for us. But he'll go to the Master before he goes to the prince—just in case anything vital has changed in the three months since the various letters were sent. Then, if the plans still stand, Justin will collect the prince as planned and return with him on the first ship available."

"Well, it's an ambitious assignment, even without the complication of Ramsay's insubordination," Simon conceded. He slipped his stockinged feet into the silver-buckled shoes that Justin set before him instead of boots. "But far be it from me to question the Master's wishes—or the King's. Justin, are you really willing to take this on?"

"Am I *willing*?" Justin gasped, as Andrew laughed aloud and Arabella smiled.

"If he were any *more* willing," Andrew said, "I should be obliged to box his ears to knock some sense into him. Tell me what young man of Justin's age would *not* relish such a mission: to be sent to the Old World under secret orders to bring back a prince!"

As Simon shrugged, clearly still dubious at this radical change of their plans, Andrew clapped him on the shoulder. "I shouldn't worry on Justin's account, son. He has a sound head on his shoulders. You've trained him yourself, after all. And unlike the good Ramsay and our other Bostonian friends, he knows how to follow orders. As for the rest, let the Master sort that out."

"Whatever you think best," Simon said, standing to look around for his uniform coat. "You can be certain I'll want to talk more about this when I return. Right now, however, I'd best think about getting back to my other master. It doesn't do for junior officers to keep their superiors waiting—and among the array of generals gathering tonight, a mere major is very junior, indeed."

"Well, at least they'll not be able to fault you on your appearance," Arabella said, producing a different coat from the one he

had worn home. "This is the new uniform being adopted for the Continental Army. Do you like it?"

The coat was a slightly darker blue than his old one, with cuffs and facings and tails turned back in buff and new gilt buttons. She had moved his major's epaulets onto the shoulders while he bathed. His black tricorn had gained a green hackle to match the green staff baldric he already wore. He could not suppress a grin of satisfaction as he shrugged into the coat, inspecting one cuff appraisingly when he had settled the coat over waistcoat and sashes.

"What a splendid surprise, my dear," he said. "I shall be the envy of every man at table—even the General, I fancy. You must have worked your pretty fingers to the bone the entire time I was gone."

She smiled and gathered up the old coat. " 'Tis not so fine as some, but you'll not be put to shame," she said. "I'll change the facings on this one in the next few days. A general's aide must set a good example."

"Ah, but you set a standard difficult to meet," he said, and took her in his arms and kissed her.

He left them shortly thereafter to walk the half mile to Wadsworth House, where the Commander in Chief would be gathering his staff before moving on to General Ward's welcome supper. The air was warm and still, the streets mostly deserted, and a brisk British cannonade punctuated the summer evening from the lines on Boston Neck—not terribly loud, at this remove, but it would allow no relaxation for the men manning the miles of redoubts and entrenchments around Boston.

As he walked, Simon tried to shift his thoughts to the men he was going to meet, and to the task that lay ahead, as they worked in the coming days and weeks to forge a proper army out of the motley troops they had seen as they rode into Cambridge earlier in the afternoon. Listening to the British artillery, he wondered whether the Continental forces would be able to keep the British contained in Boston through the rest of the summer and into the fall, until winter froze both sides into inactivity. It was true that the British could not stand many such victories as Breed's Hill, but neither could the fledgling colonial forces.

Which brought Simon back to the more momentous news of the

past hour. What were James Ramsay and his Bostonian colleagues *really* up to, in trying to force a Jacobite restoration this early in the game? Now that a Crown had been offered to Charles Edward Stuart, how would this affect the Master Plan for the American colonies?

And Washington—where did *he* fit into that plan, now that he had been named Commander in Chief? What was the true significance of the dream or vision the General had experienced as he lay semiconscious after his fall the previous spring? And did Ramsay know about the dream?

Finally, what did the Master have in mind for all of them, in his Master Plan for the New World?

Chapter Four

T he new Commander in Chief took formal command of the Continental Army on July 3, 1775. Despite the scarcity of powder, the colonial artillery offered him an impressive salvo to welcome him, and the local citizenry turned out in the thousands as he rode into Cambridge Square on a white charger, accompanied by his staff, and drew rein in the place prepared beneath a great elm.

There, drawing his sword, General George Washington assumed responsibility for an army of some seventeen thousand men, few with much in the way of formal military training. His general order for that day left no doubt that he intended a unified command among all the American fighting units.

"The Continental Congress, having now taken all the troops of the several colonies which have been raised, or which may hereafter be raised, for the support and defense of the liberties of America, into their pay and service, they are now troops of the United Provinces of North America," wrote the Commander in Chief. "And it is to be hoped that all distinction of colonies will be laid aside, so that one and the same spirit may animate the whole, and the only contest be who shall render, on this great and trying occasion, the most essential service to the common cause in which we are all engaged."

In the days and weeks that followed, Washington and his staff began working to make the order's intent a reality. Justin Carmichael sailed from Boston the day after the General took command, determined to use his own days and weeks of forced inactivity aboard ship to catch up on the studies that had been interrupted by the outbreak of hostilities in the Boston area. Since the ship was British, and Justin had taken care not to become known in British circles as a colonial sympathizer, he was able to pose as a lukewarm loyalist bound for the Mother Country to attend to family business dealings set awry by the increasing disruption in the colonies.

The cover gave him reasonable latitude to explore the sympathies of his fellow passengers. The man nearest his age, a titled subaltern carrying dispatches to Parliament from Generals Gage and Howe, proved too high-and-mighty to consort with a colonial "yokel" of mixed French and Scottish extraction, even if professing English loyalties. However, Justin found both a challenge and eventually a kindred spirit in the quiet Hessian artillery officer returning from observation duty with the British batteries at Boston. Hauptmann Hans Schiller, it emerged, was on assignment from the Landgrave of Hesse-Cassel, Frederick II—whose brother, Prince Karl, was the very man Justin had been told to seek out, in a first attempt to locate the Master.

It was an acquaintance worth cultivating. Schiller was only a handful of years older than Justin; and despite the fact that Justin's German was only rudimentary when their conversations began, it was better than anyone else's on the ship. Schiller was grateful for the companionship. As Justin's comprehension increased, he managed to learn a great deal about Hesse and Leipzig, where he was bound, and also about Parliament's intention to hire German mercenaries for service in North America, if the colonists continued their defiance. In that regard Schiller proved a thoroughgoing professional, with a keen eye for the real issues at stake in the New World and a genuine regret that war seemed inevitable.

By the time the ship docked in Southampton, in mid-August, Justin's German had improved greatly, as had his opinion of his Hessian shipmate. Not only was Hauptmann Schiller intelligent and well read, but he was a brother Freemason, having been raised

Master Mason only the year before by Prince Karl himself. Justin
was still Fellow Craft, but the two of them spent many an hour
comparing experiences in Lodge, struggling along in a patois of
German and English mixed. Justin was genuinely sorry when they
had to part, Schiller to continue on to the War Office in London
and Justin to make his way to Dover and the Channel crossing. He
was sorrier still that, in the future, he and Schiller might be obliged
to regard one another as enemies.

The journey overland to Dover took three days by coach. From
Dover to Calais was another day, by the time he worked out the
arrangements and actually made the Channel crossing. He had
experienced only a few queasy hours at the very beginning of his
Atlantic voyage, but the brief stretch between Dover and Calais
was to prove his bane. By the time he made landfall in France, he
was all but convinced that he had left his stomach somewhere in
midchannel.

He spent the night in Calais recovering. Then, following the
instructions of his mentors back in Cambridge, he hired a post
chaise and engaged the same French driver to take him and his
single trunk all the way to Leipzig. Though he felt more confident
about his German after his weeks of practice with Schiller, he *knew*
his French was fluent, thanks to his French-born mother. Best not
to risk ending up somewhere other than where he was supposed
to be.

It was an afternoon late in August before Justin reached his German destination. He had spent the previous night at a small inn on
the southern outskirts of Leipzig, where he left his trunk to be
collected once he determined he was in the right place. He had
changed the post chaise for a hired horse before leaving that morning, to avoid attracting undue attention.

His plain blue coat was well suited to that intent, though as a
traveler, he did wear a sword at his hip. His tricorn now bore a
discreet white cockade that would pass for a fashion affectation
here in Germany, where folk cared little about a rebellion in England, now thirty years past; but it would identify him as a Jacobite
sympathizer to those disposed to notice such things. His breeches
and boots had started out clean that morning, but a sheen of dust

dulled the black leather after a day's ride, and the linen breeches bore a smear of dirt across the top of one thigh, where the horse had butted its sweaty head against him as he watered it at mid-morning. He hoped his cravat was not too wilted, for the heat was far worse than he had expected—though probably not so hot as it was back in Cambridge.

Breathing a heavy sigh, Justin drew rein in a street called Ritter-strasse and briefly removed his hat to wipe a damp handkerchief across his forehead, scanning the row of elegant town houses ahead. His instructions had been explicit, both from Andrew and from the innkeeper at the Drei Könige; but operating in a foreign country, in a language still awkward on his tongue, necessitated especial caution. He replaced his hat and glanced at the scrap of paper in his hand, reviewing the description of the coat of arms he had been told to seek, then kneed his horse into a reluctant trot as he spotted the right colors on a flag farther along the street.

Closer approach confirmed the odd crowned and striped lion rampant of the House of Hesse-Cassel: on an azure field, a lion rampant, barry of ten, gules and argent, differenced by the cadency marks of a second son—which would be correct for Prince Karl, the Landgrave Frederick's younger brother. A liveried groom emerged from a stair descending to a service entrance as Justin drew rein just outside the iron gates and dismounted at the mount-ing block.

Now, if the prince was just at home—and more important, if his sometime guest was here . . .

Murmuring a properly accented "Danke schön," Justin handed over the reins and a small coin to the groom and headed up the cut-stone steps to the front entrance. Schiller had advised him that a small gratuity always helped ensure attentive service. The pan-eled door ahead was painted a tasteful soldier blue that echoed the azure of the princely banner, and the door brass gleamed like gold in the afternoon sunlight. Before Justin could lift his hand to knock, the door was opened by a liveried butler who looked him up and down appraisingly.

"Guten tag," Justin said. "Ich heisse Carmichael. Der Prinz Karl von Hesse—er ist hier?"

With a slight bow the butler stood aside to admit him.

"Your German is quite acceptable, Herr Carmichael, but perhaps you would be more comfortable speaking English. Please to come in. His Highness is not at home, but you are expected. If you please, I will show you to the library."

Both relieved and a little puzzled—for he could not think how anyone might have been expecting him—Justin let the man take his hat and sword, also suffering a silent footman to remove his spurs and dust off his boots with a cloth. After that he followed the butler along a lavish hallway paved with black and white tiles and peopled by half a dozen near life-size alabaster statues of Greek and Roman gods and goddesses perched on pedestals of porphyry. As the butler opened the double library doors, the faint scent of beeswax tickled at Justin's nostrils, along with the heartier smell of good leather bindings and an undertone of something sweeter that he could not quite identify—not tobacco, like what Andrew smoked, but something more akin to incense.

The room was paneled in pale oak, its bookshelves crowded with leather-bound volumes of russet and burgundy and forest green, stamped with gold along their spines. A baroque fireplace carved of red marble dominated the wall to the right, with a spray of carefully arranged greenery and garden flowers decorating the grate; it made the room seem cooler. A mirrored overmantel reflected the rest of the room in double. From opposite the door, sunlight streamed through mullioned windows, filtering past heavy fringed velvet drapes swagged to either side of a book-laden writing desk.

"May I inquire whether you have brought letters, *mein Herr?*" the butler asked, recalling Justin from his quick perusal of the room.

Justin only just stopped his hand from going to his breast pocket. He was under orders to deliver his letters only to the Master.

"You said that I was expected," he said, ignoring the butler's question. "By whom?"

The butler gave him a little bow. "With respect, Herr Carmichael, I am not at liberty to say. Wait here, please."

Before Justin could inquire further, somewhat taken aback by the tone of the exchange, the butler had withdrawn and closed the

doors quietly behind him. Justin glanced nervously into the mirror to straighten his cravat and slick back an errant curl that was escaping from the ribbon tied at his nape, but when no one returned within a minute or two, his attention began to wander around the room.

He had never seen so many books before. Back home in Cambridge, his father had left him and his sister a library of more than a hundred volumes, considered a prodigious collection by New World standards; but the Prince von Hesse must have many times that number, perhaps as many as a thousand. There were folios and unbound scrolls as well, the latter stored in leather tubes on a pigeonholed shelf beside one window.

The prince's tastes apparently ran to the esoteric, too. The stack on the writing desk angled in the window bay revealed an astonishing selection of titles in a variety of languages: Latin volumes by Albertus Magnus and H. Cornelius Agrippa; a French text by Paracelsus, the Swiss-born alchemist and physician; the latest edition of Culpepper's Herbal; Lilly's treatise on Christian astrology, right next to Reginald Scot's *Discoverie of Witchcraft*. And something of fairly recent publication called *Vox Stellarum*, which, when he opened its cover to flip through the pages, seemed to be about astrological predictions.

"Interesting," he murmured under his breath, bending down for a closer look at one of the charts set out at the back of the book.

"Yes, I have always found it so," said a low, faintly accented voice behind him.

Justin could feel the blood rushing to his face as he whirled to confront the speaker. Despite the butler's denial that his master was at home, the man standing before the fireplace, hands clasped behind his back, must surely be the prince. His aristocratic bearing declared him totally at home in his surroundings. His coat was of a rich black brocade, impeccably cut; his small clothes close fitting and of a startling whiteness. A diamond glittered in the lace at his throat.

"Your Highness, I—"

"Not 'Highness,' my young friend," the man said, making a disparaging gesture with one elegantly ringed hand. "At least not here, though I have answered to that courtesy in the past.

Rheinhardt tells me that you call yourself Carmichael—which may explain your interest in my books."

Justin closed the book quickly and stepped back from it, convinced that his face must be as red as the volume's cover. "I do beg your pardon, sir. I meant no offense. Is my name familiar to you?"

"It is. The Chevalier Wallace holds you in very high regard, as does his son, who is married to your sister. It was I who asked that you be sent. Incidentally, you may call me Francis, and I shall call you Justin. You were told, I hope, that the letters you carry are intended for me, and not for Prince Karl."

Justin felt his pulse begin to throb in his temples, for he suddenly had an inkling just who this elegant stranger must be—though addressing that man by his Christian name was inconceivable.

"I was—instructed to seek out Prince Karl," he said carefully. "I hoped that he might direct me to a poor widow's son, who would meet me on Weldon Square."

"I have been known as the Chevalier Weldon," the man admitted with a faint smile, "and I am a poor widow's son." Justin barely dared to breathe as he waited to see if the man would finish the recognition by making the appropriate correction to the ritual phrase.

"But if I were the man you seek," the man went on, "I think I should rather meet you upon the level than upon the square. Do you not agree?"

It was all Justin could do to whisper, "Yes, sir."

"Eh, *bon*." The man gave him an amused nod. "That said, I think it fitting that we then might act upon the plumb. If that is acceptable to you, where do you think we should part?"

"Upon—the square, sir," Justin whispered, giving the required countersign.

"Good. Andrew and Simon have taught you well." The man smiled again. "This is all quite tedious, of course, for I know perfectly well who you are, and I believe you no longer have any doubts on my account. However, such things will not always be so obvious—which is why you must become proficient in using such signs of recognition. May I have the letters, please?"

Not daring to trust himself to speak, and daring even less to

disobey, Justin fumbled inside his coat and handed over the oil-skin-wrapped packet of letters.

"I thank you." The man indicated a chair by the fireplace. "Please take your ease while I deal with these."

Gingerly Justin eased himself onto the edge of one of the Queen Anne chairs, trying not to stare as the man seated himself behind the desk and unwrapped the oilskin. The letter on top bore the name: *HH The Prince Lucien Rene Robert de Rohanstuart.* The other three were addressed to the Chevalier Weldon.

"Ramsay's letter?" the man asked, lifting the letter addressed to the prince.

"Yes, sir."

Somewhat to Justin's surprise, his host broke the letter's seal and briefly scanned its contents before laying it aside to deal with the other three. Each was composed of several pages, but he leafed through each one almost as if merely verifying the number of pages rather than making any attempt to digest and understand.

But, clearly, he had read them. When he had shuffled through the pages a second time, he set them aside distractedly and sat for some time gazing silently out the window, not moving, hardly even breathing, giving Justin ample opportunity to study the man he now knew to be the Hidden Master he had been sent to find.

It was easy to see how Justin had mistaken him for a prince. Viewed against the sunlit window, especially in profile, he resembled a classical painting by Rembrandt or Tintoretto. Both his costly raiment and his finely drawn features proclaimed aristocratic station, though unlike most men of his obvious gentility, he wore no wig; nor did he powder the dark hair pulled back in a silk ribbon at the nape of the neck, though time had brushed the temples with silver, causing Justin to estimate his age in the midforties. When at last he bestirred himself, it was to pull two separate sheets of paper before him and take up a pen in each hand, after which he began to write simultaneously on the two pages.

His utter absorption in his task invited no interruption. As Justin watched in fascination, afraid that any word or movement might break the spell, the man wrote several pages this way, glancing easily from one to the other as his hands moved independently to

dip into the ink when required and then resume their separate reckonings, occasionally setting a page aside to draw fresh paper into place.

Finally, when the graceful hands moved at last in a flamboyant signature at the bottom of two pages simultaneously, Justin looked slightly away, hoping to convey the impression that he had not been staring. His companion affected not to have noticed, but that only tended to confirm Justin's suspicion that very little passed unobserved in the other's presence.

"You will receive your own instructions in the morning, along with other documents already prepared," the Master said, addressing Justin as he applied blotting paper to his work. "You will stay the night here and start back for France tomorrow. The Prince de Rohanstuart will be found at his father's estate in Brittany. You will give him Dr. Ramsay's letter. I believe you will find him a congenial traveling companion."

"Sir, may I ask a question?" Justin made bold to ask.

"Of course."

"Has James Ramsay's action harmed our cause?"

Justin's host smiled enigmatically and half rose to tug at a heavy damask bellpull before subsiding into his chair again.

"I would rather he had not done what he has done, but it can be made to work for us rather than against. I had already determined to send Lucien to the New World on another mission. It will do no harm for him to make a brief visit to Dr. Ramsay and his impatient Bostonians, if that will reassure them that progress is being made. The prince knows what he is to do and say, and you will take him additional instructions when you go to him. Meanwhile, this demonstration of royal interest and support should keep the good Ramsay and his impetuous friends from going off further in directions that might prove truly detrimental to our cause."

"But—is our cause not that of restoring His Majesty to his throne?" Justin countered.

"We have been working toward that goal," the Master conceded. "However, as you must know, many different factors and factions are at work in the New World. The Master Plan provides for several outcomes that may prove acceptable. This Tracing

Board is a complex one. Though many things have been revealed to me, much remains to be understood as other factors take their turn. My work elsewhere does not permit me to devote my full energies to the American colonies just now, but please assure the Chevalier that I shall be available when he has need of me. In all things, we shall meet upon the level and part upon the square. Do you understand?"

"I—believe so, sir."

The other cocked his head at Justin wistfully, and the younger man had the sudden impression that he was being scrutinized with far more than mere vision.

"Yes, I believe you do," the Master finally said quietly, "—or will, as you progress in the Work. Yours is a young soul, but you stand well prepared to pass the next threshold. Are you aware of that?"

Suddenly speechless, Justin could only manage a quick nod, for he had both longed and feared to hear those words. And to hear them from the Master's lips . . .

"I have known what you are feeling now," the Master said quietly, turning his attention back to the letters on the desk before him and starting to fold one. " 'Tis both heady and frightening, to be told such a thing. However, I am confident that you will prove—"

A knock at the door cut him off in midsentence, and he smiled as he glanced at Justin and called, "Kommen Sie."

It was the butler, carrying a small lighted oil lamp, which he brought to the little writing table, bowing as he set it down.

"*Danke schön*, Rheinhardt," the Master murmured, continuing his folding. "You anticipate me, *comme d'habitude*. I am well served."

"Thank you, *mein Herr*. Will you require anything else?"

"Not at this time, no—except to bring tea to the morning room in about half an hour. Can that be arranged? I should like Mr. Carmichael to meet someone."

The butler bowed again. "I understand, *mein Herr*."

"Oh, and Mr. Carmichael will be staying the night, so his baggage will need to be collected. I assume you do have baggage, Mr. Carmichael?"

"Yes, sir, at the Drei Könige," Justin replied, a little taken aback. "One trunk."

"You travel light," the Master said with a smile, and followed the observation with a rapid-fire instruction in German, of which Justin caught only the words for "horse" and "please."

As the butler left the room and closed the door behind him once more, the Master glanced at Justin bemusedly and gestured for him to come closer as he continued folding paper.

"I have told Rheinhardt to have your horse taken back to the inn when he has the trunk collected," he said easily. "He will arrange for a carriage for you in the morning. Meanwhile, we shall reseal the letter from Ramsay. I have informed Lucien that I read it. These that I have just written are for him and for Andrew and Simon, expanding upon instructions already prepared. You will receive those in the morning. Please be so good as to light that sealing wax for me."

Next to the lamp the butler had brought, a silver wax jack held a coil of bright vermilion like a tiny, captive snake. A little nervously, Justin moved around to the other side of the writing desk to obey, carefully removing the lamp's glass chimney and then lighting the wick of the sealing wax.

While the wax began to melt, the Master produced a gold pocket watch and detached a jet fob from the chain. Diamonds glittered on the fine, graceful hands as he used the fob to imprint a seal in the wax Justin poured onto the overlap of each of the three letters in turn. Justin was not able to make out details of the seal, but he caught a glimpse of the signature on the second letter, just before the man who called himself Francis pressed its folds flat and sealed it.

It was the name Justin had been expecting, but he had hardly dared to let himself believe it. Francis was the Christian name that Andrew said the writer had borne through several lifetimes, linked with other names like Tudor, Bacon, and Rakoczy.

But the name he had signed on the letters he had just written— and by which Andrew and Simon sometimes referred to him when not simply as the Master—was the Comte de Saint-Germain.

Chapter Five

S aint-Germain was not the only illustrious personage whose acquaintance Justin Carmichael was to make on that August afternoon. After the Master had addressed the letters just sealed, he handed them into Justin's keeping and then invited the younger man to accompany him to the morning room.

"As you no doubt have surmised, I am merely a guest in Prince Karl's house while he is away. But there is a far more important guest temporarily in residence. I should like to make you known to him. I believe you and your family have served him for some years."

The Master could be referring to only one man. Justin faltered in midstride as that realization registered, but Saint-Germain was already opening the door to the morning room, stepping aside in the open doorway, gesturing for Justin to precede him.

Across the room, silhouetted against the late-afternoon light that filtered through a curtained window, an unassuming-looking older man in a powdered wig looked up from a writing desk piled high with books and papers. His coat was a quiet dove-gray, well cut but without embellishment save for silver buttons and some kind of decoration glinting on his left breast. A pale blue riband crossed his ample chest from left to right, a handsbreadth wide, just visible

through the opening of his coat. His linen and smallclothes were as snowy white as Saint-Germain's. He wore wire-rimmed spectacles perched on his nose, but he removed these and laid aside a pen as he glanced at Saint-Germain in question.

"Majesté," said Saint-Germain, with a slight inclination of his noble head, "I have the honor to present Mr. Justin Frederick Carmichael, one of your loyal supporters from the American colonies. Mr. Carmichael, His Majesty Charles III, de jure King of England and Scotland. Justin is the young man we sent for, Charles. He has come to escort Lucien back to Boston."

Justin's astonishment actually to be entering the presence of Charles Edward Stuart quite overcame his shock that Saint-Germain should presume to address the King by his Christian name. He had heard it said by detractors that the King had grown fat and dissipated in exile, addicted to strong drink; but the man who now smiled and gestured for Justin to approach, though grown old and tired in the pursuit of his rightful crown, yet retained an ample measure of the grace and charisma that had drawn men to follow him thirty years before. Perhaps it was the kindness of the light that melted away some of the years and their disappointments, but for Justin, approaching with awe to drop to one knee and kiss the offered hand, his prince had suffered little in the intervening years.

"How good you are to honor an old man, Mr. Carmichael," the King said. His English was fluent, if faintly accented. "Carmichael, Carmichael . . . The Chevalier Wallace speaks very highly of you. I believe you are related in some fashion?"

Justin bowed his head, overwhelmed with emotion. "My sister is married to his son, M-majesty."

"Ah, then, he is something of a father-in-law, is he not? I make a hobby of studying these obscure family connections."

As an amused chuckle escaped the royal lips, Justin dared to lift his head. "I—believe Your Majesty may have discovered a name for the relationship," he murmured in amazement. "It has always seemed to me that there should be one."

The King pushed his chair a little from his table and leaned back in it, gesturing for Justin to get to his feet.

"You should make a close examination of my family tree some-time, young sir. 'Tis full of second cousins twice removed and half siblings and God knows what all else." He paused a beat in recol-lection. "A Mary Carmichael served my ancestress, Mary Queen of Scots—one of the four Maries who accompanied the young Queen to France, on her marriage to Prince Louis. Is it possible that you are related?"

"I am, sir," Justin said. "My direct ancestor was a brother to that Mary Carmichael."

"Ah, then, the link of service to my House *was* made long ago," the King replied. "And you are here to carry on that tradition. I thank you."

"It is my honor, sir," Justin murmured, making him the bow he had meant to make before he had fallen to his knees.

"But, sit down, Mr. Carmichael. Please, sit, and tell me about America. Rheinhardt is to bring us some lovely tea, even though Francis will never drink any of it with me. Perhaps you will see to it, Francis?"

This time Justin was taken aback that the King should call Saint-Germain by his Christian name—though the Master himself had told Justin to do so. Even more to his surprise, Saint-Germain made the King a dutiful little bow, if with an indulgent smile on his lips, and went to supervise the tray Rheinhardt was just bringing into the room. The King, however, motioned Justin to come see what was on his writing desk.

"I follow the events in America with great interest, Mr. Carmi-chael," he was saying, putting his spectacles back on and smooth-ing the page on which he had been writing. "You see? Here I have been extracting an account of the Battle of Lexington from this Salem newspaper. One of my agents delivered it only a few days ago."

He indicated the paper from which he had been copying, then turned back several pages in the journal to point out an earlier entry, all of it penned in a fine italic hand.

"Here is another one, from the *New York Gazette*—a fairly reli-able publication, I am told. This one describes the capture in May of a fort called—Ti-con—Ticonderoga, is it?" He stumbled a little

over the unfamiliar name and looked to Justin for confirmation. "I believe it is an Indian name."

"It is, sir," Justin replied.

"I thought as much. Fascinating creatures, your Red Indians. And here is news of another American victory, at a place called Crown Point."

His gesture not only invited but almost commanded Justin's closer perusal of the pages. The younger man turned them in wonder as the King continued to recount details that only a colonist should be expected to know well. Page after page had been filled with the inimitable italic script—and there were maps as well, sprawling layers of them, spread on another table nearer the window.

"You see? I have these of Mexico and the West Indies, so I may follow the overall naval strategies," the King said, plucking at Justin's sleeve and urging him to look. "These of New York and Philadelphia and Williamsburg are useful as well. And I understand that a great deal is happening in Philadelphia."

"It is, indeed, Sire," Justin managed to murmur. "The Continental Congress meets there."

"The Continental Congress." The King savored each syllable of the name. "They are like a—a parliament for the colonies?"

"After a fashion," Justin agreed. "Each colony sends delegates to represent it. Late in June they adopted the Massachusetts militia units surrounding Boston and commissioned General George Washington as Commander in Chief of a new Continental Army. I was there. He arrived in Cambridge a few days before I left, to take up his command."

"Ah, Cambridge—Boston," the King replied, pulling out another map. "I have a very good map of Boston—perhaps the best of all. But tell me of your General Washington, and what he plans to do there."

Concerning Washington, Justin could relate only what he had picked up from Simon, for his own exposure to the General was limited to admiration from afar. But over bowls of tea that Saint-Germain presented, he conveyed the more recent news of Breed's Hill to the King. He had no firsthand knowledge of that battle, for

he had been in Philadelphia with Simon and Andrew, but he had talked to dozens of people who had.

Talk of Breed's Hill led inevitably to discussion of specific American losses, with news of the death of Joseph Warren eliciting particular consternation—for the King, though he kept a neutral public face concerning the Craft, was an avid student of Freemasonry and knew of Warren's standing in the Craft. At his obvious distress—and Saint-Germain's warning glance—Justin abandoned any thought of mentioning the visitation Andrew had received from Warren the night after the battle, but he did assure the King of Washington's intention to find the body of the slain patriot leader, once they drove the British from Breed's Hill, and eventually give him a proper Masonic funeral.

"The Grand Master of Massachusetts," the King whispered when Justin had finished, tears welling in the brown eyes. "We are none of us immune, are we? And many more brethren will fall before this conflict is resolved—just as they did thirty years ago."

"Charles, don't," Saint-Germain said quietly from his chair across the room. "You cannot change the past."

The King braced his shoulders and raised his head, seeming to gather his dignity around him with the breath he inhaled.

"I know. You are right. But this time the outcome will be different, God willing. 'Tis a different land, but the basic cause remains the same: a just struggle against an illegitimate monarch. The Elector of Hanover must not be allowed to perpetuate his error in the New World as well as the Old."

"He *shall* not, Sire!" Justin said eagerly. "The offer you received from James Ramsay and his associates may have been premature, but it reflects the dreams of all of us who work in your behalf. God grant that the day soon will come when Charlie may, indeed, come into his own again!"

The last alluded to a line from a ballad popular immediately after the Forty-Five, and Justin pronounced the name in the Highland manner, "Tearlach," which non-Gaelic speakers had anglicized to "Charlie." Recoiling almost as if from a blow, Charles Edward Stuart bowed his head, suddenly an old and weary man once more.

"Pray, do not feed my hopes and dreams on ancient fantasies, my dear young friend," he whispered. "Believe that I treasure your loyalty, and that of dozens like you, but I am well aware of the obstacles to be overcome. It may well be that a crown shall come to me before I die—and I yet have hope of an heir—but I begin to fear that time is running out for me." Again he drew a deep, steadying breath, lifting his head so that, in the failing light, Justin caught yet another glimpse of the dashing prince of thirty years before.

"Meanwhile, your struggle is here and now, young sir, and Francis tells me that those who have served me in the past can serve me now by serving the cause aborning in the New World." He rose and dug deep into a pocket in the tail of his coat to extract a small leather-bound jeweler's box.

"This is for the Chevalier Wallace," he said, handing it to Justin, who also had stood. "Many years ago, as a mark of my gratitude for his service and friendship, I gave him the Order of the Thistle. It is the premier Scottish Order, but I think that this may be far more useful to him. Go ahead. Have a look. It replaces one he gave me at Culloden. Francis suggested that I have it made."

After glancing at Saint-Germain for confirmation, and fumbling at the catch on the box, Justin eased it open.

"Careful, don't drop it!" the King said. "It's Venetian glass."

It was, indeed, Venetian glass—the finest glass eye that Justin had ever seen. Had he not been warned that it was not flesh, he might have mistaken it for a real eye nestled in the wool that padded the inside of the box. As it was, he turned it to the light in wonder, not even looking up as Saint-Germain peered over his shoulder.

"I shall be calling upon Andrew to do some delicate work for me in the next months," the Master said. "It will be important that he not be recognized as himself. For a man whom everyone is accustomed to seeing with an eye patch—who makes a flamboyant fashion statement with the variety of his eye patches—seeming to have two good eyes will be a large part of changing others' perception of him."

"It's—incredibly lifelike," Justin murmured. "I am—quite taken

aback, I must confess." He closed the box and made the King a bow, remembering his manners. "But I thank Your Majesty, on behalf of the Chevalier Wallace, who will value it far beyond its beauty and utility, for having come from his beloved prince."

The King smiled sadly. "Spoken like a true courtier, Mr. Carmichael. 'Tis a grisly reminder, I must admit. And I would far sooner have kept him his own eye at Culloden, if that had been within my power. But since it was not, I make this poor attempt at late amends. Tell the Chevalier—" The King broke off and had to swallow hard to keep back his emotion. "Tell the Chevalier that I value, and will always value, his loyalty and friendship, both then and now; and that I—hope I may see him again, wearing his new eye, before I die."

He buried his face in one hand at that, stifling a sob, and Saint-Germain, with a glance that warned Justin not to interfere, gently set his hands on the King's shoulders and guided him to a soft high-backed chair.

"Lie back and sleep, my prince," the Master murmured, easing the silently weeping King into the chair and lightly beginning to stroke the furrowed brow, down the trembling shoulders. "Sleep and forget the sadness. Dream of better Times. *Dors, mon cher Charles. Dors bien. . . .*"

As Justin watched in amazement, straining to catch Saint-Germain's words, the King's sobs gradually ceased and he slept. Saint-Germain stood over him silently for several minutes, hands now leaning on the chair arms to either side of him, staring fixedly at the closed eyes, then roused himself and turned to face Justin. The younger man found himself immobilized before that steady gaze, but he could not seem to conjure any fear.

"Do you understand what you have just seen?" the Master asked quietly. "You may speak," he added when Justin's lips parted but no sound came out.

Justin managed to swallow and found that he *could* speak.

"I—have heard of such things from Simon, and from Andrew," he said softly. "I had never seen it before, or—experienced it."

Saint-Germain smiled wearily. "You will recall that I said you were ready to cross the next threshold. I believe this may have been a preparation for that crossing. Not an official part, of course. But true Initiates know that a formal ceremony often but sets a seal on something that has already begun in the candidate. Simon or Andrew will explain it to you. In those sealed letters you carry I have requested that they raise you Master Mason as soon as possible. In terms of our Inner Fraternity, that means a great deal more than it does to the exoteric Lodge—but you shall see all of that, in due course."

He glanced at the King, still obliviously asleep in the chair, then returned his attention to Justin.

"You will not speak of what you have seen in these last few minutes, even to Andrew and Simon. Do you understand?"

"Yes, sir," Justin whispered.

"Good. I shall not require you to forget it, for you show good potential, and the knowledge may prove useful in the future, but you will not speak of it. In the outside world there are people enough who think Charles Edward Stuart a drunkard and—well, you cannot be unaware what many of them say. As you may have gathered, much of that image is a front to put off serious attention by his enemies. His interest in and understanding of the situation in the American colonies is prodigious.

"But he is not a young man. Neither is his health what it might be. Unless the chances of his success are almost guaranteed, I cannot allow him to become involved in another attempt to take back his throne. That will be for his sons to do, or his sons' sons."

"But—" Justin had to concentrate very hard to get the words out, for it was far easier just to drift in the cadence of the Master's voice. "But he *has* no sons," he managed to whisper. "Is the Queen—?"

"No, the Queen is not with child," Saint-Germain said quietly. "After three years of marriage, she has not conceived, and his apprehensions grow. I pray God it will not be necessary to put her aside, but he must have a legitimate heir. He has fathered children on several mistresses, and even a son, but the boy lived only six months. That was long ago. Only the Lady Charlotte survives." He gave Justin a piercing glance. "Does it surprise you to hear me speak of him this way?"

Justin's mind seemed to be working far too slowly. All he could think was that he had not known that Charles Edward Stuart had once had a son.

"No, sir," he said carefully. "I had—gathered that you—were aware of many things to which others are not privy."

Saint-Germain chuckled with even a little real mirth. "I am impressed, Justin Carmichael. Even under my sway you have mind enough to be diplomatic. The skill should serve you well in the future." He glanced again at the King, then set his arm around Justin's shoulders and began walking him toward the door, also reaching into a pocket.

"One further matter, before I have you seen to your rooms. Give me your hand."

As Justin obeyed, Saint-Germain pressed a small brown leather pouch into the proffered hand and closed his own around it. From the pouch dangled a long leather thong, which he looped around the younger man's neck.

"What now resides within your keeping is precious beyond any worldly riches," he said quietly, pulling Justin slightly closer by the thong to gaze deeply into his eyes. "I require you to give it directly to Andrew and no other. After tonight, once you leave this house, you will carry it this way, but underneath your clothing. You will not remove it, even when you sleep; you will not look inside it; and you will die rather than allow it to be taken from you. Are my instructions clear?"

It was all Justin could do to summon the will to nod.

Saint-Germain breathed a tiny sigh as his hand tightened around Justin's over the pouch, and he broke eye contact for just an instant.

"Excellent. In truth, I would not normally entrust this to someone of your level of training, except that I have no other means for conveying it where it needs to be. This is not meant as any slight on your abilities or your trustworthiness, but merely states a fact. You have the potential to bear it safely one day, but your talent is yet untrained. If you disobey my orders, I cannot answer for the consequences. Do you understand?"

Even without the power behind the soft, penetrating eyes, Justin would not have thought of arguing.

"I understand," he whispered.

"Excellent." Saint-Germain tucked the pouch inside Justin's shirt, then tugged at a bellpull by the door. "You will go with Rheinhardt when he comes. He will show you to a room and bring you a light supper. After eating you will bathe and retire. You will sleep soundly through the night.

"In the morning, after you have broken your fast, Rheinhardt will deliver additional letters into your keeping. One of them will be addressed to you, but you will not open it until you are on your way. A post chaise will collect you at nine o'clock precisely. The driver will be instructed to take you all the way to the prince's estate at Kilvala, and to arrange for appropriate accommodations en route. Once you are under way, you will read the letter addressed to you, commit its instructions to memory, and destroy it. Do you understand?"

Justin nodded drowsily. "Yes."

"*Bon.* You should reach Kilvala well within a fortnight. There Prince Lucien should be awaiting your arrival. I suggest that you rely upon his knowledge of local conditions in determining how best to proceed back to Boston. A French ship will probably be best, perhaps from Brest."

At the faint rap on the door, Saint-Germain opened it himself, guiding Justin easily into Rheinhardt's hands. "Mr. Carmichael is very tired, Rheinhardt. He will wish to retire as soon as he has had a good supper and a bath. Please see to it."

"Sehr gut, mein Herr," the butler said, with a bow and a click of his heels.

"Good night, then, Mr. Carmichael," the Master said. "I shall not see you in the morning, but I wish you a pleasant night and a safe journey. Au revoir."

Justin did not remember following Rheinhardt to the room prepared for him, or eating or bathing, but he awoke refreshed the next morning, quite confident of what was expected of him. He read his letter as soon as the post chaise had left the vicinity of Leipzig, easily assimilating its contents and then tearing it into tiny bits, which he scattered randomly all along the road south.

It was not until midafternoon that he realized he had not once thought to ask Saint-Germain about Washington and his most unusual dream. Nor had Saint-Germain mentioned it, though Justin was sure Simon's letter about it had been among those he'd delivered to the Master.

He concluded that it must be none of his business, at least for now, and that Saint-Germain had answered what needed to be said in one of his letters to Simon or Andrew. In the ensuing fortnight, as the post chaise bounced along the miles across Germany and into France and Brittany, he put the American Commander in Chief largely out of mind and found himself daydreaming more than once about the glory of the Stuart cause, and the thought of a Stuart restoration in the New World.

Chapter Six

T he carriage conveying Justin Carmichael to Kilvala crossed
into Brittany during the first week in September, continuing westward past Rennes and gradually threading its way
along increasingly narrower roads toward the coastal town of Ros-
coff.

The journey itself was uneventful to the point of tedium. Justin
had found the foreign scenery interesting at first, but the novelty
soon began to pall in the continuing heat and the repetition of day
upon day of dusty travel in the swaying post chaise. On the road
from just past dawn until nearly dark each day, Justin spent a great
deal of time reading or dozing—though today promised release
from the monotony at last, for his driver had informed him this
morning that, barring unforeseen mishap, they would reach Kilvala
sometime that afternoon.

He had been starting to anticipate their arrival since their stop to
change horses at noon. As the post chaise rattled through a set of
imposing gates to enter a tree-lined avenue, he closed the volume
of Cavalier poetry that had occupied his last hour and leaned out
the window to peer ahead, finally thumping on the roof of the
coach with the hilt of his sword to get the driver's attention.

"Eh, monsieur, ici c'est Kilvala?" he shouted.

"Oui, monsieur."

"Ah, c'est bon. Merci."

So. Kilvala at last. Justin had no idea how large the prince's estate might be, but it looked to be passing prosperous. In the fields to the left, farmworkers were harvesting a fine crop of wheat. The dust from their labors hung on the still air in a golden haze, shimmering in the late-summer heat. In the fields to the right, new-mown hay lay drying in the sun, some of it already gathered into neat haystacks in preparation for winter.

After a mile or so the carriage slowed to pass through a small village—probably where the estate workers lived, Justin guessed—then rattled across a fine stone and timber bridge. Ahead, the avenue ran straight as a string toward an impressive château, beautifully sited on a gentle hill. Its stone gleamed white and silver and starkly shadowed in the late-afternoon sun.

A groom and a footman seemed to materialize out of nowhere as the post chaise pulled up before the broad front entrance, the former moving to the horses' heads as the latter opened the carriage door and swung down the folding steps. The two were simply clad in breeches and shirts rather than livery, perhaps as concession to the heat, but they carried out their duties to the new arrival with precision and courtesy. The haughty-looking majordomo who appeared at the top of the stairs *was* in livery, and looked uncomfortable in it, but he became all deference as Justin disembarked from the post chaise and donned his hat with its white cockade.

"Bonjour, seigneur, que désirez-vous?" the man said, making Justin a respectful bow.

Justin favored the man with a polite nod, answering him in impeccable French.

"Je m'appelle Justin Carmichael, de Boston. Je porte une lettre pour le Prince Lucien de Rohanstuart. Il est ici?"

The man blinked. "Vous venez de Boston, monsieur? Suivez-moi, s'il vous plaît."

Justin followed, reflecting that the mention of Boston seemed to have provided his entrée, rather than any recognition of his name—not that anyone in the prince's household necessarily would have known what name to expect. Whether the prince him-

self was actually at home remained to be seen. The majordomo had not answered that question; nor would Justin have expected him to.

Another footman dutifully took his hat and sword just inside the front door, and Justin tugged at a cuff as he followed the major-domo through a stately entry hall toward a carved and gilded door. The room beyond proved to be a large and very ornate baroque drawing room, all cream and crystal and gilt, with large and airy windows looking out onto a vast formal lawn and garden that eventually gave onto a breathtaking view of the sea.

"S'il vous plaît, monsieur, restez ici," the majordomo said, ushering Justin in and then closing the door behind him.

Justin moved on into the center of the room and cast his gaze around it. His first impression was one of opulence, with pale silk hangings on the walls and cut-crystal chandeliers suspended from the ceiling bosses; but closer inspection suggested that the room had been rather more grand some years before. Most of the furnishings were of good quality, undoubtedly quite costly when new, and some of the paintings and gilt-framed mirrors and candle sconces were as fine as Justin had seen anywhere.

But the furniture was sparse, and several empty spaces on the walls betokened paintings removed, probably for conversion to needed cash. In short, it appeared that the fortunes of the present occupants of the house had been affected just as adversely as those of other formerly well-off supporters of the Stuart cause, who had stood by their liege at Culloden and elsewhere.

Turning away from his perusal of the room, Justin strolled over to the windows overlooking the gardens, his tread silent on a silk carpet adorning the polished wooden floor. Off to the right, on a grassy parterre, two men dressed all in white were engaged in a spirited *passage des armes* presided over by a third white-clad man, perhaps a fencing master. Justin watched them for a moment or two, nodding approval at the apparent skill of both combatants, then returned his attention to the room, wandering over to a baroque bookcase set into the wall nearer the door.

He had not expected to find the variety of books he had seen on Saint-Germain's desk, so he was not disappointed. The volumes appeared to be primarily French and Italian, mainly of a pious

religious nature, but a few titles in English caught his eye—some Shakespeare and Marlowe, Spenser's *Faerie Queen*, *Tom Jones*, and even a rather dog-eared copy of one of Dr. Franklin's famous almanacs.

This time, however, he did not make the mistake of picking up any of the books, contenting himself with merely scanning the titles on the spines. Consequently, he had only to turn as the door into the drawing room opened and a tallish white-clad man entered, wiping his face and neck with a linen towel draped over one shoulder.

He appeared to be one of the fencers Justin had been watching out on the lawn, perhaps as old as thirty, with a gingery mustache, a mane of sweat-darkened hair tied back with a black silk ribbon, and his immaculate white shirt open at the throat. He was not classically handsome, but the brown eyes were lively, the jawline strong and symmetrical. His well-proportioned body moved with the grace one might expect of either of the men Justin had seen fencing. The man smiled as he spotted Justin, heading toward him with right hand extended.

"My dear Mr. Carmichael," he said, in slightly accented English, giving Justin a firm handshake. "Joinville tells me that you have come from Boston, and that you have a letter for me."

At once Justin found himself ever so slightly on guard, for though the man seemed to be presenting himself as Prince Lucien, Justin had not expected so informal a first encounter. He also was remembering Saint-Germain's instructions regarding caution.

"I have business with the Prince Lucien de Rohanstuart, sir," he said carefully. "Are you that gentleman?"

The man laughed aloud and wiped his face again with his towel. "I assure you that I am, sir," he said, glancing wistfully at the gold signet ring on his left little finger, "though I cannot fault you for wondering, the way I am dressed. You have found me at my *exercice d'escrime*—my swordplay. Perhaps I should have donned more formal attire before I came to you.

"But I can tell you that the letter you bear will have come from the Bostonian Party, and I will guess that they have sent you as my escort back to Boston, where I am to speak to them on behalf of my royal cousin, Charles Edward Stuart."

All but convinced, Justin gave the man a formal inclination of his head. "You reassure me, sir," he said with an answering smile as he reached into his coat pocket. "In fact, I bear *three* letters. Two are from—the Chevalier Weldon."

Justin had substituted one of the Master's aliases at the last instant, as a final test that the man was who he said he was. The brown eyes widened slightly above the ruffled white shirt, but the aristocratic lips only repeated the name. "The Chevalier Weldon. Ah."

"Who is?" Justin insisted.

"Why, the Comte de Saint-Germain, of course."

Without further hesitation Justin took out the letters and handed them to the prince.

"You will find that Saint-Germain has resealed the letter from Boston," Justin pointed out as the prince examined the seals on all three letters and glanced at him curiously. "I was sent first to him, after my superiors learned of the offer made to the King last winter. I take it that you are familiar with the background of the situation?"

"Yes, I am," the prince replied.

"Good. That saves a great deal of explaining. Saint-Germain read Dr. Ramsay's letter before writing his second set of instructions to you. He suggests that you read it first."

With a distracted nod the prince broke the seal on Ramsay's letter and opened it, gesturing vaguely toward one of the chairs by the fireplace.

"Thank you, Mr. Carmichael, I appreciate your candor. Please, sit down. 'Tis clear I should read all of these before we continue our discussion."

A soft knock preceded the entrance of a servant with a tray bearing two silver goblets and a frosty silver pitcher.

"Ah, thank you, Michel," the prince said as the servant offered Justin one of the goblets. "In Spain they call this drink sangria, Mr. Carmichael. It is a mixture of fruit juices and good red wine. I find it very refreshing after heavy exercise, especially in weather like this. My father keeps ice all through the summer in an icehouse above an underground spring." He lifted his own goblet. "Deoch slainte an Righ."

The old Gaelic toast to the King's health surprised Justin, but a mere lifting of his glass seemed adequate response, for the prince had already turned his attention to the letters, only sipping at his wine distractedly. Moving into the window bay, where the light was better, the prince paced while he read first Ramsay's letter and then the ones from Saint-Germain. Occasionally he paused to set down his wine and mop his face and neck with his towel. He glanced up once or twice as he read, but Justin could detect no change in his expression beyond thoughtful speculation. When, at last, he had finished, he stood gazing out at the gardens for a very long time, the letters all but forgotten in one hand, before turning back to his guest.

"The Master's instructions are most interesting," he said as Justin rose expectantly. "No, please sit down, my friend." The prince waved Justin back to his seat as he, too, settled onto a chair opposite Justin, tossing the letters onto a table and taking up the pitcher the servant had left. "Saint-Germain says that I may be utterly candid with you."

Justin made the prince a formal little inclination of his head. "You may rely upon my discretion, sir."

"Yes, I am certain that I may." The prince gave him a droll smile as he leaned across to refill first Justin's goblet and then his own.

"First of all, then, may I suggest that we dispense with formality between us? Saint-Germain has suggested that I travel under the alias of Dr. Lucien Rohan. The Bostonians may know me as *Count* Rohan. I shall assume another surname later on, but that, too, will be a doctor. Such being the case, it might be prudent if you began immediately to think of me as a *docteur* and not as a prince. A slip of the tongue before the wrong people could be dangerous for both of us."

Justin gave a tentative nod, endeavoring to make the necessary change of mental gears. "Very well, s—" He caught himself before he actually said "sir" and allowed himself a faintly sheepish grin. "Fortunately, as a physician several years my senior, you *could* be entitled to an occasional 'sir,' I believe—which ought to cover most any inadvertent slip I might make." He cocked his head thoughtfully. "*Are* you a doctor?"

The prince smiled. "Let us say that I have sufficient medical training to pass for one—which is fortunate, since Saint-Germain intends that I should offer my services as a doctor to the British once I have met with your Bostonians."

Justin gaped. "I beg your pardon, sir?"

"Ah! You are calling me 'sir' again! You *must* pay attention! I have leave to tell you more, and shall, but tales of dark doings are best told after dark, preferably over a fine meal. You shall dine with me this evening, of course."

At Justin's bewildered nod of agreement, the prince went on.

"I know. Saint-Germain has said to call him Francis, and that is as inconceivable for me as it is for you. But I insist that you call me Lucien. I am a very small prince."

The last was said in such a tiny, wistful voice that Justin found himself laughing out loud.

"There, you see?" the prince said. "You do have permission to relax. It is essential, if we are to work together closely. And I hope you will not mind if I call you Justin. The name comes from 'justice,' does it not?"

Justin recovered enough to venture a quick grin. "It does."

"Ah, justice. It is what we all seek, both for our royal Charles and for the people of the American colonies—and perhaps for the two of them together." The prince snorted. "Not that you will ever obtain justice from the Hanoverian usurper in London. Are you aware that he has rejected the so-called Olive Branch petition recently offered by your Congress and now considers the American colonies to be in open rebellion?"

The news was like a dash of cold water in Justin's face, and he felt a vague, sickly sensation in the pit of his stomach as he shook his head.

"Ah, yes," the prince went on. "The London government is an evil force to be reckoned with." He cocked his head at Justin and grinned. "Shall I tell you what my father is doing right now, to confound the enemy?"

"Prince—Alexander?" Justin murmured.

The prince nodded approvingly. "Very good. Your Andrew Wallace no doubt has told you of their escapades after Culloden, before

you or I were even born. As it happens, *mon cher papa* bears an uncommon resemblance to our royal cousin." He grinned. "For the last little while he has been leading the British Secret Service a merry chase, all through Wales, so that Charles Edward may be about his business with Saint-Germain. He has done this before, and doubtless will do again."

In his astonishment Justin forgot all about deference to princes. "You mean he's doubling for the King?"

"He is. He began the chase in Paris, some months ago, so that Charles Edward might slip away from Florence unobserved. Now the chase has been shifted to Wales, where the English are convinced that he is waiting to take ship to America, to head the rebellious colonists. God willing, that shall, indeed, be my cousin's aim, when the time is right; but meanwhile, the false scent provides excellent cover for doing other necessary things."

Justin could only shake his head in amazement. "I had no idea."

Prince Lucien smiled. "Fortunately, few people do. But enough of this. You must be tired after your long journey; and Saint-Germain desires that we embark as soon as possible for the New World. Have you made arrangements?"

"He said that I should rely upon your guidance in that regard, since you are more familiar with this area. He did suggest that we might wish to leave from Brest."

"Very well. I shall have one of my men see to it." The prince stood, followed quickly by Justin. "It will not be possible to leave for several days in any case, even if a ship were waiting now. Since the time of my father's return is uncertain, I must make arrangements for my mother to manage the estate until his return. Saint-Germain knows this."

Justin inclined his head. "Whatever you think best."

"Good. Come, and I shall have Joinville show you to an apartment, where you may rest and refresh yourself." He sniffed delicately at an edge of his sleeve and made a grimace of distaste. "I shall welcome the refreshment of a bath as well.

"After that, over a quiet supper, I shall share Saint-Germain's instructions, and then we shall discuss our mutual Mother, the Craft—*la Veuve*, whose sons we are. I shall be fascinated to com-

pare practices on both sides of the ocean. And incidentally, allow me to offer my felicitations that you are to be raised Master Mason upon your return. Saint-Germain informed me," he explained, at Justin's look of surprise. "He also has requested that I be present as his representative—which will be my honor and privilege. For that matter, since we are to be in one another's company for a very long ocean voyage, I would be quite pleased to offer you instruction in the material of the Third Degree, both to profit the Craft and to help while away the time."

"I—thank you," Justin managed to reply. "Your generosity overwhelms me."

The prince shrugged and smiled. "We are brothers in the Craft, Frère Justin. It is the least I can do for you—and for Saint-Germain."

Chapter Seven

A French ship bore Justin and his royal companion back to the New World. Autumn squalls made the return crossing far more lively than his outward journey had been, but they also cut several weeks off the usual three-month sailing time. Since the port of Boston was still under British blockade, they came into Plymouth, where they arranged cartage for their trunks by wagon and hired horses from a local livery stable for the journey north to Cambridge.

It was late November when they finally arrived, and late in the afternoon of a chill, stormy day. Because of the hour and the weather, Justin decided to put the hired horses into the Wallace barn for the night; he would deal with their return to a local livery operator the next morning. The stable was empty as they led the animals out of a drenching downpour, suggesting that Simon either was still gone for the day or was keeping his mare at Washington's headquarters, so Justin and the prince unsaddled, rubbed the horses down, and fed them. When they finally gathered up their saddlebags to make a dash for the house, Justin opening the stable door to lead the way, Andrew was just reaching for the latch from outside, cloaked and hooded and with a lantern in his hand, for night had fallen.

"Ah, it *is* you," Andrew said to Justin, eyeing the stranger behind him speculatively.

"Andrew! I didn't want you to have to come out in the rain!" Justin began, turning in confusion to glance at the prince. "This is—"

"Rohanstuart, Chevalier," the prince said before Justin could finish, offering his hand to the elder Wallace. "But here I am to be known as Dr. Rohan—*Count* Rohan, if I must use an alias among the Bostonians. I am honored to meet you, sir. My father speaks of you warmly, as does my cousin."

Andrew clasped the offered hand and bowed over it slightly. "Then the honor is mutual, sir," he replied. "I trust that Justin has taken good care of you?"

The prince smiled. "He has, indeed. He is a credit to your family. After nearly three months in his constant company, I quite understand why he was chosen for his mission."

As Andrew glanced at Justin in mild question, the younger man grinned self-consciously. "It will take me several hours to explain," he said. "Meanwhile, perhaps we should go into the house. Is Simon expected anytime soon?"

"No, he's been sleeping at headquarters for the past week or so. But I'll catch you up on all of that later."

With that they dashed into the rain, splashing across the soggy yard to duck under the eaves above the back porch as Andrew opened the door. Inside, Arabella was just sending the children up to bed and gave a little cry of relief as she saw her brother.

"You *are* back!"

"Uncle Justin, Uncle Justin!" the children cried, the two younger ones swarming around him to hug his legs and jump up and down excitedly. Charles, the oldest, settled for a manly handshake and insisted upon relieving his uncle of his saddlebags, though he staggered under the weight as Justin handed them over.

"Books," Justin mouthed, to both Charles's and Arabella's delight. "And you lot," he continued, trying to get the attention of the other two. "Let's have a little decorum, please. You'll make our visitor think we have nothing but a houseful of Red Indians!" He

shook his head at their continued chatter and held up his hands for silence, which slowly came.

"Dr. Rohan, may I present my sister, Mistress Arabella Wallace. And these are her children: Charles, Sarah, and James. Children, do you think you can remember your manners enough to say hello to the doctor?"

Young Charles immediately offered the newcomer a grave hand-shake, but the two younger children suddenly went shy before the tall, self-possessed stranger, little James darting behind his mother to hide. Arabella dipped in a graceful curtsy, well aware who he really was.

"You are welcome to our home, sir," she said. "I hope your journey was not too arduous."

The prince smiled and kissed her hand in a display of Gallic charm. "Your brother was most excellent company, dear lady, and even the rigors of the storm fade from memory before your radiance."

A blushing Arabella hustled the children off to bed then, while the three men divested themselves of dripping cloaks and hats and muddy boots and warmed themselves before the fire in the parlor. Andrew made the expected polite inquiries about the prince's father, but Justin guessed that the older man's more immediate curiosity had to do with the letters Justin was sure Andrew knew he carried. Their visitor apparently sensed the same thing. No sooner had Arabella returned from bedding down the children than the prince stood expectantly.

"The Chevalier is far too polite to say it, but I know he must be eager to hear of Justin's travels, and to receive the various instructions he carries—all of which is most appropriately done in private. If I may, then, I should like to relieve you of some of the awkwardness of this moment by suggesting that I might retire upstairs somewhere for an hour or two. If someone will show me where I am to stay . . . ?"

"But you must be frozen through and starving," Arabella protested as Andrew murmured that it really was not necessary, and Justin looked uncomfortable. "What kind of a hostess would you think me, to send a man off to a cold bed and a cold room, without even a bite of supper?"

The prince smiled. "If you desire it, dear lady, I shall be delighted to come back down after Justin has had a chance to share his news. I am quite conscious that my presence here must be an imposition—and that you are nonetheless willing to accommodate me in the interests of our mutual cause," he added, holding up a hand to still her protest.

"But, please. You will find my company far more agreeable if you first have satisfied your curiosity regarding Justin and his messages. I assure you, I am not offended. I shall be offended only if you insist upon leaving all of us in an uncomfortable position."

So saying, he picked up his saddlebags and waited expectantly. After a glance at Andrew and Justin, Arabella made him a little curtsy and indicated that he should follow her upstairs.

"I shall bring you a warming pan and a tankard of mulled ale in a few minutes, sir," she said, taking up a candlestick to light their way. "I hope you won't mind that you must share a room with Justin."

"Not at all. I have found him a most agreeable companion."

When they had disappeared at the head of the stairs, Andrew nodded approvingly.

"He resembles his father," he said to Justin, easing down into one of the chairs by the fire and putting his stiff leg up on a stool. "Did you meet Prince Alexander?"

Justin shook his head, sinking down on another chair opposite. "He was off in Wales, being a decoy for the King. And guess what! The King was at Leipzig with Saint-Germain! I met him. I actually met Charles Edward Stuart!"

"Indeed?" Andrew murmured, his face going very still. "And—how did you find my prince?"

"He was incredible! I couldn't believe how well informed he is about the colonies. He follows every battle, every skirmish. He has a whole journal of newspaper items he's transcribed in his own hand—and maps. I think his maps are as good as any Washington has!"

Andrew nodded, a fond smile lighting his one good eye and melting away some of the years.

"It is a way to keep the dream alive—the only way he knows," he said softly. "Would that all this had come sooner. . . ."

As his voice trailed off, Arabella came back down the stairs and disappeared into the kitchen. Justin, recalling himself to the business at hand, pressed a hand against his chest and then against an outer coat pocket, confirming that the letters and other items he carried were still there.

"Before I give you the letters I brought," he said, reaching into the outer pocket to extract the leather jeweler's box, "I have something for you, from the King." He raised an eyebrow as he handed it across to the older man. "I warn you, it isn't just another decoration. He said to tell you that it replaces the one you gave him at Culloden, and that he—hopes to see you wear it, before he dies."

Andrew had started to open the box, but at Justin's mention of dying he looked up sharply.

"He isn't ill?"

"No, sir. But he— You'd better look at it. Apparently it will serve Saint-Germain's purposes as well, but I believe this was a gift from the King's heart."

Andrew eased the lid upward on its hinges, peering into the cushioning wool as he prodded it with one finger. Then he froze for just an instant before easing it open the rest of the way. The eye of Venetian glass looked out at them in all its pale glory, a perfect match for the single real eye that gazed down at it, suddenly tear filled.

"I—guessed that Saint-Germain would arrange for one of these," he said after a moment. "But I never thought that my prince would provide it. 'Tis a work of art."

Justin smiled, pleased with himself. "Saint-Germain sent along a bottle of special lubricant as well. It's in my bag. I believe he's provided additional instruction in one of his letters. There are several of those. I take it that this is part of some kind of disguise?"

"Something like that," Andrew murmured. Closing the box, he set it carefully on the little table beside his chair. He kept looking at it from time to time, as if to reassure himself that it still was there.

"Perhaps I'd better see those letters next," he said after a moment, clasping a monocle into his good eye.

Without comment Justin reached into his coat and produced an oilskin package from which he extracted a thick sealed packet,

which he handed to Andrew. The Chevalier opened the packet and sorted through the variously labeled items, then opened one. While he read, Arabella went back upstairs with a tankard and a warming pan. She returned just as Andrew was finishing the first letter. Justin, meanwhile, had undone his cravat and was unbuttoning his shirt to get at the leather pouch still hanging from its thong around his neck.

"Justin, what on earth?" Arabella murmured as she came to sink down on a stool before the hearth.

"This one is from Saint-Germain," he said, extracting the length of thong until the small leather pouch at the end appeared. "He put it around my neck in Leipzig and said to let no one remove it unless I were to die in the process." After looping the thong off over his head, he handed the pouch to Andrew with a profound sigh of relief.

"There. *That* duty is accomplished, at least. He—laid some kind of—compulsion on me about it. I have no idea what it is. I couldn't even bring myself to feel it through the bag. But you know what it is, don't you?" he added accusingly, as the old man and his sister exchanged knowing glances.

"Not—precisely," Andrew replied, fingering the pouch. "But I know what its purpose is. Let us see what form it has taken, shall we?"

Bending his attention to the object in his hand, he loosened the drawstring that held the pouch shut and reached inside. A wad of wool emerged between his fingers, like the one cushioning the glass eye, and he unfolded it to reveal a scrap of sky-blue silk wrapped around a beautiful moonstone, the shape and nearly the size of a pigeon's egg. Two flat, narrow bands of polished silver encircled the stone, intersecting at the two ends. The smaller of the ends also had a small silver ring soldered at the crossing. Closer inspection revealed mystical symbols engraved on each of the bands, with more engraving on the undersides, visible through the stone.

"Alchemical symbols?" Arabella murmured, not touching the stone itself but raising Andrew's hand, so that candlelight shone through it from behind.

"Hmmm, in part," Andrew agreed. "Some are zodiacal signs,

though, and others come straight from the Cabala." He adjusted his monocle and brought the moonstone closer, then fished a magnifying glass out of a waistcoat pocket to inspect the underside of the bands.

"The inside engraving is in Latin. That should present an easier starting point than the symbols. Or perhaps Saint-Germain has already done this for us." He laid the moonstone back in its nest of silk and wool and handed it and the magnifying glass to Arabella before breaking the seal on the second of Saint-Germain's letters.

"Go ahead and see what you can make of it. You, too, Justin— see what you were carrying all these weeks. It won't hurt you."

While they examined it, Arabella quite clinically, Justin with rather more caution, Andrew read his letter. When he had finished, he read it again, then folded it carefully and put it in his inside coat pocket.

"An interesting proposition, and a challenging one," he said, touching the fingertips of one hand to his breast. "I shall need to think more on this. May I see the stone again, please?"

Arabella held it out to him, still in its cocoon, and he plucked it out with bare fingers, nodding as he looked at it again—though Justin had the impression that whatever Andrew was learning came as much from touch as from sight.

"Yes. I think I understand—or will, when I have done as the Master commands. Meanwhile, I shall need to raid your work basket for some silk, Arabella."

"I'll get it," she said, rising to retrieve the basket from its place beside the fireplace. "Are you to wear the stone, then?"

"On occasion."

She grimaced, lifting the lid to rummage inside. "I'm afraid the silk I have is very fine. Would a chain not be better?"

He shook his head. "No, it must be silk. Blue would be best, but red or white will do nicely. Or purple, if you have it. Anything but black."

"Very well, here's red," she said, extracting a small ivory spool and unreeling a few inches of scarlet thread. "It's even finer than I remembered, though. Silk is strong, but I doubt one strand will hold the weight of that stone safely."

As she gestured toward the gem in his hand, her face lit with an alternative idea. "How, if I were to crochet you a chain of the scarlet? It would be much stronger, and far less likely to tangle. Or *ribbon*? I have some narrow blue ribbon in here, I'm certain!"

As she produced it triumphantly, a pale narrow length perhaps a yard long, Andrew smiled and lifted a hand to brush her cheek gently with the back of his fingertips.

"There's my clever girl!" he murmured. "The ribbon will be splendid. And thank you for not asking questions I cannot yet answer. Be assured, both of you, that I shall tell you what I may, as soon as I know myself."

His words brooked no further discussion on the subject, though both he and Arabella then proceeded to pump Justin for further details about Charles Edward Stuart. Justin shared what he could as they moved into the kitchen and Arabella set about supper preparations, but he found his tongue oddly uncooperative when he even thought about the things Saint-Germain had forbidden him to discuss.

Sometime not too long after that, Prince Lucien joined them, making certain they heard him clumping down the stairs, appearing apologetically in the kitchen doorway with a quilt bundled around his shoulders.

"I hope I have given you long enough to accomplish what needed to be done," he said, "but it was colder than I realized. May I join you?"

Any remaining awkwardness quickly disappeared this time, as Andrew made inquiry about the health of the prince's father and then shifted deftly into a discussion of how the planned meeting with the Bostonians should be accomplished.

"My original mission has been somewhat complicated by this additional task the Master has set for me," the prince said when Andrew had pointed out the need to keep his presence secret, even among most of the Bostonians, if he planned to stay on afterward as a Jacobite agent among the British. "Now that you have had opportunity to read his instructions, how do you suggest we proceed?"

Andrew considered his answer as Arabella ladled out steaming portions of lamb stew with dumplings for the four of them.

"We shall need to consult with Simon first, of course," he said, "but I think it wisest if your 'official' visit is confined to one meeting with a small, carefully selected group of local Jacobites. Ramsay's offer was premature, as you know, and only a small faction within the Bostonian Party were privy to it in the beginning, but you can imagine the excitement as word has spread that you were coming—discreet within our number, I assure you, but they all are eager to meet you. Fortunately, I've been able to make them understand why too many would be dangerous."

The prince nodded gravely. "I appreciate your caution."

"In any event," Andrew went on, "once you have made your official appearance, and 'Count Rohan' has departed for France, we shall do our best to shelter you until Dr.—Saint-John, is it?—is ready to infiltrate the British Army. I take it that the Master has instructed you in how you will pass information back to us while you play Saint-John, and how you're to avoid being taken as a deserter, once it's time to slip away and return to France?"

The prince nodded. "To a certain extent I shall be relying upon Justin and Major Wallace for that—and General Washington."

The eyebrow arched above Andrew's good eye. "He *will* need to know something about you, if you're to act as his agent behind the British lines. But not who you really are, I take it?"

"No—and not even of the Saint-John persona until after I have concluded my business with the Bostonians. A meeting is to be arranged before I go over. Justin has letters for Major Wallace that will clarify his part in this, and how he is to expedite my access to the General.

"Also following my work with the Bostonians," he went on, "there is the matter of a Master's Lodge to be convened for Justin's raising. Saint-Germain was most insistent that I be present. I would suggest that several of your Bostonians also should be included among the brethren invited, as their knowledge of Count Rohan's presence and approval will strengthen Justin's future credibility for our cause, despite his youth. Obviously, this must occur before Rohan returns to France, since I cannot return to Cambridge in any capacity once I have taken the Hanoverian shilling."

Justin frowned. "You won't simply enlist, will you?"

The prince smiled and shook his head. "No, I have letters of introduction that will secure me a respectable commission without any questions being asked. But that is Dr. Saint-John's mandate. Meanwhile, Count Rohan has much to do. First of all, I shall need to meet with Major Wallace, the sooner the better. Then we must make arrangements for the meeting with the Bostonians. As you can see, a great many details will need to be worked out."

They discussed more of those details while they ate, gradually shifting back to Andrew's reminiscences of the Forty-Five and the prince's retelling of stories his father had told him about that last stand at Culloden. By the time they were ready to retire, the prince had put them all at their ease, and even Andrew felt far more reassured about his presence.

The next morning dawned cold and clear. The prince was still deeply asleep, so Justin dressed quietly and went downstairs for a quick breakfast of porridge and ale before heading off to Vassall House, where General Washington had moved his headquarters in mid-July. He was not yet commissioned, so he wore civilian attire, but he had Simon's letters on him and came proudly to attention as his brother-in-law entered the room where he had been asked to wait.

"Brevet Lieutenant Carmichael reporting for duty, sir," he said.

"Justin, welcome back!" Simon came to pump the younger man's hand enthusiastically and thump him on the back. "When did you arrive?"

"Last night." Justin grinned as he reached into his coat to produce Simon's mail. "There have been some new permutations of what we thought was going on, however," he said. "If you'll read these first, it will probably save a lot of explaining."

When Simon had skimmed through the two letters addressed to him, he folded them and slid them into his inside pocket.

"I shall give these my fuller attention later," he said, "and I shall arrange to come home for supper this evening. What is he like?"

Justin nodded speculatively. "You'll like him, I think. I do. He isn't at all what I expected. But, then, this whole situation isn't what any of us expected, is it? Incidentally, I wonder if I might see the General for a few minutes, while I'm here. On the voyage over,

I had some very informative conversations with a Hessian officer that I think he ought to know about."

When Simon had heard a brief account, he agreed.

"Wait here, and I'll ask if he can see you now," he said. "I've already seen to your commission, but this will clinch it."

Ten minutes later Justin was entering the General's office with Simon, standing stiffly to attention.

"General, Mr. Justin Carmichael," Simon said.

"Please be at ease, Mr. Carmichael," the General said, leaning back in his chair to appraise the new arrival. "Major Wallace speaks very highly of you. Please stay, Major. Now, what's this about German mercenaries being hired by the British?"

After five months of command, Washington looked every one of his forty-three years, the craggy face drawn with fatigue, though he also looked every inch the General. As Justin recounted what the German officer had told him about negotiations between the British government and the Landgrave of Hesse, he found himself focusing on the blue riband across the great man's chest that identified him as the Commander in Chief, even if the three stars on the epaulets had not also proclaimed that fact. It was very like the King's Garter riband, though of a darker blue. The desk in front of Washington was covered with dispatches in various stages of preparation; and as Justin finished telling everything he knew, the General jotted down a few notes and turned his attention to Simon, waiting attentively a few feet behind Justin.

"Your young aide has made a fine beginning to his military career, Major," he said with a nod. "I think you'd better give him his commission and see that he gets into proper uniform as soon as possible. And, *Lieutenant* Carmichael—thank you for bringing this to my attention. Dismissed."

"Sir!" Justin said, unable to control a grin as he snapped to attention and saluted.

A brief return to Simon's office produced the promised commission, backdated to the day Washington had taken command. Simon swore him in, calling in Thomas Mifflin as witness, then sent him home briefly to don the blue and buff Continental uniform that Arabella had ready for him. Justin then remained with Simon

for the rest of the day, catching him up on further details of his absence whenever the opportunity presented itself and preparing him to meet the prince later that evening. Simon still was somewhat dubious by the time they left Vassal House, just after dark, but he was prepared to be convinced that the prince was, indeed, the powerful piece in the game that Justin now believed him to be.

At Andrew's direction Arabella had laid supper in the library for him, Simon, and the prince. She had already put the children to bed by the time Simon and Justin arrived, and laid two more places in the kitchen. Andrew and the prince were waiting in the parlor, and the latter came gracefully to his feet as the master of the house entered.

"You must be Major Wallace," the prince said, offering his hand. "Lucien Rohanstuart. I believe we have much to discuss."

"So Justin has informed me," Simon said with a smile, taking the prince's firm handclasp. "A belated welcome to my home, sir. I must apologize for my fellow Bostonians who have precipitated matters so as to require your presence. Justin has told me something of your—enhanced mission."

The prince smiled. "I had hoped that he would—and that he will not be offended if we excuse him from our meeting this evening," he added, glancing at Justin. "He will not mind dining with your goodwife, I hope—who has prepared us a very fine meal—for I think that in the last few months he has heard quite enough of what I have to say regarding the Stuart cause. Besides that, other matters requiring discussion this evening are best kept among Master Masons, regarding how and when he is to be made one himself."

Justin's momentary disappointment at being excluded was quite overshadowed by Simon's appreciative chuckle.

"Now I see why the French are noted for their diplomacy," he said easily. "Allow me to compliment you on your handling of the language, Prince."

Their visitor smiled again. "Please, no such titles among brethren," he said. "May I suggest that you refer to me as Brother Lucien, if title you must use, for both my surnames are apt to fall awkwardly upon the tongue in this context. And if I may, I shall

call you Brother Simon, since otherwise there should be two
Brother Wallaces to confuse the issue. You will pardon me, I hope,
Brother Andrew, if I occasionally slip and refer to you as Chevalier,
since that is the way my father has always spoken of you."

On this note of informality and genial fraternity, the three retired to the library and remained behind closed doors for the rest
of the evening.

Chapter Eight

I t did not take long for word of Justin's return to Cambridge
to reach interested ears. The next morning Andrew was enjoying a bowl of porridge oats with his youngest grandson
and his daughter-in-law when a determined knocking called
Arabella to the door. Simon had stayed the night, but he and
Justin had already set out for Vassall House; the prince was still
abed.

"Why, good morning, Dr. Ramsay," Andrew heard his daughter-in-law exclaim, rather louder than would have been necessary.
"Yes, Justin arrived home the night before last, very late. I believe
he intends to call on you this afternoon. He said something about a
letter for you. But do come in and have a bowl of tea."

Her warning gave Andrew time to compose his thoughts, so that
by the time she ushered James Ramsay into the kitchen, Andrew
was wearing a bland, indulgent smile.

"Good morning, James," he said easily, though he did not get
up. "I'm afraid you've missed Simon and Justin. The General
scheduled an early staff meeting. Say good morning to your name-
sake."

Ramsay's pale gaze had darted around the kitchen as he entered
behind Arabella, but he flashed a forced smile in the direction of

young James Wallace, who was feeding porridge to a small painted horse with red wheels.

"Good morning, Jamie-lad. Andrew, may I have a word with you in private?"

"Of course."

Taking his time, and leaning far more heavily on his stick than was necessary, Andrew led Ramsay into the library and closed the door.

"Well?" Ramsay whispered. "Is he here?"

"Is who here?"

"The prince!" Ramsay replied. "Don't try to tell me that he didn't come back with Justin. I know that *someone* did. He calls himself Dr. Rohan."

"Very good," Andrew said, sitting down and easing his bad leg onto a footstool. "Please sit down. Did you get the name off a ship's manifest?"

"One of my agents did," Ramsay said sourly. "Is he the prince?"

"Actually, it's *Count* Rohan, for our purposes," Andrew replied. "Do sit down, James, or I shan't tell you anything more. No one is trying to keep him from you, but the poor man was exhausted after his journey. You know what the weather has been like. I believe Arabella already told you that Justin had planned to call on you this afternoon."

Ramsay subsided onto a chair with a sigh, rubbing both hands across his face. His pale hair was almost the same shade as his fawn-colored coat and was tied back with the white silk ribbon that was his personal badge of loyalty to the Jacobite cause.

"I'm sorry," he whispered. "It's just that we've waited so long. . . ."

"Not nearly long enough," Andrew replied sharply. "We're fortunate, indeed, that the King was willing to send his cousin as a gesture of his continued goodwill, when our offer was so woefully premature. But I will not dwell on the past," he added as Ramsay looked up resentfully. "Count Rohan requests that a meeting be arranged as soon as possible and suggests that its number be limited to no more than a score."

"Why not all?" Ramsay demanded. "Surely all of us have a right—"

"Safeguarding the prince's identity will be difficult enough with twenty men knowing who he really is," Andrew interjected. "He suggests that we couch the gathering in the fiction of a Lodge meeting. This was the most plausible cover we could devise to avoid arousing undue curiosity when so many men arrive in one place. It has the added advantage that, since all of us are brethren in the Craft, an actual Lodge can be convened, if desired, with the proceedings protected under long-standing obligations already sworn by all in attendance."

Ramsay nodded slowly. "An inspired suggestion. But could we not use this ruse several times, so that all our members might meet the prince? It would do a great deal for morale."

"I am certain that it would," Andrew replied, "but the danger is too great. His Highness is more than willing to undertake this commission for his cousin, but too much exposure could bring him to the attention of the British." *And could prove fatal to Dr. Lucas Saint-John,* Andrew added to himself. "He has booked return passage on a ship leaving in ten days' time. The King will be eager to receive his report on *us* as soon as possible."

"I had hoped he would stay longer," Ramsay murmured, a little taken aback. "May I see him?"

"What, now?"

"Later today, perhaps. Certainly before the meeting."

"I think that might not be wise," Andrew replied, for Ramsay had become enough of a loose cannon that he might regard royal access as a condoning of his recent insubordination. "The prince knows that you are largely responsible for the premature offer to the King and is understandably resentful at seeing his royal cousin's hopes dashed yet again. Furthermore, and for the same reasons, you are *not* in the highest of favor with the Master just now—who has had to explain to the King why the timing is not yet right for him to try taking up his Crown. Best not call particular attention to yourself."

Ramsay had deflated like a spent balloon as Andrew spoke, and now he hung his head over his folded hands. "Is he very angry with me?" he asked quietly.

"Who, the Master?"

"Yes."

"That is not for me to say," Andrew replied. "But I believe that the letter Justin intends to give you later today is from him. If you wish to be reinstated in his good graces, I suggest that you pay careful heed to his instructions."

Ramsay nodded slowly, looking up after several seconds.

"I had already made some preliminary preparations," he said quietly. "I shall endeavor to set up the meeting as soon as possible."

Ramsay had the meeting arranged within three days. The location that he secured was a room above an inn called the Silver Tassie, where several local Masonic Lodges were wont to meet. The Sons of Liberty and other patriot groups also used the premises on occasion, when the Green Dragon Tavern was not available, so local inhabitants were well accustomed to seeing cloaked men coming and going at night, and asking no questions.

The list of potential invitees was winnowed down to seventeen before being finalized, to include Simon, Andrew, and the prince among the total of twenty to attend. Any larger gathering might have attracted too much attention, even given the usual comings and goings at the Silver Tassie. At Justin's own suggestion, since he already knew what the prince was going to say, it had been agreed that he should be the one to serve as Tyler for the ostensible Lodge meeting.

Accordingly, on the appointed evening very early in December, Justin was stationed just outside the door to the room above the Silver Tassie Inn, sword in hand, as was appropriate for his supposed office, but armed underneath his cloak with a brace of loaded pistols stuck into his belt. He was not in uniform—none of the men were—but he came to attention when, at the appointed hour, Andrew escorted the cloaked and hatted prince up the stairs from the back entrance of the tavern below.

"Is everyone here?" Andrew asked quietly.

Both he and the prince were dressed formally tonight, Andrew in his customary gray, with a black velvet eye patch and his silver-headed walking stick, the prince all in black and white, pristine linen and lace gleaming above the collar of his greatcloak. The dark green of Thistle ribands showed across the chests of both men—a rare opportunity for Andrew to wear his—and the breast stars of the Order flashed in the light of Justin's lantern. A gilt-hilted smallsword hung at the prince's side, and he wore his long hair curled and powdered for the occasion. It made him look older and more grand—a prince indeed, where before he had become simply Justin's Brother in the Craft and congenial travel companion.

"Aye, the last one arrived a few minutes ago," Justin said a little nervously, glancing down the empty stairwell behind them. "They've been trickling in for the past hour. Two that weren't on the list showed up with Ramsay, but I went ahead and admitted them rather than cause a stir. Simon said it was all right."

"Fair enough," Andrew murmured. "Has he sworn them all?"

"He has."

"Well done, then." Andrew set a hand on Justin's shoulder in reassurance, then turned to the prince. "Shall we, Your Highness?"

At the prince's nod Andrew raised the head of his walking stick to rap three times on the door, then opened it. The men seated around a long table in the paneled room beyond came to their feet in a scraping of chair legs as the two entered. Simon was waiting to take the newcomers' cloaks.

Not a sound intruded on the respectful silence save the closing of the door behind them and the measured tread of heels on wooden planks as Andrew gravely led the prince to the place prepared for him at the head of the table, where an open Bible lay beneath the square and compasses of Freemasonry. Three candles were lit on the table, arranged as if, in truth, a Lodge meeting were being held, and more candles burned in mirrored wall sconces all around.

The prince took his place without ceremony, waiting as Andrew moved in on his right and Simon took a place at the far end of the table. It was Andrew who spoke first, his one-eyed gaze sweeping neutrally over the assembled men.

"Gentlemen," he said quietly, into a silence that would have made a falling pin seem loud, "so that we need not court additional danger by speaking dangerous names, our guest desires to be ad-

dressed this evening as Count Rohan. Sir," he added, turning slightly to the prince, "I beg leave to present loyal members of the Bostonian Party, who have been working toward that day when a Stuart restoration may become possible. On your left is Dr. James Ramsay, who has convened this meeting tonight."

Doffing his hat, the prince bowed over it in acknowledgment, then put it back on as he took his seat—as was appropriate if he had been, indeed, presiding Master at a Lodge meeting, for the Master alone wore his hat during ritual.

"Thank you, Chevalier," he said quietly. "Please be seated, gentlemen."

The men sat, to further scraping of chairs and knockings of swords and heels against table and chair legs. Expressions varied from doubtful to hopeful to awed.

"First of all," the prince said, before anyone else could seize the initiative, "please allow me to present my credentials." Reaching across his Thistle riband to delve into an inside pocket of his coat, he produced a folded piece of paper, which he handed to Ramsay. "The Chevalier has already read this, Dr. Ramsay, so I shall ask you to inspect it and pass it on so that your colleagues may satisfy themselves that I do, indeed, have the authority to speak for my royal cousin."

A ripple of interest followed the document as it made its round of the table, whispered queries dying away as each man saw it for himself. When it came back to Andrew, he merely laid it on the table before them, much as a Masonic charter might be displayed at a Lodge meeting. Bold at the bottom of the page, and authenticated by his seal, was the signature of Charles Edward Stuart: *Charles III R.*

"*Et maintenant,*" the prince said quietly, "I should like to begin by making a short statement. I think there can be no argument within these walls that Charles Edward Stuart is, and by right ought to be, de jure King of England. That, de facto, Hanoverian usurpers have held the throne for most of a century is a travesty of justice whose measure may never be equaled.

"But my royal cousin has never given up his just claim, and *shall* never concede while there is breath in his body. And if, in the course of throwing off Hanoverian oppression here in the New World, a power base can be established whereby a Stuart restoration might be possible, with an eye to extending this restoration to the recovery of the Scottish Crown in particular, His Majesty has authorized me to assure you that he would be willing to consider a call to such a restored Crown."

A stir of satisfaction and approval rippled among his listeners, but the prince continued.

"The means of accomplishing such a task is by no means clear. The Hanoverian threat is vast, and great care will need to be exercised in order even to consider the King's own presence here in the colonies. In that I fear that your very generous offer is ill timed, for as yet you have no Crown to offer him.

"But come he shall, if all is properly prepared," he continued, cutting off incipient protests. "And even if that time should never come, it may well be that, at very least, your efforts on his behalf will have occupied sufficient British resources on this side of the Atlantic that a direct assault may be made in England itself, for the eventual restoration of the Stuart monarchy.

"To that end I invite your comments and questions, with the assurance that I shall report back faithfully what you have said, for His Majesty's enlightenment and consideration."

He had them eating out of his hand by the time he finished, and Andrew was able to relax a little after that, as the meeting shifted into a true discussion. Gone was any lingering resentment that the King had not taken up their offer or come to treat with them himself. The prince listened attentively to each question and concern voiced by his now avid supporters, answering their questions when he could and occasionally making comment.

By the time they moved to disperse, the entire company had been charmed and inspired by this engaging Stuart prince, and Andrew was forced to concede that perhaps, in the end, James Ramsay's unauthorized action had not been so precipitous as they had feared. Certainly, morale among the Bostonians had never been higher. It was with genuine regret that he had to inform them that another such meeting would not be possible, since pressing business required the prince's imminent return to France.

Afterward, while the attendees began slipping away by ones and twos, Andrew informed Ramsay privately that, in fact, the prince's departure would be delayed until after the following evening, when a Master's Lodge was to be convened in the Wallace library to raise Justin Master Mason.

"The prince has asked that you attend and assist," Andrew told him, "and suggests that you bring along one or two of the others who were present here tonight. The choice he leaves to you."

The request caused Ramsay to raise an eyebrow. "Am I to take it that the prince has decided to involve himself in our Masonic affairs?"

"Ah." Andrew allowed himself a wan smile. "I assure you that his interest is totally separate from what occurred tonight. On the voyage from France he and Justin apparently developed a cordial relationship, as one might expect of two bright and enthusiastic young men with common interests. They spent a great deal of the crossing time discussing the Craft. Mere discussion soon turned to instruction, with the result that he believes Justin more than ready to be raised Master. Understandably, he would like to be present when this occurs."

Which was true, as far as it went, though Andrew had omitted to mention that the prince also was following the lead of Saint-Germain's instruction.

"I see," Ramsay said. "Will the prince raise him?"

"No, he leaves that happy duty to me, since Justin belongs to my Lodge; he is content simply to be present and to assist."

"Why include me?" Ramsay asked. "I should have thought I am in disgrace for having precipitated tonight's meeting."

"You acquitted yourself well, in the final analysis," Andrew said flatly. "We seem to have minimized the potential damage caused by your premature actions. Besides that, you are still a Past Master, and a brother in the Craft, and one of the most influential members of the Bostonian Party. Your witness of Justin's perfection in the Craft can also be seen as an acknowledgment that he has come of age within the Jacobite movement. The prince was most impressed with the way Justin discharged his commission to come fetch him."

Ramsay nodded, apparently satisfied. "I shall be honored, then. Have you any personal recommendation regarding whom I should bring along?"

"Perhaps the Irishman Colonel O'Driscoll, and another of your choosing. I have tried to select only Past Masters. The time may come when it will be important that Justin's standing in the Craft has been witnessed by someone with international standing. For the same reason I have invited Dr. Franklin to assist."

"Very well. I shall make the arrangements. What time should we arrive?"

Chapter Nine

The convocation had been called for eight o'clock the following evening. It was dark by five, a cold, dry night, and the children had been sent to stay overnight with a neighbor. Arabella retreated upstairs with a book recommended by the prince, for a woman's presence at any ordinary Lodge would not be permitted—even though her training in Saint-Germain's inner order made her more than the equal of most of the men who would be participating.

By a quarter to the hour, half a dozen very senior Freemasons had congregated in the Wallace library, the outside arrivals carrying satchels and cases. A fire crackled on the hearth to keep the winter cold at bay, and fragrant bayberry candles burned on the mantel and in twin mirrored sconces opposite the windows, whose heavy drapes were drawn.

The redoubtable Dr. Franklin had been among the first to arrive, joining Andrew, Simon, and the prince to warm himself before the fire and offer his felicitations to a somewhat self-conscious Justin. Following shortly came Ramsay, an artillery officer named Murray, and Colonel O'Driscoll, who hailed from the Grand Lodge of Ireland, chartering body for most of the military Lodges operating in the colonies, both British and patriot. To all of the

newcomers, the prince was introduced only as Brother Rohan, though the Bostonians knew precisely who he really was.

Just on eight came the final arrival necessary to constitute a Lodge "just and perfect": the Commander in Chief himself, wholly unexpected by all but Simon and Andrew, but most cordially received, quietly dignified in the blue and buff of his Continental uniform and the blue riband of command. An aide accompanied him as far as the door, obtained permission to put their horses in the Wallace barn, then went off to a nearby tavern for supper.

"Good evening, gentlemen," the General said to the room at large, as Simon ushered him into the library, where the accoutrements of Lodge were being set out. "Major Wallace informed me that this was to be a special evening for young Carmichael. I approve of my young officers being active in the Craft. Congratulations in advance, Brother Carmichael." He shook Justin's hand firmly. "I am honored to be present."

"Thank you for coming, sir," Justin managed to reply. "It is I who am honored."

A somewhat flustered Justin retreated soon after to a quiet spot near the door, unable to believe his good fortune in having a Master Mason of Washington's stature present, in addition to the venerable Franklin and a prince. He told himself that if he could put aside his awe in Saint-Germain's presence, he ought to be able to do it with Washington in the room; but the two were of a similar cut, at least in the wielding of authority. Though he knew the General's reputation as an active and conscientious Freemason, Justin had never attended a Lodge with him before.

Washington's presence at this particular Lodge raised additional questions, especially in light of the very odd dream he had confided to Simon before Justin had sailed for Europe. Justin found himself wondering whether the dream perhaps had betokened some kind of esoteric awakening in the General, to be somehow harnessed and directed by his participation in the night's ritual. Since returning, there had been no time to question Simon much about further developments in that area, or to learn what Saint-Germain had said—and the Master himself had deftly avoided mentioning

Washington, at least to Justin. The possible implications were most sobering.

Of course, Simon might have invited the General strictly in his capacity as an unimpeachable witness—or perhaps Washington himself had asked to attend, impressed with the intelligence Justin had given him on the Hessian mercenaries. And he *had* said that he approved of his young officers' participation in the Craft, which Justin knew was true.

Which brought him back to tonight's ritual. It was not the outward form of the rite that concerned him—somewhat predictable, if one had paid attention to one's earlier initiations and understood the symbolism. Nor need a participant in the Craft expect to experience anything beyond the externals of any given ritual; the Craft worked on many levels, not all of them apparent until one was ready to progress from one to the next.

The prince had offered an example of multiple levels during one of their long discussions in mid-Atlantic. If one likened Freemasonry to a religious hierarchy—which he had hastened to declare that it was not—then the raising of a candidate from Fellow Craft to Master might almost be viewed as entry into a kind of priesthood. Beyond the rank of Master Mason, a man might attain no higher Masonic achievement until he one day served as Installed Master of some regular Lodge—as every other man in the room had done, Justin suddenly realized, with the possible exception of Washington. Returning to the religious analogy, an Installed Master might almost be considered a kind of Masonic bishop, in his ability to pass on the powers of his office and to initiate, pass, and raise new Freemasons.

Justin smiled faintly at the notion of that many "bishops" in one place, when there was not even one conventional bishop of any faith in all the colonies. Simultaneously, he realized that when peace eventually permitted a return to normal life—and provided he survived the coming conflict—he, too, would be called upon to take his turn as Installed Master, perhaps in this very Lodge.

Meanwhile, the very least Justin could expect of tonight's ritual was an elucidation of certain symbols and parables on an immediate and conscious level, intended to raise his awareness of truths pertinent to his spiritual growth, just as the initiations to Apprentice and Fellow Craft had done. The Master had hinted at far more than that, of course. Justin had long understood that outward ritual in any initiatory context was but a matrix in which to accomplish the real work in the candidate, often having but little bearing on what went on within—as Saint-Germain had made a point of reminding him. He had said that Justin was ready to cross the next "threshold" in some more esoteric context—indeed, the process had already begun—and had hinted that important progress, perhaps, was to be expected in the context of tonight's ritual.

Which raised the question of why Saint-Germain had made a point of instructing the prince to be present. If Saint-Germain was a mystery, then what about the charming and personable Lucien Rohanstuart, obviously enjoying Saint-Germain's confidence on levels not yet apparent, but not yet inclined—or not yet permitted—to disclose just how far that confidence extended?

Was the prince somehow deputized to act for Saint-Germain as more than witness tonight? As he thought about it, Justin suddenly realized that it was "Brother Rohan" who would receive him when he entered the Lodge to begin the actual initiation. Of all the offices the prince might have assumed, other than the Master's chair, that one alone gave him direct ritual contact with the candidate. Somehow the coincidence made Justin a little uneasy, even though he trusted the prince and would not have thought of questioning Saint-Germain.

In need of reassurance, he sank down on a straight-backed chair in a corner and made himself glance around the room to compose himself, seeking stability in familiar landmarks as he watched the physical layout of the Lodge take shape. Improvisation was the norm in the New World, for the colonies boasted few places dedicated exclusively to Lodge work—and none built specifically for that purpose.

Still, the Wallace library was far better suited for Lodge use than the usual room above a tavern, where the Tracing Boards must be sketched out in chalk on the bare floorboards and then scrubbed away when the night's work was done. And few Lodges in the New World yet enjoyed the luxury of floor cloths bearing the appropri-

ate symbolism. The one now being unrolled in the center of the room had been painted and embroidered by Arabella, working to specifications provided by Simon and Andrew. Justin found himself wondering whether it would scandalize the other men in the room to learn that a woman was privy to at least this part of their secrets.

The background was a checkerboard design of black and white squares, light and darkness in balance, just like the floors of the permanent Lodge rooms Justin had heard of in London and Paris, with a blazing star painted and embroidered in the center. The border appliquéd along the edge—the looped design called the *cordon de veuve*, or "widow's cord"—represented the Divine Providence that encompassed and protected the "widow's sons," as well as their ties of mystic Brotherhood. The tassels at the four corners recalled the four cardinal points and virtues so important to the Craft.

Arabella had embroidered and appliquéd other symbols of Freemasonry along the top of the cloth, beneath the tasseled ends of the widow's cord and before the checkered squares began—symbols of the Entered Apprentice and Fellow Craft Degrees: the rough and perfect ashlars, the three pillars, the square and compasses, the plumb, the ladder leading upward toward a seven-pointed star, the cross, the anchor, the outstretched hand reaching upward toward the cup. Symbols for the Master's Degree would be added on another cloth once the ceremony began.

None of the floor cloths were for walking on, of course—except by the candidate and his conductor, in the process of an initiation. The Worshipful Master presided from behind a table set along the top edge of the cloth, in the east, and the rest of the brethren stood and sat around the cloth and would "square" the Lodge as they perambulated during the course of the ritual.

A low admonition from Dr. Franklin recalled Justin from his contemplation, urging all present to clothe themselves for work. From satchels and cases and capacious pockets emerged white lambskin aprons, to be girded about the loins of their respective owners with tasseled cords. Most, including Justin's, were plain white, and lined with white watered silk, but embroidery embel-

lished those of Franklin and the prince, following European usage, and the linings were blue. Franklin's blue was a darker shade, signifying his status as a former Grand Officer.

Justin's apron was whiter than most, for his being newer in the brotherhood than anyone else present, but he donned it with pride and the ease of ample practice, tying the cords so that the tassels hung down in front, and then, as a Fellow Craft for the last time, folding the flap up and securing it to a button of his waistcoat. After tonight he would be entitled to wear the apron with flap folded down, as did all the other men in the room.

To these uniform symbols of membership in the Craft, a few of the men added jewels of office suspended on narrow ribbons of white silk: Andrew's square and compasses, as Master of the present Lodge, with Franklin and the prince wearing similar emblems as Past Masters of their own lodges.

The preparations were nearly complete. Andrew had already taken his place at the center of the table in the east, gavel in hand. He alone wore his hat, as presiding Master. His warrant from the Grand Lodge of Massachusetts already lay before him, toward his left, where Franklin would sit. The document had been signed by their late Grand Master, Joseph Warren, whose body still had not been found. Without such a warrant, no regular Lodge could legally function.

Also on the table, and on smaller stands to either side of the door, pewter candlesticks held three unlighted candles. And from a well-worn valise the Commander in Chief himself took out a well-thumbed and obviously much-cherished Bible, touching it reverently to his lips before laying it on the table before the Master. Opened, it would become the Volume of Sacred Law, which transformed the room from a mere library into a temple.

Beside it, ready to be set in place when the Lodge was officially opened, Franklin laid a large pair of compasses of silver and gilt, the arms opened at a forty-five-degree angle, the steel compass-points oriented toward the bottom of the book, spanning perhaps a foot. A square he placed there as well, of a similar size—this one made of olivewood from the Holy Land, with brass fittings polished to shine like gold. Both were Franklin's personal property,

collected in the course of his various journeyings around the world, and represented two of the most potent symbols of Freemasonry: the compasses, for keeping one within due bounds, and the square, for regulating one's actions. As a Past Master of one of the same lodges as Andrew, Franklin would act as Immediate Past Master for the night's working, a sort of master of ceremonies to oversee the details of the ritual and ensure that all was conducted as should be.

"Places, please, gentlemen," he said when he had given the room a final look around.

At his word those not already in place went to the positions to which they had been assigned: Washington to the chair at Andrew's right hand, Franklin to the left; Simon and Ramsay to either side of the door, as Senior and Junior Wardens in the west. O'Driscoll stationed himself directly before the door, sword already drawn, ready to function as Tyler. Murray was stationed in the south. The prince waited beside O'Driscoll, ready to become the Inner Guard when his services should be needed. Justin stayed where he was, quietly rising from his place in the northwest corner, ready to withdraw when he was bidden.

The library's fireplace lay in the south, the fire and the candles on the mantel providing ambient illumination to that side of the room. Franklin came to light a slender taper from one of the candles, pausing then to snuff out both before carrying the taper carefully back to Simon, to whom he delivered it with a bow. En route back to his place at Andrew's left, Franklin extinguished the mirror sconces on the wall opposite the windows, leaving the room lit only by firelight and the taper in Simon's hand. When he had seated himself, and Andrew had signaled his assent by laying down his gavel, Simon began the ritual.

Holding his light aloft in the silence, light bearer to the Lodge, he slowly began moving purposefully from west to east, skirting the floor cloth along its northern edge. At his approach Andrew picked up the candlestick set on the table before his chair, returning Simon's bow.

"Wisdom in the east," the Worshipful Master said, lighting his candle from the taper Simon presented.

The taper was passed to Franklin, who pinched out its flame. Andrew then gave the lighted Master's candle to Simon, who bowed in acknowledgment and carried the Master's candlestick back around the south to his own place, right of the door, to light the second candle.

"Strength in the west," he said as the new wick flared.

The Junior Warden's candle remained to be lit. Ramsay held it only a few feet to the left of where Simon stood; but to go directly to it would require moving widdershins, which was contrary to proper Lodge procedure. So, instead, Simon turned to his right and went the long way round, squaring the Lodge with military precision, skirting the floor cloth again, saluting as he passed the Master's chair, and bearing the light through their midst, until he came at last to the Junior Warden's place and bowed.

"Beauty in the south," Ramsay declared, lighting his candle from the one Simon bore.

A third time Simon squared the Lodge, returning the Master's candle to its place beside Washington's Bible. Lights now burned there and to either side of the door. When Simon had returned to his station, Andrew's hand signal bade them sit.

"Worthy Brethren, I ask now that we spend a few moments in silent meditation for our intentions, beseeching The Great Architect of the Universe to fire our resolution, that this night's work may be well and thoroughly done."

Profound silence settled on the room for a long moment, broken only by the crackle of the flames in the fireplace and faint, distant sounds from the street far outside, until at length the Master's gavel knocked once to command their attention again.

"Brethren, I pray you assist me to open this Lodge."

As all of them became upstanding, Justin was aware of O'Driscoll coming to attention in the shelter of the closed library door, ready to take up his post when directed.

"Brother Junior," Andrew said to Ramsay, who was serving as Junior Warden. "What is the first care of every Freemason?"

"To see his Lodge close tyled," Ramsay replied promptly.

"Direct that that duty be done," Andrew commanded.

With a bow Ramsay turned to the prince, who was Inner Guard.

"Inner Guard, see the Lodge close tyled."

"Brother Tyler, do your duty," the prince said, in turn, addressing O'Driscoll.

With a smart sword salute, O'Driscoll turned on his heel and went outside, closing the door behind him. When three distinct knocks had sounded from the other side of the door, the prince turned back to Ramsay.

"Brother Inner, the Lodge is close tyled."

"Worshipful, the Lodge is close tyled," Ramsay reported back to the Master.

After this the Master proceeded to question the assembly regarding the number of principal and assistant officers and their various duties. Justin knew he should be paying close attention, answering each question in his own mind and considering its deeper meanings, but he found his attention wandering, distracted by increasingly vibrant impressions of color surrounding each officer as his situation was established. It was something he had never noticed before. The color around the prince, in the Inner Guard position, was a silvery violet, but a brilliant blue surrounded Simon, and a paler gold wrapped itself around Ramsay. Justin could not quite decide what the color was around Andrew, but when, as Presiding Master, he removed his hat and declared the Lodge duly open, a rose-gold blossomed around him, punctuated by scintillating points of blue and green.

"I declare this Lodge duly open for Masonic purposes, in the name of God and holy St. John," Andrew said. Concurrent with his uttering the word "open," Franklin opened the Volume of Sacred Law and moved the square and compasses onto the open pages, the points of the compasses pointing away from the Master and the square overlapping them, as was proper for opening in the First Degree. ". . . forbidding all cursing and swearing, whispering, and all profane discourse whatsoever," Andrew went on, "under no less penalty than the majority shall think proper."

With that he rapped sharply three times with his gavel and put his hat back on, and Franklin solemnly began to recite the opening words of the Gospel of St. John:

"In the beginning was the Word, and the Word was with God,

and the Word was God. The same was in the beginning with God. All things were made by Him; and without Him was not any thing made that was made. In Him was life; and the life was the light of men. . . ."

The proceedings moved quickly after that, as Andrew demanded and was given the step and sign of an Entered Apprentice by all present. With no business to conduct besides Justin's raising, he was able to dispense with many of the usual forms and raise the Lodge from First to Second Degree by an abbreviated procedure, this time requiring that all give him the steps and signs of Fellow Crafts. The outward symbol of this conversion was the placing of a letter G in the center of the blazing star on the floor cloth, which duty Justin himself performed, amid appropriate questions and knocks from the Master and responses from his officers.

That done, and preparations having been made for further raising the Lodge from Second to Third Degree, Justin was required to leave the room, passing quietly into the Tyler's charge outside. He could hear the vague murmur of the responses being made inside, just faintly audible, but he could not understand the words, nor was he meant to. However, he *was* meant to make certain physical preparations at this time.

As O'Driscoll resumed his stern vigil before the closed door, naked sword held in readiness across his body, Justin retreated to a bench beside the window and took off his shoes, also unbuckling his breeches at the knees and removing his stockings—for he had been instructed that both knees must be made bare, and both heels slipshod. His coat and waistcoat he also shed, opening his shirt to the waist to bare both breasts and unbuttoning his cuffs to bare both arms. Then he waited.

After a few minutes all sound from the library ceased and Franklin emerged, to ensure that the candidate was properly prepared. He looked Justin up and down, adjusted the opening of the shirt more to his liking, then disappeared back inside—though not without a benign and somewhat avuncular smile meant to reassure a nervous candidate. Justin was not nervous—Franklin could have no idea that his charge had faced far more exacting initiations than what was to come—but Justin appreciated the concern. The com-

ing ceremony was still, to him, the unknown; and any traveler on an unfamiliar road ought to be grateful for company along the way.

The door closed. Presently O'Driscoll beckoned him to approach. Drawing a deep breath to fortify himself, Justin came to stand beside the colonel. As O'Driscoll turned back to deliver three distinct knocks to the door, Justin reflected that it was rather like the first time he had entered the Lodge, but with no cable-tow to guide him this time, and no hoodwink to keep him in literal darkness as he entered the Unknown.

O'Driscoll stepped behind him as the door opened. Justin was not surprised to be received by the prince, but it was a different and somehow immeasurably more powerful "Brother Rohan" who now confronted him with the twin points of the great compasses pressed to both his breasts in challenge.

"Who comes there?" the prince demanded.

The steel points at Justin's breasts threatened mortal peril if he tried to advance without leave. O'Driscoll's sword at his back forbade retreat, even if the prince's brown eyes had not held him captive as surely as had Saint-Germain's, an ocean away. Suspended between those three points of mortality, a paralysis of mind as well as body seized him for what seemed an infinity of exquisite dread, as he sensed that his very soul was being weighed in a balance of unspeakable sensitivity.

But then, as the prince's voice repeated the traditional challenge, the steel points pressing closer against bared flesh, enlightenment only vaguely connected with mere words burst into Justin's mind like a flash of summer lightning—gone from direct consciousness in an instant, but lingering as a vaguely sensed certainty that he had, indeed, passed some new threshold.

The Master had warned him to expect it; but the reality far surpassed the anticipation. A faint gasp stirred Justin's chest, for he had forgotten to breathe during that instant of testing. All the prince's mid-Atlantic coaching seemed momentarily to have gone out of Justin's head, but he somehow produced the appropriate response.

"One who hath justly and lawfully served his time as an Entered

Apprentice, and sometime Fellow Craft, now begs to become more perfect in Masonry to be made a Master."

"How do you expect to attain it?" the prince demanded.

"By benefit of a password."

"Give it me, then."

"Tubal Cain," Justin replied.

A faint smile teased at one corner of the prince's mouth, but the points of the compasses were withdrawn and he stepped back.

"Enter, Tubal Cain."

Chapter Ten

Meanwhile, in the room directly above the library, Arabella Wallace had not meant to fall asleep. It was her father-in-law's bedroom, and though she had standing permission to enter for access to his books, she had intended only to fetch a volume on ancient symbols and take it back to her own room, there to spend the rest of the evening in scholarly sleuthing while the men worked their rituals downstairs. The book lent her by the prince had suggested a new line of inquiry regarding the engraving on the silver bands binding Saint-Germain's moonstone, so several dictionaries must be consulted as well.

As often happened when browsing among books, however, looking up one item had led to looking up several more—and then to settling down cross-legged on the braided rag rug, her back braced against the bed, skirts tucked close around her knees, the great iron-bound oak chest yawning open before her and books opened to pertinent passages all around—lost in the magic of the printed word.

Thus enchanted, she looked more like a schoolgirl than an elegant officer's lady and the mother of three. Her night-black hair was plaited loosely down her back like a young girl's, caught at the end with a ribbon of blue moire silk. More blue ribbon was

threaded through the deep frill of Honiton lace at her throat, for she had changed her fashionable day dress for a flowing *robe de chambre* of heavy velvet over her shift, the same pale shade of silver-azure as the moonstone in her hand. A double-branched candlestick on a stand beside the bed shed soft golden light over her shoulder, lost in the blue-black sheen of her hair but reflecting richer gold onto her face from the new volume she lifted closer to peruse. The moonstone seemed to take on a life of its own whenever she turned it in the candlelight.

Afterward she could never be certain whether the moonstone had been responsible; or perhaps the outcome had been a part of Saint-Germain's intention all along. Whatever the cause, she drifted off to sleep after only a little while, the moonstone cupped loosely in her right hand, head lolling against the edge of the bed. At some point she huddled down on her left side, drawing her robe closer against the cold and resting her head on one of the books. She was not aware of dreaming, or even of any particular passage of time; only that, when she came to full consciousness again, the measured cadences of male voices had been with her for some time, coming from the room below, intoning ritual secrets that she was not meant to hear.

The realization paralyzed her for a moment; but even as she struggled to sit upright again, rubbing absently at her eyes with the hand that held the moonstone, she realized that she had already heard far too much. The words of the ritual came all too clearly through the floorboards, burning themselves into her memory— solemn obligations and fearsome penalties and words of power meant only for the initiated.

Hands set to her ears, her eyes tightly closed, she shook her head in useless denial—for she remembered things she heard as some people remembered things they had seen, in perfect detail. It had been thus from young girlhood, after recovering from a fever that nearly took her life. For many years she had shrugged off the ability as an amusing oddity—though of late she had found it a distinct advantage, when spying among the wives of British officers, later to be able to recall every word that was said.

But it was *not* an advantage to have engraved upon one's memory

that which one should not have heard. Right now, if she wanted to, she could pick up from the very beginning the ritual they were working below, reciting each man's part in perfect mimicry of his voice and intonation.

And the penalties to be imposed upon those who broached the secrets of Freemasonry were dreadful. She could hear the words in Justin's voice, as he took the obligation of a Master Mason, vowing never to disclose any of the secrets of the Craft, "under no less a penalty than that of being severed in two, my bowels burnt to ashes, and those ashes scattered over the face of the earth and wafted by the four winds of heaven, that no trace of remembrance of so vile a wretch may longer be found among men, especially Master Masons. . . ." The words were firmly set in her memory, in her brother's own voice.

Heart pounding, she tried to think what to do, pressing to her lips the fist that closed the moonstone inside. She did not know whether the penalties Justin had enumerated applied equally to traitorous Master Masons and to those who merely overheard, however inadvertently. Nor could she think that he or Andrew or Simon would really allow such penalties to be imposed. But she did know that she should not be hearing any more—and that there was no way to avoid hearing, so long as she stayed where she was.

And yet to move was almost certain to court discovery. The floorboards in the bedroom were creaky, and directly over the heads of the men working below. When she closed her eyes, she could visualize from their words what must be happening physically—Justin, acting out the part of the murdered Master Hiram Abif in ritual drama, being lowered into symbolic death, covered over by the darkness. . . .

She shook her head, trying to will away the images, but the words, as well as the pictures and the inner awakenings, still came through. With her psychic link to her brother—strong at most times, and amplified by the emotional focus of the ritual—she might as well have been undergoing the ritual herself.

She could feel herself being sucked into it, reeling as the Worshipful Master performed the symbolic resurrection, raising Justin's body on the Five Points of Fellowship.

"Hand to hand I greet you as a Brother," came Andrew's deep voice, speaking the ritual words. "Foot to foot, I will support you in all your undertakings; knee to knee, the posture of my daily undertakings shall remind me of your wants; breast to breast, your lawful secrets when entrusted to me as such I will keep as my own; and hand over back, I will support your character in your absence as in your presence. . . ."

She could not hear the actual word of power then imparted to her brother, but she felt the upsurge of his emotion. And thus discerning the inpouring of power, unprepared by the prior initiations of Entered Apprentice and Fellow Craft—

Inadvertently, a little cry escaped her lips. She stifled it almost immediately, but in her haste to clap her hands to her mouth, a book that had been teetering precariously on her lap fell onto the floor with a hollow thud.

The men below had to have heard that, even if they had not heard her cry—which itself they hardly could have missed. As she stared at the floorboards, transfixed by horror, their startled voices queried anxiously among themselves and then broke off at a single knock of wood against wood. The sudden silence was worse than their alarm. And the sound of footsteps coming up the stairs made her blood run cold.

She could not move. The blood was pounding in her temples, and her vision went a little blurry.

Please don't let me faint! she prayed to a childhood guardian angel, closing her eyes and pressing her clasped hands to her lips. And then, more sternly, *Arabella, get hold of yourself. They can't kill you for something like this. There has to be a way out. Simon won't let them hurt you. Neither will Andrew. They only impose those penalties on people who have betrayed their secrets. They aren't going to cut your throat, or rip out your tongue. Take a deep breath and stop shaking like a child!*

It was neither Simon nor Andrew who opened the door. The man was older than Simon and younger than Andrew, a rubicund, bandy-legged stranger with a sword in his hand and a look of horrified disbelief on his florid face. In that infinite instant Arabella could not have said which of the two of them was more appalled. Only just in time she remembered she still had Saint-Germain's

moonstone in her hand, and she stuffed it behind her and under the bed in the pretense of sitting up straighter, her eyes wide and frightened.

"Girl, girl, what are ye *doin'*?" the man murmured, the *r*'s in "girl" rolling on his tongue with an Irish lilt as he shook his head in dismay.

Close behind him came Andrew and then Simon, the father grave and concerned, the son both frightened and angry. She had never seen them in their Masonic regalia before—the distinctive aprons fashioned of white lambskin, and Andrew's jewel of office supported on a narrow white ribbon. It somehow set them apart, so that even her beloved husband seemed like a stranger.

"Oh, Arabella," Andrew said softly, his accent on the "bell" conveying a world of exasperation as he took charge of the scene. "Dear child, what are you doing here? How much did you hear?"

Addressed as "child," she felt like one, hanging her head in misery.

"I—fell asleep, Beau-père," she said in a small voice. "I came to fetch some books—very early, long before anyone started arriving. I meant to go back to my room right away, but one book led to another, and I—lost track of the time, I suppose. And then I—fell asleep."

She dared to glance up at him—though not at Simon, who had closed his eyes and was swaying slightly on his feet, one hand closed tightly on the doorjamb. The Irishman merely looked incredulous, casting indignant looks at Andrew. As Master for the interrupted ritual, Andrew was the one who must make any decision; but Arabella knew that he would never lie in the context of the Lodge, even for her sake. And he was fully aware how much she might have learned, given her unique memory.

"I think," Andrew said after a long, studied pause, "that we had better go downstairs. You're fine as you are," he added as her eyes widened and her hand clutched at the neck of her dressing gown. "If anything, your attire tends to confirm that you really were meaning to go to bed rather than eavesdrop on something you were not meant to hear."

He tried to smile as he held down a hand to help her up, but she

could see he was worried. Simon would not even look at her. Drawing her gown more closely around her, she got to her feet.

"I'm sorry, Beau-père. I'm sorry, Simon," she managed to say in a very quiet voice, not daring to look up.

The Irishman had let his sword blade come to rest on his right shoulder as he watched and listened, and now he moved in to take her elbow with his other hand.

"Best you address your good-father as 'Worshipful Master' until this is settled, lass," he told her gruffly. "And there are a number of other gentlemen downstairs who are going to be sore distressed when they hear what you've done."

"Let her be, Sean," Simon murmured, speaking for the first time, though he still would not look at her. "I think she knows all too well what she's done."

She could hardly forget it. As she followed Andrew down the stairs, Simon at her back and the Irishman still clasping her elbow, she felt like a prisoner being led to execution. Her anxiety was not relieved when, just outside the closed library door, Andrew stopped and turned to look beyond her at Simon.

"Brother Wallace, I'll trouble you for the loan of your cravat," he said quietly. "It's for a blindfold," he added, for her benefit. "We call it a hoodwink in the Craft. You've already heard things you should not have heard. I would not compound the problem by having you see forbidden things as well—though you must be brought before the brethren."

Even as he finished explaining, her husband was stripping off his cravat, laying its snowy folds firmly over her eyes. Automatically her hands lifted to help him, holding the folds and layers in place while he wrapped it several times around her head and knotted it at the back, shaking her head at his wordless interrogative of whether she could see.

"Courage," he whispered, his hand brushing hers in brief caress just before he stepped back.

"Worshipful, I would strongly recommend the cable-tow as well," the Irishman said quietly, suddenly right beside Simon—and her. "I'm thinkin' there may be a precedent to resolve this, if all agree, but we must follow all the proper procedures. If she's to

enter the Lodge, she must be hoodwinked, on a cable-tow, and at the point of a sword."

Not a word broke the silence for several seconds; then Andrew's voice said, "See to it, Brother O'Driscoll."

Footsteps receded and then returned as she waited anxiously. She knew what a cable-tow was, and even its symbolism: a token of submission to the discipline of the Craft of Freemasonry. She tensed, though, as strange hands passed a cord around her neck—from one of her curtains? an irrational part of her wondered—snugging the slipknot underneath her chin, other hands freeing her braid in the back. She could feel the loose end dangling nearly to her knees as O'Driscoll took her right elbow again and led her forward once more. A faint squeak and a brief movement of air bespoke the opening of the library door.

"Alarm, alarm," came the voice of the Irishman behind her, in what she realized was a ritual warning. "There is an alarm at the door, and a stranger approaches. Take care that the secrets of the temple are guarded."

She felt the stir of attention focusing directly on her—shocked, amazed, hostile—and she tried to keep her head up as she was led farther into the room, glad even for the unrelenting grasp of O'Driscoll's hand on her elbow, for at least the contact was human. She could feel the difference as she crossed the threshold, like a wave of otherness surrounding and enfolding her within the darkness behind the hoodwink, dizzying and disorienting. Seeking equilibrium in the familiar, she made herself visualize what would not have changed in the room: the location of the fireplace, the windows, the door. She guessed that the floor cloth she had painted and embroidered would be there too, so she took comfort from that familiarity as well.

From there, based on what she had heard from the room above, she could even venture some idea of the ritual setting—though whether her visualization bore any resemblance to reality, she might never know. She had recognized several of the voices but had no idea how their owners were configured in the room. Directly in front of her she heard Andrew's distinctive, limping footsteps continuing on toward the side of the room opposite the door. Simon, she sensed, had remained somewhere slightly behind her.

"The Tyler's post is unattended," came Andrew's brisk statement. "Inner Guard, you will take the Tyler's post for the present,
but do not close the door. We shall have need of your counsel.
Junior Warden, you will cover for the Inner Guard."

Briefly Arabella heard the sound of movement behind her; then
nothing.

"Brethren," Andrew said then, his words falling into the silence
like drops of water into a well, seeming to come from a long way
away, "the Lodge now being close tyled once more—or as close
tyled as may be, under the circumstances—I declare this Lodge
reopened in the first degree, for the purpose of dealing with this
most unfortunate situation. As is most patently obvious, we have a
problem. For those of you who may not have deduced it already,
this is Brother Simon's wife, Mistress Arabella Wallace. She is also
sister to Brother Carmichael. She also, I fear, has heard far more
than she ought to have done of our recent work."

"Perhaps the lady would care to offer an explanation for her
actions," said an unidentifiable voice from the left of Andrew.

"Indeed," said another voice from Andrew's other side, "but let
a chair be brought first. Mistress Wallace is frightened enough, I
think, without having to worry over whether she will faint in front
of all of us."

Arabella dipped her head in gratitude at that, sinking gratefully
onto the chair that quickly presented itself against the backs of her
legs. She thought the second speaker might be Dr. Franklin; she
was not sure about the first. That voice had been rather cooler than
she would wish and gave little promise of leniency.

"Very well, Mistress Wallace," came Andrew's voice. "Please tell
the brethren exactly what happened, as you related it upstairs."

She folded her hands in her lap, lifting her chin courageously.

"Gentlemen, please be assured that it was never my intention to
spy upon your ceremonies," she said. "The Worshipful Master
knows of my passion for books and learning and will tell you that I
have his permission to borrow books from his room whenever I
wish. That was all I sought to do tonight. Dressed to retire, as you
see me now, I went into his room in search of several specific
volumes, intending to take them back to my room to pass the time
while my husband was occupied in your company. I did this long

before any of you began to arrive—which is why you did not hear me walking above your heads. As—sometimes will happen, when browsing among books, I not only lost track of the time but fell asleep. When I awoke, a little while ago, it was to—to realize that your ritual had been in progress for some time."

She drew a deep breath to continue, wondering whether she should tell *all* the truth—how any word or sound she heard went instantly into memory, to be recalled at will, in perfect detail.

"Unfortunately, that room lies directly above this one," she went on, avoiding the problem for the moment. "Until I awoke, I had not realized how sound carries from the library below. I feared to stay and hear more—and feared to go, for fear of being caught for what I had already heard. While I debated what to do, a book slid off my lap, rendering my dilemma academic. The sound brought your Brother O'Driscoll to investigate. The rest is as you may surmise, by my presence here before you. If it will—ease your justifiable outrage at my all unwitting act, I vow to you that I shall never speak a word of what I have heard. Or write it down," she added, in a small, hesitant voice, when no one spoke. "Or communicate it to anyone, in any way whatsoever."

After a short silence the voice she thought was Dr. Franklin's spoke.

"Worshipful, I am minded to inquire how much Mistress Wallace actually could have heard—and more important, how much she could be expected to remember."

"Mistress Wallace has a most interesting memory," came a new voice from behind and to her right.

She knew that one: James Ramsay. She found her head turning slightly in his direction in resentment, for she had hoped none of those who knew about her memory would betray her; but even as she thought it, she realized they could hardly keep silent about something that bore on the integrity of the Lodge they all had sworn to guard and preserve. If Ramsay had not said it, Justin or Andrew or even Simon would have been obliged to do so.

"Perhaps Brother Ramsay would care to elaborate upon that remark," said the cool, measured voice from the left of Andrew. "Are we to infer that Mistress Wallace's memory is somehow extraordinary?"

"There are those who have the gift of remembering everything they see," Ramsay replied. "Mistress Wallace remembers everything she hears, *exactly* as she hears it. Many a British matron would be shocked to learn that her idle words concerning her husband's activities had been recalled verbatim by Mistress Wallace and taken down to be forwarded to our agents. 'Tis a talent well useful to our patriot cause, but it bodes ill for the security of the Lodge."

"Is this true, Worshipful?" Dr. Franklin asked. "Does Mistress Wallace have such an ability?"

"It is true," Andrew said.

"Well, then," Franklin went on reasonably, "could we not simply accept the lady's word of honor that she will not communicate what she has heard tonight? She is the wife, sister, and daughter-in-law of Master Freemasons, after all. And the offer of her oath was sufficiently specific that I believe she understands the gravity of what is at stake."

"I will concede that the lady has presented her case most eloquently," the cool voice responded. "However, I must ask the Worshipful Master and my esteemed brethren whether we would even consider accepting such an offer if it had come from a male cowan. The issue strikes to the very foundation of the Craft, gentlemen. Let us not be diverted by the charms of our fair culprit."

Arabella shivered at his words, wondering whether discussion was now about to turn to the ancient penalties delineated in the oath she had heard. But before Andrew or anyone else could respond, O'Driscoll cleared his throat behind her.

"If I may venture a suggestion, Worshipful," he said, "we are, indeed, skirting the issue. The Craft gives us a most expeditious way to resolve this unfortunate incident. If Mistress Wallace is willing, I propose that we initiate her."

"What?"

"It's never done!"

"Initiate a woman?"

Over the chorus of protests and explanations, Arabella could hear a gavel rapping for order, echoing the pounding of the pulse in her temples. She, too, had been aghast at the notion at first, for it was totally outside normal Masonic practice to admit women.

Considering further, however, she realized that O'Driscoll had, indeed, hit on the perfect solution. Initiation would bind her by the same obligation of secrecy that bound them all, invoking dreadful penalties if her oath should ever be broken.

But she would *not* break such an oath, even if the penalties were *not* so appalling. And if O'Driscoll could persuade them to agree, the solution did, indeed, present a way out of their present predicament. If *they* were willing, she was willing to swear whatever oath they liked.

"I'll have order, *please*, gentlemen!" Andrew's voice intruded, punctuated by several more raps of the gavel. "Brother O'Driscoll still has the floor. Order, I say, on your obedience to your Master!"

Immediately the uproar died down, the last mutters trailing off at one final rap of the gavel.

"Now," Andrew said, the word punctuated by the rattle of wood against wood as he cast down the gavel. "We'll have no further outbursts of that sort. Brother O'Driscoll, perhaps you would care to elaborate on your proposal."

"I would be pleased to do so, Worshipful," O'Driscoll said. "As I was about to say, there *is* a precedent for dealing with this sort of thing—if I may be permitted to acquaint you and my worthy brethren with the details."

"Brother O'Driscoll, I shall be grateful for anything you might have to offer," Andrew replied.

Arabella could hear footsteps approaching closer behind her, and O'Driscoll's next words came from directly behind.

"Thank you, Worshipful. With your indulgence I should like to relate an incident that occurred in the Grand Lodge of Ireland, early in this century. The cases are not without their parallels, as you shall see."

"Proceed."

"At that time, as is well documented in Irish Freemasonry, there was living in the vicinity of Cork an ardent Master Mason, one Viscount Doneraile by name, surnamed St. Leger, who occasionally was wont to open Lodge in his home, with his three sons and several intimate friends in the neighborhood assisting—much as we have done here tonight.

"As it happened, this Master had a daughter as well as sons: the Honorable Elizabeth St. Leger, who probably was not yet twenty at the time. One winter afternoon, Miss Elizabeth fell asleep while reading in a small library room adjoining the room her father used for Lodge meetings, unaware that he intended to hold Lodge there that night. Alterations were being carried out in the house, with the intention of connecting the two rooms by an arch, so large portions of the wall between the two rooms had been removed, to be reclosed only temporarily by setting some of the bricks back in place. Of course the room where Elizabeth slept was dark, so no one preparing for Lodge was aware of her presence.

"Imagine our young lady's distress when she awakened later that evening to find a Lodge meeting in progress in the adjacent room—and not only a Lodge meeting, but a conferring of the Second Degree. Perhaps Miss Elizabeth even removed a few of the bricks, the better to see what was going on. Perhaps, until she realized the solemnity of the obligations being undertaken by the candidate, her natural curiosity held sway over what normally would have been good common sense, knowing that she should not be watching and listening."

Arabella dared not move a muscle, wondering whether they thought that was what she had done.

"In any event," O'Driscoll went on, "escape soon became Miss Elizabeth's overweening concern—but the only way out of the little library lay through the Lodge room. Nonetheless, she made her attempt. As the concluding part of the Second Degree was being given at the other end of the room, she eased through the connecting doorway and crept softly along the shadows of the far wall, to the very door into the entry hall—only to be confronted there by a drawn sword: her father's faithful butler, serving as Tyler, who must have been every bit as horrified as she."

O'Driscoll's droll delivery produced a faint snort from Franklin's direction, almost a smothered chuckle, and Arabella had to fight an almost irresistible urge to smile, at least. Had she not been in an almost identical quandary only minutes ago, young Miss Elizabeth's plight *was* almost comical.

"Her shriek of terror raised the alarm," O'Driscoll went blithely

on. "The Tyler seized her, the brethren bore her back into the tiny library room, and several remained there to keep her under guard while the rest retired to the Lodge room to decide what to do. In the end they agreed that, if Miss Elizabeth could be persuaded of the seriousness of what she had witnessed, only one course was open to them. That very evening Miss Elizabeth St. Leger was initiated an Entered Apprentice and bound by the same oaths and obligations shared by all Freemasons."

After a short, pregnant silence, someone off to the right cleared his throat.

"Did this Lady Freemason ever function as such, Brother O'Driscoll?"

"She did, indeed," O'Driscoll replied, "and was a model of Masonic decorum and charity for the rest of her life. It is said that she often led her Lodge in processions, and that no one in need of help was ever turned away from her door empty-handed. When she died several years ago, brethren all over Ireland drank a toast to the memory of their departed sister. She is buried, I believe, at the cathedral in Cork."

"An interesting precedent," the cold voice said. "You propose, then, that we should apply the Irish precedent to our present dilemma?"

Two hands plumped themselves firmly on the back of Arabella's chair, and she could feel O'Driscoll leaning over her, toward the speaker.

"Indeed, that is precisely what I propose, Past Master."

O'Driscoll's words set off another murmur of indignant comment, silenced only by the rap of Andrew's gavel. Suddenly O'Driscoll's voice was close beside her left ear, whispering silkily just below the hoodwink still tied firmly around her head.

"Stand now, and ask for initiation," he told her. "They cannot offer it; you must request it. Do it."

Drawing a deep breath, Arabella gathered her dressing gown more closely around herself and rose.

"Please, may I speak, sir?" she said in the sudden silence her action produced.

"You may," came Andrew's reply.

"Worshipful, I beg you to forgive me if I do not frame my words in precisely the proper form, but I wish you to know that my heart is sincere even if my words fail. At this time I would make formal request of you and these assembled brethren that I be admitted to your number as an Entered Apprentice, by whatever process is customary. I have always honored the Craft and have supported it by supporting the activities of the men of my family. I beg to assure you that my esteem will only increase, should you deem me worthy to be counted among your number. Also, by swearing the obligation of an Entered Apprentice, I will have bound myself to secrecy regarding what I have heard, in terms that none here, I think, can question."

She kept her chin high when she had finished, hardly daring to breathe. After a moment Andrew spoke.

"Arabella Wallace, your petition is duly noted. Accordingly, I now must ask you, in due and proper form: Do you seriously declare, upon your honor, before these brethren, the stewards of this Lodge, that unbiased by friends and uninfluenced by mercenary motives, you freely and voluntarily offer yourself a candidate for the mysteries of Freemasonry?"

She squared her shoulders resolutely.

"I do."

"Brethren, we have now before us the petition of Mistress Arabella Wallace," Andrew went on. "The request is irregular because of her sex, but so are the circumstances also irregular. To that end I think it not amiss if our consideration of the petition is likewise irregular, in that I shall ask at this time, in the presence of the petitioner, whether anyone present feels unable to make a decision in this matter. She has the tongue of good report; her character is above reproach. I also can attest that her loyalty to the Craft, through her support of her husband, her brother, and myself, is unquestionable. Other than the gender of the petitioner, has anyone anything to offer that might cause us to look unfavorably upon her petition? For what is unknown to the many may be known to the few."

Arabella's ears strained at the silence, but not a sound intruded.

"Then we shall take the vote," Andrew's voice went on.

"Brother Wallace, would you please distribute the tokens for the balloting? Mistress Wallace, you may be seated."

She sank onto her chair again, still trying to sort out the random sounds around her as someone—presumably Simon—made a circuit of the room. When his footsteps had returned to his place near the door, movement stirred in Andrew's direction again.

"The brethren will now come forward in order of seniority and cast their ballots," he said quietly, "recalling that a white ball elects and a black ball rejects."

Chapter Eleven

Arabella was familiar with the method of balloting. Its origins lay in the mists of antiquity, before the written word. By the sounds, as the balloting proceeded, she guessed the balls to be of wood or ivory, clicking hollowly into a wooden container. She found herself trying to count the clicks as the votes were cast but gave up after ten, when she realized that either there were many more men present than she had dreamed, or else each man was also discarding his unused ballot into a second container.

She waited numbly until, at length, Andrew announced, "The vote is unanimous *for* the candidate. I therefore direct the Tyler and the Senior Warden to escort the candidate from the Lodge and properly prepare her for initiation."

So quickly was it decided. Before she could even breathe a sigh of relief, O'Driscoll's hand was under her elbow, bidding her rise. She got shakily to her feet, glad of his support, turning at his direction to walk out of the room at his side. They paused just outside; and as soon as the door had closed behind them, it was Simon who pulled off the hoodwink and took her in his arms, to hold her wordlessly for a moment before drawing back to look at her in approval, hands resting on her shoulders.

"My God, how I do love you, Arabella," he murmured, shaking his head slightly.

She might have burst into tears of relief at that, for it seemed the immediate danger now was past; but O'Driscoll was watching, eagle-eyed, and recalled them to the task at hand.

"Here now, none o' that," he said gruffly, laying aside his sword and scanning her up and down appraisingly. "You're a game lass, m'girl, but for a while there I wasn't sure the General was going to play along. Let's not give him a chance to change his mind."

"The—*General?*" Arabella breathed, wide-eyed. "You mean, W—"

Simon laid a forefinger across her lips and shook his head. "Don't worry about it, my love. You're doing fine, and he won't change his mind. But Sean is right. We have to prepare you. First of all, no metal." He briefly ran his fingers back into her hair, then down her shoulders and lightly along her sides.

"Good. No hairpins, no ear bobs, no stays. And the buttons on your gown are bone, aren't they?"

She nodded wordlessly.

"The wedding ring will have to come off, Major," O'Driscoll said.

Her wedding ring? She looked at her husband in dismay. "But Simon, I've never—"

"I know you've never removed it," Simon said, taking her hand and gently beginning to work the ring off, "but you must do so tonight. I promise to guard it with my life and to place it back upon your hand when all is done. Metal is forbidden because it's symbolic of wealth; and all who enter the Lodge must enter as equals, 'poor and penniless.'" He kissed her empty finger as the ring came off, then slipped the gold band onto the end of his little finger.

"It also has to do with the ancient notion that metal was considered ritually unclean," he went on, "and that during the building of the Temple at Jerusalem was heard no sound of ax, or hammer, or tool of iron. Further, it's an assurance that the candidate carries no weapon. All of the preparation has a meaning, my love. No other metal, I trust? It could invalidate the initiation, if we've overlooked any."

She shook her head, watching with bewilderment as he eased her back a few steps so she could sit on a bench against the wall, kneeling at her feet to uncover her slippers. O'Driscoll, she noted with gratitude, had turned discreetly away.

"Now, right heel slip-shod and left knee bare," Simon said, as he removed the right slipper and began rolling down that stocking. "This has to do with contact with the floor, when you kneel to take the obligation. It's related to standing on holy ground. And your right arm must be bare to the elbow, too; just push the sleeve up on that side."

As she complied, fighting to keep from trembling now, he removed the right stocking altogether, so that the right foot was bare, then rolled the other stocking down around her left ankle, folding the edge of her skirts back so that both feet were visible.

"Sean," Simon called over his shoulder, "will you witness that she's complied with the right-heel, left-knee requirement, or must she demonstrate that in Lodge?"

Arabella felt herself blushing furiously, but when O'Driscoll turned to glance briefly at her feet, his expression was one of bland detachment.

"I'll vouch for the lass," the Irishman said, shifting his gaze squarely to Simon's. "I—ah—believe it will also be permissible for *you* to vouch that the left breast has been bared at some time in the past, enabling you to state that the candidate is, indeed, a woman—which has to be the major purpose for that requirement, if you think about it. Besides that, we've agreed that her sex doesn't matter, in this instance.

"The other purpose has to do with presenting the blade at the breast, of course, but I—shouldn't think that a few layers of muslin constitute any particular impediment." He cocked his head thoughtfully. "I wonder how they dealt with this in Cork."

His droll afterthought almost made Arabella smile, despite the awkwardness of the situation. She also realized that O'Driscoll's words had given her at least a clue to part of what was going to happen when she went back inside. If she had harbored any misgivings before, it now became quite clear that the Irishman was on her side, trying to put her at her ease and make the best of truly

difficult circumstances. He gave her a faint smile and a nod as he and Simon each gave her a hand to help her to her feet, and she found herself smiling shyly in return and murmuring a word of thanks.

He busied himself with shaking out Simon's cravat then, readying the hoodwink while Simon himself gently undid the top buttons of her dressing gown. Arabella found herself stiffening a little under his ministrations—for though O'Driscoll had given dispensation from the requirement to bare her breast, she still would be entering a roomful of strange men, clad only in the gown and her night shift.

Annoyed with herself, Arabella made a conscious effort to relax. Whatever was she afraid of? The neckline of her shift was no lower than the gowns she wore in the evening. Not even the wildest of speculations about what Freemasons did behind closed doors had ever suggested anything untoward—no nights of debauchery and wild orgies, no deflowering of virgins or ritualized rape. And it was not as if Simon would allow any man even to glance at her with other than respect, and certainly not right here in her own house! As Simon looped the cravat across her eyes once more, she was even able to smile a little at her imagination gone totally out of control.

Again she helped him by holding it in place while he wrapped it several times around her head and knotted it behind, taking slight comfort in the dark refuge it provided—the ostrich believing itself safe from danger, because it cannot see the danger approaching— illusion, but a useful one. As Simon shifted his attention to readjusting the cable-tow around her neck, she lifted her chin and made herself drop her hands to her sides, determined not to shame him by any show of cowardice.

"There. I think we're ready," Simon finally said, presumably to O'Driscoll. "Arabella, just follow the promptings you'll receive along the way. You needn't worry."

You needn't worry. That was fine for Simon to say, who was not having to go through whatever was in store for her, Arabella thought, as he and O'Driscoll took her arms to either side and led her back toward the library door. At the same time another part of

her noted, quite dispassionately, that Simon knew precisely what was in store for her and not only had experienced it himself, at his own initiation, but had put others through the same experience. If he said she need not worry, he certainly knew what he was talking about.

She still was apprehensive as they stopped before the library door and someone—she presumed it was O'Driscoll—folded her right hand into a fist and knocked the knuckles sharply against the door three times.

The door opened. As before, she could feel the breeze of its opening as it swung inward.

"Who comes there?" Andrew's voice demanded.

"Worshipful," came O'Driscoll's voice from her right side, "here approaches one who begs to have and receive part of the benefit of this right worshipful Lodge, dedicated to St. John, as many Brothers and Fellows have done before her."

"How does she expect to obtain it?" Andrew asked.

"By being freeborn, and well reported."

"Let her enter."

O'Driscoll remained where he was—for, presumably, he would remain outside to guard the door—but Simon led her inside—to be brought up short against something pressed sharp above her heart.

"Do you feel anything?" Justin's voice demanded from directly in front of her.

She dipped her head in a careful nod. "I do."

"Mind well, then, that you hold this in remembrance for the future," Justin responded, "lest ever you should forget your oath to guard the secrets of Freemasonry."

With that the pressure was removed, and a new presence came to take her arm at the right, Simon stepping back out of reach. As the door behind her closed with a solid thump, the new presence urged her forward a step, then bore her arm downward in signal to kneel.

"Kneel and bow your head," came the whispered command. The faint accent identified him as the prince.

Grateful for his presence, she obeyed, drawing calm from his

continued touch. From far before her, Andrew's voice now offered up a prayer.

"O Lord God, Thou great and universal Mason and Architect of the World: Be with us, as Thou hast promised, when two or three are gathered together in Thy name. Grant that this our friend may become a faithful Sister, and grant, O Lord, as she putteth forth her hand to Thy holy word, that she may also put forth her hand to serve a Brother. . . . The might of the Father of Heaven be with us at our beginning and give us grace so as to govern ourselves here in this life, that we may come to His blessing. Amen."

"Amen," the brethren repeated, as did Arabella.

"In the interest of the hour and the situation, we shall skip directly to the Obligation," Andrew now declared, in a tone that brooked no dissension. "Junior Warden, please bring the candidate forward."

With his hand firmly beneath her elbow, the prince now aided Arabella to rise and guided her to the left, skirting the perimeter of the room. When they stopped, she had the impression she was facing the east.

"Worshipful," the prince declared, "I here present Mistress Arabella Wallace, properly prepared to be made a Freemason."

"Arabella Wallace," Andrew responded, "you now are offered a final opportunity to withdraw; but if you do not, the obligation which you shortly shall be required to swear is binding for life, by penalties too horrible to contemplate, and cannot be revoked. Knowing this, is it still your determination to go forward, without fear or rashness, in what you have begun?"

"It is," she replied steadily.

"Then let the candidate be brought before the altar by the pass steps," Andrew commanded, "and there properly prepared to take the obligation of a Freemason."

The steps were threefold, and of varying length, but the prince quietly talked her through: left foot first, because it was nearest the heart, then the right foot joining it at right angles, heel to heel; the process repeated twice more, each step longer than the one preceding. She heard his explanation of the symbolism, but she merely filed it away for the time being, having no leisure to ponder its full significance.

Then the prince was bidding her kneel upon her bare left knee, deftly helping her arrange her skirts so that the knee made clean contact with the floor. Her right heel likewise had to rest squarely on the floor, with the angle of the knee forming a square. He promised to explain the symbolism later.

Thus prepared, he laid an open book upon her left palm, guiding her right hand to rest on top, steadying several objects of metal and wood. As he moved the whole a little closer to her, she again felt something sharp pressing at her left breast. When she would have withdrawn, another hand pressed lightly atop hers, forbidding movement. She guessed it was Andrew's, for his voice was the next she heard, from directly in front of her.

"Now, with your left hand supporting and your right hand resting upon the Volume of Sacred Law, you will repeat the obligation after me," he said. "I—and state your full name—"

"I, Arabella Julianne Carmichael Wallace," Arabella responded.

"Of my own free will and accord—"

"Of my own free will and accord . . ."

"Hereby and hereon—"

"Hereby and hereon . . ."

"Do swear always to hele and conceal and never reveal . . . write, indite, carve, mark, engrave, or otherwise delineate . . . unless it be in a regularly assembled and properly dedicated Lodge . . . any part of the secrets of Masonry . . . that may now or at any future time be communicated to me. . . . These several points I solemnly swear to observe . . . without evasion, equivocation, or mental reservation of any kind . . . under no less a penalty . . . than that of having my throat cut across . . . my tongue torn out by the root . . . and buried in the sand of the sea at low water mark, or a cable's length from the shore . . . where the tide regularly ebbs and flows twice in twenty-four hours . . . or the more effective punishment . . . of being branded as a willfully perjured individual, devoid of all moral worth . . . and totally unfit to be received into this worshipful Lodge. . . . So help me God."

"Now kiss the Book, to seal the oath," Andrew prompted, when she had said the final words.

She obeyed, leaning forward carefully, lest the sharp something

at her breast do her damage. As soon as her lips had touched the page, book and implements were taken away.

"Now rise, newly obligated Entered Apprentice," Andrew said, "and let the cable-tow and hoodwink be removed."

The prince removed the cable-tow and helped her rise. As she did so, the hoodwink also was pulled away. The first thing she saw was Andrew, a single candle illuminating the open Bible before him. A large pair of compasses lay opened on its pages, the points toward her—clearly the source of the menace at her breast—and a square lay atop the compasses, its arms obscuring the points, the angle opening toward Andrew.

Things moved forward quickly after that. She barely had time to notice who else was in the room, though she could hardly miss the General, standing slightly to her left; and Franklin's presence on Andrew's other side was not a surprise. In what Andrew again acknowledged was abbreviated form, to be expanded at a later date, she received but a brief explanation of the trials she had just undergone. Following that, Andrew gave her the step, the sign, the grip, and the word of an Entered Apprentice: a short pace with the left foot, bringing the right heel into its hollow; a hand drawn rapidly across the throat, called the "penal" sign; a pressure of the thumb on the joint of a man's first finger while shaking hands; and the word "Boaz," signifying "in strength."

Finally they conferred upon her the plain lambskin apron which was the principal symbol of the Craft when working in the Lodge, "more ancient than the Golden Fleece or the Roman Eagle, more honorable than the Star and Garter or any other Order under the sun which can be conferred by king or prince or other potentate, except he be a Mason as well."

It was Simon's they gave her, Simon who tied it around her waist, with the flap folded inside in token of her status as an Apprentice. Its lining was a fine white watered silk, though she noticed that the prince's lining was sky-blue, and Franklin's a darker shade. She found herself noting the embroidery on Franklin's, and wondering whether she dared copy it.

More brief instruction followed, with Arabella standing at the northeast angle of the Lodge while Andrew, as Worshipful Master,

expounded on the symbolism of the floor cloth she herself had made: the situation of the Lodge itself, due east and west; the three great Pillars represented in every Lodge throughout the world; the black-and-white-checkered floor; the illustrations of the working tools. This, at least, she had already known.

But most of this blurred together in her mind by the time Andrew declared the Lodge duly closed and her new brethren began to dismantle the Lodge and disperse. Washington was the first to make motions to leave—to her readily acknowledged relief—but he called Simon to him as he put away his Bible and apron, and the two of them disappeared into the parlor for a very long time.

Shortly thereafter, with no sign that their host was likely to emerge anytime soon, Ramsay departed with Murray and O'Driscoll. Franklin stayed long enough to cajole a smile out of Arabella while she helped Andrew and Justin begin restoring the library to its usual configuration, but soon he, too, was gone, after promising to have the General's aide bring around the horses. The prince pitched in at first but soon was summoned to the parlor by Simon.

Half an hour passed. They finished in the library and sat down to wait, but no one was eager to begin any discussion of import with the General still in the house. Arabella offered to mull ale, but neither Andrew nor Justin could summon up any enthusiasm. When the parlor door finally opened, Simon wordlessly escorted a tight-jawed and shaken-looking Commander in Chief out to where his aide was waiting with the horses. The prince remained in the parlor. When Simon very shortly returned, he summoned the rest of them into the parlor as well, gesturing for them to take seats.

"I know this already has been a far longer night than any of us expected, but I believe we need to clear the air regarding several points," he said, with a sour look at the prince. "It's obvious that His Highness knows far more about a number of things than he led us to expect. Are we entitled to any explanation, Prince, or must we simply accept everything that has happened tonight?"

Simon's tone was a little sharp, but the prince only shrugged, not at all taken aback.

"I assure you, my dear major, that it has never been my intent to

deceive any of you. On the other hand, you must bear in mind that I have been constrained in what I am permitted to tell you. We all answer to the same Master. However, ask me what you will. If I may, I shall give you an answer."

Simon sighed perplexedly, his immediate annoyance defused, and searched for a less confrontational approach as the others regarded him curiously.

"Very well. Perhaps the best place to begin is by relating what happened in here with the General before I called the rest of you in." He scowled at the prince. "You knew about the dream, didn't you?"

The prince inclined his head in the affirmative.

"Did Justin tell you?"

"No, he did not."

"Saint-Germain, then?"

Again the royal nod.

"I see," Simon said. "Are you aware that part of the dream was fulfilled tonight?"

As the others looked at him in question, the prince allowed himself a tiny smile. "Which part did you have in mind?"

Simon simply stared at him for several seconds before saying carefully, "The General had a flash of memory during Arabella's initiation. He had mentioned something about a laurel wreath, that first night we discussed it, but he couldn't remember any details. He did tonight. It seems the laurel wreath was actually a victor's laurel, placed on his head by a woman—a woman wearing a Freemason's apron. He now wonders whether it might have been Arabella."

"Ah," the prince said.

"He was also mightily curious about you," Simon went on. "He seemed to think you might have been in the dream as well. Since he'd never met you before tonight, I think that unlikely—or is it? Which part of the dream did *you* have in mind?"

"I confess that I had not anticipated your good lady's involvement at this time," the prince said slowly, "though perhaps I should have done. It was Saint-Germain who suggested that it was she who would become most intrigued by the antiquarian aspects

of the moonstone and instructed me to bring the book on symbols to her attention. But he cannot have known she would fall asleep upstairs and . . ."

His voice trailed off for a few seconds; then he shook his head lightly.

"No matter. It soon became clear that her initiation was intended—and for good reason, it now appears. As for the part I *expected* to have in tonight's events, I tell you truly that it had only to do with Justin."

Justin closed his eyes briefly, aware of them looking at him, remembering that awe-full, heart-stopping instant of eternity at the end of the compasses. Almost, he could conjure up an inkling of what it meant.

"Justin is being readied to assume a fuller part in the Master's plans," the prince said quietly. "To that end I was instructed to ensure that a Master's Lodge be convened in his behalf, and to act as the Master's deputy in a very real sense, on several levels. I believe I was successful, but Justin can tell you better than I."

Justin slowly nodded, raising his gaze to the prince's dark eyes— though this time he knew he could have looked away, if he wished.

"Something happened when you received me on the points of the compasses," he said carefully, delving for meaning in the memory. "It was—it was—"

"Beyond description," the prince supplied. "Do you understand its significance?"

Justin nodded. "Saint-Germain said that I was prepared to pass the next threshold. I rather suspected that he wasn't referring only to the Craft. But not until you gave me the challenge did I realize that you were functioning as more than just a Freemason." He shook his head in wonder. "How did you do that? *What* did you do?"

The prince smiled. "One day, perhaps, we shall discuss it. For now, suffice it to say that the Master now may regard you as a full member of his inner circle. This will become increasingly important, as more of the Master Tracing Board is revealed."

"And is Saint-Germain the author or the interpreter of this Tracing Board?" Andrew asked, speaking at last.

The prince permitted himself a droll smile. "Either, both—I tell you truly, I wish I knew. I do know that all of us have parts to play on that Board. My own next task is of a less dramatic nature than what I did in Lodge tonight, but it is nonetheless a part of the Master's vision."

"You refer to your venture behind the British lines?" Arabella asked.

"I do. Which brings us to Washington, and his part in all of this. He now knows what I plan to do for him, and something of the reason, but I have not told him of my full connection with Charles Edward Stuart. I do have the impression that he is guardedly sympathetic to the Stuart cause—though Simon is in a better position to judge that than I."

"*How* sympathetic?" Justin asked before Simon could respond.

Simon permitted himself a heavy sigh. "There is no simple answer to that question," he said. "Though he commands what is now regarded as a rebel army, he yet hopes for a resolution in other coin than blood. He has held the King's commission and served with honor, but he is fast losing his enthusiasm for the man now sitting on the throne in London. Still, he is not yet ready to discard long-standing loyalties to the concept of King and Crown."

"Would he be willing to support a different king?" Andrew asked.

"I have no idea. He knows you fought at Culloden, and we once discussed what makes men cling to what seems a long-lost cause. But that was not *his* cause."

"No, the colonies have become his cause," the prince interjected. "And in due time, to serve their best interests, he may well come to believe that he cannot in conscience acknowledge any king. The Master recognizes this possibility."

"But—what of King Charles?" Justin murmured.

The prince shook his head. "I do not know. He is an important element on the Master Tracing Board, but only one of several. It is Washington who, as Commander in Chief, has taken on responsibility for securing the rights of the colonies and thus moves toward the center of the Board. For his guidance and inspiration, the Master has set the dream in place, couched in symbols that will speak to him at the proper time.

"Simon has been placed to help the General remember the various elements of this dream and guide him in gradual recognition of the Divine Pattern being laid out for the colonies. At the appropriate time it is the Master's intention that the dream should be reenacted on the physical level, in a rite of dedication that will seal Washington's destiny as defender and champion of colonial liberties, and eventual victor. In the course of his preparation, it may well be that he shall become the Stuart champion as well, preparing the way for restoring the Stuart Crown. Even the Master cannot know exactly how it all will resolve, but this is his intention."

In the stunned silence that followed these words, only Andrew finally had the presence of mind to speak.

"I believe I begin to discern his intention in my immediate instructions," he said, fixing the prince with his good eye. "Are you aware what he intends me to do?"

"I am," the prince replied, with a faint smile. "Regrettably, since I must be about my own work, I shall not be privileged to witness yours, or to support you in it actively, but I am certain you shall succeed most admirably. The stage is well set."

"Yes." As the others looked at him in question, Andrew only smiled and gave a satisfied nod. "Yes, after tonight, I do believe it is."

Chapter Twelve

The prince left them two nights hence, on the first of December, having shaved off his ginger mustache and cut off more than six inches of his hair. It radically altered his appearance, as did the patched breeches and somewhat tatty brown coat Arabella had provided.

The look was serviceable if less than fashionable, but quite in keeping for a displaced French surgeon seeking employment with the British Army. He would change his borrowed attire for a British uniform once he actually had his commission. The documents he slipped into a well-worn valise borrowed from Simon, atop a change of linen and a well-used surgeon's kit, declared him to be Dr. Lucas Saint-John, a Frenchman trained in medicine at Cadiz.

"Cadiz?" Justin asked.

The prince added a nearly worn-out set of razors and brushes formerly belonging to Andrew. His own were too fine, and new toilet items might have occasioned questions.

"I do speak Spanish," he said with a droll smile, "and it is unlikely I shall meet anyone familiar with the medical faculty of Cadiz. I am hoping that will explain away any gaps in my medical knowledge."

"Just how far does your knowledge extend?" Simon asked.

"Oh, I know basic anatomy, and I can dress a wound and cut out bullets," the prince admitted. "I fear I should find an amputation daunting—but I learn quickly. I do have other resources at my disposal, as one might expect of a student of Saint-Germain, but I must be circumspect if I hope not to draw myself too much attention. Still, even modest skills may serve to ease the sufferings of those poor wretches who find themselves the victims of war."

The prince's blunt confession of his limitations left both men taken aback, but he was determined to go. Justin accompanied him to the British lines and wished him well before seeing him off on the last leg of his midnight defection, watching and listening in the cold and dark until there was no question that he had made the crossing without mishap. Several weeks later papers captured during a skirmish near one of the British observation posts included a medical duty roster assigning a Dr. L. Saint-John, Captain, to duties in one of the British field units.

"He's in!" Simon announced to Justin before heading off to inform the Commander in Chief.

Meanwhile, British and colonial forces maintained an uneasy balance, gradually forced into inactivity as fall gave way to winter. As Justin took up his duties as Simon's aide, settling into Washington's military family, he began to acquire both a military perspective and an appreciation for the tactical situation in Boston.

First of all, as Arabella had predicted, General Gage had been replaced. Command had passed to General Sir William Howe shortly before Justin's return, though Howe seemed no more willing to press the British advantage than his predecessor had been, perhaps still haunted by the appalling cost of Breed's Hill. The Americans, on the other hand, though willing enough, found themselves unable to move against the entrenched British positions, because of the lack of artillery for bombardment.

To remedy that lack, Washington looked north to the captured Lake Champlain fort of Ticonderoga, taken by Ethan Allen and Benedict Arnold the previous May "in the name of the Great Jehovah and the Continental Congress," though one wag pointed out that neither man had produced credentials from either authority. Ticonderoga itself had not been the true prize—though there had

been real fears that the British in Quebec might seek to cut the colonies in two by moving up the St. Lawrence and Richelieu rivers, down Lake Champlain and Lake George, and then through the Hudson River Valley. The more important American objective had been to secure the heavy guns and mortars remaining in the fort from the French and Indian War.

These Washington now hoped to employ to his advantage. First, however, they must be transported southward to Boston—a task that ordinarily would have been entrusted to Colonel Richard Gridley, the engineer who had masterminded the Boston entrenchments; but Gridley's health was failing. Accordingly, Washington appointed as his chief of artillery a bright and energetic young bookseller and fellow Freemason named Henry Knox, who had been second in command of a volunteer artillery company and who now proposed to retrieve the guns.

By early December, using flat-bottomed scows and then specially constructed ox-drawn sledges to cross the snow and ice, the newly commissioned Colonel Knox had dragged his prizes southward as far as Albany—mortars, cohorns, howitzers, and cannons, both iron and brass, totaling more than fifty pieces in all. He would not reach Boston for some weeks, but Washington clearly was elated at the progress, though anxious for Knox's arrival.

Far more important than lack of artillery, however—or lack of powder and muskets and all the other supplies needed to support an army—was the impending lack of any army at all. Though *called* a Continental Army, its actual makeup defied description. The core of the army had come from volunteer militia and "minute" companies responding to the emergencies of Lexington and Concord, mostly raised by local officers whom the men themselves elected, and retaining fierce loyalties to their places of origin. Shortly before Washington's arrival, Congress had attempted to regularize the structure somewhat, authorizing an eight-month enlistment of twenty regiments, each commanded by a colonel and containing ten companies of fifty-six men and three officers—some twelve thousand men—but these enlistments were due to expire on December 31. By the beginning of December, only five thousand men had signed on for service in 1776.

Since taking command in July, Washington's growing concern had been how to induce the rest to reenlist, interspersed with the more immediate necessity to instill discipline in a collection of fiercely independent individuals. Few of his officers had experience of command, and most of the men were ill accustomed to following orders. Strict military discipline and attention to details had begun to yield results, but it took constant supervision, haranguing, and the occasional flogging or court-martial to drive the point home. It had not been an easy five months for anyone—least of all, the men who must be wooed to stay. And the traditional incentive of cash bonuses was out of the question, when Congress could not even afford to pay the army yet.

Fortunately, other factors were being set in play to help ease Washington's dilemma. Soon after Justin's return from Europe, late in November, Simon had begun sowing certain seeds; by mid-December some had begun to flower. Because of the increasing press of duties since the extraordinary events in the Wallace library, neither he nor Justin had been home except briefly, both of them sleeping on camp cots in Simon's office at Vassall House; but early in the second week of December, shortly after nightfall, Simon showed up alone and unannounced.

"I cannot stay long," he said as he warmed his hands around the tankard of hot ale that Arabella gave him, "but I have good news. As you know, there's been a great deal of concern about the enlistments due to run out at the end of the year. I've had to tread very cautiously to lay the groundwork, but the General informed me today that Congress has finally decided that a common flag might provide a rallying point. They've appointed a committee to design one."

Andrew nodded sagely and lit a pipe.

"Excellent. Who's to head it?"

"Dr. Franklin," Simon said with a smile. "You said he would. He asked whether the committee might meet here. Apparently his last visit left a favorable impression."

"Indeed. And what was the General's impression?"

Simon grinned over the top of his tankard. "Apparently the same. He asked that I convey his compliments to the lady of the

house and be certain the committee's presence would be no imposition."

Arabella rolled her eyes, then glanced from her husband to her father-in-law.

"Is this part of the Master's Plan?"

"A vital part," Andrew replied. "Because of a flag's symbolism on many levels, selection of a design can be critical—it *will* be critical, if a flag is to become a rallying symbol for the United Colonies. He wishes his guidance imparted to the committee."

"I see." Arabella cocked her head in question. "Are you to act as his agent, then?"

"After a fashion." Andrew turned his one-eyed gaze back to Simon. "Who else has been named to the committee besides Franklin?"

"Lynch and Harrison. And the General is an honorary member, of course. After all, he must fight under the flag selected."

Andrew nodded, his eye going briefly unfocused through the smoke spiraling upward from his pipe, then gestured with the stem.

"This will be an ideal setting. When do they wish to meet?"

"On Thursday evening, if that presents no problem," Simon replied. "And if the meeting is held here, I believe the General intends that I should be included as well."

"Even better." Andrew shifted his gaze to Arabella. "Practical considerations, my dear. We shall need to provide a collation for our guests before the meeting begins. In the library, I think, so that we can work while at table—and that will recall certain other events for Franklin and the General. Can you manage that?"

"Of course."

"Now for my part." Andrew resumed his study of the smoke. "It occurs to me that the Chevalier Wallace has pressing business in Philadelphia, necessitating his conspicuous departure tomorrow. Unfortunately, that will cause him to miss the arrival on Wednesday of a visitor who, just by chance, will still be here on Thursday when the committee meets."

Simon's brow furrowed. "Am I to gather that *you* would be this visitor?"

"In a manner of speaking, yes."

"I'm not sure I can arrange that," Simon said. "You're very well respected, but—"

"I said that I would be present 'in a manner of speaking,' " Andrew interjected, allowing a tiny smile to curve his lips. "I will grant you that the Chevalier Wallace might not be invited to join Congress's carefully selected committee. However, the visitor intended for this most important meeting will be readily identifiable to at least one of its members, and perhaps to a second as well. Like our friend the prince, I am not always privy to all of the Master's plans, but this one is quite clear. Now, here is what I propose. . . ."

Three nights later, early in the evening, Arabella knocked on the door of Andrew's room. It was the thirteenth of December, the Thursday night appointed. The library was arranged, the food prepared, but none of the expected guests had yet arrived. The children had been sent to visit a cousin several miles away.

"Enter," came Andrew's low response.

She found him bent over a dresser on the left side of the room, lit from behind by a single candle. The rest of the little room was dark, with heavy drapes drawn over the window on the other side of the bed. As she closed the door behind her, he picked up the candlestick and turned to face her.

For an instant it seemed that a stranger gazed at her, for Andrew's usual appearance was totally altered. Most immediately apparent was the hair, combed straight down to his shoulders rather than dressed in the fashionable peruke he usually favored. His eye patch was gone, too. The exquisite glass eye sent by the King occupied the usually empty socket, so lifelike that for an instant Arabella had to remind herself which one was real and which one artificial.

He had put on unfamiliar attire as well: clothing fashionable enough twenty years before, but far more conservative than what most folk associated with the stylish Chevalier Wallace. The black coat was of archaic cut, of good enough quality at one time, but going rusty brown at the lapels and cuffs. The immediate impression was professorial—an image instantly reinforced when Andrew

slipped on a pair of half-moon spectacles similar to the ones Dr. Franklin usually wore.

"You can't actually *see* out of both those lenses," Arabella found herself pointing out as she continued to take in his overall appearance with amazement.

"Of course not," Andrew agreed. "But our visitors shan't know that. And the spectacles tend to reinforce the difference between me and the gentleman I shall portray this evening. Everyone knows that the Chevalier Wallace uses a monocle, after all. That and his varied eye patches are his two most dramatic fashion accessories."

She looked him up and down more closely now, noting finer details of his attire—and remembering another fashion accessory.

"How do you propose to walk without your stick?" she asked. "That's as distinctive as your eye patch."

"I shan't use it," he replied. "I don't always need it. And for short periods, here in the house, I can manage not to limp."

"You'll pay for it afterward," she reminded him. "You know how your leg pains you sometimes, even when you're taking proper care."

"That's true," he agreed. "However, I'm willing to deal with that."

"Well, you do look completely different," she finally acknowledged. "But do you really think you can carry it off? Harrison and Lynch are no problem, but Franklin and the General know you— Franklin quite well. You surely can't hope to fool *them*."

Andrew smiled and came to take her hand, raising it to his lips in courtly salute.

"You don't understand, my dear. It isn't I who shall fool them; it's Saint-Germain."

Her blood ran chill and her jaw dropped.

"What do you mean?"

He smiled again and released her hand, turning back to the bureau to exchange the candlestick for the moonstone pendant Justin had brought back several weeks before.

"I told you before that the Master had anticipated this," he said softly. "This is my link with him. Part of the instructions he sent will enable me to use it as a focus, so that I may become his instrument, a channel for his power."

Heart pounding, Arabella shook her head in dismay. "Is it—like possession?"

He sat down on the edge of the bed, still smiling gently.

"Less active than that, my dear, and far less sinister. And if I were not a willing and wholly trusting partner in this venture, he could not accomplish his intent. No, it is more a—an overshadowing, perhaps. I have heard of it before, though I have never experienced it. I am given to understand that I will remain fully conscious of what is going on around me, but *he* will direct my words and movements. This will enable him to have eyes and voice where they are needed—or at least one eye. Do you understand?"

"Only a little," she whispered.

He chuckled genially, reaching up a hand to stroke her cheek. "I, too, understand only a little, my precious. But together, I believe we can carry out the Master's instructions to his satisfaction. Is this agreeable to you?"

She swallowed and lowered her eyes, covertly continuing to watch him while she affected to study the toes of her slippers.

"I shall do my best to carry out his wishes, Beau-père," she said. "Ah—what *are* those wishes?"

He smiled and lay back on the bed, swinging his feet up onto its foot.

"You shall hear them from the Master himself," he said. "Bring the candle and sit beside me."

She obeyed, trying not to think too much about what he had just said. She had met Saint-Germain just once before, in Paris; but that had been in the early years of her marriage with Simon, before she had begun acquiring any real control of her talents. She remembered very little of the meeting—odd, now that she thought back on it, because her memory usually was so precise about such things. The occasion had been a reception at Fontainebleau Palace, and she remembered *that* quite vividly. But there had been another part—unknown moments spent alone with him and Simon in a withdrawing room, of which she remembered hardly anything at all.

She had not thought too much about it at the time, gladly accepting Simon's reassurance that the incident had been benign. But now the mysterious man they thought of as their Master was about

to reinstate his acquaintance, and Simon was not here—though Andrew was. She could not decide how she felt about that. Oddly, she found that she was not afraid.

Gathering her skirts around her, she perched on the edge of the bed as Andrew had instructed, holding the candlestick above his chest as he directed.

"The flame will serve as a visual focus for the beginning," he told her, positioning her hand more to his liking and giving her a reassuring smile. "Once my eyes have been closed for about a minute, you may set it aside."

She nodded in return and tried to smile, watching as he looped the fine blue ribbon of the moonstone over his head and then closed it in his hand once more, laying it over his heart. As he fixed his gaze on the candle flame, he drew a long, deep breath and slowly let it out, repeating the process a second time and then a third. After a moment his lips began to move in words not audible to her.

Slowly his face began to relax. Slowly his gaze unfocused, lethargy stealing over every line of his body as he sought for the link with his distant Master. After a few more minutes, his eyes turned upward in their sockets, eyelids fluttering and then closing. His breath exhaled with a long, heavy sigh.

Arabella watched in awe, finally remembering to withdraw the candlestick, not daring to take her eyes from him. His breathing changed, movement beginning to flicker behind closed eyelids. His hands twitched several times, especially the one that held the moonstone.

Then, all at once, both eyes opened to fix her with a cool, implacable stare. Startled, she started to draw back, but his empty hand shot out to seize her wrist.

"Do not be afraid," he commanded in a voice that did not sound at all like Andrew, touched with a faint foreign accent. "Andrew is quite safe, so long as nothing untoward occurs to strain the credibility of this masquerade. I should like to avoid that, at all cost. For that reason I desire to instruct you in what you are to say to your guests tonight. Do you agree?"

Arabella nodded, her eyes never leaving his, any further move-

ment frozen by the clasp of the hand still locked around her wrist—familiar and alien at once. Despite the fact that she knew it was still Andrew's body, she could entertain no lingering doubt that the individual who spoke with Andrew's lips was someone else entirely. Nor did she question who that individual was.

"I thank you," he murmured, smiling slightly. "Now. You shall introduce me simply as 'the Professor.' You need not name me beyond that. Simon will follow your lead, and Franklin as well. There will be no question."

Her eyes widened in doubt.

"Surely they will not accept you without a name?" she said.

In one fluid movement he was sitting up, still holding her fast, Andrew's good eye riveting her in her place.

"I cannot predict precisely what will happen, for I do not know all the individuals involved," he said. "But I do tell you that if we, who know the truth of who I am, abide by our stories, the unknown factors will remain at least neutral. We shall leave it to those who *do* know to accomplish what must be done." His left hand reached up briefly to touch her forehead with the moonstone.

"Now close your eyes for just a moment, *ma petite*, and breathe in deeply," he whispered, in compulsion that could not be denied. "All shall be well, and all manner of things shall be well, I promise you. Exhale now, and feel all doubt leave you, and all fear."

She obeyed, disinclined to do otherwise, and felt the relief he promised. At his command she drew another breath, opening her eyes as she exhaled, now no longer afraid, either of him or of what lay ahead.

"Go down and see to the supper and your guests now," he said, lying back on the bed again after releasing her. "I shall come down after they have dined, when I have settled better into this body. All is well. Go now."

Chapter Thirteen

D r. Franklin was the first of their guests to arrive, in the company of Lynch and Harrison. Simon and the General joined them soon after, Simon briefly disappearing to put their horses in the barn behind the house, for snow was falling heavily outside. When they had all thawed in the parlor, with hands wrapped around glasses of hot cider, Simon led them into the library, where they gathered companionably around the table laid before the library fire. Pewter and china gleamed by the light of candles and fire as Arabella served up the simple but hearty fare she had provided. The aroma of a rich chicken stew and fresh-baked bread soon filled the room, along with the spicy-sweet tang of cinnamon and nutmeg from a pudding just come from the oven.

"This is a most excellent repast, Mistress Wallace," Lynch declared, between appreciative mouthfuls of stew and bread. "I would wish that several ladies of my acquaintance in South Carolina might learn your recipe."

Harrison, several inches taller than even Washington, and stocky almost to the point of obesity, lifted his tankard of ale in enthusiastic agreement.

"Aye, 'tis plain to see why Dr. Franklin suggested we hold our

meeting here, if this is the usual fare in the Wallace household. My compliments, Mistress—and to you, Major Wallace, on your good fortune of a lady not only beautiful but accomplished."

As Simon raised his tankard in smiling acknowledgment, darting a fond glance at his wife, Arabella dimpled prettily and framed a suitable response.

" 'Tis clear that the gentlemen of Virginia possess courtly manners as well as physical stature, Mr. Harrison. Tell me, are all Virginians as tall as you and the General, and as flattering?"

Harrison laughed heartily at that, and even the usually sober Washington managed a faint smile, seated between Lynch and Franklin. The easy table banter continued, interspersed with casual discussion about the state of the siege, until a knock at the door called Simon from the table. Very shortly he summoned the General to join him.

"Sir, there's an express here with dispatches from Philadelphia. He says he has orders to deliver them only into your hands."

As Washington excused himself and went into the parlor to deal with the messenger, Arabella began clearing away the supper things. As she did, Andrew came down the stairs and paused in the library doorway—only now he was even less the familiar Andrew that Arabella knew. At once she found herself thinking of him as the Professor, and immediately abandoned the table to come to him.

"Ah, Professor, will you take a dish of Indian pudding? Gentlemen," she went on, turning to address the three men still at table, "perhaps you'll permit a guest to join us for a few minutes while the General is occupied. Dr. Franklin, I believe you may be previously acquainted with the Professor."

Franklin had risen as the Professor entered the room, eyes fixed questioningly on the newcomer, and now he came around his chair to shake the other's hand. An instantaneous and mutually gratified recognition passed between them as their hands touched—*not* the perceptive Franklin seeing through Andrew's physical disguise, Arabella somehow knew—and the egalitarian Franklin even gave the older man a slight bow.

"Professor, you are most welcome," he said. "Please allow me to

present two of my colleagues from the Continental Congress, Messrs. Harrison and Lynch."

The others, too, came to shake hands, listening almost dazedly as Franklin muttered something about the academic credentials of the newcomer. A similar scene was enacted when the General returned with Simon, Franklin hastening to make the introductions before Simon could.

"My dear General, a most illustrious guest has joined us while you attended to your duties. Professor, I am honored to present General Washington, our Commander in Chief."

Again the flash of general recognition as the two men shook hands, though more bewildered for Washington than it had been for Franklin.

During the desultory conversation that followed, as the company tucked into the promised pudding—save for the Professor, who declined any refreshment—the newcomer let it be known that he was an old family friend visiting from New York for a few days, consulting manuscripts in the possession of the Chevalier Wallace—though, alas, he had missed the elder Wallace by a day and might not be able to stay until he returned. When Franklin casually mentioned the company's interest in flags, the Professor offered several observations reflecting considerable insight as well as expertise in the subject.

As a result, when supper was ended and Arabella had set about clearing the last of the dishes so that papers might be spread out on the table, the General himself exchanged a few quiet words with his fellow committee members. The Professor had withdrawn into the library doorway with Simon, clearly preparing to retire and leave the committee to their business. It was Dr. Franklin who now ventured nearer, eyeing both men in speculation.

"I beg your pardon, Major. Might I have a word with the Professor?"

The latter turned expectantly, making Franklin a little bow.

"How may I be of assistance, Doctor?"

"It is you who may assist us, if you will, dear sir," Franklin replied with a bow of his own. "His Excellency has pointed out, and Mr. Lynch and Mr. Harrison agree, that your observations at table displayed remarkable insight into the scope of our present

task. As I am chairman, then, they have asked me to invite you to join our committee as an honorary member. We would esteem it a great honor."

The Professor inclined his head in acceptance—as much the graceful gesture of a prince acknowledging his due as it was a simple statement of agreement.

"The honor would be mine, dear doctor." He lifted his gaze to include the others in his acceptance. "We are six, then? I assume that Major Wallace also is an ex officio member."

Thomas Lynch, in the process of pulling a sheaf of documents from inside his coat, sat down and plopped the papers onto the table in front of him.

"Surely you can have no objection," he said, raising an eyebrow. "He *is* the General's aide, as well as our host."

"No, no, of course not. I think it most fitting," the Professor replied. "In fact, I should like to offer a further suggestion, if I may."

"Certainly," Harrison murmured as Franklin and Washington likewise made signs of assent.

"Very well. We are six now. However, seven is a far more auspicious number for a task as important as the one set before us. To provide that number, and to add an element of feminine intuition and artistic acumen to our deliberations, I propose that we ask our charming hostess to join us, also ex officio. You have no objection, do you, Major?"

No hint of disagreement seemed to occur to any of them. Even Washington, most likely to have objected, after her unorthodox entry into Freemasonry but days before, gave only a nod of placid agreement. There being no dissent, Arabella was invited to take a seat at Franklin's right, becoming secretary for the meeting.

"Now, I propose that we first consider the ideas we have come up with as individuals, since the committee was named," Franklin said, surveying the faces around the table and bringing out his own sheaf of notes. "I have prepared several drawings of my own. I invite you all to peruse them and offer your opinions."

Several more sketches were produced once everyone had looked at Franklin's; those professing no artistic skill merely described what they liked. The difficulty was that, until now, the thirteen

colonies had been operating under at least that many different colonial flags. Indeed, some of the colonies possessed several.

Some of the devices previously used were unique to the New World. Massachusetts had long used various forms of the rattlesnake, symbol of vigilance, which "never begins an attack or, once engaged, ever surrenders," Franklin informed them. Also prominently discussed was the pine tree, even now being flown on two floating gun batteries guarding the Charles River.

A few designs incorporated variations on the British red ensign, with its canton of union in the upper corner. Most featured written mottoes as well as symbols, apt to look cluttered on a battle standard. To come up with a design that was clear, would slight no one, and would still reflect their united purpose began to appear less and less likely.

"If I may," the Professor offered, after listening to them talk, and nearly argue, for the better part of an hour, "I would submit that an entirely new design is called for, different from any single colonial ensign and different from any flag flown in Europe—for this is a New World and must reflect the new ideas that will make it flourish."

Washington leaned back in his chair, distracted and thoughtful. "I have no quarrel with that logic, sir. Many would argue, however, that it may yet be possible to resolve our grievances with the Mother Country. So long as that hope persists, it seems to me that any army I must lead against the forces of the Crown should bear a battle ensign that continues to declare our ties to England, even though her King and Parliament may consider us technically in rebellion."

"I certainly respect that aspiration," the Professor agreed. "But despite our fondest wishes and intentions, reconciliation may not prove possible. For that reason I would propose a design that, for now, can carry the symbolism of our ties to England, but which may allow for modification in the future, if separation becomes the only course of action."

"Then perhaps we might consider keeping the red ensign as part of the design," Franklin said. "Quartered with something else, perhaps."

"Yes, but what else?" Harrison wanted to know. "Perhaps it would be better to place some charge *on* the red ensign—something like Virginia's rattlesnake, and 'Don't Tread on Me.' Is that not what we want the British to know, after all?"

Washington shook his head—as a Virginian himself, the only other man in the room who could reject his fellow Virginian's suggestion out of hand without giving offense.

"I have no quarrel with that sentiment, Mr. Harrison," he said, "but British regiments use charges on the red ensign for their King's colors. For us to do the same would offer too much chance for confusion in battle, when a flag may wrap itself around the staff or even just hang limp on a still day. Add the complication of smoke and dust on the battlefield, and one red flag basically looks much like the next."

"Then what about the quartering idea?" Lynch volunteered, returning to Franklin's earlier suggestion.

Arabella looked up sharply from her minutes. "I beg your pardon, but in heraldic terms, I believe that quartering means something different from what we are trying to convey. It implies a unity of equal entities—which may be the outcome we would hope for, but it hardly represents the present state of affairs."

"Well, the red ensign conveys that," Harrison said. "It's also called the union ensign. The canton shows the union of England and Scotland, the two crosses of St. George and St. Andrew superimposed. In terms of vexillology, that's the definition of a union."

"Yes, the cross of St. George over that of St. Andrew, England over Scotland," Simon pointed out a little sourly. "Tread softly when you speak of the union ensign to folk of Scots descent, Mr. Harrison. The union of England and Scotland is still a touchy subject among those who fought in the Jacobite Wars."

"Ah, but surely you're too young to remember *that*, Major," Harrison said.

"Aye, but my father lost an eye in the Forty-Five," Simon retorted, not looking at the Professor and his steady blue gaze. "Still, I will concede that retaining some form of the union as a symbol of colonial loyalty to the Mother Country probably *is* a good idea. We could change the red of the field to some other color, I suppose—

something to make it different from anything that's being used by Crown forces."

"I do believe the major may have hit upon a useful line of reasoning," the Professor said with a slight smile, drawing all eyes instantly to him. "Rather than a solid field, however, I should rather propose something entirely different, drawing on Mr. Harrison's notion of unity."

"You have something specific in mind, Professor?" Franklin asked.

"I do. Take horizontal stripes of red and white: red from the Mother Country, for valor, justice, and the blood we must be willing to spend in defense of the cause of liberty; and white for temperance and purity, the holiness of our cause. Their number should be thirteen—one for each of the colonies united in this struggle— seven red and six white." He glanced at Washington. "You will agree, I think, my dear General, that such a field could not be readily confused in battle, whatever the wind or the smoke or the dust. Nor does it resemble any current British ensign."

Washington nodded thoughtfully, and Harrison murmured, "I like it." Lynch was sketching furiously, shading in the requisite stripes and glancing up eagerly to see what else the Professor might offer.

"Now, in the first canton," the Professor went on, leaning to oversee Lynch's sketch, "retain the British union, as Major Wallace suggested, to show that loyalty still exists, that there still is hope that the colonies will not have to break away. But if they do—" The Professor rose and went to Lynch's side, gently taking the pen from his hand and leaning down to draw.

"If, in the future, the break proves inevitable, then we simply substitute for the British union a new canton of heavenly blue, with a new constellation of thirteen stars, arranged in a circle thus. I should also point out that the circle is a symbol of eternity, thus denoting our aspiration that the new nation shall endure."

As he sketched it in, the others craned their necks to see, nodding with increasing agreement and enthusiasm as the basic shape took form.

"I like it well!" Washington declared. "I would be proud to lead an army under either banner."

"And I, to give either flag my allegiance," Franklin agreed. "I believe we need search no further, my friends." He cocked his head and scanned around the table owlishly over his half-moon spectacles. "May I take it that we are all of one mind in this? I will entertain further discussion, if anyone has a better idea."

But no one seemed inclined to debate the matter further, other than to begin considering how soon the first example of the new flag might be made and flown.

"It would be well if we could begin the New Year with a new flag," the General said wistfully. " 'Tis hardly a fortnight away, I know, but so is the end of current enlistment."

"Certainly the need is pressing," Harrison agreed. "But should we not seek the approval of Congress before we adopt the design as a fait accompli?"

"Congress gave us authority to adopt a design," Lynch replied. "We can quibble later about technicalities of procedure. The General needs his new flag *now*, to fire up recruitment. The most immediate question, then, is whether someone can be commissioned to produce such a flag in so short a time."

Casually Franklin turned his spectacled gaze on Arabella, his mouth softening in just the hint of a bemused smile. "Mr. Lynch obviously is not aware, being but new to Cambridge town, that our own Mistress Wallace is a most accomplished needlewoman. Indeed, I was privileged to see several fine examples of her handiwork only last week. I believe the General also is acquainted with her work. Perhaps we might prevail upon you, dear lady?"

Quite taken by surprise, Arabella put down her pen to stare at Franklin. She had, indeed, been thinking how the new flag might be constructed, even sketching at a schematic of the different pieces of the union in the margin of her notes—but only as an exercise in design. Yet Franklin obviously was alluding to the floor cloth she had made for Andrew's Lodge—and by doing so, he also was making a point of reminding Washington of her very awkward entry into Freemasonry. Uncertain just why, she glanced covertly at the General, who had turned his impassive gaze upon her.

"Dr. Franklin, you honor me by even mentioning my name in this context," she said tentatively, "and I will admit to some modest skill with a needle. But are you certain you wish me to under-

take so important a commission? Perhaps the honor should be offered to the General's lady, since she is recently arrived in Cambridge. I am told she is also well skilled in needlecraft."

Washington actually managed a strained smile as he glanced aside at Simon. "You obviously have not told your lady wife about the chaos at my headquarters, Major. If Mistress Washington and young Jacky manage to settle in before Christmas, that will be small miracle in its own right. I doubt she would thank any of us if we were to place this additional burden upon her time and energy—and it *is* burden, dear lady," he added, returning his gray-blue gaze to Arabella.

"I would not count it burden, sir," she found herself replying, "only that I might not be worthy of the task."

"Your modesty becomes you, Mistress," he said—and he looked her straight in the eyes. "I have seen your handiwork. In addition, having heard your contributions to our deliberations this evening, I am confident that you understand the full significance of the work to be carried out." His gaze flicked briefly to the sketch before Lynch.

"The symbolism of a flag proclaims those virtues upon which our hopes are founded. To craft such a flag is a sacred trust. No military officer under my command could boast a commission of more significance, no matter what his rank. It is my earnest hope that you will accept this commission, for which your unique qualities have prepared you so well."

"Well said, General, well said," Franklin responded briskly, looking very pleased, though Arabella could hardly believe what she had just heard. "Will you do it, Mistress Wallace?"

She glanced down at her notes, hoping her relief was not too obvious. The private meaning behind the General's words could not be clearer. By asking her to 'craft' his first battle flag, he seemed also to be affirming that he accepted what had been done in this room only days before.

"I shall be honored, gentlemen," she said. "For this first one, 'tis a simple enough task to alter an existing red ensign for our purposes. We need only apply white stripes upon the red." She cocked her head wistfully. "For that matter, if it comes to that, converting

to the later version, with the new constellation, is simply a matter of removing the two crosses from the old union and adding the stars to the blue that's left."

Lynch chuckled. " 'Tis clear that Mistress Wallace has the entire matter well in hand—and that we have a ready source of flags for our new union."

"Aye," Harrison said, "but the question remains whether a new flag can be ready by the New Year."

"Of course," Arabella replied. "White cloth is easy enough to procure—though it may be necessary to enlist help with the sewing from among other ladies of my acquaintance."

"Just so long as you are circumspect in your choice of helpers," Franklin said over his spectacles. A droll smile curved at his lips as he glanced at Harrison and Lynch to explain. "In the past Mistress Wallace has been wont to entertain the wives of British officers to tea. Sometimes they confide the most fascinating details about their husbands' military activities—as the General has cause to appreciate." He shifted his gaze to Washington. "I trust you do agree, General, that no advance knowledge of our intent should reach the British until they see the new flag fly above Prospect Hill?"

"Precisely my thought," Washington said. "And I know that we may count upon Mistress Wallace's utter discretion."

"Good, then," Harrison said, pushing back his chair as Arabella breathed a silent sigh of relief. "*That's* decided. We have our design, and Mistress Wallace shall produce the first flag for these United Colonies, to be flown on the first of the New Year. Thomas, I believe we've imposed on the lady's hospitality long enough. I, for one, am eager to seek out our colleagues at the Bull and Bush and test a few reactions. You may rely upon our discretion, Dr. Franklin, General."

Within a few minutes the two were gone into the night, but Franklin and the General stayed for nearly an hour more, deeply immersed in further converse with the Professor. Simon stayed as well, since he was to escort the General back to his headquarters, but he made himself as unobtrusive as possible, saying nothing. This was Saint-Germain's time with the two patriot leaders, laying

the subtle groundwork for the future, and it was obvious that the
seeds being sown were falling on fertile ground.

No word passed between him and Simon when the General finally announced that he must go, but a glance was sufficient, as
Simon brought the General's hat, cloak, and sword and then
headed outside to bring around the horses. The Professor rose to
bid the visitors farewell, but he remained in the library as Arabella
escorted Franklin and the General to the door and saw them off.
Franklin started out on foot, with cheery reassurances that he did
not mind walking alone, but Washington and Simon walked their
horses beside him for some distance, still talking, before they
spurred off for headquarters.

Arabella watched from the doorway until they had disappeared
from sight, then returned to the library. Andrew had sat down
again in her absence—still the Professor, surveying her with that
compelling gaze—but the flesh that was Andrew looked suddenly
very tired.

"I believe we may count this evening a success," the Professor
told her, just barely managing a faint smile. "Dr. Franklin played
his part to perfection, and the General rose to the occasion equally
well. Now that we have provided a potent rallying point in the new
flag, we shall see whether Washington meets his next challenge as
successfully. That is partly in Simon's hands."

As she looked at him in question, not entirely certain what he
meant, he laid his head against the back of the chair and closed his
eyes.

"I must end this now," he whispered. "The link stretches over a
vast distance, farther than I have ever worked before, and your
beau-père is unaccustomed to such use. You need not worry that I
shall do this again without warning, or without his active cooperation. I thank *you* for your cooperation and assistance. Au revoir for
now, *ma petite*."

So saying, he drew a long, deep breath and let it out with a slight
shudder. A breathy little gasp, and it was definitely Andrew opening his eyes, momentarily a little dazed and disoriented. He raised
a hand to his forehead as he blinked at her, only gradually able to
focus his good eye in recognition.

"Arabella," he murmured.

With a little sob she knelt beside his chair and took one hand in hers, pressing it to her lips.

"Is it really you, Beau-père?" she murmured. "Do you remember what happened?"

Andrew blinked at her again and lifted his gaze above her head, focusing on something beyond that only he could see.

"Of course I remember. I'm fine, my dear—a little tired is all. The others all have gone?"

At her distracted nod he smiled a little and stroked her hair gently with his free hand.

"Good. I'm very tired. I must sleep very soon. A most intriguing evening, was it not? And Washington—what a canny fellow! I had hoped he would come around, where you are concerned. And now you're to make his first proper battle flag. 'Tis a great honor, 'Bella."

"Is that all you can say?" she asked, almost indignantly.

He managed a weary laugh at that, but his obvious fatigue only underlined the cost of the night's work. He staggered a little as he stood, clearly favoring his game leg; and though he assured her he could manage alone, Arabella helped him up the stairs anyway. He dismissed her quite firmly at the door to his room.

Outside another door, another Wallace was not to be so dismissed.

"Please come into my office for a moment before you retire, Major," the General said when he and Simon had returned to Vassall House and were heading up the stairs.

Simon said nothing as he followed the General into the room and closed the door softly behind them. The request had almost the tone of a command, though this was not unexpected, given the tenor of the discussion they had just left.

The private meeting with the Professor had set the seal on the night's work by revealing a glimpse of the Master Tracing Board. Through Andrew, the Master had offered a compelling vision of American destiny, predicting the coming of the Novus Ordo Seclorum, a new order for the New World, predicated on enlightenment and universal brotherhood and the establishment of human rights and liberty—philosophic ideals long nurtured and perpetuated by individuals and esoteric fraternities engaged in the

Great Work, of which Freemasonry was a prime example. A nation founded upon such principles might one day take its rightful place among all the governments of the world and serve as inspiration and example for those to come. Those fated to assist at the birth of such a nation would be her guardians, her champions, her defenders.

Washington had listened avidly, for the Master's words clearly touched on hopes only beginning to take conscious shape. He could not but have further questions. And if he asked the right ones . . .

As the General set his candle on the desk and walked to the window to pull aside the curtain and gaze distractedly at the snow falling in the yard below, Simon came to stand beside him. At this hour, and on this subject, they must keep their voices low. By the light of the single candle it was just possible to make out the General's features as he turned slightly in Simon's direction.

"This—'Professor,' " he said. "I cannot recall having heard a surname. What do you know of him?"

Coolly Simon kept his gaze focused on the questioning face.

"He is a friend of my father's, as he said, sir," he said truthfully. "He is a very learned man. I have known him for some time."

Washington nodded, apparently unaware that Simon had not volunteered the Professor's surname, saying nothing as he turned to gaze out at the snow again. Then:

"Either you, or your house—or perhaps even your wife—seem to have a very odd effect on me sometimes, Major," he said quietly. "Tonight I remembered more of the dream. The setting continues to be a very formal, proper Lodge—with the exception of your wife's presence—but this time I saw the face of the man seated in the Master's chair. He was your Professor." As he snapped his head around to gauge Simon's reaction, the younger man only smiled.

"That does not surprise me, sir."

Clearly astonished, Washington blinked at him in bewilderment for several seconds, then groped behind him for the chair behind the desk and sat down, never taking his eyes from Simon.

"Who *are* you?" he whispered.

"A poor widow's son."

"And what else?" Washington insisted.

Drawing his intention from the Master's own instructions, Simon bent to set both hands lightly on the ends of Washington's chair arms, leaning down so that their faces were no more than a foot apart.

"I am a tool in the hands of The Great Architect of the Universe, directed by His Master of the Works, whom you now have seen," he said softly. "I am a pale reflection of what *you* may become, if you rise to that high destiny which is written in the stars for you. The dream you were given is the key. Remember all its parts, match all the elements, reflect the inner in the outer and the outer in the inner, and potentials shall become potencies, the victor's crown yours in fact."

"I—don't understand," Washington murmured, a little dazed looking, but not alarmed.

"Then why does the dream continue to haunt you, General?" Simon persisted. "Counting tonight, you now have mentioned it to me *three times*. Its details elude you, but you sense the importance of remembering. By its form, cloaked in the symbolism of the Craft, you suspect a spiritual significance beyond the literal meaning—and you are correct! For what is required is nothing less than the quest for enlightenment, the refinement of the human spirit that shall make you worthy to take up the sword of the champion, and eventually to wear the laurel crown of victory!"

The General had listened spellbound as Simon spoke, his expression shifting from dazed to uneasy. Now, though Simon still loomed above him, he at last managed to wrench his gaze away.

"I fear you may have placed far too much meaning on my talk of dreams, Major," he said. "The symbolism of the dream perhaps describes an ideal, even a secret longing on my part—and I cannot explain why that dream is peopled with those associated with your family—but dreams and ideals will not buy powder and muskets and food for my army. I must not let myself be swayed from the practical concerns that are my duty as Commander in Chief."

As the General at last dared to look at Simon again, the younger man slowly straightened, nodding.

"Was it 'practical concerns' that you called me in to discuss, sir, at this hour?" he asked softly.

Washington blinked and stared hard at him.

"No," he whispered, barely breathing the word.

"Then I shall speak plainly and to the point, sir, for the hour is late, and we cannot predict when a guard or another of your aides might interrupt this discussion, curious as to why a light burns so late in the General's office." Simon crouched down beside the chair to lean closer to his listener.

"Beyond a general wish to see this present struggle favorably resolved against the British, be assured that I have no 'practical concern' beyond being a loyal officer and easing the burden of command for you. It is not for me to influence the decisions which are and of right ought to be yours, or to compel or coerce you in any way. Should you come to regard me as a friend as well as a subordinate, I will deem it as a sacred trust; but I shall be content merely to serve in whatever capacity you think appropriate." He smiled. "This assumes, of course, that after tonight you do not decide that I have gone quite mad, and that you no longer wish me on your staff—in which case, I shall dutifully, if regretfully, offer my resignation.

"As for the dream—" He allowed himself a shrug and a faint sigh. "I have said what I may, at this time. I shall only add that you need not search alone for the dream's deeper meaning. If you will have me, my charge is to serve you as catalyst and guide, drawing and urging you toward that inner fulfillment which best serves the Great Work."

For a long time the General simply stared at him. Simon could almost hear the questions whirling through the other man's mind—the fears, the doubts, the uncertainties.

"You are—oddly convincing, Major," he said at last, very quietly. "Suppose that I were to accept that everything you say is true."

"If you believe that it is, you have only to take my hand," Simon said, lifting his right hand between them, never taking his eyes from Washington's. "If you do, I shall give you my holy bond, as one Master Mason to another, that I have but one ambition in this life: to faithfully execute the plans laid out upon the Tracing Board of The Great Architect—and assist you to read and execute those plans as well. Remembering the dream is the key, and the path to the victor's crown."

"I—see," the General said slowly, after a stunned pause. "And what—bond would you expect of me in return?"

"Your confidence. Your trust. And so that nothing may distract you from your Work, I would require that you put this conversation from your mind, once our hands have parted."

"Would that it were that easy, Major. I cannot forget what I have heard."

"And I do not ask you to forget it—merely to set it aside until need recalls it at the proper time."

With an audible swallow Washington flicked his gaze briefly from Simon's face. "I almost believe you have the power to make that possible," he whispered.

"If I did, would you permit it?"

Washington blinked, confusion and a little fear stirring behind the gray-blue eyes.

"*Do* you have that power?"

"Rest assured that I shall do nothing without your consent, sir."

"That does not answer my question."

"I may give you no other," Simon said quietly.

"And how . . . if I should refuse your offer?" the General asked, after a long pause.

Simon shrugged, smiling and still holding out his hand. "If you refuse, then I cannot help you."

"And if I should call a guard, right now?"

"Then this conversation has never taken place. No one will *believe* it has taken place, your credibility will be vastly undermined if you try to insist that it has, and this offer will not be made again."

For a long moment Washington simply stared at him, weighing his fears. Then he slowly lifted his right hand, though he stopped short of touching Simon's.

"You aren't some kind of sorcerer, are you?"

"No, sir, I am not."

Very cautiously, Washington drew a long, deep breath and let it out.

"Somehow, I believe you," he said—and clasped his hand to Simon's.

Chapter Fourteen

I n the run-up to the new year Washington made no further reference to his late-night conversation with Simon. Arabella worked diligently and alone on the General's new flag, though all of the Wallaces, including little James, had put in a few stitches before Simon delivered it to headquarters on the afternoon of December 31.

That night the General and Mrs. Washington attended services at nearby Christ Church, only just reopened after use as a barracks earlier in the year. Many of the General's staff officers and their families were also in the congregation that night, joined in prayer for the survival of the beleaguered colonies. The bells tolled in the new year, but there was no other music to intrude on the solemnity of the occasion, for the church's organ pipes had been melted down for bullets.

More festive ceremonial attended the military spectacle of the following day, intended as a celebration of the formal establishment of the Continental Army. To the music of fife and drum, and witnessed by many of the citizens of Cambridge, Washington marshaled much of the American Army at Prospect Hill for New Year's parade and inspection and the presentation of the new standard. Andrew took Arabella and the children to watch from their carriage as the flag was rigged to a tall pine-tree liberty pole especially prepared for the occasion. The Commander in Chief hoisted the new flag aloft with his own hands, as hats were doffed in salute and hundreds of throats shouted heartfelt huzzahs. Thirteen cannons roared their approval.

The event was noted even from the British emplacements guarding Boston, where British officers turned their spyglasses on the flag first with puzzlement and then with evident approval.

"Well, there's a rebel rag I haven't seen before," a British colonel remarked to several of his officers as he scanned his glass over the distant scene. "Strange—those red and white stripes make it very like the flag of the English East India Company."

"Perhaps it's a sign of submission, then," said one of his captains. "They will have read the King's speech by now. They cannot have failed to grasp the consequences if they do not submit."

The colonel's second in command borrowed his superior's spyglass to scan the flag for himself.

"Hmmm, it does retain the British union in canton," he conceded. "Nonetheless, there's only one rebel standard to which I shall give credence, and that's the white flag under which the traitor Washington begs leave to offer his sword to General Howe!"

"Surely a harsh assessment, Major," said a young French physician but recently come to the regiment. " 'Tis said that many of the colonists still favor reconciliation."

"General Howe certainly hopes for that," the colonel replied before the major could answer. "Perhaps you're right to be wary, Major, but this is a noble variation on a loyal flag." He took back his spyglass and closed it down with a clatter of brass fittings. "Captain, please convey my compliments to General Howe and ask whether he will permit an appropriate salute."

The captain had no opportunity to carry out his orders, for at that moment a round of thirteen huzzahs went up from the troops farther along the British line, closer to where Howe and his general staff had also been watching the American flag raising; and very shortly, the winter air resounded with the answering thunder of the British guns repeating the Americans' cannon salute.

The British reaction startled the Americans, who had no inkling

that their new flag was being viewed as a token of impending submission. Indeed, copies of the King's speech were only then being
circulated in Cambridge, eliciting dismay and anger, but never submission. Several days later, when forwarding copies to Joseph
Reed, then in Philadelphia, Washington commented:

> The speech I send you. A volume of them was sent out
> by the Boston gentry, and farcical enough, we gave great
> joy to them (redcoats, I mean) without knowing or in-
> tending it, for on that day, the day which gave being
> to our new Army, but before the proclamation came to
> hand, we had hoisted the Union Flag in compliment to
> the United Colonies. But behold, it was received in Bos-
> ton as a token of the deep impression the speech had
> made on us, and as a signal of submission. So we learn by
> a person out of Boston last night. By this time I presume
> they think it strange that we have not made a formal
> surrender of our lines. . . .

Whether from dismay over the King's speech or renewed determination sparked by the new flag, reenlistments were sufficient to
ensure that Washington's ragtag army again began growing instead
of shrinking in the coming months. But as the winter wore on, the
belated news constantly trickling into the colonies from Europe
did nothing to reassure either side. It soon became widely known
that the King had declined to receive the so-called Olive Branch
petition sent by Congress the previous July, and that he had declared the colonies to be in open rebellion, branding Washington a
traitor and threatening "condign punishment." Nor were British
governors helping matters by their occasional high-handed actions
against individual colonies. Governor Dunmore of Virginia had
dared to shell Norfolk on New Year's Day, even as Washington
was hoisting the colonies' new flag.

The possibility of reconciliation seemed increasingly remote as
spring approached. All winter the American forces had maintained
the fragile siege of Boston, determined to starve out the British and
drive them to their ships and thence away, on constant tenterhooks

lest the British learn the true state of their weakness, destitute of ammunition and even adequate clothing.

Fortunately, the British declined to test the patriot resolve, still demoralized over their near defeat at Breed's Hill—or Bunker Hill, as it also was being called, from an adjacent and better-known location also involved in the battle. Washington's determination was forging a proper army from the ragged assortment of patriots who had answered the call to arms, most of whom had never seen military service and who viewed insubordination as an expression of the very liberty for which they were fighting. The General was even making inroads on the jealousies that prevailed among the troops of the different colonies. But the bulk of the troops still were basically untried, ill equipped, and lacking in the discipline he would have wished.

Still, the situation was far better than when he had taken command a mere six months before; and both morale and his tactical strength improved with the February arrival of Henry Knox's train of artillery. By the time the spring thaws began, Washington found himself perhaps possessed of the wherewithal actually to attack the British positions in Boston—but only if bold action were taken. There was risk; but not to act was to risk seeing all his efforts thus far go for naught.

Washington's initial battle plan was bold and even audacious and provoked stubborn resistance among his command staff, but a compromise plan was soon agreed: to take possession of Boston's Dorchester Heights under cover of night, throw up breastworks, emplace the newly acquired guns, and be prepared to hold the position by the time dawn revealed their intentions to the enemy. Howe must then respond or else watch his command pounded to pieces by American artillery.

The endeavor would be supported by troops under command of Generals Putnam, Sullivan, and Greene, advancing into Boston from two positions under the cover fire of three American floating batteries on the Charles River. A light bombardment from Knox's artillery would divert British attention while the night advance began and reinforce American efforts on the actual day of battle. The date proposed was March 4, the first anniversary of the "Boston Massacre," in which four Americans had been killed and several

wounded in a clash with British troops. It had been one of the catalysts for the outbreak of open hostilities.

Knox began his diversionary cannonade of two British positions on the nights of March 1 and 2, provoking desultory answering fire. He repeated his attack on the night of the third, during which the occupation of Dorchester Heights proceeded as planned, supported by the specified infantry support at other locations. Because the ground was still frozen, timber-framed breastworks filled with straw, stones, and earth were set into position on the Heights, rather than trying to dig in. A twelve-hundred-man working party hauled the materials into place with over three hundred oxcarts and wagons, so that by daybreak two redoubts were all but complete.

General Howe was astonished and alarmed by what he saw in the dawn's early light and declared that the rebels had done more work in one night than his whole army could have done in a month. Furthermore, his naval counterpart informed him that if the Americans succeeded in placing heavy guns on the hills, the fleet would not be able to remain in Boston Harbor to give artillery support to Howe's ground forces.

Immediately Howe began to bombard the new American position on Dorchester Heights, at the same time preparing to land twenty-five hundred picked men by night to take the Heights by storm, but his guns did little damage. Washington was there on the Heights throughout the day, encouraging his troops and directing the reinforcement of their position. By the time darkness fell and Howe's picked men had boarded transports for their assault, a powerful northeast storm had blown up that prevented any landing attempt.

Howe postponed the attack until the following night, but the storm continued and even increased and blew all through the following day and night, preventing any British movement by sea but allowing the American position to be made impregnable. When the storm finally ceased, Howe was forced to accept that his position had become untenable and made preparations to evacuate his troops to Halifax. By March 17 the last British ships had sailed from Boston Harbor, taking with them some eleven hundred loyalists who dared not stay once the rebels moved in.

But a British withdrawal from Boston did not mean a British withdrawal from the colonies. Washington's first campaign had succeeded in ousting the British from their only position of military occupation in the colonies, but he knew Howe would return with the spring; the only question was where. The most likely target was New York, for a successful enemy incursion there would cut the colonies in two and give the British access to Canadian reinforcement via the Hudson River. In something of a gamble—not the first or the last of his career—Washington began making preparations to move his army and headquarters to New York.

The afternoon before he was to leave, he called Simon Wallace into his office at Vassall House. He was signing orders, but he laid down his pen as Simon came in, and indicated a chair.

"Please sit down, Major. I have a favor to ask of you. A personal favor. For the sake of the poor widow's son."

The request startled Simon, for Washington was not prone to asking favors of any sort. To invoke the Craft made it unusual, indeed.

"You have but to ask, sir," he said as he sat.

The General swiveled to gaze out the window, toward the battle-scarred heights of Dorchester.

"I've been trying to clear up the final loose ends before I leave tomorrow," he said. "One of the many things I was not able to accomplish was to see Joseph Warren's body recovered and given proper burial. Now that the British have withdrawn from Boston, that may be possible—but I cannot stay to see it done."

"Would you like me to stay on and give it a try, sir?" Simon asked quietly.

"If you will." Washington turned back to face Simon squarely. "He was a great patriot, Major. I should like him to lie in hallowed ground, with the honors due his courage and example. I've had additional information regarding the probable location of his remains. From your Dr. Saint-John."

"Ah." So far as Simon knew, this was the first intelligence to come from the prince since his defection behind the British lines. "Has he located the grave?"

"Not directly—and he couldn't have done anything about it if he had, without endangering his cover. But before he left with the

British, he managed to smuggle out a diagram and a fairly detailed description that should lead you to it. I've only just received it." Washington plucked a much-folded piece of paper from his center desk drawer and handed it across to Simon.

"Another British surgeon apparently recognized Warren on the day and saw him buried up by the redoubt on Breed's Hill. There was a British officer, a fellow Freemason, who kept the body from being mutilated. Another officer wanted to cut off the head for display."

Simon had started to glance over the letter but looked up sharply at that.

"I'd heard that they dug him up at least once, to be sure he was dead," he said.

"In a way, can you blame them?" Washington said, tight-lipped. "The British regarded him as one of the most dangerous men in the Massachusetts colony. They knew very well that he, Revere, and Samuel Adams were responsible for most of the agitation leading up to Lexington."

He sighed, recalling himself to his purpose in summoning Simon.

"In any event, I hope I may rely upon you to handle this matter with discretion," he said briskly. "I'm sure you or your father have the necessary connections with Grand Lodge to ensure that the proper obsequies are observed once the body is recovered. Identification of the remains may prove difficult after so long, so I've asked Dr. Ramsay to assist with the practical side of the search. I believe he has several of Warren's former medical students working with him in the field hospital units over in Boston, and at least one of Warren's brothers. He'll be expecting your visit."

"I'll give it my closest attention, sir," Simon promised.

The following morning, after seeing off the General and his lady for New York, Simon set out to follow up on Washington's request. Given the state of chaos left in the wake of the British withdrawal, he had asked Andrew to make preliminary inquiries regarding Ramsay's whereabouts and to accompany him to the meeting; Justin had gone ahead with the General's party. Mid-morning of the sultry Saturday found father and son making their

way up the wooden steps of a once-proud Boston home, now commandeered as a field hospital.

A bored-looking sentry directed them to a makeshift ward set up in the former parlor. Ramsay was changing the dressing on a belly wound, crooning reassurances as his patient arched under his hands with the pain and a young assistant tried to hold the man still. The grim experience of too many wars told the newcomers that such wounds were almost always fatal, usually after long and drawn-out suffering. As they moved closer, the stench that drifted toward them only confirmed this patient's probable fate.

They refrained from speaking until Ramsay had finished, watching him soothe the man into sleep with a few low words and the gentle stroking of his hands across the man's brow, waiting until he straightened up and noticed them.

"Good morning, James," Simon said quietly.

"Simon. Andrew." Ramsay's gaze flicked to his assistant, whom he dismissed with a gesture. "Please see to the amputees, Dr. Eustis. I'll take these last two head injuries."

As the man acknowledged and went into the adjoining room, Ramsay led the way to the next bed, where a man with head swathed in bandages lay comatose.

"I expected you might be here today," he said as he began undoing the bandages. "Does this mean I've been forgiven?"

Simon managed a wan smile. "Fortunately, the General didn't know you were in disgrace; and I wasn't about to tell him."

"Then I *am* still in disgrace?" Ramsay asked.

"This might redeem you," Simon allowed. "How much have you been told?"

Ramsay gave a preoccupied glance to the head wound revealed beneath his patient's old bandages, shook his head, then began rebandaging the wound with fresh linen, not looking at Simon.

"Only that information had been received that might lead to the recovery of Warren's body," he said. "Can you be more specific? Go ahead; *he* can't hear you. And I haven't time to go elsewhere with you just now."

Simon glanced at his father, then crouched down beside Ramsay, speaking very quietly.

"The General has an operative behind British lines," he said,

omitting to mention that the operative was known to all of them. "This operative had occasion to speak with a Dr. John Jeffries, who had conversation with a Captain Laurie shortly after the battle. It seems that Laurie told Jeffries of ordering a grave dug, up by the redoubt where our men say that Warren fell."

"He's sure it was Warren?" Ramsay asked.

"Aye. Laurie described the blue coat and the satin waistcoat with silk fringes that everyone agrees Warren wore into battle, though the body apparently was stripped fairly quickly. Someone did wrap him in a farmer's smock before burying him, but that could be long gone by the time we find him. Jeffries said that he heard the body was dug up at least once so high-ranking British officers could look at it, to be certain he was dead. General Gage is said to have declared that Warren's death was worth five hundred men to him." He grimaced. "There was talk of cutting off his head to display as a trophy of war, but a fellow Freemason, a British officer, apparently forbade that."

Ramsay paused in his work to exhale softly, in ironic denial. "At least some values stand, even in war," he murmured.

"Aye. Will you help us find him, then?"

"Of course." Ramsay tucked the last end of the bandage in place. "I've rounds to finish this morning, but I can organize a try this afternoon. His brothers will want to be present, and I'll see if Brother Revere can come along. He made a couple of teeth for Warren, shortly before Lexington." He sighed and shook his head again. "This isn't going to be pleasant, if we do find him."

"Dulce et decorum est," Andrew murmured under his breath, remembering his conversation with Warren's specter.

"What was that?"

"Nothing."

After a deliberately sparse noon meal, Simon and Andrew met Ramsay on the north shore, where Warren's two younger brothers and several of his former medical students were waiting with a boat to row them across the river. Paul Revere was among them, as was the young sexton of Christ Church, who had experience at digging up the dead as well as burying them.

After making introductions among those who did not already know one another, Ramsay directed the party to board the boat. Only the creaking of the oars in their locks intruded on the silence as the boat glided across the water in the sullen heat.

The sexton and several of the students carried their shovels shouldered like muskets as they trudged up the shell-pocked slope of Breed's Hill. Simon found himself thinking about other ascents of the hill, not so many months before, when the withering fire—first from the colonial forces, while their powder lasted, and then from the British—had made of the hill a killing ground. Andrew leaned heavily on his walking stick, Simon giving him an occasional hand, both of them choosing to trail behind Ramsay and Revere. They were all sweating and a little winded by the time they reached the remnants of the makeshift fort and redoubt.

The sexton stripped off his coat and began rolling up his sleeves as one of the other men with shovels began probing gingerly at one of the mounds and Simon mounted a collapsing sandbag for a look around. Nearly a year had passed since the battle. Winter had arrested the decay of the dead buried on the hill, but now the faint, sickly sweet stench of death wavered just above the ground in an almost visible miasma, floating without a breeze to stir it. Leaning on his walking stick, Andrew almost fancied he could feel the ghosts of the dead hovering around them—for Joseph Warren had not been the only one to be buried where he had fallen, after the battle was over.

Simon studied the terrain for some time, comparing it with the diagram and written description the General had given him, then directed their party toward a faint mound visible just beside the trampled entrance to the redoubt. As he came down off his sand-bag, the sexton and several of the others began to dig.

It did not take long. Like most of the graves on the hill, this one was fairly shallow. Very shortly the sexton's shovel struck something with a dull thud.

More careful digging and scooping with bare hands soon revealed a skeletal shoulder clothed in homespun, and then the decayed remnants of a bearded skull. As one of Warren's brothers turned away, the back of a grimy hand pressed to his mouth, Simon

knelt down and started digging more energetically to one side, Ramsay crouching to assist him.

"Our source said another man may have been buried with him," Simon said. "Help me look."

More of them pitched in at that, the sexton moving careful shovelfuls of earth as the others scooped with their hands. Soon their labors were rewarded by the gradual emergence of another skeletal form wrapped in a gray frock like that worn by farmers, with dark stains marking the folds of fabric shrouding the head. Ramsay carefully teased the folds back to reveal strands of once-fair hair matted against the skull. Most of the soft tissue of the face was gone, and a finger-sized hole punctured the cheekbone just beneath the left eye socket.

"I think we may have found him," Ramsay murmured.

The second of Warren's brothers turned aside briefly, quietly retching, then watched with terrible fascination as Ramsay gently lifted the head of the corpse free of the ground to peer underneath for an exit wound.

"The facial wound matches what was reported," he said, lowering the head and returning his attention to the mouth. "If it's any consolation, I doubt he felt a thing. He was probably dead before he hit the ground. Let's just have a look at the teeth now. Brother Revere?"

As he gently angled the skull upward, probing at the jaw and what remained of the teeth, Paul Revere crouched down to bend closer, a handkerchief held tightly to his mouth. He and Warren had been close friends for more than a decade, and he bit back the queasiness and tears as he peered at the upper left portion of the jaw, where silver wire held two artificial teeth in place. After a long, searching look and a tentative probe with one reluctant fingertip, he rocked back on his heels and sighed heavily, bowing his head.

"That's my work," he whispered. "I carved those teeth out of ivory and wired them in just before Lexington." He swallowed noisily. "I—wasn't able to make them very functional, except to fill the gap, but he was courting Mercy Scollay. They were going to be married, and he—wanted to look his best. . . ."

A grieving silence fell upon the company for a long moment; but then, at a nod from Simon, the sexton began digging again to uncover the rest of the body, the others with shovels pitching in. Andrew watched from behind them, braced against his walking stick with one hand, his head bowed in the other, lulled by the stagnant heat and the quiet murmur of occasional comment by the workers as they dug, letting himself drift in sorrow with his eyes closed.

Suddenly he seemed to see the figure of Joseph Warren standing before him, not disheveled by battle, as Andrew last had seen him, but resplendent in the finery he had intended for his wedding. His arms were crossed casually over the light blue coat and the distinctive waistcoat laced with silver, and the linen at his throat was immaculate, as were his white satin breeches. The handsome face wore a gentle smile, and the blue eyes gazed at him with compassion.

This was not necessary, Brother Andrew, though I thank you nonetheless, he seemed to say.

Andrew swayed slightly on his feet, suddenly light-headed, though he did not open his eyes, lest he lose the vision.

"Are you all right?" came Simon's fierce whisper, solicitous at his elbow.

"Just a little giddiness," he murmured, sinking to a crouch. "It will pass. Give me a moment."

He was aware of Simon's hand on his shoulder, intended to steady him, but he paid it no mind as he returned his attention to Warren's image, still waiting patiently. Quite obviously, the visitation was meant only for him.

Is it you, Joseph, or do I only wish you here, and hence you are? he asked in his mind.

For you I am here, Warren replied. *May I ask why this is being done?*

Brother Washington wished you to have proper burial, and the honors due you as Grand Master, Andrew replied. *Your loss is greatly mourned, a blow to the patriot cause.*

Warren nodded. *If my example can serve to inspire others, to maintain the just battle for our liberties, then I am content,* he said. *And what of you?*

I shall continue the good fight in my own way, Andrew replied. *Shall I see you again?*

Eventually, of course you shall, Warren said, with a gentle smile. *But if there is sooner need, call upon me and I shall come if I can. For now, farewell, dear friend. Blessings be upon you.*

As Warren's figure faded from his inner vision, Andrew allowed himself a sigh and opened his eyes. Simon was standing beside him, watching him covertly from the edge of his vision, and raised an eyebrow in question as Andrew stirred, but nothing had changed around them. Ramsay and the sexton were helping Warren's former students shift the remains onto a heavy gray blanket they had brought for that purpose, wrapping it in a long cylinder and lifting it by the ends to carry it in ragged procession down to the waiting boat. Revere followed with Warren's two brothers, and Andrew and Simon brought up the rear.

They took Warren's remains to the statehouse, close by Boston Common, for he had been President of the Provincial Congress. There his coffin lay in state for three days, guarded by his Masonic brethren and adorned with symbols of the Craft he had served in life: his Grand Master's jewel, a set of compasses, and a gold plate engraved with an irradiated eye within a triangle. On April 8 Freemasons from miles around gathered in full Masonic regalia at the council chambers of the statehouse and carried Warren's coffin to King's Chapel for his funeral.

Chief among the mourners were his mother, his two brothers, and Mercy Scollay, who was to have become his wife and mother to his four young children. Also prominent were Paul Revere and John Hancock. Major Simon Wallace represented the Commander in Chief, accompanied by his wife, his father, and Dr. James Ramsay. The men wore their Masonic aprons openly; Arabella wore hers beneath her petticoat. Dr. Cooper conducted the service, and Brother Perez Morton delivered a funeral oration reminiscent of Marc Antony's speech over the body of the slain Caesar.

"Our Grand Master fell by the hands of ruffians," he said, "but was afterward raised in honor and authority. We searched on the field for the murdered son of a widow and found him by the turf and twig buried on the brow of a hill."

Afterward, escorted by two companies of soldiers, Warren's brethren carried his coffin in procession to the old burial ground at the Granary, where so many of Boston's honored dead already lay. Following further Masonic and military honors at graveside, a firing party fired volleys over the coffin before it was lowered into the grave. As Simon turned away from the graveside, after tossing in his handful of earth, he found himself wondering how many more good men would have to die before peace was restored.

Chapter Fifteen

I t was mid-April before Simon could join Washington in New York, bringing with him a letter from Andrew to forward on to Saint-Germain. For the moment Andrew remained with Arabella and the children in Cambridge, though both were prepared to journey down to Philadelphia as soon as Simon summoned them—for Andrew had additional instructions from Saint-Germain, contingent upon certain developments anticipated in Congress.

The General had made his new headquarters at the Motier mansion, called Richmond Hill, some two miles north of New York City. The house commanded a superb view of the Hudson River and possessed gardens, pavilions, ponds, and a stream in addition to an ample assortment of large rooms to accommodate the General's extended military family. After reporting on Warren's funeral and briefing the General on the state of affairs in Boston, Simon settled into the new routine necessitated by the move and began acquainting himself with the new strategic venue.

His official duties were only part of a far larger picture. Once he felt he had an adequate grasp of the tactical situation in New York, he began preparing a detailed update for Saint-Germain. He had written up the events surrounding Justin's and Arabella's initiations back in December, along with his assessment of Washington's developing perceptions, but that report had yet to be sent. The prince had sent his own account before going behind British lines, via contacts he appeared to trust, but Simon preferred to use only known couriers. With the prospect of sending Justin in that capacity, he now expanded on his earlier accounts and related further details regarding the design of the flag, its reception, the recovery of Warren's body, and the shift of military focus to New York. He sent Justin to deliver the documents, along with Andrew's letter, late in April.

Meanwhile, the continued rantings of King and Parliament were edging the colonies ever closer to a breakaway, as more and more of the colonial legislatures began serious discussions of possible independence. Reports from Philadelphia indicated that in March, South Carolina had given its delegates permission to band together with other delegates to do whatever was necessary in the defense of the colonies—a tacit recognition that South Carolina was prepared to make the break with England. Later in the month, when Congress authorized the fitting out of armed vessels to "cruise on the enemies of these United Colonies," John Adams was able to remark that the colonies were now engaged in three quarters of a war, whereas before it had been only half a war.

By April copies of the King's notorious speech of the previous October had achieved broad circulation in the colonies—the speech the British had thought would spell an end to colonial resistance, for George III had described affairs in America as "a conspiracy to make a rebellious war" intended to establish an independent empire and had declared as traitors all those who supported such rebellion. The decision of Congress to open colonial trade to all the world except Britain was seen as further evidence of American defiance and intention to sever ties with the Mother Country.

Early May saw Congress summon Washington to Philadelphia to confer on the military situation, with Simon among the staff officers who accompanied him. It was a fruitful visit. To facilitate the recruitment problem that had plagued him the previous winter, Washington persuaded Congress to authorize three-year enlist-

ments and to offer the added incentive of a ten-dollar bounty per recruit. He was also granted authority to summon additional militia to be raised in the neighboring colonies. To facilitate the administration of all these measures, his trusted aide, Joseph Reed, was appointed adjutant general of the Army. Simon received a promotion to colonel.

"I have meant to do this for some time," the General said as he handed Simon the commission that evening. "If you are to continue acting in my behalf, it is fitting that you hold a rank commensurate with your responsibilities—and in your case I think I cannot anticipate how wide ranging those responsibilities might be. I especially appreciate the work you did regarding the recovery of Warren's body."

"I am grateful for your trust, sir," Simon said quietly, slipping the commission into an inside breast pocket. "I shall do my utmost to continue worthy of it."

Meanwhile, intelligence conveyed to the Commander in Chief shortly after his arrival confirmed what Justin had reported months before: that German mercenaries were en route to reinforce Howe, and to crush American resistance by force. It had not taken such confirmation for some of the colonies to make up their minds what to do about continued encroachments of colonial rights. Very shortly they learned that Rhode Island had finally taken the step of declaring its own independence, regardless of what the other colonies decided, and had given its congressional delegates leave to combine with others to annoy the common enemy.

Additional colonies gradually followed suit during the month that followed, for British response increasingly indicated that England had no intention of negotiating a reconciliation. In mid-May, when the Virginia Assembly instructed its delegates to present a resolution to the Continental Congress calling for independence, the portly Benjamin Harrison, who was six feet four inches tall and obese, boasted to a fellow delegate that when they were hanged, his greater weight would ensure a shorter agony.

The inexorable move toward independence was a scenario foreseen by the Master, for which Simon had his instructions. Late in May he sent word for Andrew and Arabella to join him in Philadel-

phia. They set out immediately, leaving the children in the care of a cousin in Cambridge. Among the items carried in the trunks that accompanied them were Arabella's sewing basket and one of the union flags to which she had added six white stripes.

When they arrived just at the end of May, they spent several late nights closeted with Simon, reviewing instructions and finalizing plans before he must head north again with the General. After he had gone, Andrew began making discreet inquiries about the whereabouts of Benjamin Franklin, and Arabella began picking out the stitching that held the red and white crosses to the blue canton, and cutting white stars to appliqué in a new constellation.

It was clear by early June, when Washington returned to New York, that the political situation was nearing the breaking point. On Friday, June 7, Richard Henry Lee of Virginia presented a formal motion to Congress, "That these United Colonies are, and of right ought to be, free and independent States, that they are absolved from all allegiance to the British Crown, and that all political connection between them and the State of Great Britain is, and ought to be, totally dissolved . . ."

The motion was immediately seconded by John Adams, with consideration postponed until the next day. On Saturday, Congress debated the resolution from ten in the morning until well into the evening. Following further debate on Monday, still torn by indecision and the unreadiness of the middle colonies, especially Pennsylvania and Maryland, the delegates decided to postpone final action until July 1, so that they could consult their constituents. But against the eventuality that independence must be declared, a committee was appointed to prepare a suitable document. It included John Adams of Massachusetts, Benjamin Franklin of Pennsylvania, Roger Sherman of Connecticut, Robert R. Livingston of New York, and Thomas Jefferson of Virginia, one of the youngest members of Congress but already with a reputation as a masterful writer. Jefferson was delegated to draft the document.

Meanwhile, in New York, Washington had to deal with betrayal within his own ranks. It was not the first instance, nor would it be the last. The previous September, evidence had surfaced that the newly appointed Surgeon General, Dr. Benjamin Church, a re-

spected patriot leader and protégé of Samuel Adams, had been selling information to the British for nearly half a decade. Washington himself had overseen Church's court-martial—and had asked Congress for authority to hang men for far lesser offenses—but he left Church's punishment to the provincial congress at Watertown, which merely imprisoned Church and denied him pen and paper, perhaps out of embarrassment that one of New England's most illustrious patriots had also been found to be a notorious spy.

The discovery of Church's activities had been shocking, but the newest betrayal was of a more personal sort. On June 12, 1776, a Sergeant Thomas Hickey had been arrested on what was at first thought to be a simple counterfeiting charge. Within a fortnight, however, it emerged that Hickey had been part of a more insidious plot to kidnap Washington and as many of his guard as could be captured, and to attack the American rear. Hickey was tried before a court-martial, convicted of mutiny, sedition, and treachery, and hanged.

The Hickey affair underlined the ambivalence still felt by many Americans and gave warning of the fragility and vulnerability of the patriot cause—for if Washington had been taken, American focus would have been badly disrupted, if not destroyed. He had moved his military operations to New York because he believed that General Howe would strike there next, and had spent the spring putting all available manpower to work building fortifications. The very day after Hickey's execution, a vanguard of forty-five British ships appeared in New York Bay, sailed through the Narrows, and began disgorging men and equipment on Staten Island, where Howe now made his headquarters.

Eighty-two more vessels joined them the following day, carrying nine thousand British Regulars and under command of Howe's brother, Admiral Lord Howe. Rumor threatened of more to come—perhaps the largest expeditionary force ever to be sent out from Britain. And against them, whatever their eventual numbers, Washington had but twenty thousand men, poorly trained, equipped, and supplied. He could not hope to hold New York, but he intended that any advantage the British gained should cost them dear.

As Washington pondered ways and means, events of an even more far-reaching nature were coming to a head in Philadelphia. On June 28, culminating nearly a month of intense work in committee, Jefferson finished the required draft document of a declaration of independence and reported it to Congress. By then virtually all the colonies except New York had authorized their delegates to approve independence, though a few qualified their instructions by stipulating that their delegates should vote *against* it unless their votes would make the decision unanimous.

During subsequent debate numerous revisions were made to Jefferson's draft, mostly to eliminate contentious points; but by the afternoon of July 4, 1776, the time at last had come for the die to be cast. The air was sultry and warm, even stuffy, in Philadelphia's statehouse, for the doors to the lower chamber had been closed and locked to prevent interruption. As John Hancock, the President of Congress, rose for a reading of the final draft, it became clear that, if the war for independence failed, every man who affixed his signature to the declaration would be subject to execution for high treason. The words Jefferson had penned were a partial reworking of the contract theory of John Locke and held that those who governed the colonies from Britain repeatedly had violated the contract and then denied the colonists redress.

"In Congress, July 4, 1776. The unanimous declaration of the thirteen united states of America," Hancock read. "When in the course of human events it becomes necessary for one people to dissolve the political bands which have connected them with another, and to assume among the powers of the earth, the separate and equal station to which the Laws of Nature and of Nature's God entitle them, a decent respect to the opinions of mankind requires that they should declare the causes which impel them to the separation. . . ."

Justin Carmichael knew nothing of these events as he drove up to Prince Karl's palace at Eckernförde, in Schleswig-Holstein, early that same morning. He had been directed thence from Prince Karl's other residence in Leipzig, for Saint-Germain had moved his operation in the spring. Again Prince Karl did not seem to be in residence, though the man who answered the door was Rheinhardt,

Saint-Germain's majordomo, whose presence suggested that his master was, indeed, in residence.

"Herr Carmichael," the man said, inclining his head. "Please to come in. You are expected, but I must inquire whether His Highness can see you immediately."

Justin had learned not to question how Saint-Germain always seemed to know people's movements in advance. Surrendering his hat and sword to a liveried footman, he followed Rheinhardt into an anteroom to wait while the majordomo withdrew to make inquiries.

Even though the shutters had been opened, the morning sun did not enter at this time of day, and the room was dim and a little musty smelling, perhaps from being closed up all winter. The decor was in a heavier, more Germanic style than the residence in Leipzig, with no books in evidence, so Justin bided his time by examining an oak cabinet carved with greenery and gargoyles, whose shelves displayed a collection of salt-glazed pottery. The stark primary colors on a cream background were not to Justin's taste, and he found little of interest in the German village scenes thus depicted, but surveying them was better than staring at the walls.

Very shortly Rheinhardt returned to usher him into a lower level of the palace, where Saint-Germain himself was waiting in a candlelit room hung with black velvet, almost invisible save for his snowy linen and the pale oval of his face. The Master threw a fringed black silk drape over a large standing mirror as Justin entered, motioning him toward a high-backed chair across from the one in which he himself settled. He looked uncharacteristically strained in the flickering candlelight.

"I am very pleased to see you, Mr. Carmichael," he said. "Your arrival is most timely. I believe you have letters for me?"

"I do, sir." Justin handed over the oilskin-wrapped packet that had traveled next to his heart all the way from Boston, trying not to gawk at the room. "These are from Simon and Andrew."

"Thank you." Saint-Germain's dark gaze swept Justin appraisingly. "Your initiation went well, then."

"It did, sir, though there was a—complication we hadn't anticipated. My sister—"

"Yes, so Lucien informed me," Saint-Germain said with a faint smile, holding up one beringed hand. "I am pleased on both counts. Meanwhile, as I have already said, your arrival is most timely. We have important work to do later this evening, so you will pardon me if I withdraw to read these and continue preparations."

As Saint-Germain stood, Justin got hastily to his feet as well, his mind awhirl at the implications of what Saint-Germain had just said.

"Sir?"

"I shall explain more this evening. I wish you to observe. Meanwhile, I shall ask you to return upstairs and have Rheinhardt show you to a room to rest. You may have water, but nothing more. Do you understand?"

Justin swallowed, wide-eyed, for the Master's instructions seemed to suggest a part for him beyond mere observation.

"Yes, sir," he managed to whisper.

"*Bon,*" Saint-Germain replied. "In that case, I give you leave to set about your own preparations. I shall have Rheinhardt summon you at the appropriate time."

Faithful to Saint-Germain's instructions, Justin put himself in the hands of Rheinhardt, who conveyed him to an apartment where his baggage had been brought from the carriage and left him to sleep if he could, or at least to rest. He did rest with his eyes closed and thought he dozed for a while, though images of the black-draped room and Saint-Germain's face kept intruding in his mind's eye.

Early in the afternoon Rheinhardt returned to conduct him to an adjoining chamber where a bath had been drawn and fresh clothing laid out—smallclothes and breeches, stockings and soft slippers, a scarlet waistcoat, and a long black velvet robe intended to belt over the rest with a scarlet silk sash. Thinking back, Justin thought that Saint-Germain might have worn similar attire, though it was hard to recollect against the blackness of the room itself.

A clock somewhere was striking four by the time Justin had bathed and dressed. He had drunk from a flask of water provided, but he was hungry—though he knew that fasting was required for

some esoteric operations. Rheinhardt was waiting dutifully outside the door and conveyed him downstairs without comment.

The room in which Saint-Germain had received him before was now lit by only two candles flanking the mirror. The air was close. Justin did not see Saint-Germain as he stepped inside and Rheinhardt closed the door behind him, and he started as the Master suddenly seemed to materialize at his right elbow.

"Please come and take a seat, Mr. Carmichael," the Master murmured, his dark gaze ensnaring Justin's. "I intend that you should only observe, but I may require your assistance."

As he led Justin to the left-hand of the two armchairs set before the mirror, Justin found his focus captured by the mirror, whose darkly roiling surface seemed to pull at him, even as he sank down in the chair.

"Close your eyes, please," the Master whispered, his hand reinforcing the command as it brushed across his brow and two fingers pressed briefly against his eyelids. The touch also seemed to distance Justin a little from his body, so that he slumped against the chair's high back without resistance, hands slack on the chair arms.

"Forgive me for taking such liberties," the Master murmured, "but powerful magic is already at work in this room, and I would not have you overwhelmed betimes. Have you any idea what is happening today in the statehouse in Philadelphia? You may speak."

Justin only shook his head, for words were not necessary to convey his ignorance.

"You are aware, I trust, that through Andrew I made my influence known when the General and other patriot leaders were designing a flag for the United Colonies. In a like fashion I have intruded certain guidance in the preparation of a document set today before the Continental Congress, which will declare American independence to all the world."

Independence! Justin thrilled to the very word, but he felt himself stilling as Saint-Germain continued.

"Yet it is a weighty undertaking that these brave men contemplate," the Master said. "Failure of the American endeavor will mean a traitor's death for all who sign this document and do not

fall in actual battle—yet sign it they must. The speeches have be-
gun, and Andrew is prepared to be my voice again. I must watch
and wait, and be ready to act if it becomes necessary. Your assistance will help me conserve my strength until the appointed time.
Are you willing to do this?"

"I am," Justin managed to whisper, both thrilled and fearful to
be caught up in such high endeavors.

"Très bon, mon ami," the Master murmured. "Then watch and
wait with me. Open your eyes and gaze into the mirror, and see
with the inner vision of your soul. . . ."

Justin opened his eyes, blinking in the candlelight, at once drawn
back to the mirror before him as Saint-Germain took a seat beside
him. As he tried to pierce the roiling mists that obscured what lay
beyond the mirror, the Master turned aside to pour a small amount
of ruby-clear elixir into a thimble-sized glass cup. This he set to
Justin's lips, bracing his other hand behind the younger man's neck
to tip his head back so that a few drops of a sweet, volatile liquid
ran onto Justin's tongue.

It numbed where it touched, then seemed to permeate his entire
mouth and explode through its roof and into his sinuses. His vision
reeled, and he grabbed at the chair arms for stability.

"Breathe in sharply through your nose," the Master commanded.

Obedience caused Justin to cough sharply several times and
made his eyes water; but then his vision cleared as his breath steadied. As he let his gaze drift back to the mirror, relaxing a little, the
mists gradually seemed to dissipate.

"Simply watch now," the Master whispered, settling back into
his chair beside Justin. "Watch and listen—and learn."

In one of the galleries of the Philadelphia statehouse, Andrew Wallace sat quietly in a back row and listened, eyelids lowered, his
empty eye socket filled by an orb of precious Venetian glass given
him by a king. Disguised by the rusty black raiment of the Professor, he was aware of Another's presence all but overshadowing his
own will, focused through the moonstone pendant hanging next to
his heart, but he was content that it be so. Arabella sat in the

opposite gallery, doing her best not to look as if she was watching him, but no one else had noted his arrival or his presence; the Master's glamour ensured that. All the galleries were packed with patriotic citizens waiting to see what would transpire, and the lower doors had been locked and guards posted to prevent interruption.

Andrew had been here for several hours already, for the matter under discussion was of grave importance. After the reading of the draft declaration submitted by Jefferson's committee, Jefferson himself had spoken at length, followed by John Adams of Boston and Dr. Franklin of Pennsylvania. As the summer hours stretched on, some of the delegates remained undecided, for passage of the matter now under consideration would have drastic implications for everyone. The conclusion of the declaration had said it all, following on the words of the motion originally made by Richard Henry Lee: "And for the support of this Declaration, with a firm reliance on the protection of divine Providence, we mutually pledge to each other our Lives, our Fortunes, and our sacred Honor."

It was late in the afternoon by the time discussion began to focus on just what the would-be signers were risking, with mention of axes and scaffolds and gibbets. As the images washed over Andrew, so also did the Presence that had been watching and listening through him; and at length he found himself rising to move to the edge of the gallery, setting his two hands on the balcony railing as all eyes lifted to him and silence fell upon the occupants of the statehouse.

In the weeks leading to this day, he had spoken several times to the framers of the declaration about the document they were preparing: that the parchment on which it would be written was, in fact, a Golden Fleece. Not the secret of immortality, like the original golden fleece, but a magic formula of human hope—the secret of the immortality of human society.

Now he spoke of the words on the document that lay before them, which would live long after the bones of every man and woman present had returned to dust, whatever means of death might claim them. They must not fear gibbet or scaffold or the most ignoble grave, for the ideals enshrined in that document would never die, if only those present had the courage to pledge their all. He spoke of a New Order, and the benevolent Providence that had decreed the proliferation of freedom in this New World, to be bought with the blood of its sons and daughters upon the altar of freedom.

"God has given America to be free!" he declared.

He was not aware of finishing, or even of much of the content of what he had said, but he found himself suddenly outside the state-house gallery, ducking into a small antechamber to change his rusty coat hastily for a blue one Arabella produced from a small carpetbag, to let her brush his hair back into a more conventional queue and apply an eye patch over the glass eye.

"Is it finished?" she whispered as she handed him his stick.

"For now, I think so," he murmured. "Let us be gone now and let them do their work."

They made their way back to the rooms they had taken in a nearby inn, across from the City Tavern, where Andrew made a more complete return to his own persona and then lay down for a well-deserved rest. Not long afterward bells began pealing all over the city; and a little while later came a sudden and unexpected knock at the door.

It was Dr. Franklin who doffed his hat as Arabella answered the door, inclining his head in a gallant little bow but setting his hand firmly on the edge of the door as he stepped slightly into the doorway to peer past her at where Andrew was sitting up on the bed.

" 'Proclaim liberty throughout all the land unto all the inhabitants thereof,' " he said with a faint smile. "That is the message cast into one of the bells you hear ringing. Leviticus twenty-five, I believe. May I come in? I thought the Professor might like to know how matters transpired after he made his rather hasty departure from the statehouse."

Arabella stiffened slightly and glanced back at Andrew, but the latter only raised an eyebrow, inviting Franklin to enter with a nod.

"Please come in, Doctor. Will you take a glass of port with us?"

"Thank you, I will." As Arabella closed the door behind him, he came to sit on a straight chair beside the bed, gazing mildly over his spectacles as Andrew poured wine into three glasses.

"I had my suspicions after the Professor's second appearance, when he assisted us with the drafting of the declaration," Franklin said as Andrew handed him a glass.

Andrew said nothing, only raising his glass slightly in salute to Franklin and taking a sip.

"It was when I saw Mistress Wallace sitting in the statehouse gallery this afternoon that I made the connection," Franklin went on. "I do believe we all take guidance from the same Master."

Andrew calmly set aside his glass, fixing Franklin with his single eye.

"I don't believe I know what you're talking about," he said.

"Oh, I believe you do," Franklin replied. "I tell you, Brother Wallace, on the level, that the personage to whom we all answer is a poor widow's son who lives on Weldon Square."

"Indeed?"

Franklin smiled and took a healthy swallow of his port. "I, too, have been instructed to avoid mention of his name whenever possible, but 'tis clear that you require further reassurance. I first met the Count of Saint-Germain while visiting a Lodge in Paris several years ago. As you know, I have lived abroad this past decade and more, looking after colonial interests."

"And?"

"It was an auspicious introduction—and no chance meeting, as I later learned," Franklin went on. "Since then I have had opportunity to meet and observe an even wider variety of interesting and useful people. Your Brother Rohan is an excellent example. I am quite aware that he is actually the Prince Lucien de Rohanstuart, whatever other names he may go by. Granted, I might have gained this information from your Bostonians, but I think by now you know that I did not. Let us say that his presence at Justin Carmichael's raising to Master Mason was no surprise to me; nor was what happened to Sister Wallace."

Had Franklin's smile been less avuncular, Arabella might have been alarmed as he turned to gaze at her over his spectacles, but Andrew's delighted laugh utterly disarmed any remaining fear.

"Very well, Brother Franklin, you have amply made your point," he said, taking up his glass again. "How may I help you?"

"I am hoping to enlist the further services of the Professor," Franklin said. "His insights regarding flags and a golden fleece were extremely enlightening, even before he spoke out today. I should like to hear his opinion regarding a Great Seal."

"A Great Seal?" Andrew repeated blankly.

Franklin inclined his head. "One will be needed to complete the evidence of the act of independence. A committee to design it was named shortly after the Professor left, following the actual approval of the declaration."

"It finally passed, then," Andrew said. "I had guessed as much, from the bells."

"Aye, the vote was unanimous—though further revisions were made, as one might expect. Poor Jefferson. He squirmed at every change—and there must have been dozens."

Andrew quirked a faint smile, well aware how Jefferson had agonized over every word of the original draft. "That will have been a sore trial for him. What happens next?"

"Ah." Franklin took another sip of his port. "The declaration will be printed tonight over the signatures of Hancock and Thomson. Tomorrow post riders will start distributing copies to the colonial assemblies, the committees of safety, and the commanding officers of the Continental Army, to be read out at public gatherings.

"Meanwhile, we have yet a few loose ends to tidy up. New York was the final sticking point, as you know, but her delegates finally went against their instructions and voted for independence. This means that a formal ratification still must be obtained, but I feel certain that will be forthcoming very quickly, now that the deed is done. As soon as that occurs, a fair copy will be engrossed on parchment—the Professor's 'Golden Fleece.' If all goes well, it should be ready for signing within a week or so."

"But it takes effect from today, even without the signatures?" Andrew asked.

"Oh, indeed. A typeset copy will be sealed into the Rough Journal of Congress tomorrow. Meanwhile, the declaration gives the newly created free and independent states the power to—let me see

if I can remember the exact words we finally adopted: 'to levy war, conclude peace, contract alliances, establish commerce, and to do all other acts and things which independent states may of right do.' Hence the need for a Great Seal—which brings us back to the reason for my coming. Might the Professor be persuaded to lend his counsel to the committee?"

By the tone of the request Franklin clearly did not understand that the Professor was, in fact, an overshadowing by Saint-Germain himself. Nor was it Andrew's place to tell him. While it might, indeed, be in the Master's plans to assist in this way, Andrew had no way to inquire save by letter—a four-to-five-month proposition at best, unless Saint-Germain himself initiated extraordinary measures. There was a further document that had accompanied his instructions regarding the declaration, not to be opened until today's mission was accomplished; but whether it related to a Great Seal remained to be seen.

"Who composes this committee?" Andrew asked.

"Myself, John Adams, and Jefferson," Franklin replied. "A proven combination. I trust that is satisfactory?"

"Oh, quite," Andrew said. "May I think on it for a few days? I would not like to overexpose the Professor. It may be that a more informal association would be more appropriate than actual participation. In the meantime, please be assured of the support of the Chevalier Andrew Wallace."

Franklin looked at him for a long moment, then slowly nodded.

"I sense that additional factors are at work here that you may not share at this time," Franklin said. "I am not offended," he added, holding up a hand. "Under the circumstances, I shall be quite happy with the assistance of Chevalier Wallace. And if the Professor can also lend his good counsel at a later time, so much the better."

Tossing off the last of his port, he got to his feet. "But I've kept you long enough, and I must be about further errands—the first of which is to drop by John Dunlap's printing shop and see how the typesetting progresses. I shall let you know when I have further word regarding the committee's plans. Meanwhile, if the bells can be ignored, I expect you would be glad of some sleep."

When he had gone, and Arabella had locked the door behind him, she came to sit on the edge of the bed beside Andrew.

"What will you do now?" she asked. "Can you summon up the Master's overshadowing at will?"

"No, he must anticipate the time when it is needed, and I must be ready to facilitate it," Andrew said. "But I do have his instructions on this general subject—and Franklin seemed willing enough to accept the Professor's assistance at a later date."

"Saint-Germain has already worked out the symbols for the Seal?" she asked incredulously.

"No, nothing that specific," he replied with a smile. "But he suggests the general forms. The shield will be simple enough—based on the new flag you have been crafting so diligently, with its starry field and its red and white stripes. But there are a number of more esoteric symbols to be considered, such as the All-Seeing Eye of Providence and the Radiant Triangle. The Master suggests several mottoes as well. I shall pass these on to Franklin and allow him to introduce them as and when appropriate. Then we shall see what falls on fertile soil."

Arabella smiled, reaching out to stroke his cheek lightly.

"Enough of this," she whispered. "You're tired. You should sleep."

"With all those bells?" he retorted.

"With all those bells," she agreed. "Sleep now, Beau-père."

Chapter Sixteen

J ustin likewise had succumbed to sleep, after being released by Saint-Germain. He remembered little of the later part of the session, for at the height of Andrew's harangue in Congress, the Master had laid a hand atop Justin's wrist and bade him close his eyes.

What followed had not been like sleep at all—rather, a faint, drawing sensation between his eyes that dizzied him and left him drained. Of what further transpired in the mirror, he had no idea; only that, when he regained his senses, slumped in his chair and with a crick in his neck, Saint-Germain was covering the mirror with its black silk drape, faintly smiling. He looked tired but satisfied and promised to convey details of the completed Work in the morning.

He was as good as his word. In the days that followed Justin availed himself of Saint-Germain's briefing on the successful ratification of the declaration and learned more of his Master Plan for the now United Colonies. By mid-July, he was starting back for Boston with new instructions for Andrew, Simon, and the prince. He also, to his surprise, bore a letter for Dr. Benjamin Franklin.

Meanwhile, the American Declaration of Independence was being promulgated throughout the thirteen colonies, to almost universal acclamation and joy. On July 9, as Howe's army continued to mass on Staten Island and the expected Hessians began to arrive, the Convention of New York formally adopted the declaration at White Plains.

Early that evening Washington paraded his regiments for a reading of the declaration and informed them in accompanying orders that the true liberty of the new union now would depend "(under God) solely on the success of our arms." Three huzzahs greeted the reading; and later that night local Sons of Liberty marched on the Bowling Green to pull down and behead the huge, gilded equestrian statue of George III—an act of riotous high spirits deplored by Washington, but he benefited in the end, for most of its lead was taken to Connecticut, where it was melted down and molded into more than forty thousand bullets.

He would need them. In early July, joining Howe's army encamped on Staten Island, another British fleet arrived in New York, followed by thirty transports and men-of-war just come from attacking Charleston, South Carolina, though Generals Lee and Moultrie had repulsed them there. Very shortly Generals Sir Henry Clinton and Lord Cornwallis joined Howe from the south.

From this position of strength, and with another fleet still to come, Howe felt justified in making one final attempt to negotiate a possible reconciliation—for neither he nor his brother the admiral were personally enthusiastic about fighting the colonies. Concurrent with their military brief to deal with the American rebellion, the Howes had been empowered to inquire regarding the causes of the colonists' complaints and to act as peace commissioners—though they possessed no authority to offer any terms. Nor did they truly understand what was at stake, as was confirmed by their very approach to the intended parley.

On July 14, in pelting rain, Admiral Howe sent out a barge from his flagship, under a flag of truce. Royal Navy lieutenant Philip Brown told the Americans who met him in the center of the harbor that he had a letter from Howe to Washington.

The Americans withdrew to confer and shortly returned with General Knox and Washington's adjutant, Joseph Reed, who asked how the letter was addressed. Brown courteously informed him that it was from Lord Howe to Mr. Washington—to which Reed

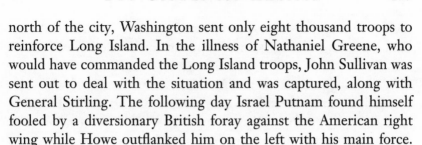

north of the city, Washington sent only eight thousand troops to reinforce Long Island. In the illness of Nathaniel Greene, who would have commanded the Long Island troops, John Sullivan was sent out to deal with the situation and was captured, along with General Stirling. The following day Israel Putnam found himself fooled by a diversionary British foray against the American right wing while Howe outflanked him on the left with his main force.

Many of the Continental troops performed superbly, but they were simply overwhelmed and outclassed by the British and Hessians. Washington brought in reinforcements and prepared to resist a British assault, but on seeing Howe's preparations for siege operations, he soon realized that the position in the Brooklyn Heights was untenable. The night of August 28 found the Americans huddled in the flooded trenches of Brooklyn Heights, short of food and ammunition, with the East River at their backs, a vastly superior force before them, and Washington and several of his ablest generals in the trap with them.

That Washington was able to extricate himself from this situation was no small miracle, though he was to prove repeatedly during the war that he was at his best when his back was against a wall. Calling on the resources of two Massachusetts regiments largely made up of Marblehead sailors and fishermen, he assembled a flotilla of small boats and, under cover of darkness and fog on the night of August 29, managed to evacuate between ten and twelve thousand men to the New York side of the river, from under the very noses of the British. His only losses: five heavy cannons that became mired in the mud and three stragglers who had remained behind to plunder. Reporting the escape to Congress the day after, he apologized for the delay in informing them and noted that for six days "I had hardly been off my horse and had never closed my eyes."

New York clearly was lost. General Greene and others of his command staff urged Washington to burn the city before withdrawing, to prevent establishment of a permanent British base, but Congress forbade it. On learning that Howe meant to winter in New York, Washington again consulted with his generals and made the decision to begin the evacuation as soon as possible. To assist in

their planning, he sent a young captain named Nathan Hale behind the lines to Long Island to spy out further details of Howe's
troop positions.

Justin caught up with the American command staff while the
evacuation plans were still taking shape, having arrived in Philadelphia a few days before. Discovering that Andrew and Arabella had
set out for Cambridge earlier in September, he came directly to
Harlem to deliver Simon's new instructions from Saint-Germain.
The letter for Andrew was sent on to Cambridge by post rider, and
another, intended for the prince, was locked away in a strongbox,
for Simon had had no word from him for some months and knew
his position must be precarious. With luck it might be possible to
smuggle the correspondence to him during the winter, when military activity was negligible; it certainly could not be gotten to him
while an evacuation was in progress.

Meanwhile, the Americans were to be given no opportunity for a
leisurely withdrawal. By September 21, as the evacuation was just
getting under way, the British attacked again at Kips Bay. Under
cover fire of eighty guns from British ships along the East River,
the impending landing of seemingly uncountable flatboats loaded
with Redcoat and Hessian infantry so demoralized the defending
militiamen that they threw down their muskets and fled.

Washington was furious, and with several aides galloped the four
miles from the Heights to the landing site in disbelief. The men
were retreating in blind panic, convinced that even the sound of
the British guns would blow them to pieces. Ordering them to
stand and fight, the General and his aides drew their swords and
charged into their midst, but to no avail.

"Take the walls! Stand and fight!" Washington shouted, indicating fences behind which they might still make a stand.

But his exhortations fell on deaf ears. Though a few tried to do
as the General directed, most continued to surge up the Post Road,
their flight hampering an orderly retreat. Washington swung at
them in rage with his riding crop, finally throwing down his hat in
sheer anguish and crying, "Are these the men with whom I am to
defend America?"

Meanwhile, not eighty yards away, the British were advancing at

the run, and the Commander in Chief seemed not to recognize his danger, perhaps not even to care.

"General, we must withdraw!" Simon shouted, catching the eye of one of Washington's other aides and kneeing his horse closer. "General, come away *now*!"

But Washington seemed stupefied at the defection of his troops, blind with rage and frustration, and briefly railed at Simon and the other aide when they seized his bridle and led him to safety. As the Americans were gradually forced to withdraw to Harlem Heights, British troops marched down Broadway virtually unopposed. Later that night Simon remonstrated with the General for taking such risks.

"I beg you not to place yourself in such danger, General! What if you had been taken or killed? You *must* take more care!"

But Washington's mind was still focused on New York—and on the fire by then consuming the city, of which he wrote to Congress, "Providence, or some good honest fellow, has done more for us than we were disposed to do for ourselves."

It was never determined who was responsible for the blaze, which broke out in some wooden warehouses along the East River and destroyed some five hundred houses—about a quarter of the city's dwellings—but the British apprehended at least one good honest fellow who was to pay a terrible price for other work carried out in Washington's behalf, that night when New York burned. Washington did not learn of the cost until several days later, when Simon ushered a haggard, unshaven, and exhausted Prince Lucien into the upstairs room commandeered as an office by the Commander in Chief. The prince wore civilian attire somewhat the worse for wear and appeared not to have slept for some time. Both he and Simon wore somber expressions.

"General, Dr. Saint-John has just come from behind the British lines," Simon said quietly. "I fear he brings distressing news."

"Sit down, please, Doctor," Washington said, noting the prince's condition and laying his pen aside. "Pray, be plain in your reporting."

The prince inclined his head in bone-weary acquiescence. "The gist of the news is this, General. Nathan Hale is taken and has been hanged without trial. I witnessed the execution and have spent the past three days making my own escape."

"Hale taken?" Washington repeated dumbly. "And executed?"

"That is the usual fate of spies, sir," the prince replied, "though the doing of it went beyond the usual coldness. He was captured the night of the twenty-first and executed the following morning, allowed no Bible or benefit of clergy. He had all but completed his sketches of the British troop positions and had the incriminating papers on his person. There was no question of his fate, and nothing I could do to save him. As it is, I dare not go back."

"Hale dead," Washington murmured, still reeling with the shock. "And I sent him to his death."

"He knew the risk," the prince retorted, then added, more gently, "You must not blame yourself. *He* did not blame you. He was a brave soldier, and a true son of liberty. Would you hear his last words?"

Washington nodded numbly.

"He said that it was the duty of every good soldier to obey any order from his Commander in Chief. He said it with pride, and he bade the men around him to be ready for death in whatever shape it might appear. Then he said, 'I only regret that I have but one life to lose for my country.' If many display his courage and devotion, I think you need not fear for the final outcome of this war, General—though many more will fall before all is resolved. The price will be dear."

"Well do I know that," Washington whispered. "All too well do I know."

Official word of Hale's fate did not come for several days, by which time Washington had succeeded in withdrawing the remainder of his troops from New York and had even inflicted a minor setback on the British at Harlem Heights. By then the prince had studied his instructions from Saint-Germain, acquainted himself with Washington's general intentions through the approaching winter, and decided that his best course of action now lay in returning to France, for Congress was preparing to send a delegation to join Silas Deane in Paris. Deane had been sent in April, as an agent of two secret committees of Congress, to buy guns and equipment for the Continental Army—all on credit. Now Franklin and Arthur Lee were to join him, with Franklin as senior American negotiator. Their mission: to secure additional credit and to present a proposed treaty of alliance to the French government.

"I know most of the men with whom they must deal," the prince told Simon the night before he was to leave. "It may be that I can ease certain introductions, open certain doors. I have useful financial contacts as well. If I may, I should like to take Justin with me."

"But he has only just returned," Simon began as Justin looked at the prince in surprise. "I had hoped to have the services of my aide for a few weeks, at least—perhaps even through the winter."

"He is an American who speaks fluent French, in addition to his many other talents," the prince said with a smile. "For what I have in mind, he will be able to do us far better service in France. Believe me, I have the Master's own word in this regard."

"Very well," Simon said, though a trifle dubiously. "And what happens here in the meantime?"

"You must continue to safeguard the General," the prince replied, "and to guide him toward his high destiny. For now it is a deadly game of cat and mouse, with many cats who, happily for us, are somewhat complacent. Cats also do not like snow—and winter will soon be upon us. Let us hope that the mouse continues to be exceedingly clever and agile, and that he does not underestimate the cats."

He and Justin left the next day, heading south for a ship out of Philadelphia. Meanwhile, Washington's scarce-gained success at Harlem Heights was to become the pattern for many a future military encounter: to harry the British without any hope of actually winning, because of the sheer superiority of British numbers, but to tie up British forces with uncertainty. Though Howe never had fewer than twenty-seven thousand troops under his command, once the fleets arrived, he remained wary of advancing too strongly against the Americans, forever imagining hordes of American troops ready to fall upon his army. Perhaps with this in mind, both he and his brother, the admiral, began to talk of reconciliation again and let it be known that they desired to negotiate a peace.

But the events of the past weeks had taken Washington beyond what he called "this fatal idea." Though pushed from Westchester, and subjected to betrayal that resulted in the loss of Fort Washington before Fort Lee also fell to an attack by General Cornwallis, he continued to resist even under pursuit by Cornwallis across the flatlands of New Jersey. (He had withdrawn from Fort Lee with Generals Putnam, Mercer, and Greene just half an hour before the enemy surrounded the fort.)

Urgently and repeatedly he sent word to General Charles Lee to reinforce him; but Lee was convinced that he was the better commander—and perhaps was—and was sufficiently engaged in trying to convince other generals of this fact that he continued to ignore the requests of his Commander in Chief. Joseph Reed, Washington's adjutant general, had also become embroiled in the intrigue and, based on the recent withdrawals, was suggesting a change in the high command.

By December 8, with only three thousand men, Washington retreated to Trenton and crossed the Delaware to escape, the last boat embarking just as the British arrived. Of Lee there was no sign—though he would be captured five days later by a British patrol while attempting to subvert General Gates via Gates's aide. Shortly thereafter Washington shifted his headquarters to the Keith house, about ten miles from Trenton, to be nearer the headquarters of Generals Greene and Knox while he pondered what to do next.

By then, because of British pressure, Congress had adjourned and fled to Baltimore. As the weather turned bitter, promising worse to come, General Howe ordered a chain of manned outposts set from Trenton to Hackensack and withdrew to set up winter quarters in New York. Mostly Hessian units would be left to hold the chain, with command headquarters based at Brunswick. A garrison of three Hessian regiments was posted to Trenton, under a German colonel called Johann Rall, who had distinguished himself at White Plains and Fort Washington.

Howe's withdrawal did little to reassure Washington, who could not yet afford the luxury of taking up winter quarters. If the Delaware River froze over, he was still fearful that Howe would march

troops across the ice and move on Philadelphia. Furthermore, he was again facing the evaporation of his army when their enlistments expired at the end of the year. As he had written to John Hancock on December 20, "Ten more days will put an end to the existence of our army."

What was desperately needed was some semblance of success, to bolster morale and offset the series of defeats and near disasters that had followed Washington across New Jersey. The British seemed convinced that the American Army was in no condition to launch an attack and were settling in confidently to await its collapse, further lulled into a sense of security by the approaching winter. What Washington had that the British did not was boats with which to cross the Delaware while it remained unfrozen. But could he come up with a plan to use those boats that had any hope of success?

Late on the afternoon of December 22 he was still pondering his slender options, poring over maps with Simon and half a dozen other members of his staff, when a commotion in the hallway outside his office interrupted their deliberations. Simon was sent to ascertain the cause of the commotion: two cavalrymen with a muddy, sullen-looking prisoner, hands trussed behind his back and a pistol held to his head by one of his captors.

"Says he's a cattle dealer, sir," one of the troopers said to the lieutenant on duty, lowering the pistol and uncocking it as two sentries took up posts just inside the door to the outside. "We caught him down by the river. Says he was looking for one of his cows, but he ran when we tried to question him. I expect he's a Tory spy."

Simon had left the office door ajar as he stepped into the hallway to hear the circumstances of the capture. To his surprise Washington himself now emerged, nodding his thanks to the two cavalrymen.

"Excellent work, gentlemen. I'll question him privately, in my office. Shoot him if he tries to escape," he told the watching sentries. "Colonel Wallace, perhaps you'll be so good as to move the staff meeting to another room."

The office was quickly vacated, the prisoner was ushered in, and

Washington closed the door. Bewildered speculation superseded
military discussion for several minutes before the staff meeting resumed, but after half an hour Washington emerged, turned the
prisoner over to the guards, and ordered him locked up. He volunteered no explanation as his staff trooped back into his office, re-
suming the meeting as if there had been no interruption. But when
he adjourned for supper, another hour later, he asked Simon to
remain, waiting until all the others had gone out and the last one
had closed the door.

"That fellow in the guardhouse—I want him to escape later tonight," he said quietly as he drew Simon as far as possible from the
door.

"He's your agent, then?"

"Aye. And he's brought me some very useful information. Can
you get him out?"

Simon nodded grimly. "I think so."

"You *think* so?"

"Leave it to me."

They went on to supper after that, and the General and his staff
retired at their usual times thereafter. But later that night fire
broke out in some hay piled near the guardhouse. The sentry at the
guardhouse was among those who came running to help put it out,
but on returning to his post he discovered that the guardhouse
somehow had been unlocked and his prisoner had escaped.
Though he roused other guards, and a figure seen fleeing into the
woods was fired at, the prisoner was neither hit nor apprehended.
When told of the escape the next morning, Washington appeared
to be furious, but he became increasingly preoccupied as the day
wore on, closeting himself in his office with one and another of his
staff and scribbling on scraps of paper as he fleshed out a plan.

And it was an audacious one: to cross the ice-clogged Delaware
River under cover of night and take Trenton. The night he selected
was Christmas, when the Hessian garrison might be expected to be
less vigilant, for the Germans were known to make much of their
Christmas celebrations. Before embarking upon this ambitious endeavor, and as a winter storm blew up that Christmas night of
1776, the Commander in Chief assembled his troops and caused to

be read to them a message published not a week before by Thomas Paine:

"These are the times that try men's souls," Paine had written. "The summer soldier and the sunshine patriot will, in this crisis, shrink from the service of his country; but he that stands it now deserves the love and thanks of man and woman. Tyranny, like hell, is not easily conquered; yet we have this consolation with us, that the harder the conflict, the more glorious the triumph. What we obtain too cheap, we esteem too lightly. 'Tis dearness only that gives every thing its value. Heaven knows how to set a proper price upon its goods; and it would be strange indeed, if so celestial an article as Freedom should not be highly rated. . . ."

Washington's troops rose to the challenge. The password for the night was "Victory or death." Ferried across the ice-choked Delaware by the Marblehead men who had evacuated them from Long Island, in sleet and bitter cold, they landed above and below Trenton by four in the morning. Henry Knox supervised the moving of eighteen vital artillery field pieces. The crossing had taken nine hours instead of the expected five, and few men had managed to keep their powder dry.

"Then we must rely on the bayonet," Washington ordered. "The town must be taken, and I am determined to take it."

The delay meant a brief rest might be allowed for food before they moved out. The General took his own meal on horseback, then rallied his men to their feet and pressed onward, for dawn was approaching. They had no other option but to go on, for if they lost the element of surprise, retreat would be cut off by the river at their backs.

Despite several last-minute setbacks, the Americans still managed to surprise the British garrison at dawn, in a blinding storm, killing or wounding about thirty and capturing a thousand, without loss of American lives. Colonel Rall, the German commander, was among the casualties.

Withdrawing across the Delaware to recover, Washington dined with some of the captured Hessian officers the following day before sending them on to Philadelphia with the rest of the Hessian prisoners, and two days later was recrossing the Delaware to occupy Trenton. Besides the badly needed victory, he had taken spoils that included a thousand weapons, three wagons of ammunition and four of baggage, six brass cannons, forty horses, and twelve drums.

On the thirtieth, with the enlistments of all but a handful of his men set to expire, the Commander in Chief assembled his ragged troops and begged them to stay for just six more weeks, praising their success at Trenton and lauding them as the soldiers of whom Thomas Paine had written—not sunshine patriots, but the men who were carrying the revolution forward while others stayed at home. It took two appeals, and the inducement of a bounty that Washington had no authority to offer, but in the end some twelve hundred men agreed to extend their enlistments for another month—long enough, Washington hoped, to see hostilities all but suspended for the winter, and to await the arrival of new recruits with the spring.

His audacity was vindicated the following evening when an express arrived from Baltimore with new instructions from Congress. After reading them the General withdrew into the room serving as his office and shortly called Simon in.

"It appears that I was only a day early in offering bounties for extending reenlistment," he said, waving Simon to a chair, "though God alone knows where we shall find the hard money to pay them. Furthermore, I have leave to raise a formidable force for the new year: sixteen additional battalions of infantry, three thousand light horse, three regiments of artillery, and a corps of engineers."

"This should be welcome news," Simon replied, noting the General's somewhat strained demeanor. "Or is there more you wish to tell me?"

Washington grimaced and handed the dispatch to Simon. "They have given me the powers of a military dictator."

Simon's gaze flicked over the catalog of powers, not only to muster the troops already mentioned but to decide on their rate of pay and for what duration, to appoint their officers, to appeal directly to the states for additional militia as required, and to take "whatever he may want for the use of the army"—and to arrest those who refused to sell.

"These are far-reaching powers," Simon agreed, "but clearly Congress realizes how desperate are our straits, if the war is to be carried to a successful conclusion. And with Congress several days' ride away, you cannot always afford the time to consult with them every time a decision must be made. 'Tis clear that you have their utter trust." He consulted the document and selected an illustrative sentence. " 'Happy is it for this country that the General of their forces can safely be entrusted with the most unlimited power, and neither personal security, liberty, nor property be in the least degree endangered thereby.' They *do* limit this power to a period of six months," Simon added with a smile, "unless sooner determined by Congress."

"Still, a formidable responsibility," Washington said bleakly.

"Is it that you fear you may misuse those powers?" Simon asked. "They have given you the authority to do what you must to see this venture through. I know of no man better suited to the task. And I believe Providence will confirm that, in the end."

Washington closed his eyes hard, then looked back at Simon.

"Do you really believe that?" he whispered.

"I do, with all my heart, and unto death." When Washington only looked away, Simon added, "I hope and pray that you may receive confirmation of this destiny in the very near future, but meanwhile, you must trust that you are doing the right thing."

"Am I?" Sighing, Washington rose and moved to the curtained window, twitching it briefly aside to gaze out at the snow-covered yard. Another sigh escaped his lips as he leaned heavily against the window casement to bury his face in one hand, rubbing wearily at the bridge of his nose.

"Dear Lord, I am weary!" he murmured. "We have respite now, but Howe will not wait long to respond to what we have done here. Will I have the men to answer him? Can we continue to stand against such opposition?"

Rising, Simon came to stand beside the General, daring to lay a hand lightly on a blue-clad elbow.

"You should get some rest, General," he murmured, nodding toward the camp bed set in a corner of the room. "A little sleep will help you gain a little perspective."

Washington shook his head, but it was halfhearted. "I must respond to Congress."

"Sleep first," Simon urged. "I shall wake you in a few hours and help you deal with the necessary correspondence. Please, General. Without sleep you will be no good to any cause, no matter how honest your intentions."

That argument produced the desired response. Sighing, Washington removed his sword belt, handed it to Simon, and sank down onto the bed, not minding his boots as he shifted his long legs up and reclined. His eyes closed as soon as his head had settled on the pillow.

Briefly setting aside the sword, Simon shook out a blanket and draped it over Washington, who was already deeply asleep, then settled down on a chair near the door with the sword across his lap. He had tried before to gain some psychic impression from the sword, and tonight's attempt was no more successful than the previous tries. But he did dream of Washington when he lapsed into sleep for an hour. More strongly than ever before, he saw the General with a laurel wreath across his brow. When he snapped back to wakefulness, and then shortly roused the Commander in Chief, he hoped it was a portent for the days to come.

Rain ushered in the first day of January, 1777, far milder than the previous week. By the next day, in preparation to meet the British riposte he knew must come, Washington had reinforced Trenton with nearly five thousand men. However, more than two thirds of them, though fresh, were untried and untrained militia.

Cornwallis meanwhile had reinforced nearby Princeton with sufficient numbers to bring his strength to about six thousand crack British and Hessian troops, and began to move on Trenton. As intelligence came in from Washington's scouts and spies, it soon became clear that he dared not give direct battle or even remain in Trenton; but perhaps another encounter on terms of his own choosing stood some chance of success. A cache of British supplies lay at Princeton, relatively unprotected—a most tempting target.

While a detachment of Pennsylvania riflemen fought a delaying action along the road from Princeton to Trenton, holding Cornwallis until dark, Washington withdrew his troops and artillery to a

strong position across the Assumpink. Then, in another of his typi-
cally innovative desperation moves, he left decoy watch fires and a
token force in his assumed campsite and attempted to bypass the
British defenses in Princeton by marching his forces around Cornwallis's flank, along a little-known alternative route reported by
one of his spies.

But the British got wind of the plan before Washington was
ready to engage, nearly routing the Americans until their Commander in Chief took personal command, mustering an American
attack and riding out between the two battle lines on a white horse.
As he dashed to within thirty yards of the enemy, waving his hat to
urge his militiamen forward, a volley was fired from the enemy
line, and several of his officers covered their faces with their hats,
for they could not bear to see him shot.

But he was still there when they dared to look again, still motioning them to advance; and his reckless exposure again inspired
his men to wrest victory from defeat, in what soon would be acknowledged a military masterpiece. Demoralized, and with a substantial portion of his command shattered, Cornwallis withdrew
from western New Jersey to take up winter quarters, though desultory skirmishes would continue for another week.

Only then did Washington dare to withdraw to the shelter of
Morristown, New Jersey, where he would set up his own winter
headquarters. Whether by Divine Providence, blind luck, or his
own military savvy, he somehow had managed to survive his first
full year of campaigning and now could hope to use the winter to
reorganize and to remedy some of the glaring inadequacies of his
battered army.

Chapter Seventeen

Justin and the prince arrived in Paris in time for Christmas, following a stormy Atlantic crossing and a wet slog across France from Brest, while Washington's assault on Trenton was still in its planning stages. Lodgings appropriate to the prince's station had already been engaged in their behalf, apparently by Saint-Germain, but Justin was learning not to question the Master's ability to anticipate events.

Actual instructions arrived shortly after they did, addressed to the prince, along with invitations to a succession of gala Christmas and New Year's celebrations to be held at court in the coming weeks. Justin soon found himself moving in somewhat more exalted circles than he had expected—though the prince advised him not to wear his American uniform.

He soon discovered why. The Declaration of Independence had reached Europe in early October, to general approval by most of England's traditional enemies, and Deane's first shipment of supplies had gone out very shortly: thirty thousand guns, one hundred thousand balls, two hundred cannons with full trains, twenty-seven mortars, three thousand tents, and a large consignment of much-needed gunpowder, all of which would be greatly welcomed back at Morristown.

But since then had come the news of Washington's defeats in and around New York, and his subsequent withdrawal, tempered but little by the minor successes he had managed to wrest from mounting disasters. Franklin and Lee had arrived on the heels of this news, only days before Justin and the prince, to learn that the King's ministers had forbidden French officers to join the insurgents—though Franklin pointed out several who were determined to go anyway.

"The Marquis de Lafayette is the highest ranking of them," Franklin confided to Justin and the prince at a New Year's fete at Versailles. "He's over there, pumping my grandson for information about Washington."

Lifting his glass slightly, he indicated a tall, somewhat gawky-looking youth engaged in animated conversation with the sixteen-year-old William Temple Franklin, who had accompanied his grandfather as secretary on the mission. Though young Franklin's companion was as elegantly attired as any of the courtiers present, powdered and bejeweled in the latest of fashion, there was an awkward quality to his movements and his very carriage that bespoke extreme youth.

"He looks very young," Justin observed, casting an appraising eye over the distant figure. "Lucien, do you know him?"

"Not for some years," the prince allowed. "I remember hearing how his father had been killed by the English at Minden. It was very tragic, for Gilbert was not yet two at the time, and I believe his father had never seen him. But when he was twelve, he inherited the entire estate of his maternal grandfather, the Marquis de La Riviere—which left him a very wealthy young man. And I believe he has married extremely well."

"Interesting," Justin murmured, returning his attention to Franklin. "And how old is he now?"

"Just nineteen, I believe," Franklin replied. "However, he is not entirely without military experience, despite his youth; he's held a captaincy in the very prestigious Noailles Regiment for more than two years. He's also reasonably well educated, and fairly fluent in English."

"So are many men," Justin pointed out.

"Yes, but he is also full of zeal for our cause. Coupled with his family connections and his not inconsiderable wealth, that makes him potentially very useful. And I believe a mutual acquaintance of ours has additional plans for him, does he not, Prince?"

The comment startled Justin, for though he had suspected for some time that Franklin's interests and talents ran far deeper than initially assumed, he had not expected even a veiled reference to Saint-Germain in this context. The prince, however, seemed quite nonplussed.

"Yes. I was told that a new agent was being prepared," he allowed.

"Well, you see him before you," Franklin said. "Mind you, I don't believe the young marquis is meant to know he's being guided. Why don't you make his acquaintance, Lieutenant? Perhaps the prince will introduce you. You aren't that much older than he is; and when he learns of your close association with our Commander in Chief, I expect you'll find you have a most attentive new friend. He's quite taken with the idea of serving under Washington."

"How will he be able to do that, if French officers are forbidden to serve in our army?"

"Why, I believe he intends to purchase a ship. And my colleague Silas Deane has been induced to offer him a commission as major general. Come the spring, I expect that Paris shall see little more of Monsieur le Marquis de Lafayette."

Prince Lucien performed the introductions that very evening, then faded quietly back to Franklin's side to watch the two younger men interact.

"You actually *know* the General?" the marquis murmured, when they had sampled the punch and Justin had confided his standing in the Continental Army.

"I cannot claim him as a friend," Justin admitted. "Few men can. But my brother-in-law is one of his aides, and I serve *him* as aide. I've had occasion to perform the occasional service for the General."

"Tell me what he is like," Lafayette urged, drawing Justin into a mirrored alcove where they could speak more privately. "He seems to me the most admirable of commanders. I intend to offer him my services as soon as I can arrange passage to America—and against the orders of my king, though I would ask that you not betray me in this matter," he added with a meaningful look around the assembly before them in the mirrored hall. "I have agreed to take no salary, if only I may serve at his side. This is my most fervent ambition!"

Containing a smile, and assuring the marquis that he would not think of revealing his plans, Justin spent the next hour describing the general circumstances of the American struggle, and of their Commander in Chief in particular. By the end of the evening he had a firm new friend. Within the week Saint-Germain had informed him just how firm he intended that new friend to be.

"His part extends even beyond what is unfolding in the New World," the Master told Justin as the prince listened but said nothing. "Others are attempting to use him, but I have already set him apart for my own use. Have you met a gentleman called the Comte de Broglie?"

"He is hardly a gentleman," the prince remarked with a sniff of disdain.

"But his rank does give him important connections," the Master pointed out, returning his attention to Justin. "The Comte de Broglie commands the French army at Metz. He is both ambitious and disappointed. He served Louis the Fifteenth most ably as head of his secret diplomacy, but Louis the Sixteenth has not shown him the favor he feels he deserves. Since that state of affairs is not likely to change, the Comte de Broglie has conceived a plan whereby he shall become King of America, after leading the American Army to a glorious victory. Of course it has not occurred to him that the Americans might have other ideas."

Justin's jaw had dropped as Saint-Germain spoke. "He wants to be king?"

"Oh, indeed. He has positioned several of his aides to treat with your Silas Deane for commissions—at which they may succeed, since Deane is desperate and fears that only European officers have the skill to stand against the British."

"Is Lafayette one of Broglie's aides?" Justin asked.

"No, Broglie considers him a means to an end, of limited usefulness because of his youth and inexperience. His principal lieuten-

ants are a German called Johann De Kalb, of some ability, and a minor French nobleman called Mauroy—rather an unpleasant fellow.

"Broglie intends that Lafayette should be used as a stalking horse, to secure American commissions for De Kalb, Mauroy, and a cadre of additional French officers selected for their loyalty to Broglie. Then, when the time is right, these men would call in Broglie to take over as Commander in Chief—a laughable plan, but it could create problems for Washington that he does not need. Yet he does need Lafayette. So we shall use Broglie and his minions for now, for our own purposes."

"Which are?"

"First of all, to get Lafayette out of France and attached to Washington," Saint-Germain said with a smile. "This will be more difficult than it might appear, even without Broglie's intrigues, for not only the King and his ministers but also his family are opposed—and he will be leaving a young wife who, I believe, is with child.

"Fortunately, young Gilbert du Motier, Monsieur le Marquis de Lafayette, was determined to go to America long before I set my hand upon this matter. These are early times yet, but if all proceeds as planned, I intend that he shall become a brother in the Craft, to ensure his discretion, and eventually a vital link within our Inner Circle."

"The Craft is strong here in France," the prince remarked. "I am surprised he has not yet embraced it."

"He is young yet," Saint-Germain replied. "Besides that, far better that Washington should start him upon that path, since his function in the New World will revolve around Washington. I shall hope to see him guided gently in that direction over the coming year. Simon will also be apprised of this intention, since he is apt to have even closer contact with both men.

"In a related vein, I desire Arabella to continue in her masonic work. I would hope to see her made Fellow Craft before next winter, if that is possible. I am sending instructions to Andrew in that regard."

The prince nodded. "I understand. And Lafayette—how much is he to know?"

"For now, only what is necessary. As I said, he is young. I intend that he should spend this year and the next in America, establishing his relationship with the General. Then I shall want him back in France for a time. By then, we shall have more precise assessments of the part it will be necessary for him to play." The Master glanced at Justin. "Does anything in this plan give you cause for concern?"

Justin shook his head. "He seems an agreeable young man," he said. "If he endears himself to Washington as he has to me, his placement will be ideal for whatever you intend for him."

"Excellent." Saint-Germain smiled. "Then, make the most of these next few months, until he departs for America. Though I intend that you shall continue as my principal courier to and from Andrew and Simon, I wish you to maintain a cordial relationship with the marquis. I shall instruct you in more specific terms as this becomes appropriate."

The next months proved more enjoyable than arduous for Justin, for what young man could fail to be caught up by the excitement of carnival season in Paris? Especially if one's introductions came via a prince—albeit of modest means—and a dazzlingly wealthy marquis. Seen increasingly in the company of the smart set usually attendant on the young Queen, Marie Antoinette, Justin found his days filled with riding, hunting, attendance at racing meetings, and leisurely carriage rides through the many parks in Paris. By night, his growing association with the Marquis de Lafayette opened doors to the best parties and salons and balls in Paris, where he and Prince Lucien helped further the illusion that the marquis had given up his plans to go to the New World.

While Broglie's men became convinced they were manipulating the young marquis, inducing him to buy a ship and helping lay false trails to facilitate his flight from France, in fact Saint-Germain was manipulating them all; so that by April, when Lafayette set sail with a handful of young French officers and De Kalb—who was convinced he had masterminded the affair—in fact Lafayette was doing precisely what Saint-Germain had always intended. As soon as he was safely away, Justin and Prince Lucien took ship for Boston, arriving in mid-June.

They did not know to what port Lafayette was headed, but he

had not yet arrived in Boston. What *had* arrived, as the winter wore on, were Silas Deane's first shipments of muskets, ammunition, and other desperately needed supplies from France, sent thence to the army wintering in Morristown. After delivering letters to Andrew, the prince and Justin visited with Andrew, Arabella, and the children for a few days, catching up on the news current in Boston; then they headed southward, skirting New York. En route they learned that Washington had moved the army to Middlebrook, on the Raritan River above Brunswick, and that Howe's army had ventured out from Staten Island to New Jersey, hoping to lure Washington into battle, smash him, and advance on Philadelphia.

But Washington avoided the traps set for him, for he had learned a vital lesson in the previous year's campaigning: that the British preferred not to march through open country, for fear of the Americans' increasing propensity to wage guerrilla-style warfare from behind every hillock and wall and derelict building. Under constant harassment by American forces, Howe soon withdrew again to Staten Island, pulling out even the Hessian outposts he had left guarding throughout the winter, leaving New Jersey completely unoccupied by British troops.

Meanwhile, in the north, though the British under Burgoyne had succeeded in taking back Ticonderoga and had hoped to push down along the Hudson and cut off New England, they had lost other important battles. With General Schuyler and then General Gates continuing to harass Burgoyne, Howe could expect no help from that quarter.

Yet Philadelphia still lay in rebel hands—a nagging symbol of colonial rebellion, since it continued to serve as the insurgents' capital. Howe had learned the hard way that approaching across the Jerseys was not feasible. But perhaps transporting his troops over part of that distance by sea would prove the edge he needed— especially if it came as a surprise.

When British ships began massing in New York Harbor in early July, it was first assumed that they would sail up the Hudson to aid Burgoyne. Howe loaded around eighteen thousand troops but then let the ships sit for nearly a fortnight. At the same time he encouraged rumors that his intended objective for the rest of this battle season was Boston. He even arranged for a letter to fall into Washington's hands confirming that plan. But Washington was not deceived.

Justin and the prince arrived in Philadelphia along with the news that Howe's ships had not sailed up the Hudson but had gone to sea, destination unknown. The two still had learned nothing of Lafayette's whereabouts. The prince, after briefing Simon, volunteered the services of Dr. Lucien Rohan as an additional surgeon until the winter, for he had learned sufficient battlefield skill during his months with the British to make him useful. Once both armies went into winter quarters, he would turn his hand to assisting with the financing of the war effort. Justin, meanwhile, acquainted Simon with the Master's plans for Lafayette, then settled down to wait for his arrival.

The young marquis at last reached Philadelphia on July 27, after landing six weeks previously in Georgetown, South Carolina. His reception in nearby Charleston had been cordial, once it became known that he was both a genuine aristocrat and rich, but the journey north through South Carolina and Virginia was arduous. The band of eleven French officers that finally arrived in Philadelphia was travel worn and bedraggled, and the reception there was hardly what Lafayette had been led to expect.

For Broglie's ambitions were by now known to Congress, who had had enough of foreign officers seeking American commissions. Some of them were discredited adventurers no longer welcome in Europe. Many were greedy, arrogant, and not particularly well trained. Some, while competent, had only disdain for their American counterparts; and many senior American officers fiercely resented the commissions being dispensed so freely in Paris by Silas Deane.

Lafayette was an unknown to Congress; but the fact that he had come with De Kalb, who was Broglie's agent, tarred him with the same brush. Undaunted by initial rejection, the marquis approached individual members of Congress with letters of introduction and managed to convince them that he was no adventurer. While no commissions were forthcoming for any of his companions, Congress offered Lafayette an appointment Deane had promised as a major general.

"Whereas the Marquis de Lafayette, out of his great zeal to the

cause of liberty, in which the United States are engaged, has left his family and connections, and at his own expense comes over to offer his services to the United States, without pension or particular allowance, and is anxious to risk his life in our cause; *Resolved*, that his services be accepted, and that in consideration of his zeal, his illustrious family, and connections, he have the rank and commission of a major general in the army of the United States."

Of course, his youth precluded the former French captain from actually commanding a division for the time being, and he declined even the offer of reimbursement for his expenses, but Lafayette was elated. No sooner had his commission been conferred than he was taken to the house where Washington had established his headquarters outside Philadelphia.

Much of the resolution of Lafayette's fate in the last few days had been orchestrated by Simon, acting on Justin's intelligence from Saint-Germain. It was with profound relief that the pair observed the first meeting between marquis and general, as the starry-eyed young Frenchman was presented to his new Commander in Chief. Lafayette's reaction bordered on the reverent; and Washington, who enjoyed being surrounded by bright young officers, warmed to the younger man's adulation with noble affability.

The invitation to move into his house and join his military family was no more than the General extended to all his staff, whenever possible; but at Versailles, the granting of such accommodation would have been accounted a singular sign of favor. Lafayette was enchanted. The next day, during a review of troops that also paraded the newly official flag, with its new constellation of thirteen stars now replacing the British union, Lafayette was given the sash of a major general and was invited to dine with Washington. The day after that he rode at his new chief's side to inspect the city's fortifications.

His French companions railed at the show of favoritism—especially De Kalb, who needed to be in a position to note Washington's shortcomings if he was to recommend Broglie as a replacement. Blissfully unaware of this hidden agenda, Lafayette dutifully tried to secure the commissions promised by Deane; but when John Hancock assured him of eventual appointments for his aides-de-camp, Lafayette thought little more of De Kalb and settled enthusiastically into military life.

"We must be embarrassed to show ourselves to an officer who has just left the French Army," Washington told him as they drove through the camp outside Philadelphia, where his motley army of perhaps eleven thousand was quartered.

"I am here to learn, not to teach," came Lafayette's diplomatic reply.

It was no more than the truth, for Lafayette knew himself to be young and yet untried, but such modesty soon endeared him to Washington's staff as well as to the General himself, for he showed himself earnest and enthusiastic, willing to do whatever he was asked, if it should forward the patriot cause. While he let it be known that he was eager for a command of his own when his commander should judge him ready, meanwhile he was content to serve in whatever capacity he was needed.

Both cheerful and civilized, he soon became a favored companion at the General's table and proved himself a trustworthy sounding board. Only weeks after his arrival, over one of the long, leisurely suppers that were Washington's main source of relaxation, the first inkling of his future connection began to emerge, though Lafayette himself was unaware of it.

"The landing of British troops in Delaware confirms Howe's intentions for Philadelphia," one of Washington's senior aides was saying over the wine and nuts customarily passed around after dining. "I think it can be only a matter of days before we are drawn into battle. The men are eager to fight, but I could wish for more of the essentials for them—food, clothing, ammunition. Monsieur Lafayette must think us veritable scarecrows."

"Ah, but scarecrows who have frightened the British greatly," Lafayette replied, "and cost them much. One must hope that uniforms can be obtained before the winter—or at least adequate clothing. Still, uniforms would do much for morale."

"Adequate ammunition would do much for morale," Simon said archly. "Adequate food would also help. But we shall have to fight to procure those necessities."

"True enough," Lafayette agreed. "It is my fond hope that supplies will soon be forthcoming from France. Mr. Franklin, Mr. Lee, and Mr. Deane have been working most judiciously to secure the necessary lines of credit. But there is a way that one could create the illusion of uniformity now, without waiting for outside aid."

"Indeed?" Washington said, toying with the stem of his glass. "And how might that be?"

Eagerly Lafayette turned toward his idol. "You are familiar with the hackles worn by many armies in their helmets and hats, *mon général*?" he asked. "Or Colonel Wallace can tell you about the white cockades worn as a sign of Jacobite sympathies in former times."

"In these times even such simple things are difficult to obtain, my dear marquis," Washington said gently.

"Yes, but we have here an abundance of growing things," Lafayette said eagerly. "The Scots were ever wont to wear plant badges in their caps. Our army may lack uniforms, but the most humble soldier wears a hat of some kind. How, if we were to have them wear green sprigs in their hats as uniform badges for the American Army? Would it not make a brave sight, to march thus into battle?"

At the odd look on Washington's face Simon was quite prepared to hear the idea rejected out of hand, but to his surprise the General slowly nodded.

"We shall speak further on this," he murmured before turning the conversation to other subjects.

Later, when his officers had withdrawn for final duties of the night, preparatory to retiring, the General drew Simon into his office, motioning for him to close the door, though he did not invite him to sit.

"This idea of Lafayette's, to have the men wear green sprigs in their hats," he said. "Was that your doing?"

"Mine, sir?"

A look of disappointment washed briefly across the craggy face.

"I had thought, for a moment, that it might allude to the laurel wreath of my dream," he said, almost to himself. "I had even dared to hope that it might portend a coming victory, when we must face the British again."

"I know of no such connection, General," Simon said carefully—and truthfully, "though it may well be that the marquis has a part to play in your destiny. It is certain that he came to you despite unlikely odds, and that he worships you like a father and a god. And his wealth and connections in France do much to recommend him to your favor."

"Indeed," Washington said with a wistful smile. "Would that I had a son like him." He exhaled gustily and seemed to pull himself back to a more expected focus as he sat down behind his desk. "But perhaps I place too much importance on a chance discussion of greenery—though I shall certainly consider Monsieur Lafayette's proposal. Thank you, Colonel. You are probably eager to retire."

The dismissal, though affable enough, did not invite further discussion, and Simon saw no reason to belabor the issue. After wishing the general a pleasant night, Simon made his way back to his own quarters—though his mind continued to examine the conversation he had just left.

He himself would never have made the leap of logic between sprigs of greenery and laurel wreaths, but Washington had—perhaps an indication that he was willing and even eager to connect Lafayette with the dream. Of course that was Saint-Germain's eventual intention, but Simon thought it unlikely that the connection was meant to surface so soon, with so much still to set in place in Lafayette himself. On the other hand, the incident could be a sign that Providence already was laying the appropriate groundwork. It would be fascinating to watch the Master Plan continue to unfold.

Meanwhile, Howe's plans were also unfolding. The British commander had landed troops in Maryland and was advancing even then on Philadelphia. Washington knew he must fight, to delay Howe as long as possible, but he also knew it was not possible to stop him. Nonetheless, to hearten the local people, he marched his troops through Philadelphia on his way to oppose Howe—and had them wear sprigs of green for uniformity. Lafayette rode proudly at his side, with Generals Knox and Greene; and when Simon fell in with the rest of the aides, Washington gave him a sharp but approving look as he realized that Simon's sprig of green was laurel.

The days that followed became a succession of desultory skirmishes. Less than a fortnight later, on September 6, the young marquis celebrated his twentieth birthday in the field, having seen light action against Howe's advance positions several days before. By the ninth the Americans had withdrawn behind Brandywine Creek, whence Washington now sent all the army's baggage back to Chester, indicative of doubt in his ability to stop Howe. Two days later Howe, Cornwallis, and Knyphausen advanced on Brandywine, which was to be Lafayette's true baptism by fire.

It was late in the afternoon, with most of the American Army engaged in a frontal attack by Howe's main army, when Washington noticed that Cornwallis had begun a flanking movement, and sent the experienced General Sullivan to deflect it. Lafayette had ridden with Washington thus far but now asked to accompany Sullivan—to which Washington agreed.

Taking nominal command of Sullivan's center division, Lafayette rode fearlessly into battle, though it soon became apparent that Cornwallis had the superior force. With encouragement from Lafayette, his men stood their ground for a time; but while trying to rally his men on foot in the French manner, he was wounded in the leg, just below the calf.

Only when blood began filling his boot did he remount and retreat. On encountering Washington he dismounted long enough to let the General's personal physician apply a hasty field dressing, but then he was in the saddle again, soon swept up in the general retreat toward Chester. He had just finished restoring order among troops falling back on a bridge across the Chester River, some twelve miles to the rear, when Washington and his staff caught up with him again and took over. After one look at the white-faced Lafayette, now reeling in the saddle from loss of blood, Washington immediately ordered him to see his injury properly attended to and dispatched Simon and another aide to make certain that he did.

Despite his blood loss, Lafayette's wound had threatened neither life nor limb, but it was sufficient to keep him off his feet for the better part of two months—a restriction that pleased neither him nor Washington. The General's personal physician, Dr. John Cochran, looked after him for the first week or so, but James Ramsay was among the several other physicians who tended him during the weeks of his convalescence. It was Ramsay who drew Simon aside a few days after the battle, after looking in on the wounded Frenchman.

"I just learned something that made my blood run cold," Ramsay said. "Apparently young Lafayette was more fortunate than he or anyone else knew. So was Washington." As Justin approached, he motioned him to join them.

"What are you talking about?" Simon said. "What has Lafayette's wound to do with the General?"

Ramsay glanced around to make certain they would not be overheard, then drew them closer.

"I believe the General rode off on a recce with Lafayette, the morning of the battle?" he said.

"Yes, he did. They weren't gone very long. Why do you ask?"

Ramsay sighed. "I was talking to some of the other surgeons the day after," he said. "One of them told me how he'd had occasion to put a field dressing on a British officer of rifles who'd had his elbow shattered by a musket ball—a Major Ferguson. It seems Ferguson and three of his sharpshooters were scouting out Chad's Ford before the battle, just ahead of Knyphausen's Germans, when the approach of hoofbeats made them take cover. Two horsemen soon came into their sights—obviously high-ranking officers, though Ferguson had no idea who they might be—but he said he felt it unchivalrous to kill an unwary enemy, especially from ambush, so he forbade his men to fire.

"The men soon turned about and trotted out of sight, but imagine Ferguson's shock when he learned that it was Washington and Lafayette he'd spared."

Justin's jaw had tightened as the identity of the two horsemen became apparent, and Simon bit back an oath, shaking his head.

"Thus moves Providence," he whispered, almost inaudibly. Then he drew a deep breath and let it out with a wan smile. "I expect Ferguson was mortified."

Ramsay shrugged. "Interestingly enough, my source said he

seemed to have no regrets. 'The fortunes of war,' he termed it."
He pulled a mirthless smile. "It's good to know that there is still
some honor in this world. Anyway, I thought you should know.
Perhaps the General should know as well. Perhaps it will convince
him to take fewer chances."

"Perhaps," Simon said, though he doubted it.

What did make a difference to Washington's attitude—though
not about taking risks—was an incident that occurred perhaps
three weeks later. The British had occupied Philadelphia shortly
after the Battle of Brandywine, but despite advance information of
a planned American operation in the area of Germantown, Howe
failed to act upon it.

The American attack seemed to come as a complete surprise and
looked certain to succeed, except that a thick fog suddenly required
an immediate withdrawal, at the very instant when victory should
have been theirs. American morale remained high the day after the
aborted battle, but Washington was still puzzling over the fog
when he visited Lafayette's sickroom that evening, in the company
of Simon and Justin.

"In retrospect, perhaps our plan was too ambitious," the General was saying as he stood aside for Dr. Ramsay to attend to a
dressing change. "Yet we did manage to bring together four prongs
of our army to embrace the British. But the fog—the fog." He
shook his head. "We lost communication among our units. We
knew not who was friend or foe. . . ."

Washington fell suddenly silent as he watched Ramsay dress the
marquis's wound with oil, a strained look momentarily flickering
across his face.

"It is not so very painful, *mon général*," Lafayette assured his
commander, noting the latter's reaction. "The oil keeps the flesh
supple while it heals. My chief regret is that I am unable to ride at
your side while I am forced to play the invalid. Dr. Ramsay is a
harsh master."

"I am certain his only care is for your recovery," Washington
murmured dutifully, though with something of an air of distraction
as he watched Ramsay rebandage the wound. "And I, too, regret
the loss of your company. Pray, forgive my momentary lapse. I had

remembered something else I must attend to. All of your physicians tell me that they are most pleased with your progress."

Lafayette accepted the explanation without hesitation, but an air of preoccupation attended the General even when he left the room. Simon had noted the comment about remembering something, so was not surprised when Washington bade him and Justin accompany him back to the privacy of his office as soon as he reasonably could.

"Close the door, please, Mr. Carmichael," he murmured, "and be certain we are not interrupted or overheard."

"Yes, sir," Justin replied. "Shall I watch from outside? It seems to me that you have just requested the services of a Tyler."

A faint smile accompanied the question, and Washington exhaled softly, relaxing a little.

"If you would, please, Brother Carmichael. It is not that I would exclude you from what I must say, but the time of evening makes interruptions likely. You need not tyle with a drawn sword," he added, with a faint smile of his own.

With a nod Justin withdrew and closed the door softly behind him, leaving Simon facing the General across a desk piled with dispatches. At a gesture from the Commander in Chief, Simon dragged a chair around the end of the desk to sit knee to knee with him.

"Colonel, I have taken a great deal on trust," Washington murmured, "and I have no reason to question that trust," he added, lifting a hand in reassurance. "I accept that my dream has meaning on some level not yet understood, and that when you bid me forget fragments of memory that return, it is for my own peace of mind, that I may not be distracted from my work. I even accept that you have the ability to cause me to forget—and have long since ceased wondering how this is possible."

"But?"

Washington's gaze shifted uneasily to the big hands folded between his knees. "Thus far I have been content to put aside these memories as you bid me do," he said. "But it seems that their weight grows more with each new remembering. And sometimes the returning memories are more troubling than at other times."

"What did you remember?" Simon asked quietly.

"There was—a flagon of oil in my dream," Washington said. "Aromatic oil." His gray-blue gaze took on a faraway dreaminess. "I remember its sweet perfume as someone—anointed me with it."

"Was it Lafayette?" Simon asked, for the future role of the marquis was yet unknown.

"No. I saw only hands, and they were not his."

"Ramsay's, then?"

"I don't know." Washington drew a deep breath before going on. " 'Tis the anointing that troubles me, Colonel. Kings are anointed, and priests—and sacrifices. Is this a warning for the future? Was the fog at Germantown my first warning that even my meager victories now are past? Has our effort been too late?"

"No, and no, and no," Simon said softly, leaning closer to set his hand atop the General's clasped ones. "I do not yet know what it means, but none of that. Close your eyes now and put it from your thoughts." Washington's eyelids fluttered and then closed obediently. "Put away all anxiety, and all memory of this conversation. What will come is in more powerful hands than ours. I believe this; and you must believe it too. All shall be well, and all manner of things shall be well. . . ."

He did not move as the General's breathing gradually slowed, the craggy face slowly relaxing. Only after several tranquil moments did he finally tighten his hand slightly on the General's.

"When I get up to leave, you will turn around to your desk and lay your head down on your arms to rest. After a few minutes I will send in Justin with correspondence for you to sign. You will rouse refreshed and untroubled by any memory of dreams, ready to resume your duties. Nod if you understand and agree."

The powdered head slowly nodded.

Without further word Simon slowly withdrew his hand and stood, moving quietly to the closed door. Washington had stirred as Simon stood, but only enough to turn in his chair and lay his forehead on his crossed forearms on the desk. As soon as he had done so, Simon slipped outside and gave Justin instructions to fetch the afternoon's correspondence.

Ten minutes later the General was dealing with that correspon-

dence and receiving reports from his other aides as if nothing untoward had happened. A little later, when Simon had retired to his
quarters, he set his pen to correspondence of his own, relating the
incident to Andrew for inclusion in the growing body of information they eventually must incorporate into recreation of Washington's dream.

Germantown and its fog effectively signaled an end to serious
campaigning for 1777. Despite a technical victory at Germantown,
the British gradually wound down their efforts in what remained of
the year, for news of Burgoyne's surrender in mid-October had
been extremely demoralizing. Furthermore, despite continuing
skirmishes, the exhausted American Army managed to stay just
ahead of Howe's forces—who did not seem eager for another battle.

The two armies came close to a confrontation in early November, some twelve miles west of Philadelphia, but the Americans had
the high ground. After several days spent looking at one another,
Howe marched his men back to Philadelphia for the winter.
Within a fortnight, and only twenty miles away, Washington had
withdrawn his battered army into winter headquarters at Valley
Forge. That winter would be both the nadir of American morale
and the flowering of legend that would sustain American efforts
throughout the remainder of the war.

Chapter Eighteen

B y the beginning of 1778 the Master had set most of his principal players in place. Now he waited through the long winter of Valley Forge and the campaigns of the year that followed for the most junior of his players to grow into maturity.

And Lafayette rose to the challenge as the months of 1778 unfolded, proving himself repeatedly in battle, blithely weathering rivalries and upheavals within the ranks of Washington's generals (and often unaware of those who tried to use him in their own intrigues), winning a place of affection and respect in the hearts of many besides his Commander in Chief.

The year was a coming of age for the American Army as well as for its youngest general. Despite appalling conditions in the Valley Forge camp, with uncertain food supplies and desperate shortages of adequate clothing, shoes, and blankets for the men, Washington proved the binding force that held them together through that long and dreadful winter. Until huts could be constructed to house his men, built of logs and sealed with clay, he lived in a tent and shared the army's hardships.

His table remained austere even when he moved into a cramped stone house at the head of the valley, for provisions were almost nonexistent until well into February; and even though he had the authority to seize food from the surrounding area, he was reluctant to do so, since he felt that such behavior would undermine the very cause for which his army was fighting. When times were particularly lean, the men subsisted on water and firecake, a thin bread made of flour and water and baked on sticks held over campfires. On three particular occasions, in late December, early January, and mid-February, even firecake was in short supply.

Such austerity at least was conducive to the fasting and meditation that Washington had come to adopt increasingly as a means for refining and clarifying his inner perceptions, seeking ongoing guidance for the task stretching before him. Long convinced of the efficacy of daily prayer, and hopeful that official endorsement of it would help to elevate the general tone of demeanor among his men, the Commander in Chief had instituted morning and evening prayers for the army as early as Cambridge, with officers required to make certain that their men attended, especially on the Sabbath; and on Sundays when no chaplain was available, Washington himself read the Bible to his men and led them in prayer.

Of necessity, such improvisation characterized the majority of religious observances in the field, for clergy were few and of varied denomination. Even so, Washington sometimes found opportunity to indulge his personal preference for more traditional Sunday worship. On one occasion, upon learning that a nearby Presbyterian Church would be celebrating the Lord's Supper on a certain Sunday, he paid a call on the pastor, accompanied by Simon.

"Tell me, Pastor," he said, "does it accord with the canons of your Church to admit communicants of another denomination?"

"Why, certainly, General," the pastor replied. "Ours is not the Presbyterian table, but the Lord's table. Therefore, we extend the Lord's invitation to all His followers, of whatever name."

"That is as it should be," Washington replied, "but as I was not certain of your practice, I thought to ask you directly, since I propose to join with you on that occasion. Though I am a member of the Church of England, I have no exclusive partialities."

The General's attendance at divine services on the designated Sunday, in the company of several of his officers, bolstered a long-established pattern of religious participation that was to accord him repeated spiritual refreshment and renewal as the war wore on.

Fortunately, February marked a turning point in the winter at Valley Forge. Supply lines had improved by midmonth, and clothing and other necessities began to arrive, in addition to food. February also saw the arrival of a Prussian baron called von Steuben, who quickly won the respect of the Commander in Chief and began, with drill and discipline, to transform the ragtag Continentals into a proper army.

The inflow of supplies, coupled with improving military discipline, gradually began to alleviate some of the most squalid living conditions of the winter encampment. The General's lady and some of the other military wives arrived in February, as they had each of the previous two winters, to spend the inactive winter months with their husbands. As always, Martha Washington took the reins of the General's household with cheer and competence, helping nurse the sick, sewing and mending for the "boys," and fostering an air of gentility that was mostly absent when only the men were in camp. Arabella came with Andrew for a few weeks in April.

Times were never harder, but somehow Washington managed to keep morale from plummeting; and as during the previous winter, he continued to invoke the focus and solace of the rituals of Freemasonry to while away the long winter nights, conferring the degrees of the Order on his comrades-in-arms. Among those so honored was a young lieutenant colonel of exceptional promise named Alexander Hamilton, who joined Washington's staff as a confidential aide. On a less public occasion, at the request of Simon, the Commander in Chief witnessed Arabella's passing to Fellow Craft, with Andrew presiding and Justin, the prince, and Ramsay assisting. Shortly thereafter, with spring approaching, Andrew and Arabella headed back for Cambridge.

By May the emerging order had enabled Washington to reorganize his staff to better reflect his own preferences, with von Steuben as Inspector General. Spring had also seen the return of two of his generals—Charles Lee, finally exchanged for a British general after being held for fifteen months in New York, and Benedict

Arnold, wounded at Saratoga and growing increasingly bitter at what he saw as repeated slighting of his abilities. Several of Washington's other generals involved in the Saratoga campaign, including Conway and Gates, made power plays and failed; and General Lee shortly would attempt another that would bring him before a court-martial and cost him his command.

The British remained quiet throughout the winter. General Howe, with the specter of Bunker Hill still before his eyes, remained convinced that the Americans had taken up an impregnable stronghold and, though encamped only twenty miles away, did nothing to harry them through the winter. By early May, Clinton had arrived to relieve him of command.

The change of command was due, in part, to the February signing of a treaty between America and France, and the subsequent declaration of war between England and France. When news of the French alliance reached the American camp in May, to universal rejoicing, Washington was startled to receive an exuberant kiss on both cheeks from the elated Lafayette. During the celebration that followed, Simon thought he had never seen the Commander in Chief look so delighted.

General Clinton had also received the news, with predictably less enthusiasm. With a French expedition presumed on its way, he became convinced that Philadelphia was untenable and began preparations to evacuate and shift his attentions to the harbors between New York and Halifax.

At the behest of Congress, Washington now held a council of war to decide on a response. Having determined to harry the enemy while he withdrew, Washington then began to entrust small commands to Lafayette, who managed them ably. Late in May, because of a betrayal by spies, the Frenchman was nearly taken by the British, but he managed to take up such a strong position that his attackers were obliged to return to Philadelphia after only a short skirmish.

Hampered by rain and heat, and harried increasingly by the Americans, the British continued to fall back. Though plagued by intrigues within his own officer corps, Washington continued to demand and receive performance. The Battle of Monmouth

Courthouse marked the end of the British war of conquest in the north, but it also exposed the intrigues of General Lee, who had disobeyed direct orders and traitorously fallen back in the heat of battle. The situation demanded Washington's personal intervention and a harsh exchange of words between the two generals before the Americans were rallied and reinforcements could be brought up to win the day. Many of the losses that day were from the heat, not bullets; and on the last night of that campaign, late in June, the exhausted Washington and Lafayette slept side by side under a tree on a shared cloak. Simon was no less exhausted, but he was content to keep watch over the pair through the night, well pleased with how matters were progressing.

By early July, now two years after independence had been declared, Clinton had taken his army off by ship to New York. A few days later the expected French expedition under the Count d'Estaing arrived at the mouth of the Delaware River with twelve ships of the line, six frigates, and four thousand French troops. Since Washington spoke no French and d'Estaing no English, and the latter was distantly related to Lafayette, whom Washington trusted, Lafayette was deemed ideal as liaison between the French and American commanders. Colonel Hamilton functioned as the Commander in Chief's confidential aide.

The original plan had been for the French fleet to follow the British into New York to do battle, but d'Estaing judged the New York waters too shallow, so Newport, Rhode Island, was designated as the alternate target. To support a French landing in Newport, Washington deployed New England militia companies to join more seasoned Continental and state troops under General Sullivan, naming Lafayette to command one of its divisions—a formal acknowledgment that in the test of actual service Lafayette had proven himself worthy of a high command over American troops in the field.

But weather and the British conspired to thwart this plan. D'Estaing's fleet approached through the narrow middle channel only to be confronted with a reinforced British fleet under Admiral Howe. To avoid confrontation with a superior force in narrow waters, d'Estaing put to sea, intending to offer battle in the open, but while the two fleets were maneuvering for position, a storm scat-

tered both fleets and wrought sufficient damage on the French ships that the French commander was obliged to limp into Boston for refit—which pulled out the four thousand French troops intended to reinforce the Americans. Though many of the American generals protested this seeming abandonment of the operation, Washington supported d'Estaing's decision.

The naval contretemps marked the end of campaigning for the year. With the arrival of another British squadron in the area, d'Estaing soon withdrew to the West Indies for the winter. Sullivan was obliged to pull back to Providence, and very shortly, in early December, Washington took himself and his army into winter quarters in Middlebrook, New Jersey, where Lafayette soon joined him.

The young marquis had grown into his role as the months of 1778 passed and had proven himself under fire as well as at the General's table. He had spent his twenty-first birthday in the field, attempting to keep peace among the American generals who resented d'Estaing's withdrawal. Now, in the days immediately following his arrival at winter headquarters, he conferred several times with Justin and then with Simon. A few nights later, when they were the only others to linger with the General over wine and nuts, he presented his concerns to the Commander in Chief.

They were ensconced in the dining room of the comfortable white frame house where Washington had established his command headquarters. Justin had topped up the General's glass with the last of a very fine Madeira brought over by the Count d'Estaing, and Washington was holding it to the candlelight to admire its color, relaxed and at ease among his favorites.

"*Mon général,*" Lafayette said, raising his own glass slightly, "if I may, I should like to ask two favors of you."

"Two?" Washington replied, smiling slightly. "Most men would be content to ask one at a time."

Lafayette ventured a mirthless grin and took a fortifying swallow of his wine. "I ask two at once, because I pray that the one will sweeten the other," he said.

"Then one of the favors is apt to be less than sweet," Washington said cautiously. "What is it?"

Lafayette set down his glass. "I should like leave to return to

France," he said bluntly. "And it is, indeed, leave that I ask for, *mon général*, for I hope to return with additional aid for your cause. D'Estaing's arrival would have made a great difference had it not been for the ill luck of the storm. How much better if I could bring you troops and arms and equipment? I believe I *can* do that, especially if I work with Dr. Franklin and his delegation. I have the wealth at my disposal, and it would please me greatly to put it at *your* disposal."

Washington had turned his gaze to the wine in his glass as Lafayette spoke and did not look up as he finally answered.

"It cannot have been easy for you to come here so young and to be tried so sorely," he murmured. "And you have a young wife at home, and a baby daughter whom you have never seen."

"I have been more than willing to put those pleasures aside for a time, in your service," Lafayette said quietly. "I am still willing to do so. But I believe that I can make an even more useful contribution to the war effort if you will allow me to employ my newfound fame with my wealth. It—might take some time, and I should miss the camaraderie that I have shared with all of you. But if I could bring you men, and the prestige of international allies—please do not refuse me out of hand, *mon général*."

Washington took a sip of his wine and set the glass carefully on the table, then looked up at the Frenchman, careful to betray no emotion.

"You mentioned a second favor," he said quietly, "and that it might sweeten the first. It will need to be sweet, indeed, to counter the bitterness of your loss. I regard you as I would a son."

"It—shall only be for a time. I *shall* return—I promise it!" Lafayette risked a glance at Simon and Justin, both of them watching him sympathetically, then flicked his attention back to Washington.

"You must bear with me while I find the words, *mon général*," he said. "I wish to speak of Freemasonry. I am told that if a man wishes to affiliate himself with that noble Brotherhood, he must ask for admission. For more than a year now I have observed from the outside what contentment this affiliation gives to you—to all three of you and, indeed, to many of the officers and men of this

encampment. It has come to my mind that if you were to allow me to share this bond of Brotherhood with you, it would also serve as a link of our affection while I am absent. I have—discussed this with Colonel Wallace and Lieutenant Carmichael, and they have instructed me to approach you on the matter.

"I therefore ask that I might be admitted to the Brotherhood of Freemasons, and that I might receive initiation at your hands. If I—have not asked this in the proper manner, then I pray that you guide me in what I should say."

Washington's eyes had lifted to Lafayette's at the first mention of Freemasonry and kindled with a fiercely burning joy as he realized what the younger man was asking. He closed his eyes for a moment, exhaling softly. When he opened them again, the fire was somewhat banked, but a warm affection remained in the gray-blue gaze.

"The second favor does, indeed, sweeten the first," he said. "And while I may grant the first only with great reluctance, it will be my honor and my privilege to confer the second."

"Thank you, *mon général*," Lafayette whispered, his eyes bright with emotion. "I shall try not to disappoint you on either count."

"Oh, I am sure you will not," Washington replied. "But tell me one thing, my friend. Why did you wait so long to ask?"

Lafayette stared at him in some confusion.

"I was very young, *mon général*, with much else to learn. . . ."

Washington choked back a chuckle at that and glanced archly at Simon and Justin.

"Gentlemen, you obviously have not instructed our young friend as fully as you ought to have done, for he does not realize how much else there is to learn regarding the Craft."

Smiling, Simon inclined his head in acceptance of the gentle reproof. "I felt that further elucidation was best left to your good offices, Worshipful, since *you* will be initiating him."

Washington laughed aloud at that, reaching across then to clasp hands with Lafayette in congratulation before ordering Justin out for another bottle of wine.

After Lafayette had retired, Simon was delegated to make the arrangements—which suited very well, since both he and the

prince had an additional mandate from Saint-Germain concerning
the Masonic initiation of Monsieur le Marquis de Lafayette. Most
of those who assembled on the appointed night in mid-December
were members of Washington's military family, but Simon also had
summoned Andrew down from Cambridge, so that his father could
"happen" to be visiting in the camp and thus be invited to attend.
The prince's invitation came by dint of the fact that many of the
officers now knew that the aristocratic French surgeon serving under the nom de guerre of Dr. Lucien Rohan was, in fact, a friend of
Lafayette's and a high-ranking French Freemason—and apparently
a sometime agent of the General, often absent for weeks at a time
on errands of which no one ever spoke.

Washington himself would preside, of course, under warrant of
Military Lodge Number Nineteen. As the Lodge assembled, don-
ning lambskin aprons and assorted jewels of office, Simon scanned
the room to be certain he had not forgotten anything. The setting
was not so grand as the Wallace library—only a humble dining
room above the premises of a local tavern, with the Tracing Board
of the First Degree sketched out in chalk on the wooden floor—
but no greater dignity could have attended the occasion if the
General had presided from the dais of a formal salon in Paris or
London instead. Lafayette was waiting downstairs with the innkeeper, who was also a Freemason, though the latter would have
no part in the night's activities beyond acting as an unofficial second Tyler, stationed at the foot of the stairs.

Perhaps two dozen men were present, all in uniform save Andrew, who had been given a place of honor at Washington's right
by dint of his seniority. Washington fidgeted a little behind a small
well-scrubbed table at the east end of the room, watching as the
accoutrements of the Lodge were set in place: the three candles,
Washington's own Bible, and the square and compasses, all laid out
on a white cloth. Simon and the prince waited in the west, as
Junior Deacon and Senior Warden respectively, so that only those
of Saint-Germain's Inner Circle should handle the candidate when
he first entered the room, though even Washington was not aware
of this.

When all was in readiness, Washington called the Lodge to or-

der and opened in the First Degree, Justin being stationed outside
the door as Tyler. When he had examined the officers as to their
duties, he dispatched Simon to fetch the candidate.

"Brother Junior Deacon, you will prepare the candidate for the
first degree of Freemasonry and cause him to make the regular
alarm at the inner door."

Simon obeyed, leaving the room to slip past Justin and fetch
Lafayette up to the small landing just outside the door. There the
marquis was required to strip to his shirt and breeches and divest
himself of all metal and valuables. When he had bared his right
arm and left breast as directed, Simon tied a black scarf over his
eyes as a hoodwink—stark against the neatly powdered wig—and
Justin set the cable-tow in place around his neck, its end hanging
down in front. What little could be seen of his face between cable
tow and hoodwink was tense and solemn. His hands hung loose at
his sides, but the fingers of one hand clenched and unclenched in a
nervous gesture.

Simon let him wait in silence for a long moment, knowing that
the anticipation would only heighten what was to come, preparing
in his own mind for his part in the candidate's very special reception. After a hundred of his own heartbeats, he took Lafayette's
right wrist and sharply rapped the knuckles three times against the
door. Justin had moved behind and to Lafayette's left, with his
sword drawn.

"Worshipful, there is an alarm at the door," came the prince's
voice from within.

From farther away Washington's voice ordered, "Attend to the
alarm, Brother, and see who comes here."

Almost immediately three sharp raps from inside echoed the
three the candidate had made. Still clasping Lafayette's wrist, Simon rapped the knuckles sharply against the door one more time,
to be answered by another single knock. After that the door swung
open several inches, squeaking slightly.

"Who comes there?" Washington demanded, making the ritual
challenge as presiding Master.

It was Justin who answered for Lafayette from the Frenchman's
left side, naked sword in hand.

"A poor blind candidate, who has long been desirous of being brought from darkness to light. He begs to have and receive part of the benefit of this right worshipful Lodge, dedicated to St. John, as all true fellows and brothers have done who have gone this way before him."

"Is this of your own free will and accord?" Washington asked.

"Answer, 'It is,' " Simon prompted in Lafayette's ear.

"It is," the marquis repeated.

"Is he duly and truly prepared?" Washington demanded.

"He is," Simon replied.

"Is he worthy and well qualified?"

"He is."

"Is he of lawful age, and properly vouched for?"

"He is."

"By what further right does he expect to obtain admission into this Lodge of Entered Apprentice Masons?" Washington demanded.

"By being freeborn and well reported," came Simon's reply.

"Let him enter."

The door opened wider, but as Simon led Lafayette forward a few steps, the prince stepped into place directly before him, to set one of the points of the compasses against the candidate's bared breast. Lafayette bit back a faint gasp and flinched slightly, but Justin's blade was at the center of his back, forbidding retreat. Simon could feel the energy course briefly through Lafayette's body and steadied him as the prince softly asked, "Do you feel anything?"

What Lafayette had felt, poised within the triangle of three of Saint-Germain's most trusted agents, was more than just the bite of steel at breast and back, but he only nodded jerkily and murmured, "I do."

"Then mind well that you hold this in remembrance for the future," the prince replied, "lest ever you should forget your oath to guard the secrets of Freemasonry."

As the prince stepped back, withdrawing the compasses to replace them upon the Bible that now lay open before the Master, Simon conducted Lafayette into the center of the room and bade him kneel to receive the benefit of a prayer. The marquis swayed a

little as Simon helped him down, and seemed grateful for a steady-ing hand on his shoulder. Three raps from the Master's gavel brought all present to their feet while the prayer was intoned, after which the General came to lay one hand lightly on Lafayette's head.

"In whom do you put your trust?" he asked.

"In God," came Lafayette's answer at Simon's prompting.

"Your trust being in God, your faith is well founded," Washington replied, taking the candidate's right hand in his. "Rise up and follow your leader," he continued, placing Lafayette's right hand in Simon's and urging him to his feet. "And fear no danger."

As Simon then led the blindfolded Lafayette three times around the Lodge room, Washington returned to his place in the east to take up the Volume of Sacred Law and read from Psalm 133.

"Behold how good and how pleasant it is for brethren to dwell together in unity! It is like the precious ointment upon the head, that ran down upon the beard, even Aaron's beard: that went down to the skirts of his garments. As the dew of Hermon, and as the dew that descended upon the mountains of Zion: for there the Lord commanded the blessing, even life for evermore."

Simon and his charge finished their third circuit at about the same time Washington finished reading, but Simon then led the candidate back to the Junior Warden's station in the south, where he was instructed to repeat the alarm of three distinct knocks that he had given before. As had been done at the door, Simon and the Junior Warden then exchanged the same litany of questions and answers. Simon repeated the process twice more, with the prince in the west and then with Andrew in the east, behind the Worshipful Master.

"Who comes there?"

"A poor blind candidate, who has long been desirous of being brought from darkness to light . . ."

"Is this of his own free will and accord?"

"It is. . . ."

But when Simon and Andrew had concluded the third catechism of questions and answers, Washington took up a new line of questioning.

"Whence came you?" he inquired.

"From the west," came Simon's reply, speaking for Lafayette.

"Which way are you traveling?"

"To the east."

"And why do you leave the west and travel to the east?" Washington persisted.

"In search of light."

"Since this is the case," Washington replied, now addressing himself directly to Simon, "you will conduct him back to the west and teach him to approach the east, the place of light, with one regular and upright step to the first step of Masonry, his body erect, his feet forming the right angle of an oblong square. He will then kneel in due form to take upon himself the solemn oath and Obligation of an Entered Apprentice Mason."

Dutifully Simon conducted the candidate to a point between the door and the altar and instructed him in the appropriate steps, concluding with Lafayette kneeling on his left knee before the altar, his right knee forming a right angle and his slip-shod right heel resting flat on the wooden floor. But after laying the open Volume of Sacred Law in Lafayette's left hand, with the square and compasses atop it, Simon reached into his own coat to withdraw a small leather-bound Bible with silver mountings at the corners, and a heavy silver clasp.

"With your permission, Worshipful, the candidate has asked that he may be allowed to make his obligation upon this Bible, which was his father's."

Before Washington could get a clear look at the smaller book, Simon had opened it and slipped it between the larger Bible and the square and compasses that Lafayette was steadying with his right hand. Washington looked somewhat startled at the unexpected addition to the ritual paraphernalia, but Simon's next words precluded inquiry unless he wished to interrupt the ritual.

"Worshipful, the candidate is placed at the altar in due form to receive the solemn oath and Obligation of an Entered Apprentice Mason," Simon announced.

Though emotion flickered briefly on the General's face, personal uncertainty gave way to duty. At the signal of three sharp raps from his gavel, the assembled brethren came quietly to sur-

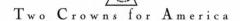

round Lafayette and witness his oath. In the expectant silence the General's voice was quiet but sure.

"Gilbert du Motier de Lafayette, you are kneeling at the altar of Masonry for the first time in your life. Before we may communicate to you the mysteries of Masonry, you must take an obligation that you will never reveal the secrets of the Order. I assure you, as a man, as a Mason, and as Master of this Lodge, that it will not interfere in any way with the duty you owe to your country or your Maker. If you are willing to proceed, you will repeat your Christian and surname, and say after me: I—"

"I, Marie Joseph Paul Yves Roch Gilbert du Motier de Lafayette."

"Of my own free will and accord—"

"Of my own free will and accord . . ."

His voice growing stronger with each line he repeated, Lafayette made his Obligation in a clear voice lightly tinged with his French accent, vowing without reservation never to reveal the mysteries of Freemasonry by any means whatsoever, and invoking upon himself most terrible penalties should he fail in this endeavor. "So help me God, and keep me steadfast, in the due performance of the same."

"You will now kiss the book on which your hand rests," Washington prompted.

Lafayette did so, bending to press his lips to both books; but before the General could get more than a fleeting look at the smaller one, Simon whisked it back into his coat. Though Washington affected not to be concerned, a darkling expression briefly rippled across his face.

"In your present situation," he said to Lafayette, "what do you most desire?"

"Light," came Lafayette's firm reply at Simon's prompting.

"Brethren, will you stretch forth your hands and assist in bringing this candidate from darkness to true Masonic light?" Washington said, nodding to Simon to remove the hoodwink. " 'And God said, Let there be light, and there was light.' "

The hoodwink was removed at the word "light," and those around Lafayette simultaneously clapped their hands once and stamped their feet.

The marquis blinked in some astonishment as he was restored to light, listening a little dazedly as Washington then proceeded to instruct him in the symbolism of what lay before him on the altar, and to raise up the newly obligated Mason by the grip and word of an Entered Apprentice and instruct him in the Due-Guard, or Sign. After Lafayette had demonstrated his understanding of these things, he was escorted outside to restore his clothing, shortly reappearing in full uniform. When he had returned thanks for the honor done him in making him a Mason and admitting him to the Lodge, Washington then summoned him to the northeast corner of the Lodge, at his own right hand, to be invested with the symbol of his new status.

"It is the emblem of innocence and the badge of a Mason," Washington said, letting the prince tie the plain white lambskin apron around Lafayette's waist, with the flap turned up. "It has been worn by kings, princes, and potentates of the earth who have never been ashamed to wear it. It is more honorable than the diadems of kings, or the pearls of princesses, when worthily worn. It is more ancient than the Golden Fleece, or Roman Eagle; more honorable than the Star and Garter, or any other order that can be conferred on you at this, or any other time, except it be by a just and lawfully constituted Lodge."

Following further instruction regarding the working tools of the Entered Apprentice, Washington rose in his place to close the Lodge.

"If there is no more business before the Lodge, we shall proceed to close. Brother Junior, what is the last as well as the first care of congregated Masons?" he said to that officer.

"To see the Lodge close tyled, Worshipful," came the reply.

"Attend to that part of your duty and inform the Tyler that we are about to close this Lodge of Entered Apprentice Masons."

The officer obeyed, conferring briefly with Justin and then turning to report.

"We are tyled, Worshipful."

"How tyled?" came Washington's query.

"With secrecy and brotherly love; also a brother of this degree without the door, with a drawn sword in his hand."

"His duty there?"

"To keep off all cowans and eavesdroppers, to see that none pass or repass but such as are duly qualified and have permission from the chair."

Two raps from Washington's gavel brought the rest of the officers to their feet, after which they recited the duties of their offices in turn. It was the prince, as Senior Warden, who finally related the Master's duties.

"As the sun rises in the east to open and adorn the day, so rises the Worshipful Master in the east, to open or close his Lodge."

"After that manner, so do I," Washington said, rising in his place. "It is my will and pleasure that this Lodge of Entered Apprentice Masons be now closed, and stand closed until our next regular communication, unless convened by some sudden emergency. Attend to the charge, brethren: 'May the blessing of heaven rest upon us, and all regular Masons; may brotherly love prevail, and every moral and social virtue cement us. So mote it be. Amen.'"

He then ordered, "Attend to the signs, brethren," and responded to the signs that all others present gave him. And finally he addressed the prince again.

"Brother Senior, how do Masons meet?" he asked.

"On the level, Worshipful," the prince replied.

"And Brother Junior, how do Masons part?"

"On the square," came the reply.

"So let us meet, and so let us part, in the name of the Lord," Washington responded. "Our work being concluded, it is now my happy privilege not to order but to invite that this Lodge be called from labor to refreshment, that we may greet our new brother in more festive spirit. I am pleased to inform you that Brother Lafayette has provided several bottles of captured Madeira for our delectation. They await us back at headquarters. I invite you to repair thereto, where I shall join you directly. Colonel Wallace, please stay a moment, if you would."

Simon could guess what the summons was about, but he feigned nonchalance as he took off his apron and began packing away the accoutrements of Lodge. Two of Washington's younger aides took

charge of Lafayette and laughingly directed him in application of a damp mop to the Tracing Board chalked on the floor—the traditional first task of any newly obligated Apprentice.

As the others also divested themselves of the ornaments of Lodge and drifted out, Lafayette surrounded by a dozen well-wishers, Simon extinguished the three candles that were the three Lesser Lights and set them aside to cool, lingering then over wrapping up the square and compasses and putting them into their protective bag. Washington thanked Andrew for attending and conferred briefly with the last of his aides to leave, promising to join them shortly in his quarters, then returned to collect his Bible from Simon and slip it into the valise where his apron and Master's jewel already resided.

"Brother Wallace, I should like to see that other Bible," he said, turning to face Simon squarely. "Was there some reason I was not informed ahead of time that there would be an addition to the ritual?"

There was, but a verbal explanation would not be half so effective a demonstration. Reaching into the breast of his uniform coat, Simon produced Lafayette's Bible, careful to keep it mostly shielded with his hands as he held it out to the General. Without thinking, Washington stretched out his hands to receive it—and gasped as he felt its weight and his eyes beheld it, eyes closing then as he swayed slightly on his feet, his face going white beneath his neatly powdered hair.

"Steady, sir," Simon murmured, seizing his upper arm and guiding him back a few steps until the backs of his knees made contact with a chair. "Sit down slowly. That's fine. Take a deep breath now and let it out completely. . . ."

To his relief Washington obeyed, his fingers relaxing their death grip on the book as he exhaled. After a moment he opened his eyes almost fearfully to look at what lay between his hands, at length flicking back the silver clasp to open the book randomly at several different spots, as if to verify that it was, indeed, a Bible.

"You said that this belonged to Lafayette's father?" he said after a moment.

"So he claims," Simon replied.

"This is—the Bible that was in my dream, Colonel. I remember

the clasp, and the silver corners on the cover—the filigree work. But I hadn't even met Lafayette then."

"You're asking how you could have seen this particular Bible," Simon said, "and I can only answer that I don't know. However, I do know that this is the Bible intended for the ultimate ritual, just as I know that Lafayette is to be a part of that ritual. This, tonight, was part of his preparation for that role, since we have already established that everyone who appeared in your dream was a Freemason. I cannot tell you more than that at this time, because I do not know myself."

"And how do *you* find out these things?" Washington whispered, a thumb absently caressing the filigree of one of the corners. "I allow you to direct me, but it becomes clear that you, too, are being directed. By whom? And what interest does he have in what is unfolding in these United States?"

"I may not tell you that," Simon replied. "I can but assure you that his interest is benign, and his perspective larger than ours."

"How can I believe that?" the General whispered. "You are asking me to accept on faith what concerns the lives of thousands under my command, my care. Who *are* you, Simon Wallace, and whom do you serve?"

"I told you before, when we first spoke on this matter: I am an instrument of The Great Architect of the Universe, directed by His Master of the Works. And I give you my word, as a man and as a Master Mason, that nothing I or He shall require of you will interfere in any way with your duty to those thousands under your command, or to this country, or to our Maker. I gave you my bond three years ago to assist you in unlocking the guidance of your dream, and you gave me yours, of faith and trust. I have not withdrawn my part of the Obligation, and I do not believe I have given you cause to withdraw yours. Remember now the progress we have made."

As he lightly touched one of the hands clasping Lafayette's Bible, Washington's breath caught softly in his throat and he blinked, a look of amazement coming across the craggy features.

"I remember," he said. "We *have* made progress. But—how is this possible? You *are* a sorcerer!"

"No, not a sorcerer," Simon replied with a smile. "My Master

works upon a Greater Tracing Board, and mine are the greater
tools with which he entrusts me on occasion. To put things from
one's mind for the moment can be a blessing, as you have cause to
know. Whenever there is need, I can bring back the memories.

"But now there is need to put the memories from mind again.
Our brethren are waiting. And one dear to you and to our cause
has more reason than he realizes to celebrate what has happened
tonight."

"You mean Gilbert?" the General murmured tentatively.

Simon nodded. "His, too, is a great destiny, though never so
great as these days when he serves at your side. He truly is like a
son to you, isn't he?"

As Washington slowly nodded, Simon quietly took the marquis's
Bible from him and slipped it into his valise, then held out his right
hand to the General.

"We must go, General. You remembered when there was need,
and you shall remember again. Another piece is set, and another
time of waiting is upon us. Take my hand now, on the bond you
gave me."

Washington's handclasp was firm in his, without further hesitation, and no inkling of concern clouded the General's brow as he
and Simon shortly quit the room above the tavern and made their
way back to headquarters to join the celebration.

Chapter Nineteen

The winter settling in at Middlebrook proved harsh, but not nearly so grueling as the previous one at Valley Forge. Shortly after Lafayette's Masonic initiation, Washington betook himself and key members of his staff to Philadelphia to meet with a committee of Congress and consult on plans for the war in the coming year. There he met Martha, en route from Mount Vernon, so the couple spent part of the ensuing fortnight in celebration of the Christmas season before returning to the more cramped and Spartan conditions at the Middlebrook camp.

When Washington returned after a three-week absence, he had also secured official permission for Lafayette to return to France. In addition, Congress had voted to award the young marquis a sword of honor encrusted with diamonds, to be ordered by Franklin in Paris; and Henry Laurens, the new President of Congress, wrote a glowing recommendation to King Louis XVI of France, praising Lafayette's services.

"Great, faithful, and beloved Friend and Ally," Laurens wrote. "The Marquis de Lafayette, having obtained our leave to return to his native country, we could not suffer him to depart without testifying our deep sense of his zeal, courage, and attachment.

"We have advanced him to the rank of major general in our

armies, which, as well by his prudent as spirited conduct, he hath manifestly merited.

"We recommend this young nobleman to Your Majesty's notice as one whom we know to be wise in council, gallant in the field, and patient under the hardships of war. His devotion to his sovereign hath led him in all things to demean himself as an American, acquiring thereby the confidence of these United States, Your Majesty's good and faithful friends and allies, and the affection of their citizens."

Washington was equally complimentary in the letter he sent with Lafayette to Franklin, essentially asking the new American minister to defuse any lingering royal anger over Lafayette's earlier disobedience in leaving France without permission.

"The generous motives which first induced Lafayette to cross the Atlantic; the tribute which he paid to gallantry at the Brandywine; his success in Jersey before he recovered from his wounds, in an affair where he commanded militia against British grenadiers; the brilliant retreat by which he eluded a combined maneuver of the whole British force in the last campaign; his services in the enterprise against Rhode Island are such proof of his zeal, military ardor, and talents as to have endeared him to America, and must greatly recommend him to his prince. Coming with so many titles to claim your esteem, it were needless for any other purpose than to indulge my own feeling to add that I have a very particular friendship for him."

Lafayette would sail from Boston aboard the thirty-six-gun frigate *Alliance*, which had been selected by the government to convey him back to France. In addition to his various commendations, Lafayette carried letters of a more private nature from Simon, Andrew, and the prince, to be forwarded to Saint-Germain. But before he set sail, on January 11, 1779, he sent a final, short letter to the Commander in Chief he was leaving behind.

"The sails are just going to be hoisted, my dear General, and I have but the time of taking my last leave from you. . . . Farewell, my dear General, I hope your French friend will ever be dear to you, I hope I shall see you again and tell you myself with what emotion I now leave the coast you inhabit, and with what affection

and respect I'll forever be, my dear General, your respectful and sincere friend."

The winter dragged on much like the last, if somewhat milder than Valley Forge had been. Again the gallant officers' wives did their best to relieve the tedium of the long inactivity with modest social gatherings, undeterred by continuing shortages of food.

As she had the previous winter, Arabella joined Simon for a few months, Andrew this time bringing the children for a two-week visit at the end. Charles had grown into a strapping lad of twelve, begging to be taken on as a drummer boy—which petition was refused by his father. Sarah was a self-assured nine-year-old, a miniature copy of her mother. Little James had become a sturdy boy of five, grave and courteous as he was introduced to the General one windy April morning.

Before they all went back to Cambridge in early May, Andrew again convened a private Lodge to raise Arabella to Master Mason, though only Simon, Justin, the prince, and Ramsay were invited to assist. With that accomplished the prince traveled back with them to Boston, to begin shifting his energies to the financial arena, for he had several banking contacts disposed to assist the American cause.

On the military front it was anticipated that the spring would see British offensives shifted to the Southern Department, with Clinton remaining stubbornly dug in in New York until the bitter end. Meanwhile, it seemed likely that the British would hold their present positions, at least for the foreseeable future, and restrict action to coastal raids in the north. Accordingly, Washington turned his immediate attention to decreasing the danger from Indians, putting General Sullivan in charge of that expedition.

But in March, British troops began shifting northward from Georgia into South Carolina; and in May they moved to sack and destroy Norfolk and Portsmouth. By the end of May a strong British expedition from New York captured Stony Point, New York, where American defenses had been still under construction and ungarrisoned.

The early summer became a war of nerves in the south, as the two forces watched one another. Aware that he must make some move, Washington conferred with his generals. Taking back Stony Point was not of particular strategic significance, so far as the defense of West Point was concerned, but its recovery would constitute a great boost to morale. To carry out the operation, Washington chose General Anthony Wayne, who expressed his confidence in Washington's strategic ability in unequivocal terms: "General, I'll storm hell if you will plan it!"

The plan depended on the utmost secrecy, right up to the last minute. Half an hour before midnight, on July 15, 1778, Wayne made his move. The surprise was a brilliant success, throwing utter confusion into the British ranks, and the garrison soon surrendered. American losses were only 15 killed and 83 wounded. The British lost 63 killed, with 554 taken prisoner.

Washington sent Simon to observe and report on the aftermath of Stony Point, accompanied by Justin. Since he had no further intention of establishing an American presence there, the fortifications were to be dismantled and destroyed, the captured guns and stores taken away to West Point. Almost as an afterthought, the General decided to send along Dr. Ramsay to evaluate the medical situation of the wounded.

The day after they arrived, while Simon was riding over the battle site with General Wayne, Ramsay and Justin went with one of Wayne's aides to inspect the field hospital facilities. Justin did his best to remain detached as he wandered through a crowded ward behind Ramsay and another surgeon, teeth set in sympathy for the suffering of the wounded and dying, most of whom lay on makeshift pallets on the floor, and who could expect only the most rudimentary of care. He was about to follow Ramsay into the next room when a groan for water drew his attention to a figure lying on a pallet in a dim corner. He was shocked to realize that he recognized the man.

"Angus?" he murmured. "Angus Murray?"

At the sound of his name Murray turned his head to squint in Justin's direction, the pain-glazed eyes only slowly focusing as Justin moved in to crouch beside his pallet. He was one of the Bostonians who, with Ramsay, had made a premature offer of a Crown to Charles Edward Stuart. He had also been present at Justin's raising to Master Mason. Bandages swathed bloody stumps at both elbows, and the flattened silhouette beneath the lightweight blanket told of a lower leg lost as well. Justin's face drained of color as he realized the extent of the man's injuries—surely beyond any hope of recovery.

"Young Carmichael?" the man breathed. "Water, I beg ye—for the love o' God!"

Quickly Justin ran to the water barrel set in the center of the room and dipped with a wooden gourd. His urgency caught the attention of Ramsay, just pausing in the doorway from the room, who joined him as he slid an arm under Murray's bandaged head and held the dripping gourd to his lips.

"It's Angus Murray," Justin murmured, rationing the water to one sip at a time, to keep the man from choking. "How can he still be alive?"

"Sheer stubbornness," Ramsay muttered, crouching down beside Justin as his eyes assessed the man's obvious injuries and a hand sought a pulse below the jaw. "Sweet Jesus, Angus, how have you come to this? It's James Ramsay."

Murray managed another sip of water, swallowing ponderously, but it seemed to ease him a little. Breathing out with a sigh, he turned his face away from the gourd to look at Ramsay.

"Jamie," he breathed. "I didnae dare to hope ye'd come. So much I should've told ye. . . . The gold . . . it wasnae just a drunken dream. . . ."

Ramsay flicked a glance at Justin, then shifted his hand to clasp the dying man's shoulder in comfort.

"I know, Angus," he murmured.

"No, listen to what I'm saying," Murray insisted, a bandaged stump lifting as if the phantom hand that once had graced it could tug at Ramsay's lapel. "I've told ye before that my da told me where he buried it—forty thousand louis d'or meant fer Prince Charlie, but come too late."

"And still too late," Ramsay replied. "Be easy, Angus, and let it go."

"No, ye dinnae understand. . . ." A feverish luster had begun to brighten Murray's eyes, but his voice became more intense, if more labored.

"Angus—"

"No, listen! I still can serve my prince, e'en though I die far frae Scotland," he gasped. "We tried before tae bring him here tae take up his cause in the New World, but we didnae offer him the gold. It might make the difference. An' I can tell ye how to find it. . . ."

"What's he talking about?" Justin whispered.

Shaking his head to fend off questions, Ramsay bent closer to their patient's lips.

"Tell me, Angus," he said.

"Six braw casks o' Spanish oak, filled wi' gold," Murray replied, his voice growing weaker. "Forty thousand louis d'or. Archie Cameron buried 'em at Loch Arkaig—some at Caillich, near Murlaggan, an' some at the foot o' the loch. But some—"

He paused to gasp for breath, his gaze going unfocused, but Ramsay raised him up with an arm under his shoulders and turned the face to his once more.

"But some *what*, Angus?" he demanded. "Don't stop now, old friend."

"Some o' the gold did nae stay there," Murray managed to whisper. "My da's kinsman, Murray o' Broughton, was charged wi' looking after it, but too many knew about it. Broughton had my da shift about half the gold to a ship at Borrodale an' take it across the sea. . . ."

"What are you saying?" Ramsay demanded. "Stay with me, Angus. What do you mean, *across the sea*? Are you saying the gold is *here*, in America?"

"Aye. . . ."

"Dear God, how much?"

"Near . . . twenty thousand. . . . Prince Charlie's gold. . . . Waitin' for the King to claim it. . . ."

"Twenty thousand—*where*, Angus? *Tell me where!*"

"Safe an' waitin'," Angus whispered. "Two braw casks now . . . all hidden where they'll be safe. . . ."

But his voice trailed off before he could be encouraged to be more specific, and though both Ramsay and Justin tried to rouse him, Lieutenant Angus Murray slipped into coma and expired later that afternoon without regaining consciousness. When, as friends of the deceased, they had recovered what few personal belongings had been with Murray, the two returned to the quarters assigned to them at General Wayne's headquarters. Simon was writing up a preliminary report to Washington on the status of Stony Point but laid aside his pen as the two came into the room and Justin closed the door.

"The two of you look like you've just come from a funeral," he said.

"No, that's for tomorrow or the next day," Justin said as Ramsay plopped down Murray's knapsack onto the desk in front of Simon. "This was more in the nature of a deathwatch."

"And the deathwatch of someone known to us, by your expressions," Simon said, glancing at Ramsay. "Who was it?"

Ramsay sank into a chair. "Angus Murray," he said. "I didn't know he'd come to Stony Point. I think he'd been with an artillery company. Angus—" He heaved a heavy sigh. "One of the surgeons said there'd been a mortar explosion. He'd lost a leg at the knee and both arms above the elbows. He shouldn't have held on as long as he did, and there's no question but that death was a mercy, but I can't help wishing he'd lasted a little longer."

At Simon's startled expression Justin shifted restlessly in his chair.

"Do you remember how, when he was in his cups, Angus used to talk about the Loch Arkaig treasure, and we were all convinced he was dotty?" Simon nodded. "Well, now I'm not so sure—for all the good it will do us."

Simon furrowed his brow. "He said his father helped bury it after Culloden. But that was more than thirty years ago."

"Yes, but apparently the story doesn't stop there," Ramsay replied. "Angus said that some of the gold was brought to America."

"What?"

As Ramsay recounted that last, fragmented conversation with the dying man, Justin pulled Murray's knapsack closer and began halfheartedly to examine its contents. The knapsack contained pitifully little to account for a man's life; but nestled in a change of clean linen, amid the expected shaving paraphernalia and other toilet items, his fingers closed around something small and angular, wrapped in a handkerchief.

What emerged as he unwrapped it was a silver snuffbox, once heavily engraved but now worn nearly smooth from years of use. Holding it to the light of one of the candles on Simon's desk, Justin could just make out a name etched inside the lid.

" 'Charles Stuart Murray,' " he read aloud as Ramsay looked at him sharply, his recitation complete. "Would that be Angus's father?"

"Let me see that." Ramsay took the snuffbox and examined the engraving, then probed the snuff with a forefinger. With a muffled exclamation, he tipped the snuff onto the floor and peered inside, then blew into it sharply.

"Now, this *is* a piece of luck," he said.

"Why luck?" Simon asked.

"It's proof that Murray's father at least had contact with the gold." Ramsay turned the open snuffbox toward them. Affixed to the bottom with four silver prongs was a shiny gold coin: a louis d'or.

"Don't you see?" Ramsay went on. "We all had relatives who were out in the Forty-Five, and we've all heard how the Loch Arkaig gold arrived too late for Culloden and was hidden against the time when it could be recovered and used to finance another attempt to put the prince back on the throne."

"But it wasn't recovered, and there wasn't another attempt," Simon pointed out. "And unless I'm misremembering, Murray never said anything about some of the gold having been brought to the New World."

"No, but he always said that he was the last man alive to know where the gold was buried—which doesn't preclude some of it being buried here. It *could* be true."

"Yes, and it may just have been wishful thinking at the bottom of too many tankards," Simon replied. "You know what he was like when he'd taken drink. In any case, the point is moot, since you've just said that he died before he could give you any details."

"He did," Ramsay agreed. "But with this he could be called back to tell us what we need to know." As he held up the snuffbox, Simon's face went very still.

"Do you know what you're proposing?"

"Yes."

"This is preposterous," Simon said, pushing back his chair in exasperation. "And it still doesn't address the probability that Murray was lying, or at least fantasizing. If he'd known where the gold was buried—especially gold here, in the New World—don't you think he would have gone after it by now?"

"That had occurred to me," Ramsay conceded. "But he'd sworn to his father to guard it, not to take it. And even if Angus didn't actually know, or we can't connect with him, his father certainly knew—and this was his snuffbox before it belonged to Angus. One couldn't ask for a much better connection. I *know* we can find that gold."

"Not without a great deal more information, whose acquisition would be difficult, quite possibly injurious to Murray, if not to us, and certainly morally—"

"It's in a good cause," Ramsay retorted. "We're talking about twenty thousand louis d'or! With that much gold in our possession, we could make Charles Edward Stuart an offer he'd find impossible to turn down."

"You know what happened the last time—"

"We need him here, Simon! Washington functions well enough as a *dux bellorum*, but he isn't a king. And don't even suggest that the gold should go to him. It rightfully belongs to Charles Edward Stuart!"

Simon said nothing in answer to that, stunned by the scope of Ramsay's proposition, even if such a thing were possible. Justin stared at his elders in unabashed amazement, for if Ramsay's suggestion had shocked him, Simon's reaction—actually considering the idea—was equally astonishing.

"Well, the gold does belong to Charles," Justin ventured after a moment. "Maybe it *would* be sufficient inducement for him at least to come to the New World and see for himself the support he has. Haven't we been working toward that day, when Charlie comes into his own again?"

"That is not our decision to make," Simon replied. "*If* the gold could be recovered, there are a number of places where it might be profitably employed. But we have all sworn oaths that give another the authority to direct our endeavors in such a determination. Are you suggesting that we set those oaths aside?"

Justin hung his head, and Ramsay sullenly shook his, lowering his gaze to the silver still winking between his two hands.

"Of course not," Ramsay said. "I have no wish to incur Saint-Germain's displeasure again. Suppose that, for the moment, we set aside the question of what would be done with the gold and concentrate instead on whether it could be recovered. I believe that it could, by the method I have suggested. But I cannot do it alone, and certainly not in opposition to you."

Simon drew a deep breath and held out his hand for the snuff-box, holding it to the light to read the inscription inside, then closing his hand around it as his eyes closed briefly. Both Ramsay and Justin watched anxiously, until at length Simon opened his eyes and slowly nodded.

"We have two links," he said quietly. "The snuffbox itself to Angus and his father, and the gold coin to the gold. It *could* work." He let out a heavy sigh. "Very well. I shall make you this proposition, James; Justin, bear witness. The three of us are not sufficient to attempt such an operation, and I cannot delay my return to the General. This war goes on, whether or not some of us engage in exercises that probably are futile.

"I therefore propose that the two of you take the snuffbox to Andrew and Arabella in Cambridge. Explain what has happened, and what you propose. I shall send my written assessment of what I understand of the procedure and the likelihood of success. I suggest that Prince Lucien be consulted as well; Andrew will know where to find him in Boston."

Ramsay scowled heavily. "What has he to do with this," he demanded, "and what is he doing in Boston?"

"He is a Stuart and Saint-Germain's agent—which is what he has to do with this," Simon said sharply. "As for why he is in Boston, that is not your concern. In any case, I consider Andrew senior in this matter, even if the prince may be more skilled. I bind you both to abide by Andrew's decision. Is that understood, James?"

Ramsay breathed a sigh of resignation, then nodded. "I understand."

"Very well. Justin, I'll give you the snuffbox when I've written the letter to accompany it. I want you ready to leave tomorrow; I'll also write orders to cover your absence."

"They'll be burying Angus tomorrow," Ramsay said quietly. "May we stay until that's done?"

"Of course," Simon replied. "James, I don't *like* having to be heavy-handed with you, but I have obligations, as do we all." He shook his head and slipped the snuffbox into the top drawer of the desk. "Off with both of you. I have letters to write."

Chapter Twenty

Murray's funeral was held the following day, with Ramsay rendering token Masonic honors to their fallen comrade at the graveside. That evening Justin took the opportunity for one final private conversation with his brother-in-law before he and Ramsay left for Cambridge the following morning. Both of them were concerned about Ramsay's outburst regarding the gold, for it tended to confirm an instability of which Saint-Germain had warned them, after Ramsay spearheaded the premature offer of a Crown to Charles Edward Stuart.

But the Master had also hinted at a future role for Ramsay on the Master Tracing Board, which precluded simply writing him out of the equation unless there was very good cause. Justin suspected it had something to do with Washington, though none of his elders had yet been able to pin down anything.

"Do you think the gold really can be recovered?" he asked as he tucked the snuffbox and Simon's letter to Andrew into an inner pocket of his uniform.

"God only knows," Simon replied. "And if it could, I have no idea how Saint-Germain would want it disposed of. So far as I know, recovering Prince Charlie's gold was never in the Master Plan—but as you know, he tends not to tell us things until we need to know them."

"Well, what if we do manage to find the gold? You don't think that James would try to take it to the King anyway, do you?"

"I don't know what he might do!" Simon retorted. "I didn't think he'd strike off on his own and send that letter to Charles, either. Just keep an eye on him, Justin. Cultivate his confidence. And maybe be ready to take his side, if it's a choice of that or letting him go off half-cocked."

"You're joking, surely," Justin murmured, wide-eyed.

"I don't know whether I am or not," Simon replied. "Just be careful."

They arrived in Boston nearly a week later, just at the end of July. Justin let Simon's letter speak for itself as he and Ramsay tucked into large bowls of Arabella's chowder with fresh-baked country bread and butter. The elder Wallace read the letter aloud, Arabella listening in astonishment.

"It's an appalling notion," she said when Andrew had finished reading.

"Perhaps not as appalling as it might seem," the Chevalier replied. "But the prince will be far more competent to assess the situation than I. I'll go to him tomorrow."

He disappeared early the next morning with the Wallace pony and trap and did not return that night or all the following day. Ramsay disappeared too—visiting family, he said—but never for more than a few hours at a time, for he feared to miss something once Andrew returned.

Justin took the opportunity to visit with his sister and renew his relationship with a niece and two nephews who had grown considerably since his last trip home. Young Charles now could be trusted to run errands alone on Justin's bay mare, and little Sarah easily persuaded her handsome Uncle Justin to escort her into town to buy ribbons for her hair. Little James was discovering the joys of reading and became Justin's shadow when he discovered that his uncle could be coerced into helping him puzzle out new words in the family Bible.

Early on the evening of the second day, summoned by the sound of a carriage pulling up outside, Justin twitched back a parlor curtain to see Andrew and the prince alighting from the pony trap,

young Charles already at the pony's head. Ramsay had not yet returned.

When the children had paid their respects to "Dr. Rohan" and retired to an early supper upstairs, the adults congregated in the kitchen, where guarded discussion ensued over the informal meal that Arabella set out.

"I tell you this, there will be no middle ground if we attempt this thing," the prince informed them as he set the snuffbox on the table amid the supper clutter. "I have some little experience in summoning up the dead, but I cannot claim to be an expert. Justin, you were present when this Angus Murray passed on, but it appears that Ramsay knew him best. Where *is* Dr. Ramsay?"

"Out," Arabella said. "It's just as well, because Justin and I wanted to talk to you before he got back. None of us are certain we trust him anymore, Lucien."

The prince nodded. "Andrew has told me of your concerns. But touching on practicalities, what harm could he do without the snuffbox? Or do you think he might attempt to find some other link, procure something else associated with one of the Murrays?"

"And use that instead of the snuffbox?" Justin asked. "Could that be done?"

"Not easily," the prince replied. "And I do not recall having felt that Ramsay was particularly powerful, though I have only Masonic ritual from which to judge. As a physician, he is competent—but no more than that. He has not the spark of a genuine healer."

"Are you saying he isn't a danger?" Andrew asked.

"No. But we perhaps malign him without cause. He has been long absent from his family, as are we all in time of war. I assume that he will return here to sleep; we shall make plans to work tomorrow night."

Ramsay duly returned within the hour, ostensibly from supper with a sister, and submitted to the prince's questions for an hour after that. Satisfied that Ramsay intended to cooperate, the prince soon released all of them to make an early retirement, for the following night would be both long and arduous.

He and Andrew remained in seclusion for much of the following

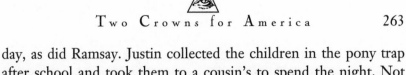

day, as did Ramsay. Justin collected the children in the pony trap after school and took them to a cousin's to spend the night. Not until nearly eleven, when it was full dark outside, did the five repair to the parlor, where Arabella had drawn both the shutters and the curtains and set a small round table in the center of the room. Five straight-backed chairs surrounded the table, and a turkey-work shawl covered it. The room was lit by candles in wall sconces and on the mantel shelf. A handsome grandfather clock ticked out its slow, regular rhythm in a far corner.

"I hope this will be satisfactory," she said, glancing around. "I can stop the clock if you think the sound will be distracting."

"Quite the contrary," the prince replied. "The sound will serve to help us concentrate—though perhaps Justin would be so good as to stop the chimes."

While Justin moved to do so, the prince pulled out the chair nearest the door. "Mistress Arabella, I shall ask you to sit here, and Justin to your immediate left. Then the Chevalier and Dr. Ramsay—and I shall take the remaining place."

The other four took their places as directed while the prince moved around the room extinguishing all the candles except one on the mantel, which he brought to set in the center of the table. Before sitting down he produced the silver snuffbox from an inner pocket and set it at the base of the candlestick. The candlelight seemed to make it glow as he scooted his chair closer and laid his hands to either side on the table before him, right palm up and left palm down.

"Now do as I do, and join hands around the table," he said, observing as they complied. "It is very important that you maintain these links while we work, both for protection and to keep the flow of power constant as we channel it. Have you any questions before we begin?"

There were none.

"Then I ask you now to gaze into the candle and let your thoughts still. We must strive for perfect harmony if the spirits are to attend. Breathe deeply once . . . and out. . . . And again. . . .

"Now listen to the ticking of the clock, just on the rhythm of the

human heartbeat, and let your own heart take its rhythm. Close
your eyes if you wish and let yourselves drift, in perfect harmony
with one another. . . ."

He fell silent for a long moment, letting each of the participants
find a balance point. Andrew had closed his eyes, as had Arabella;
Justin and Ramsay continued to gaze at the candle.

"Very quiet," the prince finally continued softly, "and very bal-
anced, ready to reach out now and summon that one whom we
have come to seek. As we turn our thoughts to the snuffbox, we
may hope to discern some faint flickering of him who owned the
box before. The name was Angus Murray in this life, and all of you
knew him. Before that his father owned the box—a man called
Charles Stuart Murray. Reach out to what you know of either man
and ask in the silence of your mind that he make his presence
known. Call to him. . . ."

Only for Andrew did an answer come, and it was not from the
one whom he sought. Behind closed eyelids he seemed to see the
familiar image of Joseph Warren take form, this time wearing
the apron of Freemasonry over his festive attire and the jewel of his
rank as Provincial Grand Master around his neck. He appeared to
be standing directly across the table, between the chairs where
Andrew knew the prince and Arabella to be sitting. Neither they
nor the others seemed aware of the manifestation, Andrew realized
as he cautiously opened his eyes.

"Joseph?" he whispered softly.

The others looked up sharply at his word, but Warren's image
did not waver, though it seemed somewhat less substantial than at
his previous appearances.

I greet you as a brother, the figure replied, raising a hand in the
sign of a Master Mason.

"I greet you as well, though I dare not break the circle," Andrew
said aloud. "Can the others not see you?"

Warren glanced down at Arabella and the prince, then at Justin
and Ramsay, all of whom were peering at where Andrew was looking, searching for some trace of what he obviously saw.

Apparently they cannot. He glanced wistfully at Arabella. *This dear
lady could learn to be my voice—and could speak for him they hope to see.
But the one you seek has not heard your call.*

"Can you not summon him?" Andrew asked.

Alas, I cannot. However, this man knows of one who can. Warren nodded toward the prince. *His ears cannot hear me, but I sense a capacity of spirit which may permit a prompting of his memory in another fashion.*

So saying, he stretched out a translucent hand and passed it gently *through* the upper part of the prince's upturned head. Though the touch seemed to cause no harm, a flicker of bewilderment registered briefly in the prince's searching eyes—which glazed and then rolled upward in their sockets as Warren bent to whisper in the prince's left ear. As Warren drew back, the prince's head lolled onto one shoulder, his body going limp.

"Lucien?" Arabella whispered, clutching hard at his hand, her eyes darting to Andrew's in alarm.

"Do not break the circle!" Andrew ordered, holding more tightly to Justin's and Ramsay's hands, for Warren still was visible. "You haven't harmed him, have you?"

Of course not, Warren replied. *I have helped him—and you. I can do none any harm. But take care that he makes good use of what I have given him, for returning to this plane becomes increasingly difficult. Perhaps once more may I come. Until then, adieu, dear friend.*

"No, wait!"

But Warren was already fading, one graceful surgeon's hand lifting in farewell. When no trace of him remained, Andrew drew a slow, careful breath and looked around. Arabella was still staring at him in alarm, her glance flitting between him and the unconscious prince. Both Justin and Ramsay were grimacing from the strength of his grip on their hands. He relaxed his hands enough to relieve the pain, but not enough for them to withdraw, drawing a deep, sobering breath to address them.

"Our conductor being temporarily incapable, I shall assume guidance of this working," he said carefully. "No one has been harmed. I shall explain in a moment. So that we may bring this working to a proper close, I ask that you all close your eyes and focus for a moment. On my backward count from five to one, return in spirit to this time and place, no longer open to whatever forces have been at large in this room. If you close your eyes, I will assume that you agree."

A glance around him confirmed three pairs of closed eyes besides those of the prince.

"A deep breath now, in . . . and out. . . . And five . . . four . . . three . . . two . . . one! This working is ended."

He paid no attention to their stirrings as he released hands with Justin and Ramsay and lurched to his feet to go to the prince. Arabella still retained one hand, but Ramsay had released the other and drawn back in his chair, staring at the prince in alarm. As Andrew stepped between them, he took the prince's face between his hands and tipped it back so that he could look at the closed eyes.

"Lucien?" he murmured. "Lucien, look at me. Open your eyes and—"

The prince's eyelids fluttered and opened and he raised his free hand to his forehead. "I am unharmed," he murmured. "What an extraordinary experience. Whoever you saw, Andrew, he whispered in my ear. I could not see him, nor could I exactly hear him, but—"

"What did he say?"

"I don't know. Something. . . ." The prince freed his other hand from Arabella's and scrubbed both hands over his face and eyes, obviously still seeking to regain his equilibrium. "I *have* thought of something that may be useful, though."

"Did Warren tell you?"

"Warren who?"

"Dr. Joseph Warren. That's who was present. He died at Breed's Hill. Don't you remember? You sent back information that helped us locate his body. He was a very dear friend. He's appeared to me twice before."

"Ah." The prince nodded, still looking a little dazed. "Well, I could not say yea or nay to that, but something certainly jogged my memory. An acquaintance of mine has spoken of a man who may just be able to help us."

"Who is he?" Ramsay demanded.

"I cannot recall his true name—I have only heard of him—but he is known as the Ba'al Shem of London. 'Ba'al Shem' means Master of the Name—in this instance, Tetragrammaton, the Di-

vine Name. A Ba'al Shem is a Jew of particular sanctity of knowledge, able to make use of the power of that Name in the writing of amulets and in prescribing cures for various ailments.

"What makes this particular man of interest to us is that he is said to be an expert at locating lost treasure—which, in this instance, may be less of a problem than it might appear, since we have a coin to use as a link. That may be considerably easier than trying to call back either of the Murrays, based on tonight's experience."

"That may still be necessary," Andrew murmured. "Warren indicated that Arabella could learn to function as a medium. His exact words were, 'This dear lady could learn to be my voice—and his'—presumably referring to Murray. I can't imagine why he should tell me that unless he felt that it would be necessary for her to do so."

"That may present additional problems," the prince said, before Arabella could comment.

"How so?"

"I assure you, I mean no slight upon our Arabella and her abilities," the prince replied, with a reassuring glance in her direction. "Rather, I am concerned with how our Ba'al Shem may receive the notion of working with a woman, however gifted she may be. It is a question of propriety, of ritual purity. Though a Ba'al Shem may command extraordinary powers and abilities, he yet functions at least within the periphery of orthodox Judaism, which places women in a position that is both exalted and restricted. In short, he may refuse to work with you."

Arabella gave a wry smile. "Such resistance would hardly be new in my experience," she said drolly. "Outside our own Lodge, I would not be accepted in the Craft."

"No, you would not," the prince said after a beat. "Yet opposition was overcome, at least within that group." He glanced at the others and seemed to make a decision.

"We shall set that aside for the moment," he said. "Our first concern must be to gain access to the Ba'al Shem. The man who can give us an introduction is here in Boston—a man called Eli Levi. I shall meet with him as soon as possible."

"You seem very confident," Ramsay said. "Suppose he won't help you."

"Oh, *he* will help us," the prince replied. " 'Tis the Ba'al Shem who is the unknown quantity. What I think and hope will open the necessary doors is that both he and Eli are Initiates of Freemasonry. Eli, at least, will not refuse to help a poor widow's son."

Two days later, in a handsome parlor office in a Boston town house, the prince laid out his proposition over tiny cups of thick, strong coffee.

"I would not ask this of you if I were not convinced you are an honest man, and that you share my own zeal for this American cause," he concluded. "I assure you that I seek this treasure on behalf of its rightful owner. And there is every reason to expect that the treasure eventually would be used in the support of the war effort." Which was true, whether Charles Edward Stuart or Washington eventually benefited from the funds. "I am, of course, prepared to go to London."

Eli Levi nodded slowly. He was a big, powerful man in the prime of life, with only a trace of silver showing in his neatly trimmed beard and mustache and in the side curls clubbed back with the rest of his thick black hair. Apart from the distinction of a small black skullcap, almost invisible against his hair, he looked little different from any other prosperous banker in Boston; but his influence was felt across an ocean. As part of the financial network centered on Haym Salomon, now working out of Philadelphia, Levi helped broker most of the funds starting to funnel across the Atlantic to finance the war. Vast sums had already been lent to the United States government on pure good faith, much of it from Salomon's personal resources and mostly without interest. Levi was no less capable, and no less a friend of the fledgling United States. He was also distantly related to the Ba'al Shem of London by marriage.

"You are, of course, aware that this request is hardly within the usual scope of the Craft," Levi said. His English was faintly inflected with a Middle European accent.

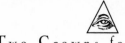
"Quite aware," the prince replied. "Nonetheless, I know of no other who could help this poor widow's son."

A faint smile briefly lit the Jew's dark eyes. "You need not reiterate that appeal, my friend," he said. "You knew when you came that I would not refuse you. And if anyone can find your treasure, it would be Dr. Falk. However . . ."

"However?" the prince prompted when Levi did not go on.

Levi frowned, a big hand toying with the cup before him, its contents long gone cold.

"You must remember that I cannot speak for him," he said. "You will appreciate that he is extremely cautious regarding gentile seekers after occult knowledge—and who can blame him, given the history of our two peoples? It will help that you go to him as a brother in the Craft—and, of course, I shall write him a glowing letter of introduction in your behalf. You are prepared, I trust, to render me a service in return?"

"I am always happy to assist a brother," the prince replied. "What was it you had in mind?"

"Only the delivery of certain letters of credit in London, and one in Paris," Levi said with a smile. "I would sooner trust them to a brother than to any ordinary courier. I advise a certain degree of circumspection in London, since the British authorities do not look kindly upon agents conveying succor to the enemy. However, the Paris trip should prove a pleasant enough diversion. And you may convey my personal greetings to Brother Franklin."

"I shall, indeed," the prince agreed, inclining his head in a bow. "And I thank you kindly. When may I collect those letters?"

"Tomorrow afternoon," Levi replied. "And I know of a Dutch merchantman that sails for London in a week's time. Shall I have space booked for you?"

"Thank you for the offer, but I shall make my own travel arrangements," the prince replied. "I may be taking several associates with me."

Chapter Twenty-one

The scheduled sailing of the Dutch ship Levi had mentioned left scant time to confer with Simon before a decision had to be made regarding who should go with the prince to Falk in London. Accordingly, it fell to Andrew to make the selection and hope that Simon would concur.

Ramsay obviously had to go, since it was he to whom Murray had first tried to confide the location of the gold. By similar reasoning, though the prince had been careful not to mention it to Levi, it seemed clear that Arabella must go along to serve as Murray's voice. And for propriety's sake, as well as for the wisdom of his own training, Andrew himself must be a part of the company.

"Justin, I know you would like to accompany us," Andrew informed him privately after supper that night, "but I think you will be of more service if you return to Simon. With Lafayette gone back to France, the General will be more vulnerable to doubts—and it will be Simon who must assuage those doubts. Your presence will lighten *his* burden. I want you to leave for Philadelphia at first light. I shall prepare a full report of what has happened and what we intend. Barring unforeseen adversity, you should have time to reach him and return before we sail if he has some objection or further instruction. Is that agreeable to you?"

It was not the decision Justin had hoped for, but he accepted it in good grace. He did return in time to convey Simon's reaction and recommendations, and to watch the ship slip out of Boston Harbor before he headed back south.

The voyage was uneventful, if tedious, the monotony of endless days interspersed with equally tiresome nights, though the wind remained fresh and they made good time. The balmy weather brought most of the passengers above decks during the day, to walk or read or play at draughts or chess. Arabella was particularly pleased to absent herself from her cabin whenever possible, for she was obliged to share it with the garrulous wife of a British officer returning to London, who spent most of her waking hours complaining when she was not being seasick.

Andrew was a proven companion of many years' standing, and the prince proved amiable and amusing, but Ramsay became withdrawn and sparing of conversation as the voyage wore on and was often to be seen far up in the bow, staring at the distant horizon. Nor did he often join them in the evenings, when the prince gathered them in the cabin the three men shared to give advanced instruction in the tenets of Freemasonry or, occasionally, to polish their proficiency by working the rituals of Lodge in whispered undertones.

They made landfall at Southampton in late September, arriving in London on the heels of news that the American John Paul Jones had defeated HM warship *Serapis* off the east Yorkshire coast on the twenty-third. Though Ramsay's air of preoccupation seemed to dissipate once they reached London, he remained a cause of concern for the prince and especially for Andrew, who knew the Jacobite physician far better than any of the rest.

Accordingly, Andrew had set himself to chronicling events as soon as Ramsay presented himself in Cambridge, confident that Saint-Germain would want to know about the potential situation developing. He had continued his chronicle during the Atlantic crossing, penning a detailed description of his own experience on the evening they attempted the seance and appending his assessment of Ramsay's mental state and recommendations for caution. This he dispatched to Germany shortly after reaching London, by way of a young assistant recommended by one of the brokerage houses to which he and the prince delivered Eli Levi's letters of credit.

Ramsay was unaware of the transaction, for neither he nor Arabella accompanied the prince on the errand to the financial district. Similarly, the prince took along only Andrew on the crisp October morning when he hailed a hansom cab and set out to meet the Ba'al Shem of London, armed with Eli Levi's letter of introduction.

Hayyim Samuel Jacob Falk lived in a comfortable terrace house in Wellclose Square, not far from Whitechapel, the Tower of London, and Tower Bridge. Architecturally similar to the other houses in the square, if perhaps marginally better maintained, it yet conveyed a sense of being different from all the others as the cab pulled up in front of its wrought-iron fencing.

Alighting from the cab behind the prince, and letting the prince hand him down, Andrew let himself drink in first impressions as his silver-headed cane tap-tapped up the granite steps to a blue-painted front door. When the prince rang the bell, the door was shortly opened by a middle-aged man with a bushy gray-streaked beard and spectacles pushed up on his forehead.

"Yes, what is it?"

"Good morning," the prince replied. "I have a letter of introduction for Dr. Falk. I believe this is his residence?"

The man's eyes flicked over the pair of them.

"Who gave you this letter?"

"A distant relation of his by marriage, Mr. Eli Levi of Boston."

"I'll ask if he can see you," the man said, standing back from the door. "Come in off the street and wait here."

They stepped into a small, neat vestibule lit by the fanlight above the door. A marble-topped hall table bore a large crystal vase brimming over with gold and russet chrysanthemums; a multicolored rag rug adorned the scrubbed honey-colored planks of the wooden floor. Several calling cards lay on a silver salver beside the vase, but the top one was printed in Hebrew, and the man returned before Andrew could do more than think about shifting it to see whether they were all like that.

"Dr. Falk has just finished morning prayers, but he will see you in the library very shortly," the man said. "Please come with me."

Exchanging a glance with the prince, Andrew fell in behind the man, who led them through a sturdy paneled door, along a gracious hall, and into a painted library, whose shelves were crammed from ceiling to floor with books. Indicating two bow-back chairs to either side of a more massive wing chair, the man withdrew.

Andrew contented himself with sitting on one of the chairs while the prince casually perused some of the titles on the shelves, but came immediately to his feet as the library door opened again to admit a small, gray-bearded man in a rumpled black suit.

He surveyed his visitors curiously over the tops of glittering spectacles as he closed the door behind him and came into the room. The white fringes of a prayer shawl showed beneath his coattails, and he wore side curls and a black skullcap. Though he looked to be quite elderly, with liver spots mottling his face and the backs of his hands, the dark eyes behind the spectacles were bright and alert.

"Moshe says you have a letter from Eli Levi, my wife's sister's grandson," he said. His English was excellent, if heavily accented— a rich baritone.

"I do, Rabbi," the prince replied, making him a little bow as he reached into his coat. "My name is Rohan, and my colleague is the Chevalier Wallace."

"And I am Falk," their host replied, not favoring them with any of his other names as he took the letter the prince handed him. "Sit, sit."

He indicated the two lesser chairs, himself taking the wingback, and immediately broke the seal on Levi's letter and began reading. Again exchanging glances, Andrew and the prince sat where they were bidden. Partway through the letter, Falk looked up at them, adjusting his spectacles on his nose, then returned to his reading. When he had finished, he sat for some time tapping the pages against his hand and staring off into space. Finally he roused himself to fold the letter and slip it into an inside pocket, flicking his gaze from one to the other of them.

"Because Eli has asked it, and for the sake of the poor widow's

son, I will try to help you," he said. "Which of you is senior? I perceive a difference in abilities, but neither seems subordinate to the other."

"Say that we function as part of a team, Rabbi," the prince said before Andrew could defer. "And that we answer to the same higher authority."

"Yes, so do we all answer to that Great Architect of the Universe," Falk said impatiently. "This treasure—Eli says that you seek it on behalf of its rightful owner. Who is that rightful owner?"

"Charles Edward Stuart," the prince said cautiously. "And we are all too aware that even to accord him his rightful style as king is reckoned treason in this country. I must also tell you that if the gold is recovered, there is every reason to expect that it will be used to further other interests besides those of George of Hanover. If, under these circumstances, you prefer not to become involved, we will withdraw our request. But we will not come to you with lies."

"No, students of Saint-Germain would not presume to lie to me," the old man said, a faint smile curving at his lips within the wiry gray beard.

Andrew had stiffened at the mention of Saint-Germain's name, but the prince only nodded, leaning back in his chair to steeple his fingertips before his chin.

"We are as you suggest," he admitted. "May one presume to ask how you became aware of this?"

"One may." Still smiling, Falk lifted a deprecating hand. "Be at ease, my brothers. I have surmised it from the nature of your request, coupled with your championship of Charles Edward Stuart. Ba'al Shem I may be, but mastery of the Sacred Name is not to be employed in frivolous displays of occult knowledge. Suffice it to say that I have long been aware of your Master's interest in the Stuart prince and in the New World. These are not my own interests, so I have given them little concern, but I am well acquainted with Saint-Germain. Does he know what you are proposing?"

Andrew shifted in his chair, fingering the silver head of his walking stick. "I have written to him, outlining all that is known to us thus far, sir, but the letter left only a few days ago, and I do not know for certain where or when he will be found."

"Nor do I," Falk replied. "Still, that cannot be helped." He pursed his lips. "You do realize, I hope, that what you ask will still be difficult, even though I can expect you to possess the advantage of Saint-Germain's training. Are there more of you?"

"Yes, two," the prince replied, deliberately neglecting to be more specific. "They and another were present when we attempted to contact the spirit of a man believed to know the location of the gold, but we were unsuccessful. We *did* make a contact," he added. "Or rather, the Chevalier did. It was not the man we sought, else we should not be here, but that contact does seem to have been responsible for putting it in my mind to ask Eli Levi about you. Eli and I have been involved in some business transactions of late, and your name came up in the course of conversation."

"Hardly the sort of conversation one might expect of a business acquaintance," Falk observed, surveying the prince over his glasses.

"Indeed not," the prince agreed. "But he and I have sat in Lodge together many times. It soon became clear that we shared certain esoteric interests—though I doubt I would have recalled that particular conversation had it not been for the seance."

"But you are not a medium," Falk said—a statement, not a question.

"No."

"And you, Chevalier?"

"No, but my contact indicated that another of our number has the capacity to be one, given suitable instruction," Andrew replied, following the prince's lead in avoiding direct reference to Arabella. "Meanwhile, my contact chose a different sort of communication through Dr. Rohan. I believe it was a rather startling experience," he added with an arch glance at the prince.

Falk chuckled and leaned back in his chair to twist at a side curl. "Such an experience usually *is* startling, even when one is prepared for it. Tell me, Chevalier, do you know the identity of your contact?"

"I do, indeed." Briefly Andrew described how Joseph Warren now had appeared to him three times, in each instance providing information previously unknown to Andrew.

"I have no idea how he knew of Dr. Rohan's connection with

Mr. Levi, or of Levi's connection with you," Andrew concluded. "So far as I am aware, he was acquainted with neither man in life— nor with Murray, the man we were trying to contact—yet he seemed quite confident that the link would bear fruit, and that you would prove equal to the task we proposed. Yet when I asked, at one point, whether he could summon Murray to attend us, he said that he could not."

"Yes, sometimes the spirits' abilities are limited in ways we do not comprehend," Falk murmured. "At other times they are oddly omniscient. We shall certainly attempt to employ the medium he brought to your attention. Tell me, what did you use as a focus for your working?"

"This silver snuffbox," the prince replied, removing it from his pocket and unwrapping the silk handkerchief that protected it. "It belonged to Angus Murray, the man who tried to tell us the location of the gold, and to his father before him, who supposedly had actually buried the gold. We believe the gold coin inside to be from the hoard that was buried in the New World."

He handed the snuffbox to Falk, still nestled in its silk swathings. The old man turned it carefully in the strong light from the window, running an aged finger across the coin set in the bottom, then set it aside on a small table.

"If your spirit contact has spoken truly regarding your medium, this should prove an excellent focus," he said briskly. "The coin provides a particularly potent link, if its provenance is as you suggest. Return here one week from tonight, at nine o'clock. I shall need some time to consult several sources. Bring along your other two. May I take it that all of you are Master Masons?"

"We are," the prince said.

"Good. Then come prepared to clothe yourselves for work. Bathe beforehand, to purify yourselves, and wear fresh clothing of conservative color, preferably black. I shall provide what else is needed. For further preparation I ask that you undertake a light fast for the three days preceding: only one small meal per day, taking neither meat nor spirits, and only bread and water on the final day.

"This is especially important for your medium, who should take only water on the third day," he went on. "See that he spends the day in solitude, preparing himself for his holy work—as should all of you be prepared to give me your utmost focus and concentration. Go now. I have much to do."

"He was certainly specific once he had made up his mind," Andrew said to the prince as they walked along the Thames beside the Tower, after leaving Falk's residence. "I wonder if we should have told him that our medium is a woman."

"I debated that myself," the prince replied, "but I feared that total candor might end the discussion before it began. Now he has committed himself. After making preparations for a week, it will be more difficult to back out on the night."

"Do you think he'll try?" Andrew asked. "How orthodox do you think he is?"

"That is difficult to say, based on our relatively short contact of today. One would hope that the—unique nature of a Ba'al Shem's activities would lend a certain flexibility, especially in a high initiate like Falk, but many very orthodox Jews will avoid the presence of any woman who is not wife or daughter or—"

His voice trailed off and he stopped walking, a slow grin curling at his lip as he turned to regard Andrew.

"My dear Chevalier, I suddenly understand why Saint-Germain insisted that Arabella should take her additional degrees in Freemasonry. I had assumed it was for the sake of Washington, and her role in the eventual enactment of his ritual—but no, not even he could have anticipated this development!"

He unfolded the logic of his proposition as they continued along the Embankment. By the time they reached Temple Bar and their hotel, they had resolved the form their rebuttal must take when Falk met Arabella.

Arabella herself showed no particular anxiety once Andrew had outlined the form of their persuasion. After rehearsing several different scenarios, according to Falk's likely objections, she declared herself content to lay the affair in the hands of The Great Architect of the Universe, at Whose direction they deemed Warren to have intervened in the first place. And if, despite their best arguments,

Falk still refused to employ her, they would worry about other arrangements at that time.

That having been decided, they availed themselves of the sights and pleasures of London for the next four days. The weather was turning too cold to enjoy London's parks and walks along the Thames, but there were museums and art galleries to sample, and the theater to enjoy. One afternoon the prince hired a carriage to drive them past the Abbey and the Palace of Westminster, where Parliament sat, and then along toward Whitehall and the Admiralty, whence issued many of the orders concerning the war in America.

Ramsay declined to join them much, declaring his wish to explore the city on his own. He had been briefed as thoroughly as possible on what they might expect when they went to Falk and was in agreement regarding the need for Arabella's participation, but a vague, brooding undercurrent ran beneath the surface. Most nights he returned only late to his room.

Andrew let him go, because he had no cause to forbid him; but he continued to wonder what was going on inside Ramsay's head. He mentioned it to Arabella and the prince, but they agreed that nothing could be done save to continue their vigilance. Even in a worst-case scenario, Ramsay was not likely to bolt until he knew the location of the gold and had a chance of getting to it before anyone else—which meant that he probably would make no move until they returned to America. Beyond that, they must simply wait and see.

Their schedule changed on the fifth day, the third before their return to Falk. Thereafter, all four of them kept to their rooms save to venture out each afternoon to nearby St. Paul's to hear Evensong. Otherwise, they occupied themselves with reading and writing in their rooms, each making his or her individual preparations for a powerful occult working.

Tempers at first grew frayed as the days passed and hunger began to assert itself; but with the hunger came a light-headedness and then a sharpening of senses, as was intended. By the evening of the third day, as four dark-cloaked figures disembarked from a carriage in front of Falk's home in Wellclose Square, at least a semblance of harmony bound them in sober fraternity.

A servant took hats and cloaks and the men's swords as they came in through the little vestibule, though he stared at Arabella as she surrendered her cloak. All of them had dressed in dark clothing as instructed, and Arabella had chosen a high-necked black gown that would not have offended a Roman pontiff, with her black hair covered by a black lace cap. Despite this demonstration of propriety, she sensed outraged disapproval in the servant's gaze as he led them through the candlelit hall and into the library. Ramsay carried the valise that contained their Masonic gear, his eyes darting constantly around him, taking in each new detail of the strange surroundings.

More candles burned behind glass chimneys around the room, but the library still was mostly in shadow. Arabella hung back behind Andrew and the prince as the door opened and an elderly man entered, the candlelight glinting on his spectacles. From Andrew's prior description, it could only be Dr. Falk, the Ba'al Shem of London.

"Good evening, gentlemen," Falk said, extending his hand to the prince and then pulling up short as he spied Arabella slightly behind him. "And who, may I ask, is *that*?"

"These are the other members of our delegation," the prince replied, including Ramsay in the sweep of his gesture. "I have the honor to present Mistress Arabella Wallace and Dr. James Ramsay. Both are in the confidence of Saint-Germain."

"Saint-Germain mentioned no woman," Falk said coldly. "Nor did you."

The prince glanced at Andrew, somewhat taken aback by the implication that Falk had been in contact with Saint-Germain in only a week.

"I do not recall that you asked, Rabbi," he said neutrally. "Nor has there been time for Saint-Germain to mention *anything* concerning this venture. Or is he here in London, unbeknownst to us?"

"He is not in London," Falk said. "Suffice it to say that we have been in communication. Both you and the Chevalier are well regarded—though now I must wonder why. Had I realized that a woman was among your number—" He shook his head, candlelight winking off his spectacles as he muttered, "Utterly impossi-

ble. I cannot permit it. The ritual *might* work with only four, but—"

"Will the ritual work without a medium, Rabbi?" Arabella asked quietly, moving from behind Andrew.

Falk stared at her dumbstruck, then turned to the prince in appeal.

"Surely she is not saying that *she* is the medium," he said.

The prince nodded. "I fear she is, Rabbi. Believe me, we would not have exposed her to this, or imposed her presence upon you, if she had not been designated by our contact as being necessary for this working."

"How can I expect you to understand?" Falk muttered, half under his breath. "High magic is an art of great intimacy. By the customs of my faith, even to speak to a woman not my wife or daughter or sister—"

"Ah," Andrew interjected. "But she is *my* daughter, by virtue of being married to my son. And she is sister to all of us—including you, Rabbi."

Falk's bushy eyebrows lifted in question. "What do you mean?"

"What he means," the prince said, suppressing a smile, "is that she is a regularly initiated Freemason, and therefore a sister to every man in this room. I will admit that the circumstances of her making were unusual, but precedent was offered that satisfied nine Master Masons at the time, including Dr. Benjamin Franklin and General George Washington, as well as ourselves. Since then she has been both passed and raised. I assure you, Brother Falk, on the level and on the square, that she is every bit the Freemason that any of us are."

"Impossible. Utterly impossible," Falk whispered, shaking his head.

"These brethren will attest that it *is* possible, Brother Falk," Arabella said very quietly. "They have made, passed, and raised me. Or do you suggest that their regard for their Obligations is less than your own? I am clearly a woman, Rabbi, even as God made me, but I am also a Master Mason in the service of The Great Architect of the Universe."

"No," Falk said weakly, still shaking his head.

"Will nothing convince you?" Arabella continued, her voice still

barely audible. "Shall I give you signs and tokens? Shall I greet you on the Five Points of Fellowship, and impart to you the Master's word?"

As he recoiled, his face going ashen, she proceeded to do just that. Boldly seizing his right hand in hers, she shifted her fingers so that her nails pressed into his wrist in the Master's grip. Her other hand she closed over their joined ones so he could not pull away.

"Hand to hand I greet you as a brother," she said quietly, looking him in the eyes. Deliberately moving her right foot forward against the inside of his, she said, "Foot to foot, I will support you in all your undertakings."

When he only stared at her in shock, too stunned to pull back, she shifted forward so that her right calf lay close alongside his, ankle to knee. Her voluminous petticoats muffled any actual contact, but the symbolism was clear, and well Falk knew it. She felt him flinch as she murmured, "Knee to knee, the posture of my daily undertakings shall remind me of your wants. Breast to breast—"

He gasped and stiffened as she leaned her right shoulder against his, his eyes squeezing shut as if to shut out the words.

"—your lawful secrets when entrusted to me as such I will keep as my own," she said. "Hand over back"—her left hand finally released their clasped ones to lift and circle lightly over his back, clasping him firmly, trembling with him—"I will support your character in your absence as in your presence."

He still did not move, stiff and rigid within her embrace, eyes tightly closed; but as she leaned closer to his ear and softly whispered the Master's word, the resistance seemed to drain out of him with a faint sob.

Slowly the fingers of his right hand shifted to echo the Master's grip against her right wrist, his left hand lifting to lightly clasp her back. Then his forehead dipped briefly to rest against her shoulder.

After a few seconds he drew breath and raised his head, his eyes stormy with confusion as he dropped his left hand and drew back slightly. But he kept her right hand in his, shifting it to a more conventional handclasp, patting it awkwardly with his left hand, shaking his gray head in bewildered respect.

"Madame," he said, his voice a little unsteady, "I am seventy-

one years old, a Ba'al Shem, a high Initiate in Freemasonry and in many secret sciences of which you have not even dreamed. Yet never did I think to see the day when I should greet a woman as my sister in the Craft."

"I feel privileged to greet you as a brother, Rabbi," she said quietly, finally lowering her eyes in the deference usually expected of women. "I am truly sorry if my presence has caused you discomfort, but we feared that if you knew my gender beforehand, you might reject my assistance out of hand. And since I was the one pointed out by the Chevalier's contact . . ."

She let him fill in the sense of the sentence she failed to finish, not offended when he dropped her hand, again shaking his head.

"Yes, there is still that question," he said.

She quirked him a brief, mirthless smile. "It would not have been my choice either, Rabbi. And if you can provide a better candidate, I shall be happy to step aside and support my brethren in whatever manner you may direct. But in this it appears that other agencies are at work besides our own."

"Indeed." Falk exhaled gustily and raised an eyebrow. "Well, I had already allowed for working with an untrained medium—and I cannot deny that, as a Master Mason, you cannot fail to have the basic preparation I would require of any man.

"Yet you were present before and failed to make contact with the Messrs. Murray," he went on. "Nonetheless, a contact was made. Curious."

He drew a deep breath, pulling off his spectacles to polish them against a voluminous handkerchief he produced from somewhere inside his coat, then cast his glance over the four of them as he put the spectacles back on.

"Very well," he said. "I like it not, for we invite far more variables than I would wish in an operation of this kind. Nonetheless, our numbers seem ordained; and the auguries for finding your gold will not be so good for many weeks if we use not this night. Come. We shall make the attempt. A place has been prepared."

Without further ado, he took up one of the candlesticks and led them out of the library, back through the polished hall and along a carpeted corridor, passing through a succession of waxed and pol-

ished doors. At length they came to a door that was grander than all the previous ones, banded in polished brass and surrounded by an architrave carved with marble pillars to either side, the right one white, and the left one black.

By the light of his candlestick Falk unlocked the door with a small brass key and pushed it open. A small silver mezuzah gleamed on the doorpost on the right, and he kissed the fingertips of his right hand and then touched them to the object before entering.

"Shema Ysrael, Adonai Elohenu, Adonai Echad," he murmured, bowing his head as he stepped across the threshold.

The prince followed immediately after, also kissing his fingertips as Falk had done and touching them to the object as he glanced back at the rest of them.

"That prayer is called the Shema," he murmured. "Say after me, and do as I do: Hear, O Israel, the Lord is our God, the Lord is One."

They repeated his words dutifully, each copying the prince's gesture of respect as they followed him inside. Ramsay was the last one in, setting the valise at his feet as he pulled the door closed behind him.

By the light of several candles in the vestibule beyond, Falk was taking off his shoes. Without prompting they followed suit, for the context made it clear that they were preparing to walk upon holy ground. As further reinforcement of tradition, Falk handed out black skullcaps to the other men, noting Arabella's lace cap with apparent acceptance.

He then bade them clothe themselves for work, surreptitiously watching Arabella put on her apron while he donned his own. The lining of his was blue, Arabella noticed, as was the prince's, as she had learned was European custom. He moved to a china basin to wash his hands, drying them on a linen towel.

"I ask that when you enter the temple beyond, you go to the places I indicate and sit in silence," he said as they washed and dried their hands after him. "Before beginning our work tonight, it is fitting that each of us pray individually, even as we prayed before being raised as Master Masons, asking God's strength to bless our

endeavor and sustain us in our work. After a suitable interval I shall then direct you in the opening of the temple, invoking the sacred Names. Have you any questions?"

There were none, though the Ba'al Shem looked long into each solemn face. When he had satisfied himself as to their readiness, he turned to open the arched door into the next chamber.

It was a perfect cube of a room, perhaps fifteen feet on a side, with heavy blue velvet wall hangings beneath the plastered cornicing, tall alabaster columns set in the four corners, a ceiling painted like the night sky, and a black-and-white-tiled floor mostly covered by a painted floor cloth. Mirror facets marked out constellations on the ceiling, catching points of light from a hanging center lantern of brass set with blue glass that also revealed the dark bulk of several chairs arranged in the center of the room.

They stepped inside at Falk's gesture of invitation, though they hung to either side while he locked the door behind them, letting their eyes adjust to the watery light. As Arabella glanced up at the ceiling, seeking out familiar patterns, she noticed that the pointers of the Big Dipper indicated north to the left—which gave the room a traditional east-west orientation.

Closer perusal of the center of the room revealed the chairs to be five in number, set astride five of the painted points of a six-pointed star formed of interlocking triangles of gold and silver. Rather than a chair, a small table occupied the easternmost point, supporting the familiar symbols of Freemasonry: square and compasses laid atop an open Volume of Sacred Law, with three lighted candles set across the back of the table. A painted circle of vermilion contained the star; a second, slightly larger one defined a band like the rim of a plate, on which were painted Hebrew letters that spelled out sacred names.

Silently Falk moved before the westernmost chair, facing the east, directing the rest of them to the positions he deemed most suitable: Arabella to the chair immediately to the right of him, with Ramsay beyond her; the prince and Andrew to the two more northerly chairs, the prince immediately to Falk's left. As Arabella nervously sat in her designated place, she cast her gaze over a small wooden pedestal standing between her and Falk, supporting a

small incense brazier, a small bowl of incense, and Angus Murray's silver snuffbox.

Slowly and deliberately, Falk closed his eyes and bowed his head. Profound silence ensued as the others followed his example and settled into prayer.

Chapter Twenty-two

T he silence deepened as the minutes ticked by, until finally Falk raised his head and stood, the rustle of his movement recalling them from meditation.

" 'Except Adonai build the house, they labor in vain that build it,' " he said, quoting from the Psalm. " 'Except Adonai keep the city, the watchman waketh but in vain.' My brothers and my sister, assist me to open this temple, in the name of Adonai, for the purpose of seeking knowledge from one who has passed beyond. Be upstanding as I invoke the Sacred Names and summon the heavenly Protectors."

They rose at his bidding, facing east with him as he moved into the center of the circle and lifted his right hand both in salute and in the beginning gesture of a familiar ritual. The equal-armed cross he began to trace across his body was no Christian symbol; rather, a glyph of the four elements in balance, the four cardinal points, known among Initiates as the Cabalistic cross.

"*Ateh*," Falk intoned, touching his forehead. "*Malkuth*." His hand dipped to his solar plexus. "*Ve Geburah . . . Ve Gedulah*." The hand swept to his right shoulder and then to the left, joining the left at his breast as he spoke the final words, "*Le Olahm*."

"Unto Thee . . . be the Kingdom . . . and the Power . . . and the Glory . . . unto all the ages. . . ."

His head dipped as he whispered, *"Amin,"* which the rest of them repeated.

A moment he stood thus, with head bowed, then lifted his eyes again to the east. Extending his right arm downward and across his body, he swept it upward in the first stroke of a banishing pentagram, carrying down then to the right, up and across to the left, directly across to the right, and then returning to the starting point off his left hip. His watchers had followed the motion and set the symbol in memory, but as he stabbed a forefinger at the center of the figure he had traced, intoning the first of the sacred Names, the Tetragrammaton itself, visual confirmation seemed to shimmer briefly before them, the air vibrating with the power of the Name.

"Yod He Vau He . . . !"

Tracing to the right with his outstretched hand, Falk turned to face the south, west, and north respectively, repeating the outline of the sacred pentagram and charging each one with a different name of power: *"Adonai Tzabaoth!"* Lord of Hosts. *"Eh-Ei-He!"* I Am. And finally, *"Agla!"* a name of great potency formed from the initials of a Hebrew phrase, *Aieth Gadol Leolahm Adonai,* Thou art mighty forever, O Lord.

When he had again returned to face east, he invoked archangelic protection for their work, declaring each entity's position relative to their circle and intoning the name:

"Before me, *Rafael.* Behind me, *Gabreel.* At my right hand, *Meekahel.* At my left hand, *Awreel.* Around me flame the pentagrams. Above me shines the six-rayed star."

He then repeated the Cabalistic Cross, again intoning the sacred formula: *"Ateh, Malkuth, Ve Geburah, Ve Gedulah, Le Olahm. . . ."*

Reverberations seemed to hang on the air long after the final *"Amin,"* enveloping their working space with potent protection, felt but not seen. A moment Falk stood with head bowed; then he lifted both palms to the east.

"Let us now adore the sacred Names," he said, "that we may be upheld in our endeavor.

"We adore the Lord of Air: *Shaddai El Chai.* Almighty and Everliving, be Thy name ever magnified in the Life of all. *Amin.*"

"Amin," they repeated, bowing with him to the east over folded hands and turning with him to face south.

"We adore the Lord of Fire: *Tetragrammaton Tzabaoth!* Blessed be Thou. 'The Leader of Armies' is Thy name. *Amin.*"

Another bow, then turning to face west.

"We adore the Lord of Water: *Elohim Tzabaoth!* Glory be to the *Ruach Elohim*, who moved upon the face of the Waters of Creation. *Amin.*"

Another bow, and a turn at last to the north.

"We adore the Lord of the Earth: *Adonai Ha-Aretz, Adonai Melekh.* Blessed be Thy Name unto countless ages. Unto Thee be the kingdom, and the power, and the glory, now and forever. *Amin.*"

When they had saluted the north, again echoing his "Amin," they turned once again to the east, lifting their faces with his as he said, "In the Name of *Yod He Vau He Tzabaoth*, I declare this temple open for the purposes we require. *Amin. Selah.* So be it."

He gave the sign of a Master Mason before moving back to his chair, confirming that what was to follow came under the same circumspection as more usual work in Lodge. They repeated his sign, sitting as he did in silent contemplation for several minutes, each seeking focus in his or her own way, until at length Falk lifted his head and reached to the pedestal beside him to pick up Angus Murray's snuffbox. Rising, he came before Arabella and bent to set it in her hands.

"I give you charge of this, that it may be a focus for the work we now set about," he said. "Have you any questions before we proceed?"

She had none that he could answer. Lifting her chin resolutely, she looked him in the eyes.

"None, Rabbi," she whispered.

To her surprise a faint smile stirred his lips and he gently touched the flat of his right hand to the top of her head.

"*Ruach Elohim* shall be thine inspiration," he whispered.

Before she could react, he was turning away to move the pedestal and incense burner to the center of the circle, taking a position directly behind it and facing her. His expression was composed again, as if nothing had happened, but she sensed a barrier had fallen from between them.

The change of attitude seemed not to have gone unnoticed.

Across the circle Andrew was tight-lipped in the manner that told
her he was actually doing his best not to smile; beside him, the
prince had lifted one hand to a cough that was actually cover for a
grin. Only Ramsay appeared unaffected by what had just transpired, brooding and dour as he turned his face toward the Ba'al
Shem, who now lifted both hands in the invocation that would
begin their serious night's work.

"*Boruch ato Adonai, Elohenu melekh haolam*. . . . Blessed art
Thou, O Lord our God, King of the Universe, Who hast sanctified
Thy great Name and hast revealed it to Thy pious ones to show its
power and might in the language, in the working of it, and in the
utterance of the mouth."

He paused to take up a pinch of incense from the bowl beside
the brazier, casting it on the glowing charcoal within.

"We offer up this work by Thy holy Names: By *Yod He Vau He.
Adonai Tzabaoth. Eh-Ei-He. Agla. Adonai Ha-Aretz. Shaddai El Chai.
Elohim Tzabaoth. Ruach Elohim. Kadosh*. . . .

He intoned the names, he did not just say them, savoring each
syllable in its fullest measure, drawing out the sounds. With each
new name he cast another pinch of incense onto the brazier. The
scent of frankincense and myrrh filled the air, underlaced with the
spicier sweetness of cinnamon, heady and potent.

Arabella could feel the web of energy building upon the drone of
words, the swirl of smoke, the focus of all present. In the watery
blue light the incense smoke seemed to meander gently upward in
a lazy spiral, softly dispersing against an invisible umbrella form
that could not be seen save by where the smoke was turned.

Lulled by the drone of his words, she let her vision go unfocused, sensed a skewing of her faculties that at once blurred and
sharpened all senses as her mind detached from the sights and
sounds and smells around her. Her head grew heavy on her neck,
weaving slightly, entranced by the random ebb and flow of the
smoke, heady with the air's sweet scent.

Not only the air was responding to his invocation. In her lap,
between her two hands, Angus Murray's snuffbox seemed to grow
colder. As she let her gaze drift toward it, she could see the chill
sheen of the silver, felt the damp slick of condensation under her
fingers.

"I now send forth my call unto the spirit world," said the Ba'al Shem, beginning the actual summoning. "I conjure and command thee, O spirit of the man known as Angus Murray, by Him who spake and it was done, by the names *Adonai, Elohim, Tzabaoth.*" Again he cast incense on the brazier with each of the holy names. "Come at once from wherever thou now dwellest and answer my questions, for thou art conjured by the Name of the Everlasting, Living, and True God. . . ."

He continued to summon the spirit of Angus Murray, shifting easily between Hebrew and English, his voice growing in intensity, though its volume remained steady. The air now was heavy with incense, all but aglow in the watery blue light, the sweetness of the frankincense and cinnamon tempered by the myrrh, lending counterpoint to the languid, slightly dizzying detachment slowly coming over Arabella.

She was not aware when Falk stopped his chanting; only that silence suddenly enveloped her, close and muffling but somehow comforting as well. Her eyes sought him through the incense haze and found him still standing behind the brazier, but her lids were very heavy. It took a great deal of effort to bring him into focus, more effort to fathom that he was looking beyond her, his lips parted in anticipation. And in her peripheral sight she suddenly realized that the rest of them were staring directly behind and above her. She wanted to turn her head to look, but she could not seem to summon up the will to do so.

"He comes not in body," Falk breathed, slowly lifting both hands in a gesture both of protection and command. "Fear not, Spirit, for we mean you no harm. Nor will we suffer you to harm any present. There was that which was left unfinished when you departed this sphere. You sought to impart certain knowledge to this man." He indicated Ramsay, sitting white-faced and rigid beside her.

"The one before you has the gift of tongues and can serve as voice, if you wish to speak," Falk went on, opening his hands toward Arabella in a gesture of offering. "She is willing, if ye swear by the name of Adonai to do her no harm, and to go when I command it. Is this your intent and true endeavor?"

Arabella could hear and feel nothing behind her save a vague tingling of the air, but Falk's face seemed to relax a little, as did the others.

"He gives the pass signs of a Master Mason," Falk murmured. "I take that as a sign that he stands by his previous obligation as our brother. Sister, if you are willing to proceed, I bid you offer up what was his."

She could feel the snuffbox tingling in her closed hands. She closed her eyes. She had known Murray slightly and had no reason to fear him, especially with his Obligation reaffirmed, but she had no idea what to expect in the present circumstance. Trusting that Falk and the others would allow her to come to no harm, she commended her soul to the keeping of The Great Architect and slowly opened her hands to offer up the snuffbox.

A dull buzz began to vibrate at the base of her skull and then to spread throughout her body, along with a lethargy she no longer had any will to resist. After a few seconds her chin lifted slightly of its own volition and her eyelids fluttered and then opened, but she seemed to see through a heavy veil.

"*I . . . am here,*" she said, though the whispered words were muffled in her ears, of deeper timbre than her own voice, and some outside agency stirred her lips.

"What is your name?" Falk demanded.

"*Murray . . . ,*" came the labored answer. "*Second . . . Artillery . . .*"

"It's him! It's Angus!" Ramsay murmured, subsiding at Andrew's sharp glance.

"Do you acknowledge the power of Adonai and affirm in word the oaths you have sworn before His altar in another place?" Falk persisted.

"*I do.*"

"Then, speak. This vessel is untried, her capacity unknown."

Arabella felt her face turn slightly toward Ramsay, the words from her mouth coming muffled through her dulled perception. It did not occur to her to worry whether Falk's comment hinted at some danger to herself.

"*James,*" the name whispered from her lips. "*So much . . . should have told before. . . .*"

"Then tell me now!" Ramsay dared to blurt. "Angus, we have

traveled many weeks to be here and are eager to recover the gold for the King. Where may it be found?"

"*New York . . . two oaken chests. . . . This way . . . too diffi-cult.*" Arabella felt her head gently turn from side to side. "*The coin . . . must point. . . .*"

"What does he mean, 'The coin must point'?" Ramsay murmured.

Arabella felt herself draw breath, a dizziness making her reel as she clutched tightly at the snuffbox.

"Murray, the vessel tires," Falk said, watching her closely. "Is there no way to speed this telling?"

"*Aye . . . but it will seal . . . the knowledge . . . to her alone. 'Tis burden . . . I would spare. . . . Have you . . . stronger vessel?*"

"There is none available at this time," Falk replied. "Does the burden offer danger?"

"*None. But she must go . . . with those . . . who seek out the gold.*"

The prince leaned closer, his voice softly interposing. "This is acceptable," he said. "Seal the knowledge. I believe she would agree. Andrew?"

Vaguely Arabella was aware of their words, of the sense of them, and knew that the prince had spoken her truly. At the same time, she felt her thumbs prying at the lid of the snuffbox, then probing inside to make contact with the gold coin fixed to the bottom.

"*Amin, Selah, so be it!*" she heard Falk declare.

She closed her eyes as the coin grew suddenly cold beneath her two thumbs, a subtle tingling slowly spreading up her arms and into all her extremities. She set her teeth as the tingling intensified, her head snapping back as power suddenly surged up her spine to fountain at the base of her skull in an exquisite wave of giddiness that overwhelmed all other sensation before it drew her down into sweet oblivion.

She came to her senses with a start, recoiling from the pungent goad of smelling salts that someone was holding under her nose. Her hand lifted to push it away, even as her gaze sought out the person responsible.

"Easy, lass."

It was Ramsay who ministered to her, Andrew watching from behind and to one side of him. Both looked concerned, but not overly so. As she jerked her head aside again to avoid the smelling salts, wrinkling her nose in distaste, she realized she was back in Dr. Falk's library, stretched out on a chaise longue. Across the room, at one end of a food-laden hunt table, Falk and the prince were bent over something she could not see. Beyond them, steam wafted upward from a large blue-and-white lidded tureen surrounded by several domed silver covers, the aroma of a rich beef stew reminding Arabella of her fast of the past day.

"Don't sit up too quickly," Ramsay said, easing a helping arm behind her and setting a glass of red wine in her hand. "Drink some of this."

"What is it?"

"Just wine. How do you feel?"

She drank down about half the wine and gave the glass back.

"I'm fine," she murmured. "I must have fainted."

Andrew eased Ramsay aside and sat beside her, taking one of her hands in his as Falk and the prince drifted back to gaze down at her.

"How much do you remember?" Andrew asked.

"All, up to the moment I passed out," she said. "But the details are hazy once Angus Murray began to speak through me." She swallowed. "Did he—tell what was needed?"

"In a manner of speaking," the prince said. "Hold out your hand."

She obeyed without hesitation, blinking as he pressed a small gold coin into her palm. It tingled slightly, and she suddenly knew what it was.

"This came from the snuffbox," she said, closing it in her hand at his nod of confirmation. "He did something to it, didn't he?"

Falk handed her the snuffbox as well.

"He was very clever, your Angus Murray," he said. "He sensed that your link to him was fragile, your being but new to mediumship, so he imbued the coin with—vibrations from its fellows, the

other coins in the hoard buried in New York. I can make you the
loan of an amulet that will amplify these vibrations.

"But first we must eat," he said, laying a hand on the prince's
arm and gesturing for Andrew to help Arabella to her feet. "Food
and drink will refresh us. We are all light-headed from fasting."

Over food they discussed what had happened and what might be
expected when they returned to America. Falk disappeared briefly
but soon returned bearing a carved wooden box the size of two
fists.

"New York was still under British occupation when we left," the
prince was saying, refilling his glass from a crystal decanter. "Until
Clinton pulls out, trying to recover the gold will be extremely
risky."

"Well, it does us no good until it *is* recovered," Ramsay said.
"We may have to risk infiltrating occupied territory."

"That risk will have to be weighed when we know more about
the current situation," Andrew said. "Moving prematurely could
put the gold into the hands of the British—which would not serve
any of our interests."

"You will find nothing without the guidance of the coin," Falk
said pointedly, setting the wooden box on the table before them,
"and for that you must take Madame Arabella into whatever danger may prevail. She is not yet strong in reading such guidance, but
this should help."

He opened the wooden box and reached into the folds of a white
silk handkerchief inside to extract the end of a substantial chain of
dull silvery metal. Dangling from the end of the chain was an iron
ring set with an oval lapis lazuli the size of a man's thumbnail.

"I shall require the return of the talisman when your mission is
completed," Falk said, rolling the end of the chain between thumb
and forefinger so that its pendant turned in the candlelight. "I shall
devise a mounting for the coin so that it may be suspended on the
same chain. Together, the two should provide a powerful indicator
to lead you to the gold. As an extra measure, to keep the link as
strong as possible, I should also carry the snuffbox on my person, if
I were you."

"But how—?" Arabella began.

"I shall instruct you when you return to collect it; I cannot do

the work tonight," Falk said. "Once the talisman has been keyed to you, and the coin to it, you will find it quite simple to use. Needless to say, it will show nothing in any other's hands. That assumes, of course, that there is something there to show," he added. "It could well be that others have been there before you."

A sudden silence fell upon them.

"What do you mean?" Ramsay said.

"Simply that some years have passed since the gold was hidden," Falk said. "It is conceivable that Murray's father may have told others of its location. I refrained from mentioning this before the working, lest doubt undermine your focus."

After a moment of stunned silence, Andrew said, "Then why did you help us?"

Falk shrugged. "Because you asked it for the sake of the poor widow's son. Because Saint-Germain spoke in your behalf. And in the hope that you might find my assistance worth a modest commission, if the gold is recovered," he conceded, with a tiny smile. "We shall discuss this further when you return for the talisman and coin. For now, I think we all shall benefit from rest, to let tonight's work settle in our minds. I shall have my servant summon a carriage."

They collected the talisman with its pendant coin two days later. Two days after that, they crossed the Channel to Amsterdam, where Andrew and Ramsay set about arranging return transport to America while the prince took horse for Paris, to deliver the last of Eli Levi's letters. He had hoped to see Lafayette but learned from Franklin that the marquis temporarily had been posted to Le Havre by the King.

"Gilbert views it as a trial," Franklin told him, "but in fact, it is a measure of his success. As you probably know, there were plans all through the summer and well into the fall for France to attempt an invasion of England. If that had occurred, 'tis said that Lafayette would have been appointed to lead the vanguard."

"Then he is back in favor," the prince said.

Franklin allowed himself a grim chuckle as he polished at his spectacles with a clean handkerchief.

"He continues to be headstrong and single-minded, but the stories of his valor in America have not gone unnoticed. Shortly following his return, the Queen saw to it that he received a promotion from captain to colonel. After that he was allowed to purchase a regiment of the King's Dragoons. If the invasion had gone forward, he was hoping to win himself further glory; but in his defense I should say that he has continued to badger anyone who will listen—and many who will not—regarding funds and other support for the American war."

"And has he been successful?"

Franklin shrugged. "Who can say what specific action has caused what specific result? At least young Gilbert's enthusiasm has never been in question. Meanwhile, the French government has all but promised a proper expedition in the spring—though I expect that Lafayette will return as an American officer; they won't give him command of the expedition."

"I doubt he really expects that," the prince said with a smile. "It will be enough just to be reunited with his beloved general. But poor Gilbert. How he must have chafed, these past months, to be banished to Le Havre, while exciting things happened elsewhere."

Franklin chuckled again. "Hardly an arduous banishment, unless one is twenty-one and eager that life not pass one by. But the appointment has not been entirely without compensation. His young wife is expected to present him with another child sometime in December. And there was a bright reminder of former glory a few months ago, when my grandson finally was able to deliver the sword awarded by Congress."

"Ah, the diamond-studded prize," the prince said.

"Indeed." Franklin shook his head bemusedly. "But in all, I am pleased with young Gilbert's progress—which is well, because I understand that conditions are still precarious in America."

"And may well grow worse before they grow better," the prince replied. "We can but carry on and trust that we will be guided as is meant to be."

He had already received some additional guidance. Franklin had given the prince letters from himself to Washington and Simon, but also a letter received but days before, inscribed to Dr. Rohan c/o Dr. Franklin, that bore the seal of Saint-Germain.

"We're to inform him when the gold has been found," the prince told his companions the night before they were to sail from Amsterdam. "He will direct what happens next."

"Did he say anything about a contact with Falk?" Andrew asked. "*Was* there a contact?"

The prince managed a faint smile. "He did not say. Nor did I expect that he would. It will be very interesting to see how events unfold."

Chapter Twenty-three

T hey arrived back in Philadelphia in mid-December, traveling on immediately to Morristown, where Washington
again had established his winter headquarters, this time in
the gracious Ford mansion. Martha Washington had already taken
up winter residence, for the previous season's campaigning had
been light. Washington had never fought a battle, though there
was activity in the Southern Department.

The four of them met Simon and Justin over supper in a private
room at the Old Freeman Tavern, on the north side of the village
green, reporting details of all that had transpired and what they
planned to do next. Later, when Arabella had retired to her room
at a nearby inn to share a more intimate reunion with her husband,
she confided her ongoing concerns about Ramsay.

"He's putting on a very earnest face, but I'm convinced he has
his own plans that he isn't sharing with any of the rest of us. I think
even Falk may have sensed that something was not quite right.
Several times he seemed to make a point of reminding us that only
I could read the directing of the coin and talisman. I almost had the
feeling he feared that James might try to take it and recover the
gold on his own."

Simon played with a tendril of her raven hair, part of his mind still preoccupied from their earlier pleasures.

"It sounds unlikely that he can actually do that," he murmured, "though he might try to bolt with the gold once you've found it. I'd rather have Saint-Germain's guidance before we let him do that, but I do have one contingency plan in reserve, involving Justin; and I have little doubt where James will take the gold if he does seize it. Besides, you could track it with your coin and talisman, in any case," he added with a smug glance.

She laughed mirthlessly. "You seem to have a great deal of faith in abilities I've never even used," she said.

"I have great faith in all your abilities," he replied, passion again stirring him as he bent to nibble kisses along the curve of her throat. "That includes your ability to bewitch your husband."

"Simon, we need to talk about James—"

"Not now," he whispered. "He can't do anything until you've found the gold."

Simon spent most of the next week sounding out the situation in New York, for recent military intelligence suggested that the British might be preparing for a major offensive elsewhere. If General Clinton pulled troops from the New York area, the risk in going behind the British lines to search out the gold would be considerably reduced. Though Ramsay chafed with the delay, even he agreed that a few weeks would make little difference.

Meanwhile, lest the time be entirely wasted, he and Andrew set about compiling the most accurate maps of New York that could be made, with Justin gleaning several to copy from the papers regarding Washington's campaign of 1776. Arabella let herself be persuaded to try out the techniques Falk had taught her over a map of the general New York area, but the talisman seemed to indicate that the gold lay almost squarely in the center of the area of heaviest British occupation. The information was tantalizing, but not enough to risk an immediate foray into enemy territory—especially if the new year might bring a lessening of the British presence in that area.

Their patience was rewarded. Clinton made his move on De-

cember 26, sailing from New York Harbor in relative calm with a
fleet of some ninety transports and fourteen warships, carrying
some seventy-six hundred men bound for Charleston. The departure was duly noted and express riders sent south to warn General
Benjamin Lincoln, but fierce winter storms were already lashing
the eastern seaboard by the time Washington received the news in
Morristown.

Aware that the weather would hamper British progress southward—and perhaps prevent it altogether—Washington shifted his
concern to the worsening conditions at Morristown, as winter set
in with a vengeance. Temperatures plummeted as the old year
wound toward its close, and food and clothing were in ever shorter
supply. Most reluctantly, Washington began to consider measures
he had always rejected in the past: to commandeer supplies from
the surrounding area. But he could not allow his army to starve.

On the last day of the old year, hoping to boost morale, he
attended the Festival of St. John's Day at American Union Lodge
in Morristown. Simon was among those who attended with him.

Afterward, when everyone else had retired, the two of them retreated to the General's office and drank the best part of a bottle of
very fine brandy while they reminisced about the times they had
shared as Freemasons over the past five years. Though their conversation was far ranging, touching on Lafayette's initiation and
even skirting close to Justin's occasional function as a very special
kind of Tyler, Washington never once alluded to his dream.

But he did drink Arabella's health, shortly before bidding Simon
a somewhat less than steady good night. Long after the General
had gone up to bed, Simon sat finishing the bottle and wondered
how matters were progressing in New York, where his Freemason
wife was embarked upon an unorthodox and very dangerous game.

She had gone north with Andrew, Ramsay, and the prince as
soon as the British fleet sailed. Shortly after the new year the four
of them infiltrated British-occupied Manhattan and took accommodations very near the area indicated by Arabella's map work.
The owners of the house were loyalists who, until the departure of
the fleet a fortnight before, had billeted several British officers as a
means of supplementing their income. With the winter deepening,

and the availability of supplies dwindling with the lessened British presence, they were glad to have paying tenants to supplement their income. Andrew and Arabella posed as father and daughter, sharing a large room on the second floor in the back. The prince and Ramsay occupied a room adjacent, with Justin joining them after a few days.

Narrowing the focus of their search took most of a week, for they could work but slowly, lest their movements arouse suspicion. The prince must take particular care not to be recognized, for he had served as a British surgeon and might be taken as a deserter. To change his appearance, he had dyed his ginger hair black.

Each day saw them trolling up and down the streets in a closed carriage, stopping periodically for Arabella to employ the coin and talisman. Their driver was the son of one of the prince's financial contacts, and well paid not to ask questions.

The procedure varied but little. Flanked by Andrew and the prince, with Justin consulting their maps and Ramsay poised to relay instructions to the driver, Arabella would hold the end of the talisman's iron chain and concentrate on the gold coin suspended beside the piece of lapis lazuli, bidding the coin to incline toward the others hidden away by Angus Murray's father.

Within seconds the double pendulum would begin swinging in a particular orientation, though always with a slightly stronger inclination in one direction or another. Always its swinging pointed them toward a center point that did not change, no matter how they approached it. On the day they narrowed its prompting to a single building, she watched it as she had so many times, then drew a resolute breath.

"Have the driver head off to the right at the first opportunity," she said to Ramsay, not taking her eyes from the coin.

The order was given and the carriage lurched forward, wheels muffled in the snow. They had been working their way closer to the area worst burned out during the fire of 1776, praying that their search would not take them into the canvas town of tents and lean-tos that still sheltered many of the inhabitants of New York. At length their meanderings led them along a side street past a faded and somewhat dilapidated two-story frame house whose un-

kempt front garden and shuttered and boarded-up windows pro-claimed it long unoccupied.

By now Arabella had learned to feel the tug of the pendulum as well as to see it, when she concentrated on the coin and the rest of the gold. Bidding Ramsay tell the driver to make a great circle around the block the house occupied, and to return to their start-ing point, she closed her eyes and let the pendulum dangle from her fingertips, feeling it incline always to the right as they circled the house in that direction.

"Unless I've been doing this entirely wrong, that has to be the place," she said, when the driver had nearly reached their starting point. "I don't think I can narrow it any closer without actually going in. We'll pray that the casks are in the house, not buried in the garden somewhere. The only way to know for certain is to go inside."

The prince chanced a look past the curtain over the carriage window and gave a slow nod. "We'll need a closer look at the surrounding area before we actually try to go in. The house looks abandoned, but the neighbors or a British patrol still might object to housebreaking."

"Justin and I can scout it on foot," Ramsay said, muffling a scarf more closely around his throat and preparing to disembark. "Meet us in about an hour, up by the crossroads. We'll bring you a full report."

The logic was sound. After brief discussion as to how the obser-vation would be divided, the two dismounted from the carriage and headed off casually in different directions. The prince watched them go, then instructed the driver to take Andrew and Arabella for a leisurely drive along the river while he made his own inspec-tion of the more general area around the house. They collected him an hour later, not far from where they had left him, then headed for the rendezvous site agreed by Ramsay and Justin.

"The front door is boarded up and much too exposed," Ramsay said, settling into his seat as the carriage lurched off. "However, there's an enclosed garden in the back, walled off and over-grown, and a back door opening onto a low porch. It's boarded up, too, but it doesn't look as formidable as the front."

"Any neighbors in the back?" the prince asked.

"One house," Ramsay replied, "but they'd need to be looking down into the garden from upstairs. The problem is that we may not be able to force that door. What looks far more promising is a boarded-up cellar window on the side where the alley runs. The adjacent house appears to be occupied, but there aren't many windows on that side."

"How exposed is it?" Andrew asked.

"Not very," Justin said. "There are weeds and a hedge obscuring it at ground level, and the angle would make it difficult to see anything from an upstairs window, unless one happened to be looking down just at the wrong time. The biggest drawback is that it's very small. I *think* I can get through; but the rest of you wouldn't stand a chance. Arabella would fit, but I don't know what she might have to contend with once she got in." He glanced at his sister. "If the door between the cellar and the rest of the house has to be forced, I don't know if you'd have the physical strength."

"I'm perfectly willing to let you try it," Arabella said with a smile. "I'm no longer the girl who used to climb trees with you when we were children."

"We'll leave it to Justin, then," the prince replied. "If necessary, we can always try to force the back door and pray that no one hears or sees."

"Pray that the snow keeps up, then," Andrew said. "It will cover our footprints and probably keep most folk inside. God knows it's cold enough already. We'll want to bring some shielded lanterns, as well. The shutters look relatively intact, but we still should be careful about showing lights inside."

The prince nodded. "We seem to have a workable plan, then. Let's go back to our quarters and get some rest while we can. We'll come back on foot, once it's well dark."

They gained access to the house without major mishap, though they had to resort to their backup plan of entering via the cellar window. The night was wind whipped and bitter cold, with snow falling heavily, the streets even more deserted than they had dared to hope. Gloved and well muffled in cloaks that also concealed a

shielded lantern and several pry bars, Ramsay and Justin crept along the alley and made their way into the back garden only to remove the boards from the back door and confirm that it could not be easily forced.

Back they went to the cellar window, which proved larger than anticipated once they got its boards off. While Ramsay kept nervous watch, it was a relatively simple matter for Justin to wriggle through, take the lantern Ramsay then handed him, and disappear into the inner darkness.

As soon as Justin was inside, Ramsay set about replacing the boards loosely over the window, then circled around to the rear to keep watch. The others were already huddled in a sheltered part of the back garden that could not be seen from the alley or the house behind. Ten minutes later the back door eased open a crack, and the low call of a barn owl floated briefly on the snow-muffled stillness.

It was the agreed signal. Immediately the prince glided up the steps and inside. When, after a few minutes, no alarm disturbed the silence, a second owl call briefly screeched and then was silent. A minute later Arabella eased her way along the edge of the garden, another shielded lantern under her cloak, and ghosted up the back steps and inside. Andrew followed a few minutes later, with Ramsay entering last and lingering to close the door and make the lock secure.

He found the others crouched in a small parlor whose only window, well shuttered, faced the house across the alley. The cold was bone chilling, even sheltered from the howling wind. The prince had unshuttered one of their lanterns far enough to cast a sullen pool of light directly onto the floor, where it was also screened by the dark-cloaked bulk of their bodies. By that light Arabella was drawing the talisman from around her neck, stripping off her right glove and blowing on her fingers to warm them, grasping the end of its chain between thumb and forefinger as she drew a breath and half closed her eyes.

The talisman seemed to move more erratically now that they were inside the house, sometimes quite strongly in a given direction, sometimes in tiny circles. It took them most of an hour and

two complete circuits of both the ground and first floors of the house to realize that their talisman was drawing them downward, toward the cellar level. Justin muttered under his breath as he led them down the steps—hardly more than a ladder with wide rungs—a shielded lantern in his hand. He had come this way to enter and perhaps had walked right over the gold.

Again he picked his way through the debris littering the earthen floor, feeling the cold suck the warmth through the soles of his boots, sweeping the lantern light from side to side as the rest gathered around Arabella, to see which way her talisman would move. It was the back wall of the basement, lined with battered paneling of tongue and groove boards, that seemed to draw her most strongly. As she held the iron chain alongside the wall, they could see the talisman and coin visibly incline in that direction, tapping lightly against the wood.

"Behind there?" Justin said softly.

"Only one way to find out," Andrew replied.

Eagerly Ramsay slid a narrow end of his pry bar into one of the cracks between the boards and bore down. The first board screeked as it began to move, so that he had to pause often lest the noise be heard outside. But as it came free and Justin worked loose a second board, the light of Andrew's lantern spilled into deeper darkness—and glinted on the metal-bound corner of something within.

Ramsay stifled a little cry and tried to contain his excitement as they continued working loose boards until the opening at last revealed the side of a wooden casket, perhaps a foot long and nearly as high, banded with iron. Grinning fiercely, he began to drag it out of the opening, Justin and the prince giving a hand while Arabella held the second lantern closer.

The weight of it was promising. As they pulled it free with difficulty and lowered it to the earthen floor—rather faster than intended, and hissing with the exertion—an ancient lock on the side away from them rattled against a sturdy-looking iron hasp. No sooner had the casket touched the ground than Ramsay's eager hands were all over it, stripping off his gloves to caress the ancient oak, to brush lightly the icy-cold lock. The wood was damp with green mildew, the lock red with rust. As Andrew bent for a closer look, holding his lantern nearer, its light shone into the space from which they had pulled it—and revealed a second casket.

"Look!" Arabella whispered. "There's another one!"

They were panting with their exertion by the time they manhandled the casket to the edge of the opening and carefully drew it free. It was even heavier than the first. Like the first lock, the second looked to be rusted solid. Ramsay was ready to apply a pry bar and try to break it, but the prince bade him wait and produced a tiny bottle of oil and a sliver of brass from somewhere inside his coat. Soon the first lock fell open in his hand. As he unhooked it from the hasp, he glanced at the others, then smiled and gestured pointedly for Arabella to do the honors.

Heart pounding, she slipped Dr. Falk's talisman around her neck for safekeeping and set both hands on the lid of the casket. It was heavy and moved stiffly; but as she slowly lifted it, then turned it fully back, the light of Andrew's lantern revealed the unmistakable gleam of gold.

"Prince Charlie's gold," Ramsay breathed, reverently reaching out to pick up one of the coins—a louis d'or that could have come directly from the royal mint at Paris, not from a casket hidden away for more than thirty years in the damp.

"Prince Charlie's gold, indeed," said Andrew, sitting heavily on the floor beside the casket, then pulling at a folded piece of paper that protruded from one side. "And what's this?"

He set down his lantern and unfolded the paper, holding it nearer the light. It was limp from the damp, and mildewed along the creases, but his face went very still as his eye skimmed down its length.

"Ah," he murmured. "Now *here* is something I have not seen for a very long time."

His hands trembled as he tilted it closer to the light, and Arabella, too, leaned closer to read aloud over his shoulder.

"It seems to be a proclamation," she said softly. " 'Whereas we have a near prospect of being restored to the Throne of our Ancestors . . . impossible for us to be in Person at the first setting up of our Royal Standard . . . therefore esteem it for our Service, and

the Good of our Kingdom and Dominions, to nominate and appoint our dearest Son CHARLES, Prince of Wales, to be sole
Regent of our Kingdoms of England, Scotland, and Ireland, and of
all our Dominions, during our Absence—' Dear God, it's a copy of
the prince's commission of regency," she murmured. "Listen to
this.

" 'It is our Will and Intention, That our said dearest Son should
enjoy and exercise all that Power and Authority, which, according
to the ancient Constitution of our Kingdoms, has been enjoyed
and exercised by former Regents. Requiring all our faithful Subjects to give all due Submission and Obedience to our Regent
aforesaid, as immediately representing our Royal Person, and acting by our Authority. And we do hereby revoke all Commissions of
Regency granted to any Person or Persons whatsoever. . . .
Given under our Sign-Manual and Privy-Signet, at our Court at
Rome, the Twenty-third Day of December 1743. In the Forty-
third Year of our Reign. J.R.' "

Ramsay had been quietly fingering a small handful of coins as
she read, the prince working on the second lock. Now, as the lock
fell away, Ramsay let his coins clink softly back into the first casket
and moved to lift the second lid. Another piece of folded paper lay
atop a second lot of new-minted golden coins. As Ramsay plucked
it out and hurriedly unfolded it, Arabella turned the lantern to give
him light.

"This one is different," he said, his eyes skimming over the text.
" 'James the Eighth, by the Grace of God King of Scotland, England, France, and Ireland, Defender of the Faith, etc. To all our
loving Subjects of what degree or Quality forever: Greeting.' " He
shook his head. "This is incredible. It's the manifesto announcing
what the King hopes to accomplish. I remember my father telling
me how they read these documents when they raised the royal
standard at Glenfinnan."

"I remember *hearing* them read," Andrew said quietly. He took
the copy of the regency proclamation from Arabella and gently ran
a fingertip over the print, blurred slightly from the damp.

"It was a Monday, the nineteenth of August, 1745. I remember
that day as vividly as I remember this morning's dawn, when our

prince was young and fair and our dream was bright with hope. I remember the waiting, as the first of us rallied to his presence at Glenfinnan, wondering whether anyone else would come."

His eye closed briefly, his mouth working as he remembered . . . and slowly began to speak again.

"I had joined the prince the day before, at Kinlochmoidart," he said softly. "I had ridden down from Banffshire with old Gordon of Glenbucket. He was seventy-two, a veteran of the Fifteen, but he'd brought one hundred fifty men for the prince's service, and several captured British prisoners. I remember his long gray hair and mustaches, and his antiquated armor—and his fierce devotion to the royal Stuart line. . . ."

His voice trailed off for a few seconds, but then he shook his head lightly and resumed, slowly refolding the copy of the regency proclamation, not seeing anything except the past.

"The prince had a personal bodyguard of fifty men from Clanranald, so we were two hundred when we reached Glenfinnan, at the head of Loch Shiel. MacDonald of Morar was waiting with another hundred fifty, but by four o'clock no others had appeared.

"Then, from beyond the gloom of the heathered hills, we heard the distant wail of pipes—a Cameron war pibroch—and soon Lochiel himself appeared, marching at the head of nearly eight hundred Camerons in their tartans and bonnets. MacDonald of Keppoch had brought another three hundred, and we felt the chills race up our spines as the two columns followed a zigzag path down the mountainside, the war pipes skirling and the men around us shouting their huzzahs."

Ramsay was listening in fascination, the manifesto all but forgotten in his hands, Justin likewise enchanted by the picture Andrew wove.

"And the Prince—what hope must have stirred in his breast as he watched them come," Andrew whispered. "He was twenty-four years old, and born to be our king—tall and handsome and fair, our bonnie prince, indeed. Later on he would adopt Highland dress, but on that day he wore a dun-colored coat with scarlet waistcoat and breeches, with a yellow bob on his hat.

"Someone brought the royal standard and placed it in his hands, and he gave it over to old Tulliebardine, who should have been Duke of Athole but had been attainted by the British for his part in the Fifteen. He was so crippled with rheumatism that he had to be supported by two attendants as he presented the banner to be blessed by Bishop Hugh MacDonald; but no power on earth could have induced him to give that honor to another. When he then unfurled the banner and raised it proudly above his head, the glen erupted to a chorus of huzzahs and shouted exclamations in Gaelic, and a jubilant schiming of blue bonnets that nearly blotted out the sky. *Prionnsa Tearlach Righ nan Ghaidheil!* they shouted. 'Prince Charles King of the Gael!'

"Then Tulliebardine read out the prince's commission of regency from his father," Andrew indicated the folded paper in his hand, "followed by the proclamation—that King James the Eighth of Scotland and the Third of England and Ireland was asserting his just rights to claim the throne of three kingdoms. After that Charles himself said a few words."

He smiled, a sad, wistful smile. "I doubt most of those present understood a great deal of what was said, for many spoke only the Gaelic, but there was no mistaking their cheers as they tossed their bonnets skyward again. I was with the Prince right through until Culloden and saw him welcome many victories, but never did I see him more cheerful than on that day. . . ."

His voice trailed off as he dipped deeper into memory, until Arabella gently laid a hand on his sleeve and said, "That was many years ago, Beau-père. For now perhaps we should see about getting the gold to safety, having found it. This place is not secure."

"Yes, of course." Swallowing, Andrew laid the folded proclamation back in one of the caskets and closed its lid, then gave it a tentative push to test the weight. It did not move until the prince added his strength to the effort.

"These are far too heavy for one man," the prince said, "and moving anything that requires two men to carry it will arouse suspicions. *Two* such burdens would certainly invite unwelcome interest. We would be taken for thieves in the night."

Justin sifted his fingers through the top layer of coins in the still-open cask, listening to the musical chiming that only gold could

make. "We could all fill our pockets," he said. "That would lighten both casks."

The prince shook his head. "They would still require two men—or many sacks."

"But we *will* need to divide it, in order to transport it," Andrew said. "I should have thought of this. I should have brought extra sacks. I suppose I must have doubted that we'd actually find it."

"We can still bring extra sacks," Ramsay said. "A couple of us can stay with the gold, and the rest go and get sacks and arrange for the carriage to be ready at a precise time. I'll stay."

"No, you are better acquainted with this area," Andrew said, speaking before the prince could reply. "I think it better if Justin and I stay. And Lucien, if you could see Arabella safely to our rooms, I shall be in your debt. You have done your part, my dear, and most admirably," he added at her beginning protest. "Without you we could not have found this. But now you must allow brawn to take over from beauty."

She agreed, if reluctantly. Very shortly she, the prince, and Ramsay were easing back up the creaking cellar stair, each carrying as much gold as could be accommodated easily—for that would ease their later task. When their footsteps no longer creaked on the floors above, Andrew gently raked his fingers through the gold remaining in the open casket, then glanced at Justin in the dim light of their single lantern.

"I have just taken a calculated risk which I hope I shall not regret," he said.

Justin gawped at him. "What do you mean?"

"I believe James has gone along with us because he had no other way to find the gold," Andrew replied. "From the start he has wanted to take the gold directly to Charles, if it could be found. When I allowed myself to reminisce about Glenfinnan, I very much fear that I may have rekindled his Jacobite hopes. It would not surprise me if he attempts to seize the gold, take it to Charles, and again offer him the Crown of America."

"Then why did you let him go?"

"I don't *know* that he will do as I suspect; but if I were James, I expect that I should be thinking about it."

Justin sighed, closing the lid on the open casket. "Can we stop him if he tries?"

"Perhaps. But it might put at risk those of us who are vital to the Master's plans for Washington. And I hesitate to take drastic measures against James himself without leave from Saint-Germain, since I do not know the ultimate plans for him."

"Then what can we do?" Justin asked. "What happens if he does try and we can't stop him?"

Andrew raised the eyebrow above his good eye. "That question has concerned me almost from the beginning," he said. "My concern became more focused on the voyage home. On three different nights, precisely a week apart, I dreamed the same dream. And we know from Washington's experience that the Master is capable of using dreams for guidance."

"You think *he* sent the dreams?" Justin whispered, wide-eyed. "And he knew that James would betray us?"

Andrew chuckled and shook his head. "Even we do not know that James will betray us," he replied. "But if he does—if he strikes out on his own and seizes the gold—I think it almost certain that he will take it to Charles. So long as we take certain precautions, that keeps it somewhat in our control. Now, here is what I have in mind."

Ramsay showed up two hours later with a bundle of sturdy homespun sacks under one arm and a shuttered lantern that he thrust cautiously into the darkened cellar from the doorway above. At the first hint of his approach—creaking floorboards above the whine of the wind outside—Andrew had shuttered their own lantern, he and Justin melting back into the shadows at the foot of the stair.

"Andrew?" came Ramsay's whispered query.

Immediately Andrew unshuttered his lantern to reveal himself and Justin. They had moved the two oak caskets into the center of the cellar, and Andrew had been sitting on one of them.

"We thought it best not to advertise our presence if the wrong folk should come poking around," he said as Ramsay joined them. "Where is Lucien?"

"He's seeing to the carriage," Ramsay replied, thrusting a hand-

ful of sacks into Justin's arms. "Let's parcel out the gold into these—no heavier than one man can carry without being obvious. We debated several methods of getting the gold out, but dividing it still seemed the best way. The caskets can go out last, lightened to the point that they can also be carried by one man each, hidden under a cloak. We shouldn't waste too much time."

"You're probably right," Andrew murmured as he bent to help Justin and Ramsay begin shifting the gold into the sacks.

They worked in silence for several minutes, only the musical clink of the coins disturbing the hush of the cellar. After a little while Justin shook his head, a faint smile stirring at his lips.

"Prince Charlie's gold," he mused. "If only it could have come to him in time, back in 'Forty-Five."

"I don't see why it shouldn't go to him *now*," Ramsay muttered.

"That is not for us to decide," Andrew replied.

"And who better than his loyal supporters?" Ramsay said, pausing to glare at Andrew. "By what right does Saint-Germain presume to decide on its disposition? It doesn't belong to him; it belongs to Charles Edward Stuart, the King we have all sworn to uphold."

"I would not presume to argue its ownership," Andrew said mildly, tying up the neck of a sack. "But if the King is to be restored, it will be accomplished at least partially through the offices of Saint-Germain, who is a very powerful patron. That gives him every right to be consulted, at least, regarding its disposition. And better to do that by correspondence rather than by dragging the gold itself across an ocean, when it may well be needed here, in the end."

"To give it to Washington?" Ramsay pulled a sullen scowl. "I cannot believe that after all these years of loyalty to the Stuart line, you would abandon our lawful prince—"

"But no one is abandoning our lawful prince," Justin said reasonably. "The gold has been lost for thirty-five years. Will another few months—"

"How many months does he *have*?" Ramsay retorted. "I say take the gold to him now and let *him* decide." With sudden decision he pulled a pistol from his pocket. "That's what I intend to do—and I don't think either of you want to try to stop me."

Justin froze, glancing anxiously between Ramsay and Andrew, and the latter slowly raised his hands to chest level. They both had been caught on their knees.

"I wondered whether it would come to this," Andrew said softly. "James, where is Lucien?"

Smiling nervously, Ramsay pulled a small coil of rope out of a pocket and tossed it to Justin. "I left him bound and gagged in his room. Arabella is asleep. I'm afraid she needed a bit of encouragement, in the form of a sleeping draft. When she wakes up, she'll release Lucien and they'll come and release you as well. I left a note in his pocket." He jerked his chin toward Justin. "Tie his hands, and do a good job of it."

"And then you'll tie me up, too?" Justin asked, a faint quaver in his voice.

"I'd rather take you along," Ramsay replied. "I think you still share the dream. But I won't hesitate to leave you trussed up as well. Which is it to be?"

"You'd let me come along?" Justin murmured, wide-eyed.

"Justin, don't!" Andrew said sharply.

"Justin is quite able to make his own decisions!" Ramsay snapped, glancing nervously over his shoulder. "Cluny, are you up there?"

For answer, a big man in a dark cloak came down the stairs and into the lantern light, followed by a bandy-legged smaller man with a second lantern and another coil of rope. The first man produced a stout cudgel from under his cloak, and both had pistols stuck in their waistbands.

"You daren't fire," Andrew said, calmly returning his one-eyed gaze to Ramsay. "You'd bring down the British on all our heads."

"If I must, I'll gamble that one shot won't be heard in the storm," Ramsay replied. "Or if they hear it, they won't be able to locate it. Justin, make up your mind. Do you tie him up and come with us, or does Cluny knock you on the head and he and Archie tie up both of you?"

"Cluny, I expected better of you!" Andrew said sharply as the other moved a step closer, eyeing Justin as he tapped his cudgel purposefully against his other hand. "Could you not have waited?"

"Seems like we've waited too long already, Chevalier," the man

replied. "We figure our mistake the last time was in sending the King a letter. This time we aim to go in person and sweeten the offer with the gold. What do you say, Justin?"

As Cluny's partner set down his lantern and began shaking out his coil of rope, Justin swallowed nervously, then eased slowly to his feet and awkwardly began straightening out the rope Ramsay had tossed him.

"I'm sorry, Andrew. I have to do this. If you'd seen him recently—how sad he was, how bereft of hope—"

A sob caught in his throat, but he bit it off angrily and came to pull one of Andrew's arms behind him, binding him with brisk efficiency, avoiding the older man's gaze. Andrew did not resist, only regarding Ramsay with something that might have been pity.

The smaller man, Archie, murmured an apology as he tied Andrew's feet, pulling his cloak more closely around him before rolling him onto his side so that ankles and wrists could be lashed together. When they were done, Ramsay thrust his pistol into his waistband and produced a pair of handkerchiefs, one of which he stuffed into Andrew's mouth before tying the other around his head to keep the first in place.

"I'm sorry we've had to do this, Andrew," Ramsay said quietly as his two henchmen helped him turn Andrew to face the wall. "I hope you don't get too cold while you're waiting. Next time we meet, I hope to be speaking for King Charles of America."

Ramsay soon left with Justin and the two Bostonians, each of them apparently carrying a small sack of gold. Andrew knew they would be back for the rest, so he made only a tentative testing at his bonds, but he was not surprised to find that all the knots were secure and beyond his reach.

He heard them come back twice more before they took out all the gold. He thought two or three more men might have joined them to assist, but he could not be certain. Someone put a blanket over him before they left the last time, but no one spoke to him.

Once they had gone for good, he tried not to doze, for he feared falling asleep in the cold and freezing to death, but it was difficult after the first hour or so, especially in the dark, and with wrists and ankles already numb from being bound. The whine of the wind gradually died down, but the cold did not diminish. He roused sluggishly some little while later at the sound of intruders making their stealthy way across the squeaking floorboards upstairs.

The narrow beam of a shielded lantern soon came probing down the stair, followed by cautious footsteps. He kept very still until low voices confirmed the newcomers to be Arabella and the prince. Then he grunted to attract their attention and tried to wiggle under his shrouding blanket.

Arabella bit back an exclamation and flew to his side, her gloved fingers tugging at the gag. The prince approached more slowly and grimaced as he dropped to his knees to cut the ropes binding Andrew's wrists. A bruise shadowed his left temple.

"You were certainly right about Ramsay," he muttered, wincing as the rope parted and his whole body rocked backward slightly. He steadied himself against Andrew's shoulder and paused briefly to press the back of his knife hand to the bruise, grimacing again before shifting to cut the ropes still binding Andrew's ankles. "Are you all right?"

Andrew spit out the last of the gag and nodded, himself gasping through clenched teeth as Arabella helped him sit and he brought his arms from back to front to rub his wrists where the ropes had chafed.

"I'll be fine," he murmured. "And I can see that Arabella seems to have suffered little harm. What about you? Did you really need to make your part so convincing?"

"Believe me, it was not my decision," the prince said sourly, still sawing at the ankle ropes. "He certainly wasted no time once he decided to bolt. I gather that Justin went with him?"

Andrew nodded, groaning and stretching out his legs as the prince freed his feet and circulation began to return.

"Aye, and he'll need to be very, very careful. James is no simpleton, nor the men with him."

"That much is certain," the prince said. "Clearly, he had planned this in advance. He even took the talisman, so that it could not be used to track him. Do you know who they were?"

"Aye, two of them, at least," Andrew replied. "I saw only Cluny Richardson and Archibald Campbell, but several more came to help carry away the gold. I would guess that he has at least half a dozen or so, if he hopes to get the gold away safely."

He let the prince help him to his feet, leaning on both him and Arabella as circulation slowly returned.

"We must return to Philadelphia as quickly as possible and book passage on the first available ship. I shall also send word to Simon regarding what's happened. I should like to bring him with us, but we dare not leave Washington unguarded."

"Does he *need* guarding, through the winter?" Arabella asked, collecting Andrew's walking stick and pressing it into his hands. "Morristown should be safe enough, and he has his bodyguards."

"But no one else in whom he can confide regarding what has been building these five years," Andrew replied, letting them help him toward the cellar stair. "I sense that what James has done may affect what is planned for the General. No, Simon must stay. It is Justin on whom much now depends."

Chapter Twenty-four

Justin knew they were watching him closely for the first few days after leaving New York, so he was especially careful to do nothing that might make them doubt the sincerity of his apparent defection. A total of four more Bostonians besides Cluny and Archie had aided in the removal of the gold from New York, all of them well-known to Justin, most of them signatories to the original offer that Ramsay had made to Charles Edward Stuart in 1775. They were wary of him when they first started back to Boston; but when he made no attempt to stop them or flee or communicate outside their immediate circle, everyone began to relax a little.

He did his best to encourage their confidence and to convince them that he shared their single-mindedness. One night, affecting overindulgence in drink, he let himself be drawn into a maudlin reminiscence of his face-to-face meeting with Charles Edward Stuart—for none of the rest had ever actually met the King. By the time they set sail for France, the gold now repacked in two well-trussed oaken casks amid their baggage, he had half convinced himself that he really was the ardent Jacobite they believed him to be, ready to set aside loyalties even to family, in the furtherance of the Stuart cause.

They made port at Marseilles late in February, and reached Florence in early March. The day was cold, but bright with the promise of the coming spring. Riding up the Via San Sebastiano in the carriage they had hired to carry their baggage—especially the two casks of gold—Justin cast a covert glance at James Ramsay, sitting anxiously at his side. The casks lay under their seat. Four of the Bostonians were riding ahead of the carriage and two behind, all well armed with pistols at saddlebows and swords at hips. All of the men sported white cockades in their tricorns, even the driver hired with the carriage.

Justin kept silent as they drove through the colonnaded entrance to the Palazzo San Clemente and pulled up in the courtyard, though he was as impressed as the rest of them. Several grooms came running to see to the horses, and the Bostonians moved quickly to take charge of the oaken casks as Ramsay and Justin disembarked from the carriage. Ramsay led them briskly up the front steps as a butler appeared from between the double front doors.

"We have come from America to see His Majesty," he said as the Bostonians began to congregate behind him, two pairs of them struggling with the casks. "Please ask if he will receive us."

When the butler displayed some uncertainty over the English, Justin repeated the request in French. Immediately the man bowed them inside, conducting them through a fine entrance hall painted in the Pompeian manner. Above the door leading into the remainder of the house was rendered a lavish depiction of the British Royal Arms, retaining the fleur-de-lis of France but omitting the detested white horse of Hanover. A thistle and a rose flanked the traditional supporters of lion and unicorn, and above was painted the King's own name and style: *Carolus III Mag. Britaniae et Hib. Rex*, and the date of his accession, *1766*.

Through a succession of airy and elegant salons the servant led them, under the scrutiny of frescoed heroes, gods, and goddesses who lounged amid classical landscapes or peered down from trompe l'oeil balconies. After ascending a wide stone staircase, they found themselves at last admitted to a more intimate reception chamber that was a departure from the classical splendor of the rest

of the palace, hung with crimson damask and with family portraits gazing down from lavish gilt frames.

At the far end, flanked by golden doors, a gold-and-crimson canopy of state overhung a gilded chair set thronelike on a small riser. Behind the throne a rich tapestry again displayed the rightful Stuart arms as King of Scotland, England, France, and Ireland. A silk rug covered the riser, another larger one spread directly before it, covering most of the white marble floor.

"Attendez ici, messieurs, s'il vous plaît," the butler said, before withdrawing.

The minutes lengthened into half an hour, punctuated by the ticking of an ormolu clock on the mantel of a white marble fireplace along the right side of the room. Ramsay directed the placement of the casks slightly behind him, flanked by his Bostonians, and fidgeted. Justin kept his own sober counsel, well aware what was likely to occur once the King emerged, if all had gone according to plan.

The golden door to the left of the throne opened. First to appear was the King's longtime manservant, John Stewart, followed by the King himself. Another retainer brought up the rear: Saint-Germain's servant, the faithful Rheinhardt, though no one in the room besides Justin would be aware of that.

Allowing himself to relax just a little, Justin turned his full attention on the King, who slowly made his way to the riser and its waiting throne. He had aged considerably since Justin last had seen him, and the intervening years had not been kind. His black suit was of fashionable cut, the smallclothes of a dazzling whiteness against the light blue of his Garter sash, but the familiar face was puffy and drawn beneath its formal wig, the brown eyes tired and lusterless. A slight stoop accompanied his gait as he made to mount the riser, leaning on John Stewart's arm, but suddenly recognizing Justin, his face brightened and he changed direction.

"Mr. Carmichael, how very pleasant to see you again," he said, holding out his hand in greeting.

Emotion choked at the back of Justin's throat as he knelt to kiss the royal hand, and he had to work at recovering his composure as he rose, bowing again.

"Your Majesty is kind to remember," he murmured. "May I present my companions? This is Dr. James Ramsay, from Boston."

Ramsay, too, knelt, ducking his head over the royal hand, then proceeded to introduce the other awestruck Bostonians, who also had sunk to their knees. Charles moved graciously among them, giving each his hand and inquiring about their connections with the Jacobite cause, finally moving back to let himself be handed up the riser so he could take his seat. When he had done so, and at his gracious gesture, all of them rose. Justin had faded to one side as the King moved among the others, well content to let Ramsay have center stage for now.

"Gentlemen, this demonstration of your loyalty brings unexpected pleasure to an old man," the King said quietly as Rheinhardt and the other servant took up posts to either side of him. "Would that I might have given you greater cause, in these years since your fathers gave so much for me in our beloved Scotland. How may I serve you today?"

Visibly bracing himself, Ramsay took a step forward and bowed nervously.

"Sire, half a decade ago I and several others present were among those who offered you a Crown in America. In your wisdom you chose to decline it at that time, but we come now to extend that offer once again. Come to America and become our sovereign Stuart prince, and from there direct the redemption of your Kingdom of Scotland from the British usurpers."

"A generous offer, Dr. Ramsay," the King replied. "But what makes this offer different from the previous one? We all are five years older now, and alas, no nearer to recovery of the rightful Crown of my ancestors."

Boldly moving to the foot of the riser, Ramsay dropped to one knee in entreaty.

"Sire, early in 1746, just before Culloden, word reached Scotland of French gold finally on its way to aid your cause," he said. "Alas, it arrived too late for that venture, but some of your loyal followers took charge of it, to keep against the day when another attempt might be made. I speak of the forty thousand louis d'or buried by Archibald Cameron at Loch Arkaig, only part of which

was ever recovered, and for the loss of which several honest men were accused unjustly of having taken it for their own purposes."

"There was much confusion in those times," Charles said neutrally.

"Indeed, Sire. What was little known is that approximately half the gold was taken to the New World and hidden there, against the time when Your Majesty might be persuaded to use it for another attempt to take back your Crown. Recently, on his deathbed, the son of one of the men responsible was able to give us information regarding the whereabouts of that gold. We here present it to Your Majesty—nearly twenty thousand louis d'or—and pray that this will serve as added inducement to join your loyal subjects in America, and a means to mount a successful assault against the British usurpers."

As he gestured behind him, two Bostonians raised the lids of both casks to reveal the bright glitter of gold. At the same time, Ramsay reached into his coat and produced a folded piece of yellowed paper, which he extended to the King.

"We found this in one of the caskets, Sire," he said, handing it to Charles. "I believe Your Majesty will find it of interest."

It was the proclamation of Charles's regency. The King put on the spectacles that John Stewart handed him and scanned down the faded print, his face going very still. When he had finished reading, obviously much moved, he folded the document carefully and handed it back to Ramsay, his gaze shifting again to the casks and the men kneeling hopefully around them. In silence he removed his spectacles and gave them back to Stewart. His halting movement showed his years as he slowly stood, gesturing for Ramsay to rise.

"I should like to speak with you in private, Dr. Ramsay," he said, moving to the edge of the riser and letting Rheinhardt hand him down off the step. "Mr. Carmichael, please join us." He glanced at the second attendant. "John, please see that wine is brought for the refreshment of our guests."

Justin fell in behind Ramsay as they followed Rheinhardt and the King through the golden door. The small chamber beyond, fitted as a robing room, gave into a short corridor, down which

Rheinhardt slowly led them, matching his stride to the King's halt-ing gait. He paused to open the first door on the right, standing aside with a bow for the King and his companions to enter.

Justin was prepared when Ramsay came to a dead halt in front of him, and set his hands firmly against Ramsay's shoulders when the doctor would have backed away from the black-clad man waiting for them. Ramsay's head snapped around wildly, hurt betrayal in the look he gave Justin as Rheinhardt closed the door behind them and leaned against it.

"Good morning, James," said Saint-Germain. His hands were clasped behind his back; his gaze was cool and inscrutable. "I wish you had not done what you did. Fortunately, the situation is not beyond redemption. Sire, will you join us in Lodge?" he asked, turning to gesture toward a door behind him.

Ramsay gave no resistance as Justin took his arm and moved him forward, following Saint-Germain and the King. Saint-Germain himself opened the door, leading into a candlelit chamber whose furnishings and black-and-white floor tiles declared it a permanent Lodge room. Mirrors and mirrored wall sconces reflected back the light of dozens of candles all around the room, revealing several others seated to either side of the vacant Master's chair—Andrew Wallace, Arabella, and the Prince de Rohanstuart. They rose as the King entered.

Saint-Germain nodded to them as he ushered the King across the checkered floor. Rheinhardt remained outside to tyle the door, closing it behind them. Installing the King in the Master's chair, Saint-Germain took that of Past Master, directly to the King's right hand. The prince was farther to his right, Andrew at the King's left. Arabella had the chair to Andrew's left.

Justin, after bringing Ramsay to the center of the room, moved quietly to the empty chair next to the prince. Though it was the King who formally presided, no one present could have any doubt who was really in command—and who was on the carpet.

"I regret the necessity for this interview, James," Saint-Germain said, settling in his chair. "It is not a trial, but it *is* a hearing to discover the reasons for your actions and to determine what must be done because of them. Dispensing with overmuch formality, I

declare this Lodge open in the degree of our Inner Circle, reminding all present of your oaths to keep silent regarding what
shall pass within these walls." A casual gesture with his right hand
brought a deeper hush to the room as Saint-Germain added, "Justin, please bring a chair for our brother."

Justin complied with alacrity, taking up a gilt-framed straight
chair from beside him and moving it behind Ramsay, who sank
down on it gratefully, eyes averted.

"First of all," Saint-Germain continued when Justin had
regained his seat, "allow me to congratulate all of you on the zeal
with which you set about to recover His Majesty's gold. You cannot
have known that I have been aware of its existence and even its
approximate location for some years; nor can you have been aware
that I had particular reasons for allowing the gold to remain where
it was."

His gaze swept them mildly, then returned to Ramsay.

"That having been said, I wish to reassure you that the mere
recovery of the gold presents no obstacle to the greater strategy
now unfolding upon the Master Tracing Board. Indeed, the circumstances by which you were led to seek the assistance of the
Ba'al Shem suggest that the time had come for the gold to reenter
the equation—and Andrew's report had assured me that he intended no decision to be taken regarding its disposition until my
instructions were received.

"You were aware of this intention, James, and of my broader
instructions regarding anything to do with His Majesty's affairs,"
the Master said softly. "Nonetheless, you made a unilateral and
precipitous decision to act as *you* saw fit: to take the gold by force,
bring it here, to His Majesty, and reiterate your offer of five years
ago."

"I thought it was the timing you disapproved of before," Ramsay
murmured, defiance smoldering in his eyes as he dared to look up.
"I thought we were all working toward a Stuart restoration. If it
does not happen soon, it cannot happen!"

"I quite agree," Saint-Germain said mildly. "An eventual Stuart
restoration has been and is a goal fervently to be sought, but it
must be accomplished in due season or not at all. By repeatedly

tantalizing His Majesty with hopes unsupported by actual where-withal, you but add to his burden, at a time when years and personal disappointments only underline the precarious nature of his position."

The King had bowed his head during Saint-Germain's recitation, steepled fingers lightly tapping across his lips, but he raised his head and glanced aside as the other paused for breath.

"Francis, I should like to say something here, if I may," he murmured.

Saint-Germain inclined his head. "Of course, Sire."

Charles drew a deep breath and let it out gustily.

"Dr. Ramsay. No king could ever ask for more loyal subjects or friends," he said quietly, "but I must acquaint you with some of the realities of my present situation. Five years ago, when you and your Bostonians first offered me a Crown, it seemed clear to me that though the time was not yet, it still might come. I was then but recently married and held fervent hopes of an eventual heir—for without a son to carry on my royal line, any Crown I might wear would be of the most ephemeral sort, especially as the years pass and my life winds toward its close."

He drew a deep breath before continuing, as if bracing himself against painful recollection.

"I must accept that the years are passing, and I yet have no male heir—nor chance of one, if I leave Europe, for my queen would never follow me to the New World. In whatever time remains to me, I can spare concern for but one Crown—if I can secure it—and that must be the Crown of Scotland. This can be accomplished only from a European base. And if, by chance, I should be blessed with a son, his place will be here, not in the New World. I was foolish to think otherwise."

"It could have worked," Andrew murmured.

"Twenty years ago, perhaps," the King allowed, touching a grateful hand to Andrew's sleeve. "But I trust that all of you see why I must again decline Dr. Ramsay's kind offer, even sweetened by the gracious gift of gold he has recovered at such effort."

"You can at least take the gold," Ramsay broke in, appalled and nearly in tears at the King's rejection. "It is yours. It has always been yours."

Charles shrugged, a tiny smile playing across his lips. "No, it was French and Spanish gold raised in my behalf, but it was never mine. And though it might have made a difference had it reached me even twenty years ago—but no. It did not, and it can make little difference now, in the purpose for which it was intended. Again, I fear it comes too late."

"Not entirely," Saint-Germain said, intervening at last.

All eyes turned in his direction.

"Sadly, His Majesty is correct in stating that there now is little likelihood of regaining his Crown, whether from an American base of operations or from here," Saint-Germain said. "But there is a way in which the gold might still be employed against the Hanoverian Usurper, if not directly to Stuart benefit."

At the King's look of question Saint-Germain went on.

"Let the gold be used in the American war effort, Sire. You know from your own studies that the American Army is in desperate need of the most basic necessities—of muskets, powder, and even the barest essentials of warm uniforms and boots. Such a sum as Dr. Ramsay has procured could make a vital difference for General Washington's cause. And who knows? Perhaps he is destined to wear the Crown that you have been denied."

Andrew glanced aside at Saint-Germain, concern creasing his forehead.

"Is it a Crown for which you have been preparing him, sir?" he murmured.

"For a victor's Crown, yes," Saint-Germain replied. "For any other—that must be for him to decide, or perhaps for a Higher Authority than any in this room. You have seen Washington placed upon the Master Tracing Board. You have assisted in preparing him to choose wisely regarding his destiny. I had intended him as a *dux bellorum,* and perhaps a Stuart regent. With Stuart aspirations now to remain focused in Europe, that same man might make a wise and benevolent King of America—if he will take the Crown. But I must remind you that America is but part of an even larger plan, whose scope extends across an ocean and includes France and, indeed, all of Europe."

"Francis is correct," the King whispered into the silence following the Master's words. "I know now that the quest to regain my

Crown does not lie in America; I think it never did. The colonies of the New World provided a safe haven for many of those who supported my cause in 'Forty-Five, and kept alive a dream far larger than any one man.

"Most sought only the restoration of my Stuart line—and I myself saw only in those terms for many years. But far more important is that one day Scotland should become an independent nation once again, free of Hanoverian tyranny. I think and pray that this desire for independence shall endure for as long as there is a Scotland, whether or not another Stuart King of Scots is ever fated to wear fair Alba's Crown.

"As for your United States, you have yet the hope of throwing off the yoke of the Hanoverian oppressor. More battles are still to come, but in General Washington you have a noble leader who can lead you to the final victory. Whether it will be as king, I do not know. My studies lead me to wonder whether a new dispensation perhaps is intended for the New World, in which kings shall have no part. Perhaps the time of kings is past, even here. Francis can tell you of stirrings even now in the rest of Europe—in France, in particular."

He paused as Saint-Germain laid a hand lightly on his sleeve.

"Yes, I know, I digress," he murmured.

"No, it is important that they hear these things," Saint-Germain replied. "But Your Majesty's loyal Bostonians are waiting for your response to their offer, and I think you must be less candid with them than you have been with James and the others. Fortunately, their discernment will be somewhat diminished from the very excellent wine they have been imbibing for the past little while. Perhaps you would allow me a few minutes with Dr. Ramsay in private, before he accompanies you back to the audience chamber."

Inclining his head for answer, the King got to his feet, everyone else rising as well, as the King set his hand on the arm Andrew offered and started toward the door.

"Justin may stay," Saint-Germain added, forestalling Justin's departure as the rest, save Ramsay, started to follow the King.

Justin turned in time to catch the gesture that Saint-Germain sketched in the direction of the door, aware of a lessening in the tension of the air around him. When the others were gone, leaving Ramsay standing alone in the center of the room, Justin subsided quietly onto his chair again, trying to be as unobtrusive as possible, for Saint-Germain now was approaching the apprehensive Ramsay with single-minded purpose.

"I now require your utmost cooperation," the Master said softly, fixing Ramsay with his darkling gaze as he stopped a few feet away, hands clasped behind his back. "It is not my intention that your Bostonians should learn the details of what has just transpired. Most especially, I do not wish them to learn what is to happen to the gold. It is the King's, to dispose of as he chooses, but I think they would not understand the larger perspective in which our Stuart prince has learnt to move, while others focused on a lesser dream. He will make a gracious speech, declining the Crown but accepting the gold for use in the Stuart cause. You must make no indication, then or later, that any further agenda is in operation. Will you give me your assurance in that regard?"

Slowly Ramsay nodded, his eyes never leaving Saint-Germain's.

"Excellent. I know that you will not disappoint me again. I wish your attitude to be disappointed but resigned—and confident that the King best knows his mind in the pursuit of his Crown. If you offer no further speculation, I believe your followers will not dispute the point. Are these instructions clear?"

Ramsay swallowed self-consciously, aware that Justin saw and heard all.

"Your instructions are clear," he murmured.

"And given that the King's decision has been freely made, have you any hesitation about accepting it? Answer truly."

Ramsay sighed and shook his head.

"Good. I think we understand one another at last. One final thing."

"Yes?"

"I believe you have a talisman not belonging to you. I must ask for its return."

Looking shamefaced and embarrassed, Ramsay delved quickly into a waistcoat pocket and produced the lapis pendant and gold coin on their iron chain.

"I never meant to keep it," he said hastily, dropping the mass into Saint-Germain's outstretched hand. "I only took it because I was afraid they'd use it to track me." He grimaced, looking even more abashed. "Of course, I'd already told them what I was going to do. It wasn't difficult to guess where I was going, or to get here before me. Did they set me up from the beginning?"

"No, they prepared for contingencies," Saint-Germain replied. "From the moment you first mentioned the possibility of recovering the gold, they guessed that you might attempt to take matters into your own hands. That is why I had Simon send Justin to help search out the gold. Andrew and Justin also had their instructions."

Ramsay sighed and bowed his head, shaking it slowly.

"I didn't know," he murmured.

"You were not meant to know."

"No, I mean that I didn't realize that we were part of such an enormous plan," Ramsay said. "And maybe I wasn't meant to know that, either. Perhaps if I'd had more faith . . ."

Saint-Germain nodded slowly, silent for a long moment.

"I think," he finally said, "that perhaps your vision is clearer now than it has ever been. I should like to ask a favor of you."

"A favor? Of *me*?"

Saint-Germain inclined his head. "Some years ago you gave me your obedience in the Great Work set before us. For whatever reason—and perhaps my guidance was unclear—you deviated from the Tracing Board set before us."

"I truly regret that."

"I know that you do. And I see a place for you still, if you desire to continue in the Work. Indeed, I was counting on your assistance in the weeks and months to come—but only if you freely choose to participate, and only if you give me your unqualified promise to abide by my direction in the future, even if you do not always understand it."

"You—you're offering me another chance?" Ramsay whispered.

"I am."

"But—I betrayed you!"

"And have repented," Saint-Germain replied.

A sob escaped Ramsay's lips, his tight-leashed composure deserting him at last. Burying his face in his hands, he started to sway on his feet. Saint-Germain caught him under one elbow and signaled Justin to come take charge of him, the two of them guiding him back to sink down onto the chair he had occupied earlier. While he sobbed, Saint-Germain returned to his own chair, tendering a sympathetic nod when the doctor at length dared to lift his tearstained face from his hands, his eyes red with weeping.

"You haven't yet said whether you accept my offer," Saint-Germain said, not unkindly.

Wiping a sleeve across his eyes, Ramsay rose a little unsteadily and came to kneel at the Master's feet, offering his joined hands in a sign of homage.

"If you will have me, I give you my obedience in the Great Work," he said as the Master's hands enfolded his. "I regret my previous lapse, and I vow not to repeat it, God aiding me."

"I receive your obedience in the Great Work and vow to uphold your endeavors in good faith," Saint-Germain replied. Removing his hands from Ramsay's, he briefly laid them on the doctor's head in blessing, then bent forward to kiss him on both cheeks and raise him up.

"Now," the Master said, rising and beckoning to Justin, "please see that Rheinhardt provides a basin and towels so that James can wash his face. Lucien and I shall accompany His Majesty, since the Bostonians know him as the King's cousin and will assume that I am a royal adviser, but I wish a few words with His Majesty before we go in."

The return of King and courtiers to the audience chamber a short while later gave no hint of what had transpired a few doors away. The prince and Saint-Germain accompanied Justin, Ramsay, and Rheinhardt as the King made his way back to the gilded chair on its riser. Andrew and Arabella observed through spy holes accessible from the adjacent robing room.

"Gentlemen, I thank you for your patience," the King said as the Bostonians set aside wineglasses and congregated at the foot of the riser, where the casks of gold had been pushed against the step. "Dr. Ramsay and Mr. Carmichael have presented a fascinating ac-

count of the state of affairs in America, and of General Washington's growing success against the Hanoverian forces.

"However, I must allow that I find the situation entirely too precarious yet to risk what is likely to be my final bid to regain my Crown. I am grateful for your continued support and pray that one day I shall be able to fulfill your hopes regarding my royal line, but for now I fear I must again decline your very gracious offer. In the meantime, be assured that the gold you have recovered in my behalf shall be used in no wise other than to torment the House of Hanover."

As the King went on, wooing and encouraging, Justin marveled at his skill, for never once did the King stray beyond the literal truth, or say anything other than complimentary to the efforts of his loyal listeners. Concluding with an invitation to dine with him that evening, and to stay the night before departing on their journey home, he gave them into the care of the faithful John Stewart to arrange accommodations, and retired for well-earned rest before he must face them again as a gracious host.

The next morning, after Ramsay and Justin had set out with the Bostonians on the road back north across France, Saint-Germain summoned the remaining members of his Inner Lodge to an upstairs sitting room for a final briefing before they also should set out for home. The King had remained abed after the previous day's exertions—indeed, after the exertions of the past several days, for Andrew, Arabella, and the prince had arrived nearly a week before Ramsay and his party.

Their first night there Andrew had worn the glass eye the King had sent him, underlining their reunion with a poignancy that seemed to revitalize the King. Charles had borne up well in the days that followed, spending many a contented hour walking in the palazzo's gardens with his old friend, but they had known the reunion must end abruptly once Ramsay arrived, for the Master had his schedule, which must move forward. The strain of finally meeting with the Bostonians gave Saint-Germain the perfect excuse to insist that the King keep his leave-taking brief and retire early with a sleeping draft. He would not wake until long after all of them were gone.

Consequently, the atmosphere at table that morning was as if the King had departed, not as if Andrew, Arabella, and the prince were preparing to depart. A noble sword lay on the table around which they gathered—the King's contribution to the ritual still to be enacted in behalf of George Washington, an ocean away. Also under scrutiny were copies of a proposed scenario for the ritual, which Saint-Germain had prepared.

"This is the Sobieski sword," the Master said, pushing it across to Andrew. "It has come down from the time of the King's great-great-grandfather, King John the Third of Poland, who stopped the Turks at the gates of Vienna in 1683. The victory was a notable one, against great odds. Afterward the King is said to have declared, 'Venimus, vidimus, Deus vicit'—'We came, we saw, God conquered.' Accordingly, Charles felt that it would provide a fitting symbol of sovereignty, a potent link between the Old World and the New—and also a token of his personal endorsement of what is to be done."

Andrew closed his hand around the wire-wrapped hilt and withdrew the blade a few inches from the scabbard, then shoved it home and laid the weapon back on the table.

"I take it that this is to represent the sword the General saw in his dream?" he said.

"As part of the matrix, yes," Saint-Germain replied. "But you will wish to pair it with his own."

"How much am I to say of its source?" Andrew asked. "Do you wish him to know of the Stuart connection with all of this?"

Saint-Germain smiled. "I think that if you are to offer him a true Crown, not just a victor's laurel, he had best know the whole of it. He is aware of your Jacobite connections. He'll not remark on the fact that you have been in contact with Charles. I will give you further on that, before you leave."

"What of the other elements?" Arabella asked. "Do you truly mean us to retain James, as originally intended?"

"I do," the Master replied. "This has been a time of testing for him, but I believe he shall prove equal to the challenge. But if he should prove false after all that has happened, and after the assurances he gave me yesterday, Lucien is prepared to step into his

place. The adjustments would be troublesome, but not insur-
mountable."

Andrew had been glancing over the pages of the scenario and
glanced up at the Master's comment.

"What of Washington himself?" he asked. "Will *he* make the
necessary adjustments? Not to James, but to this whole situation."

"Not even I can predict that with certainty," Saint-Germain said
with a tiny smile. "All of you know him far better than I. Is he
inclined toward an earthly Crown, or has the war taught him that
America is not for kings?"

Andrew nodded slowly. "The precise form of our offer will need
to be carefully considered. Perhaps it's well that we have a sea
voyage during which to refine every aspect of the plan." He
glanced at the prince. "You'll take the gold to Lafayette?"

The prince smiled. "Actually, I shall take the gold to one of Eli
Levi's brokers here in Florence and obtain a letter of credit, which
I shall take to Lafayette. The broker can also arrange to transmit
the commission still owing to Dr. Falk. I fear that, amid all the
diversion of our recent chase, Dr. Ramsay neglected to compensate
the good Ba'al Shem for his services."

"The Ba'al Shem will be grateful," Saint-Germain replied.
"Which reminds me: Dr. Ramsay returned the Ba'al Shem's talisman before he left. I shall be certain that it reaches its rightful
owner—though without its golden companion." He produced the
gold coin with a sleight-of-hand gesture, still with its frame and
ring attached, and placed it in Arabella's hand.

"A remembrance of your service to your prince, my dear," he
said with a tiny smile.

Arabella smiled back as she closed the coin in her hand.

"And now, Lucien." The Master returned his attention to the
prince. "You have no questions regarding Lafayette? He now could
become our weak link if he is not properly prepared."

The prince arched a reddish eyebrow. "You need have no fears
on that count. I sent to Franklin as soon as we made landfall. He
will have our marquis well in hand by the time I join them in Paris.
I then intend to attach myself to young Gilbert's party and travel
with him back to America. You may be certain that he will be

primed and ready by the time he is reunited with his beloved General."

"Excellent." Saint-Germain allowed himself a slow, lazy smile, the dark eyes caressing each of them in turn. "I am well pleased, *mes enfants*. Would that we could spend more time together, but your carriage will be waiting. Please convey my kindest regards to Simon. His, perhaps, has been the most difficult part of all, serving as the anchor point around which the General and all else revolves. I know he will continue to rise to the challenges he is given."

Chapter Twenty-five

The winter of 1779–80 passed but slowly for Colonel Simon Wallace, who had to wait many long months before he could expect news back from his wife and the others who had pursued Prince Charlie's gold across the Atlantic.

The previous season's fighting had been sparse and had wound down ominously. Convinced that Clinton was preparing to shift his focus to the South, Washington had detached the North Carolina brigade and the whole of the Virginia line to reinforce General Lincoln at Charleston—a move that was vindicated when Clinton sailed south from New York with nearly eight thousand men. But then the true waiting began—and the worst winter yet.

Though the General remained housed at the Ford mansion, with his wife and his military family, he had moved the army's winter camp a few miles southwest of Morristown, into a mountainous area called Jockey Hollow. Within a month winter set in with a vengeance. January snows buried the camp under six feet of snow, cutting off all supplies for more than a week; and even afterward few supplies were available.

As the winter progressed, conditions became even worse than two years before at Valley Forge. The men suffered dreadfully from lack of clothing, fuel, and food. Many stumped about barefoot or on feet muffled in rags, with empty stomachs adding to their misery. During the worst of the isolation, the men were reduced to eating black birch bark, roasting old shoes, and even killing and eating a favorite pet dog. Even the officers went on short rations when times were very lean; and many was the bitter winter night when Martha Washington would find her small kitchen invaded by upward of a score of men—all of her husband's military family of officers and servants—for it was one of the warmest places available for a staff meeting.

Some few diversions there were, to while away the long winter nights. The rituals of Freemasonry continued to be a staple of winter life in camp, especially among the officers. Occasionally musical evenings could be arranged. The General loved to dance, so he and several dozen other officers put together a dancing assembly, encouraging the girls from neighboring farms to join the military wives. If refreshment was scarce, the conviviality, at least, was plentiful—and dancing helped to keep one warm. Often the General would dance until two in the morning, sometimes for several hours without a break, amazing all onlookers with his stamina.

But not all the nights were filled with such diversions; and even Washington's favored pastime of tableside chats diminished as the winter deepened and the fare even at the General's table grew more sparse. When shortages were at their worst, Simon sometimes would accompany the Commander in Chief on unofficial walks about the camp, visiting with the men and offering quiet words of reassurance and comfort. Usually the two of them would talk afterward, on the way back and then in Washington's office, the General unburdening his fears and his frustrations and Simon offering what encouragement he could.

More poignant moments there were, as well. Returning from one such foray on a snowy moonlit evening, when Simon thought the General had merely drawn apart to answer a call of nature, he discovered his Commander in Chief kneeling in the snow amid a circle of pines, bared head bowed over the hilt of his sword in prayer. Withdrawing quietly to give him privacy, Simon had waited with his own head bowed until the crunch of booted feet on new snow warned him of Washington's return. The General cer-

tainly must have been aware that he had been observed, but he had said nothing, only laying a grateful hand on Simon's sleeve as he passed, leading on toward the path back to the horses.

Thus did the nights pass—respite of a sort, when the days must be occupied with the never-ending challenge to get the men through another day, scrounging provisions and fighting the ongoing battles to stop desertions. Floggings there were aplenty, but discipline had to be maintained.

Only once did Simon see the facade of confidence and fortitude begin to slip, late in February, when even the officers had been on bread and water for several days. Simon had brought in the latest commissary reports, and no one else was in the office. Washington sighed as he bent his gaze over the dismal figures.

"Stay, Colonel, and close the door. I must confess that I sometimes come perilously close to despair, when I must deal with numbers like these, day after day."

"General Greene has hopes of foraging livestock farther to the north," Simon said. "I know you prefer not to take what we need from the citizenry, but men are starving."

"Do you think I don't know that?" Washington snapped. "I am so weary of—"

A knock at the door came simultaneously with its opening, and the General barked at the intruder with uncharacteristic sharpness. "Not now, Colonel Hamilton! I'll let you know when I'm free."

Immediately the door closed, and immediately Washington regretted his momentary lapse. Simon said nothing as the General briefly buried his face in his hands, elbows resting on the desk as he rubbed at his eyes. After a moment the powdered head lifted, apology written all across the craggy face.

"It is times like this when I truly begin to appreciate all those times when Lieutenant Carmichael served as our Tyler," he said quietly. "I have not asked you about him, because I know that he has gone abroad and you can hope to receive no word from him for several months yet, but I cannot help wondering about his mission. It—relates to that other matter that you and I have often discussed, does it not?"

"It does," Simon replied, "and I regret that I may tell you nothing more at this time. It is—possible that when he returns, we will be ready to move forward."

The gray-blue eyes searched his; then Washington sighed and leaned back in his chair, setting both hands on the chair arms.

"I pray it will come soon," he whispered. "Five years is a long time to labor, fueled only by hope. In these dark days, when fatigue and doubt are constant companions, the dream intrudes almost nightly—never in detail, but niggling with the tantalizing prospect of the victor's Crown, which is always just beyond my reach. I have been blessed with some of the bravest men ever to offer service to a commander—and thus far we have always managed to snatch survival from the jaws of utter disaster, even in the face of momentary setbacks. But how long this can continue, I honestly do not know."

"You must not expect that reenactment of the dream will prove a magical solution to the problems, that the course of the war will suddenly change," Simon cautioned.

"No, I do not expect that," the General replied. "Perhaps I only hope for an easing of my mind, a clearer vision for what can be achieved for these United States. It is such a green and fertile land. If only we could be allowed to live our lives in peace. It has been five years since I left Mount Vernon to take up the warrior's sword. I had hoped never to have to do that again, when I returned from the Indian Wars.

"Yet here I am, Commander in Chief of what must be the most amazing ragtag army ever to be mustered in the history of mankind. And thus far we have managed to prevail—just—against the most powerful army in Europe. I tell you truly, Colonel, it mystifies me."

Their conversation soon returned to the report that had sparked Washington's unusual diversion. The subject of Justin and his mission did not come up again. Nor did the conversation change anything in the way either man approached the ongoing problems of supply and discipline in the camp.

Meanwhile, even the spring brought little respite. Rations had been cut and cut again to one eighth of normal, and two Connecticut regiments mutinied for full rations and back pay. Their colonel shamed them by pointing out the immortal honor they had won by their performance, patience, and bravery to date—all for naught, if they took to their heels and deserted. The men backed down, but two of the leaders were hanged, and Washington was forced to pardon all except the ones who had actually left camp. The wonder was that he succeeded in retaining any army at all.

Militarily, the winter had seen little activity on either side. Once New York Bay froze over, trapping the British warships in the ice, Washington authorized a surprise foray across the ice to harass the British on Staten Island, giving General Stirling twenty-five hundred men to throw against a British force of about twelve hundred.

But the British discovered the advance in time to pull back in their defensive works, so that Stirling was obliged to withdraw, though with little loss. For their part, the British raided Paulus Hook and Elizabethtown, taking a few prisoners in each instance; but like similar raids into Westchester County, which became known as the "neutral ground," they had little effect on either side.

Unfortunately, the campaign in the South had more disastrous consequences. Answering the demands of the government of Charleston to defend it, General Lincoln allowed himself to be hemmed in and besieged. (In a similar situation in 1776, Washington had avoided being penned up in New York and had kept his army from being lost, even though the British occupation of New York went forward.)

But Lincoln believed that he could keep the British from entering Charleston harbor. By May 9 he had been proven wrong and was forced to surrender his army of more than three thousand. British losses for the entire siege did not exceed two hundred sixty-five killed or wounded.

Washington would not learn of the Charleston defeat—perhaps the worst American loss of the entire war—for many days, but he had already sent more reinforcements southward under De Kalb: two thousand Maryland and Delaware troops, who would form the nucleus of a new army in the Southern Department.

Amid all this activity, military and domestic, the Master's Inner Circle finally had begun to report in to Simon. Andrew and Arabella were the first to arrive, very early in May, taking up temporary accommodations in an inn in Morristown until they could brief Simon regarding the events at the Palazzo San Clemente.

"It will be for Lucien to set the scene when he returns with Lafayette," Andrew said when Simon had skimmed over the scenario for the intended ritual. "And I should imagine that we'll see Justin and Ramsay any day."

The pair arrived only days later, even as Lincoln was surrendering at Charleston. Thanks to Simon's careful backdating of appropriate paperwork, Ramsay's unscheduled absence had been covered by official leave, the same as Justin's. Now Simon sent him off immediately to the house where Andrew and Arabella had taken up lodgings to begin preparations. Justin he took into his own quarters at the Ford house, where the two of them talked late into the night and Justin embroidered on the account Andrew and Arabella had given by adding his perspective from among the Bostonians.

"They're disappointed, as you can imagine," he told Simon, "but they had no idea what was going on behind the scenes at San Clemente. And Ramsay certainly rose to the occasion after we left Florence. He seems to have made a complete turn-around."

"And about time," Simon muttered. "Much of this to-ing and fro-ing could have been avoided if he'd stayed in line in the first place."

"Well, one can't fault patriot zeal," Justin said, "so long as it's properly focused. Speaking of which, have we any idea when Lafayette will be arriving?"

"Soon, I should think," Simon replied. "Andrew said that when he went through Paris, he'd heard it was all but certain that a French expedition would be leaving very shortly, with the marquis in the advance party. Lucien planned to attach himself to that party as part of Lafayette's staff and do his best to encourage early action. That's been Lafayette's aim for some time, of course—to return to Washington's service."

That return came only two days later, on May 10, when the ebullient Lafayette rode into Washington's Morristown camp armed with his King's instructions and commitments: the promise of six thousand French infantrymen soon to be on their way, with arms, clothing, and ammunition. The expeditionary force would be led by Lieutenant General the Comte de Rochambeau but would be considered an auxiliary corps of the American Army, and hence under Washington's command.

Delighted, Washington greeted his young friend as a returning son. Lafayette, in turn, threw himself into the General's arms with Gallic exuberance, then spent the rest of the day and evening closeted with the Commander in Chief and various of his officers while they acquainted one another with the most recent state of affairs. The Prince de Rohanstuart had traveled amid the marquis's party as one of his aides, now wearing French uniform and introduced as Major Rohan. Simon was among the General's aides invited to sit in on parts of the briefings, and Justin also was in evidence.

The General's table was more festive than usual that evening, even if the fare was still frugal. Simon was in attendance, of course, as was the prince; and Justin, too, was among the few junior officers present. After supper and its attendant table talk, when the General's military family began to disperse, the marquis asked privately whether he might have the honor of the General's further presence in his quarters; his aide, Major Rohan, was prepared to open a very fine bottle of brandy, which, alas, was enough for only a few. Perhaps Colonel Wallace would join them to help assess its quality?

The atmosphere relaxed further as soon as the four had repaired to Lafayette's quarters. The General did not seem to notice that the marquis's aide casually locked the door behind them as he closed it, or that Justin had followed them and taken up guard duty outside the door. As Lafayette drew four chairs around a small table and bade his guests sit, the prince produced crystal glasses from a traveling canteen and set them on the table, filling them from a dark-green bottle. After distributing them, Lafayette took up his own glass and raised it in salute to his Commander in Chief.

"I drink to your very good health and to old friendships, *mon cher général*," he said happily.

"And to the survival of these United States," Washington replied. "Gentlemen."

He lifted his glass slightly to all of them, and everyone drank the toast. It was a fine brandy. When Simon had savored its flavor, he set his glass aside and glanced at the prince, sitting directly across from him. The prince nodded and reached behind him to pull Lafayette's Bible from under a cloak. This he handed to Lafayette, who set it gravely on the table before Washington.

"I have come with more than the promise of troops, *mon général*," the marquis said softly. "I am told that this means something to you beyond the sacred words it contains."

Washington's eyes had widened at the sight of the book, and now he turned a questioning gaze to Simon, sitting at his right hand.

"Forgive the somewhat dramatic introduction, General," Simon said. "Both these gentlemen are party to what is unfolding and are here to assist you. If you will be so good as to lay your right hand upon the Volume of Sacred Law, much will be revealed."

Jaw tightening, Washington returned his gaze to the book, then slowly reached out to lay his palm atop it. He stiffened as he touched it, his eyes closing, then was silent for a long moment before breathing slowly out, his head bowing over the book. After a moment he looked up at them uncertainly.

"I remembered," he said softly, his fingers caressing the silver corners and clasp of the book. "Not all, but much more. Gilbert was in the dream." His gaze flicked to Lafayette, his brow furrowing. "But I had not even met you when I first had the dream."

Lafayette shrugged sheepishly, but with no evasion. "My own awareness of all that is unfolding is but new, *mon général*. But you yourself started me on the road by which I may hope to understand. Since leaving you nearly two years ago, entered as an Apprentice in the Great Work, I have been further instructed regarding the Master Tracing Board from which we all take our instruction. I am awed and humbled to have been deemed worthy to assist in this great endeavor."

Washington's jaw had dropped as Lafayette spoke, and now his gaze flicked warily to the prince.

"And what of you, sir?" he whispered. "I know you for a Master Mason and a friend of the American cause, but it seems there is more to which I have not been privy."

The prince inclined his head, one hand toying with the stem of his glass. "I apologize for the need to mislead you when first we met, General. My full name is Lucien Rene Robert, Prince de Rohanstuart. I am a distant cousin of Charles Edward Stuart. When I first made your acquaintance, I had come to America to meet with certain Bostonians who had written to my cousin and

offered him the Crown of America, as inducement that he should come to the colonies and use this as a base from which to take back the throne of his ancestors."

At the General's beginning start of protest, the prince held up a hand. "Please allow me to finish, General. For a variety of reasons His Majesty had declined the offer at that time, but already Providence had placed you upon the Master Tracing Board. In what capacity we still cannot be certain, but *dux bellorum* of these United Colonies you certainly were to be, as was confirmed by your appointment as Commander in Chief."

"What of my dream?" Washington asked warily. "Am I somehow to infer that you caused it?"

The prince shook his head. "Not I—though I am now prepared to assist Simon and the others in duplicating its ritual, to confirm you as champion of America's liberties."

"Yes," Washington said slowly, "I sense that you should be there, though I cannot say why. But—what has all of this to do with your Stuart Pretender? I have long been aware of Colonel Wallace's Jacobite sympathies, but—"

As he shook his head, the prince leaned slightly forward, his dark eyes very intent on Washington's.

"At very least, George Washington, you have been prepared to serve as America's defender, champion of her liberties, to wear the victor's laurel Crown. As an alternative, it was planned that you might assume the role of Stuart regent, if King Charles had seen fit to take up his Crown here in America."

"But—"

"The King recently has declined that option for a second and final time, for a variety of reasons; but the very qualities that have prepared you as America's defender make you also fit to take up a Crown of your own—a royal Crown, not just the victor's laurel wreath. America could do far worse."

Washington's face had drained of color as the prince spoke, the big hands closing around Lafayette's Bible. Now he brought the book to his breast as if its very touch conveyed comfort, but his eyes looked a little glazed as he slowly shook his head.

"No," he whispered softly. "I cannot think that this land will again bow to kings. All that first year of the war, I prayed that we might be reconciled with the Mother Country—but that was before it became clear that King George himself was no less an impediment to the liberties of this country than his ministers and Parliament."

"A different George might prove a far different kind of monarch," the prince observed.

"No." Washington shook his head as he put Lafayette's Bible back on the table. "I do not know what form of government will best serve when we have truly won our independence, but I think that it will not be a monarchy—and certainly not with me at its head."

"And, pray, why not?"

"I have told you one good reason," Washington said sharply. "There is the additional fact that, like your King Charles, I have no heir of my body. Nor does one ever know that one's heir will be competent; this is one of the many uncertainties of monarchy. No, I shall wear no Crown save a victor's laurel, if that is vouchsafed me."

"Yet a Crown will be offered you, and more than once, and by those far better able to deliver it," the prince said quietly. "Already many sing 'God save great Washington,' where before they sang, 'God save the King.' Many there will be, when this conflict is ended, who will wish you to be their king in fact, by right of conquest—for without you, I think this struggle could come to no happy ending. I accept that you have your reasons for declining now. But will you always have the courage of your present convictions, to refuse such earthly glory?"

Washington had closed his eyes as the prince spoke, a look of anguish on his craggy face, and pain shone in his eyes as he looked up again.

"Nothing was ever said before of earthly Crowns," he whispered. "I only ever sought the victor's laurel. That is all I have ever wanted—and not for myself, but in fulfillment of the duty I assumed when called to serve. Why do you continue to tempt me?"

"Untested virtue is little worth," the prince replied, smiling faintly. "True virtue must be tried and proven."

"As has been done," Simon said, speaking at last. "And having done, the time now has come to reinforce the dedication you declared when you first told me of the dream. General, with the return of Monsieur de Lafayette, we are now prepared to proceed as has been proposed from the beginning and reenact the dream. You have come to a major branching point upon the Master Tracing Board, and decisions must be made.

"If you would seek a royal Crown, we are prepared to support you in that endeavor. If the victor's crown is still your goal, then let the purpose of our working be to anchor your resolve—for the lure of an earthly Crown can be a heady one."

Washington breathed out very slowly, obviously awash with emotion, his swallow audible in the silence.

"I—pray you will allow me a few days to think on this, gentlemen," he said quietly. "I shall speak of it to no one else—in truth, who would believe me?—but clearly the time has come when I must face my destiny squarely. Will you indulge me in this?"

The prince inclined his head, then picked up his brandy, all but untouched. "We shall await your direction, General. In the meantime, may I wish you serenity, wisdom, and clear vision, as you ponder what could be the most important decision you may ever be called upon to make?"

He stood and drained his glass with those words, then dashed the empty glass into the fireplace with a suddenness that made the rest of them start at the sound of breaking glass. But then Lafayette and Simon also took up their glasses and rose, their eyes never leaving Washington as they, too, drank the toast, then tossed their glasses after the prince's, that no lesser toast might ever be drunk from them.

Stunned, Washington stared at the debris, at the shards of crystal glittering before the fire on the hearth, at the three men gazing at him, waiting. Then he slowly lifted his own glass and drank down the potent brandy as if it were water. He gazed long into the empty glass when he had finished, running a thumb across the crystal facets, then stood and tossed it into the fireplace with the others, where it shattered.

"I shall endeavor to give you an answer in the next few days,

gentlemen," he said softly, not meeting any of their eyes. "Colonel Wallace, I think perhaps it is time we left the marquis his privacy. It has been a very long day for him."

"It has, indeed," Lafayette said cautiously, inclining his head in a bow. "But I must remind the General that I am ordered by my government to journey on to Philadelphia as quickly as I may. I must acquaint Congress with the recent developments and receive instructions from the new French minister. It may be many weeks before I am able to return. It would be well if I at least knew your decision before I depart; and better still, if we could have done what is necessary."

Washington nodded dully, slowly moving with Simon toward the door.

"I will give you my decision as soon as I may," he whispered. "Please understand that it is not one I dare make lightly, so I pray that you will be patient with me." He paused at the door to glance back at Lafayette and the prince, drawing himself into a semblance of professional demeanor. "I—should like to invite both of you to ride with me in the morning for an inspection of the Morristown camp, immediately after breakfast. Good evening, gentlemen."

The General said but little as Simon and Justin escorted him back to his quarters, and what was said pertained only to the proposed inspection the next morning. He bade them good night with his customary courtesy and did not leave his quarters again that night, though Justin made periodic checks through the night, and in the morning reported that a thin line of light had been visible from under the General's door until the dawn washed it to invisibility. Simon might have kept the watch himself, brooding on what dark doubts might be going through the General's mind, but he made himself accept Justin's offer to take on that lonely task, for he knew he must be fresh and ready to act once the General gave them his decision.

Fortunately, Washington did not keep them long wondering. Though he looked to have slept but little the next morning, he drew Simon briefly aside while they waited for their horses to be brought up.

"I confess a part of myself still skeptical of the necessity to do what you have asked," he said under his breath, "yet there is that which almost compels me to agree. It is nothing of your direct doing, I assure you," he added at Simon's sharp look, "for since the very beginning of our association, you have been most conscientious in insisting that I do whatever I have done of my own free will."

"Then, is it your will that I proceed, sir?" Simon asked quietly.

Washington gave a faint inclination of his head as Justin approached leading Simon's black mare and the General's big gray.

"I place myself totally in your hands in this regard," he said. "Do as you think best."

Simon nodded. "Tomorrow night, then, under guise of a private farewell supper in honor of the marquis—a very private supper. We have a house prepared, and the others are standing by. I shall give you further details this evening or tomorrow morning."

"I shall hold myself in readiness," the General replied as Justin brought his horse alongside. "Thank you, Lieutenant."

He said nothing further as he mounted up and moved off to join Lafayette, but Simon's nod to Justin as he, too, mounted was enough to ensure that the latter would remain behind and ride to inform Andrew. The prince had noted the exchange and held back as the General and Lafayette rode out at the head of the inspection party, falling into place briefly beside Simon.

"Tomorrow night," Simon murmured as he leaned down, as if to adjust a stirrup leather.

Chapter Twenty-six

The house in which Andrew, Arabella, and Ramsay made their preparations had belonged to an old friend of Andrew's, now several years deceased. Upon his arrival in Morristown, Andrew had arranged with the widow Johnstone to take over the house for a few weeks while she went to visit a daughter in Philadelphia. Ramsay had joined him and Arabella a few days later and pitched in with an enthusiasm they had not seen for several years.

The house was admirably suited to their purposes, but half an hour's ride from Washington's headquarters and set far enough off the beaten track that it received few unintentional visitors. Twenty years before, the Johnstone library had been the scene of many a Lodge meeting and the occasional more clandestine gathering of fellow Jacobite sympathizers.

A party intending even more clandestine activities arrived at the house just before eight o'clock on the appointed night: General Washington, General Lafayette, Simon, the prince, and Justin. They had brought no other escort. En route, Lafayette had chattered nervously about the privations he had observed in the camp over the previous two days—the appalling lack of proper clothing and shoes, the shocking shortages of weapons and ammunition—

but he wound down as they drew rein beside the house and dismounted, Simon removing a set of saddlebags and slinging them over one shoulder.

While Justin took the horses around to the barn, Simon ushered the others to the front door. Ramsay was waiting to admit them, smartly turned out in the Continental uniform he had not worn in months. As soon as they were inside, the prince excused himself and Lafayette and followed Ramsay through a door at the far end of the entry hall, while Simon led the General into the parlor and closed the door. Washington had said but little in response to Lafayette's comments en route and watched with a taut intensity as Simon set down the saddlebags on a bow-backed chair.

"I wish that Gilbert had been less garrulous," the General said quietly. "I think I need not tell you that I feel very apprehensive about tonight."

Simon smiled faintly and began unbuckling one side of the saddlebags. "I should be surprised if it were otherwise," he said. "Would you like a glass of wine to steady you?"

Washington shook his head distractedly, pacing the room with nervous energy that the day's activities had done nothing to sap.

"No. I wish nothing to blunt the edge of my perceptions." He turned to watch Simon take out a folded Masonic apron. "Can you *really* have managed to assemble all the elements of my dream?"

"All that you have related to me, and some that have eluded memory thus far," Simon replied, handing the General his apron.

Washington fingered it uncertainly, the gray-blue eyes lifting questioningly to Simon's.

"Are you—permitted to tell me anything of what I may expect?" he asked.

Simon cocked his head thoughtfully. "Recall for me, if you will, sir, the answer to this question, which you have asked of many a candidate in Lodge, and which you yourself have answered many times before: Why do you leave the west and travel to the east?"

"In search of light," Washington replied. "In search of *more* light."

Before he could pursue the point, a knock at the door froze him in his place.

"Come," Simon called.

As Justin entered, bobbing a brief nod of apology to the Commander in Chief, Washington seemed to relax just a little.

"The outside is secure, sir," Justin said. "I'll be serving as Tyler for this evening, so you won't be seeing me about for the next little while. But I wanted to offer you my very best wishes."

A hint of what might have been disappointment touched Washington's craggy face, but then he nodded and set aside his apron to extend a hand to Justin.

"Thank you, Lieutenant Carmichael—Brother Justin," he said quietly, retaining Justin's hand in his. "It had not occurred to me to wonder who would tyle our work this evening. While I would have welcomed your presence within, I am reassured to know that you will be on guard outside our door. You have come a very long way since I was privileged to be present at your raising to Master Mason."

"So have we all, sir," Justin replied, not flinching from the gray-blue gaze.

Smiling faintly, Washington briefly clapped his left hand to their joined ones in affirmation, then drew back, watching fondly as Justin departed and closed the door behind him. His manner was thoughtful as he turned back to Simon.

"Have we, indeed, come that far?" he asked quietly.

"I think only you can answer that question, sir," Simon replied. He picked up the saddlebags and gestured toward the apron. "You'd best clothe yourself now, while I see if they're ready for us. You needn't worry what to do. I'll be at your side all the way."

"As you long have been," the General said quietly. "Thank you, Simon."

Simon said nothing, only nodding acknowledgment as he ducked out the door, but inside he felt a flush of unexpected pleasure, for it was the first time Washington had called him by his Christian name. He found himself smiling as he paused in the entry hall to deposit the saddlebags on a side chair and pull out his own apron and Washington's personal Bible, also taking off his spurs. Lafayette's smaller Bible was already tucked into an inner breast pocket, where he had carried it for Lafayette's initiation.

Before entering the library, he extinguished all but one of the candles in the entry hall.

The room was a little larger than the Wallace library and normally did double duty as a sitting room, but all the chairs had been removed save for the one set aside at the far end for the presiding Master. Andrew was standing just inside, surveying the final preparations, and turned to greet Simon as he entered. His white hair hung loose on his shoulders, and the glass eye given him by Charles Edward Stuart glinted behind the Professor's wire-rimmed spectacles. He was dressed in the rusty black clothing he had worn as the Professor, five years before, with a Masonic apron girt about his waist and Saint-Germain's moonstone around his neck instead of a Masonic jewel. A dusty black tricorn was in his hands, for Masonic custom decreed that the presiding Master should wear his hat.

At the far end of the room behind him, beside the Master's chair, Lafayette was spreading a white cloth on the small table that would serve as an altar, and Ramsay was taking a familiar-looking pair of compasses out of a flannel bag. A square and another mound of flannel already lay in the seat of the chair, across the arms of which the prince had just laid the naked Sobieski sword.

"Are those Franklin's?" Simon asked, indicating the square and compasses.

"Aye." Andrew paused to put on his hat. "Lucien obtained the loan of them when he was in Paris. If the General recognizes them, as he may well do, it should reinforce the connection between what happened at Justin's raising to Master and what happens here, tonight. How is he?"

Simon handed him Washington's Bible and paused to put on his own apron. "Very apprehensive, to use his own words; but apparently determined to go through with it. How soon will you be ready to begin? I don't want him to have too long to worry."

"We're nearly ready." Andrew held up the Bible to catch Lafayette's attention, but the prince came instead and took it, retreating wordlessly to open it on the altar. "Shall I acquaint you with the basic arrangement?"

At Simon's nod Andrew took his arm and led him a few steps

farther into the room. Besides the three candles required for ritual as the Lesser Lights of Freemasonry, presently lined up on one of the bookcases, the only other light source was a pair of mirrored candle sconces to either side of the fireplace. The flickering light was not enough to make out details of the painted floor cloth in the center of the room, provided by Saint-Germain and brought back by Andrew and Arabella, but Simon had seen a drawing of the design. The encircling mottoes and the symbolism within the large circle of thirteen stars would be explained to Washington during the course of the ritual, and the candles set at the center of each of those stars would provide more than enough light for all their purposes.

"The Masonic altar will remain outside the circle," Andrew said, gesturing toward it. "Its purpose is symbolic only, to anchor a framework for the rest of the ritual. Washington's personal altar will be the back of the chair he'll use as a kneeler." He gestured to one side, toward an odd, squat chair with an upholstered seat, very short legs, and a narrow shelf across its back that formed an arm-rest if one knelt on the seat.

Simon nodded. "You'll move that into position at the appropriate time?"

"Yes. Working within the circle of candles will be logistically difficult enough, because the stars are less than three feet apart, but Saint-Germain was adamant about wanting the symbolism and about keeping the design as unobscured as possible. So we'll move the appropriate furniture and people in and out of the circle as and when needed. The circle isn't a protective one, so it doesn't matter that it will be breached repeatedly."

"I see." Simon glanced around the rest of the room. "Where is Arabella?"

"She's changing her clothes. I believe you'll approve of the over-all effect—but I don't want you to see her until *he* does. I'm depending on you to bolster him."

Simon nodded. "And what about you? Is it going to work?"

Andrew gave him a sly smile. "Come and watch," he said. "We're about ready, otherwise. You'll still have a few minutes with the General, while we light the candles."

So saying, he headed slowly toward the far end of the room, where Ramsay and Lafayette had finished arranging the Masonic altar, with the square and compasses laid atop the open Bible in proper configuration for a Master's Lodge. The three candles now burned along the back edge of that altar.

As Lafayette retreated to a chair on the left side of the room, and the prince took up the Sobieski sword and went with Ramsay to the right side, the library door opened briefly and Arabella entered, muffled in a dark cloak. En route with Andrew, Simon glanced in her direction, but he could see only the pale oval of her face. As she took a seat at the back of the room, mostly in deep shadow, he caught a glimpse of a flag propped in the corner nearest her, identifiable only by its cascade of dark and light stripes.

"Sit beside Gilbert," Andrew murmured, gesturing toward the empty chair beside the marquis.

As Simon obeyed, Andrew settled into the Master's chair and set his hands on the chair arms to begin composing himself. After a moment he took the moonstone pendant between his fingers, holding it so that one of the altar candles could be seen through the milky lens of the stone. He stared long at it, his breath slowing, his eyelids drooping, until finally his eyes closed. After another few breaths the moonstone slid slowly to rest on his chest, his head nodding slightly. Then he slowly raised his head and opened his eyes.

Or—the Professor, Saint-Germain, opened his eyes. For Simon had no doubt that it was, indeed, Saint-Germain and not Andrew who cast his gaze over the setting laid out before him, then turned to look directly at Simon.

"Simon, my son, it has been far too long."

Simon felt a quiet joy surge within him as he rose and came to kneel before the Master's chair, taking the hand the other offered and briefly dipping his head to touch it to his forehead. Though the others had worked with the Master directly over the past few years, some of them repeatedly and dramatically, Simon had accepted less direct service at home—entrusted with work of the utmost importance, gently guiding Washington onto the Master Tracing Board, but perforce outside the Master's presence. He

found himself trembling with long-suppressed emotion, with relief that, even for a time, another had taken on the burden of responsibility for what was unfolding. He had to steady himself with both hands against the arm of the chair before he could lift his head to answer.

"It has, indeed, been far too long," he whispered. "How I have missed your counsel."

"And I, yours," Saint-Germain replied. "But you have served the Great Work in ways you may never know. Go now to your pupil and prepare him. We will require perhaps five minutes to ensure that all here is in readiness, but he may have more time, if he requires it."

With a duck of his head Simon got to his feet and retreated to the entry hall, pausing for a moment to compose himself before he stepped outside to alert Justin that they were nearly ready to begin. The General's staff back at headquarters had been informed that Washington was holding a private supper for Lafayette that night—the Commander in Chief dared not simply disappear for several hours—but the duty aide had instructions not to allow any interruptions except in case of dire emergency. With luck, there would be none.

"We'll be starting very shortly," Simon said to Justin, glancing out into the night. "Any activity?"

Justin shook his head. "Very quiet. We'll hope it stays that way. Good luck."

Smiling, Simon clasped a hand to Justin's shoulder, then went back into the house. Though he knocked lightly on the parlor door before entering, he found the General on his knees in a far corner where the candlelight barely reached, powdered head bowed over the hilt of his sheathed sword.

The image recalled that night in the snow, not so very long ago—and then Justin's description of that day when Washington had realized that he was about to be nominated as Commander in Chief; how the General had fled to the solitude of the little library in the Philadelphia statehouse, there to kneel in prayer, his head bowed against the hilt of his sword.

It was for this moment, and the hour that would follow, that

Washington had begun that road nearly five years before. Out of respect for that truth, Simon, too, dropped to one knee just inside the door, to wait until the General should be ready to end his meditation.

He waited for perhaps five minutes, his hand on his own sword hilt, silently asking for strength to be what Washington needed him to be, praying that they had not misjudged the man. At length Washington sighed deeply and raised his head, glancing back at Simon sidelong and then getting to his feet. He had removed his spurs and put on his apron in Simon's absence, and had unbuckled his sword belt to wrap it around the scabbard, for he had been told he would be required to surrender it at the start of the ritual. As he turned to face Simon, who had risen as he did, his knuckles were white where they gripped the scabbard beneath the hilt.

"Is it time?" he asked quietly, his face very still and taut.

Simon inclined his head. "If you're ready."

Washington closed his eyes briefly, then conjured an attempt at a smile. "I know of nothing further I can do to prepare," he said softly. "Let us begin."

Bowing, Simon turned to open the door, falling in at Washington's left side when they had gone through into the entry hall. As they came before the library door and halted, Washington glanced at Simon in question.

"You are to announce your presence with three distinct knocks," Simon said quietly.

Exhaling audibly, Washington squared his shoulders and knocked three times on the door.

The knock was answered from the other side, after which the door opened inward. The room was a blaze of light compared to the dim entry hall. Silhouetted against that blaze was Prince Lucien de Rohanstuart, in the uniform of the French Army and wearing the breast star and dark green riband of the Order of the Thistle, lifting the tip of the Sobieski sword to Washington's throat.

"You are expected, General Washington," the prince said. "But if you would pass, you must first surrender your sword. May it be the last time you will ever surrender it."

Looking past the prince, Washington set his gaze on the man he knew as the Professor, sitting motionless in the chair far in the east. To him he lifted his sword under the hilt, for the Professor clearly was Master in this place.

"Sir," he said, "I surrender my sword to the Divine Wisdom I believe you represent."

The Master inclined his head.

"I accept your sword in trust, General, and will return it in due time. Please deliver it to Brother Lafayette."

At this cue the marquis stepped out from behind the door, apron-clad like the others, to bow and receive the General's sword. He then turned to walk slowly toward the circle of candles behind the prince, the sword across both hands, passing easily between the candles and across the circle to lay the sword on the altar on the other side. Watching Washington, Simon saw his eyes widen as his gaze followed Lafayette's path and finally registered the designs painted on the floor cloth.

"You see before you a part of the Master Tracing Board upon which you were set some years ago," the Master said. "Advance, if you would be instructed."

The prince had lowered his sword as Washington surrendered his, and now stepped slightly aside to gesture with it, indicating that the General should approach to the edge of the circle. Washington obeyed, apprehension yielding to fascination as he came closer, eyes restlessly searching the symbols painted in the center of the floor cloth, straining to read the mottoes painted in the band outside the stars. He halted with a start as the prince laid the flat of the Sobieski sword against his chest to bar his way.

"Look now and learn, General," the Master said. "Much of what you see before you has come to pass; much is still to come. *Annuit Coeptis*, He hath prospered our undertakings. And *Ex Pluribus Unum*, Out of many, one. You see before you the thirteen stars representing the thirteen colonies, now the thirteen states. The Great Architect hath, indeed, prospered what has begun. And here, before His All-Seeing Eye, building upon the sure foundation of liberty, shall you pledge your faith.

"Your brethren charged you to be America's defender when they named you Commander in Chief. *Dux bellorum* have you become—this nation's war leader. But to be confirmed as champion of her liberties, and eventually to wear the victor's laurel crown, you must understand what it is you take upon yourself. For the victor may claim his crown only by declaring his faith upon the Master Tracing Board."

He indicated the center design, which Simon now could see displayed the All-Seeing Eye and a very literal foundation—a partially built pyramid of thirteen courses, with the Roman numerals spread across the bottom course: MDCCLXXVI, the year of declaring an independence that had yet to be won.

Both symbols held powerful associations among Freemasons. The All-Seeing Eye in a radiant triangle had been one of the first devices to be proposed as part of the Great Seal, immediately after the Declaration of Independence, though no design had yet been finalized, nearly five years after the fact. Simon recalled seeing another All-Seeing Eye engraved on a golden plate that lay atop Joseph Warren's coffin. Remembering Warren, Simon fancied he caught just a fleeting impression of Warren's presence with them tonight, though a part of him dismissed the notion, for only Andrew had ever seen Warren's shade.

"Do you understand, General?" the Master asked softly, cutting off Simon's further speculation.

"I understand what has gone before," Washington said. "I seek no earthly Crown, but only the laurel crown of victory, which comes when Britain has set aside her claim."

The Master inclined his head in approval. "You have spoken well, *Dux bellorum*. Advance now into the fuller presence of The Great Architect and kneel to be invested with the symbols of your leadership, by which you shall come to your goal."

At his words the prince stepped in front of Washington, lifted the Sobieski sword to a position of salute, and did a precise about-face to lead the General into the circle. At the same time Ramsay brought in the kneeling chair and set it on the courses of the unfinished pyramid painted in the center of the circle, he and the prince both fading back then as the Master approached and Washington knelt before him.

"I first present to you the banner under which you have fought, and under which victory shall be obtained," the Master said.

From behind them, moving along the left side of the room, outside the circle of candles, Lafayette brought forward the Continental flag, under which five of those present had fought, and whose design had taken shape half a decade before under guidance of the man presiding and the man who knelt before him. Like the interim banner the General had hoisted on a long-ago New Year's Day in 1776, the present flag had been crafted by Arabella Wallace.

The white of the stripes and the thirteen stars seemed to shimmer in the candlelight as the marquis paraded the flag behind the Master's chair, then turned to process directly toward his Commander in Chief, halting at the Master's left side. He started to dip it to the floor in salute, but Washington suddenly caught up an armful of red-and-white stripes before it could touch the floor, bowing his head to touch it to his lips. A moment he remained thus, then straightened enough to pull it closer and lay his right hand on the blue of the union, with its circle of thirteen white stars.

"May I speak?" he whispered as his eyes sought the Master's.

At the Master's nod Washington straightened, both hands now resting gently on the mass of bunting before him.

"I realize now that your guidance helped to shape this flag," he said, clearly addressing the Master, not merely the Professor. "Nor is it any ordinary flag that you have given us. In other lands the country's colors belong to its king, and his subjects dip it to the ground in his honor. But these United States derive their sovereignty from the people. Americans abase themselves before no man, so it is not fitting that their colors should ever touch the ground."

The Master gazed at him for a moment, expressionless, then inclined his head, controlling a smile.

"Your observation shows great insight," he said quietly. "Have you a pledge to make concerning this flag? If you have not the words, I can direct you."

Inhaling deeply, Washington shook his head and drew a handful of red-and-white stripes to press against his heart.

"I make this solemn pledge, here in the presence of The Great Architect of the Universe: that I shall strive to bring only honor to

this symbol of the nation I have sworn to defend. And while there is breath in my body, I shall never allow it to come to disgrace."

When he had bowed his head to kiss it again, Lafayette slowly raised the flag at a gesture from the Master and circled around to stand behind Washington and slightly to his right. The General kept an edge of it in his hand as the marquis moved, as if to ensure that it should remain close by, releasing it only when Lafayette grounded the staff and let the flag hang close beside him, still within reach, if he should wish to touch it. The General's gaze was ardent and wholly focused as he lifted it again to the elderly, dark-clad man standing before him.

Smiling faintly, the Master inclined his head in a slight bow, then turned to approach the Masonic altar, where he picked up Washington's sheathed sword in both hands, lifted it briefly to the east as if in oblation, then returned to stand once more before the Commander in Chief. As he did so, the prince brought the So-bieski sword from the west of the circle, where he had been guard-ing at Washington's back. Simon, too, moved forward, to stand between the Master and the prince, between the two swords. He had been given no precise words beforehand, but he knew what he wanted to say to Washington, and what must be done before he laid a sword across the General's hands.

"General George Washington, Commander in Chief of the Ar-mies of these United States," he said quietly. "It is given that a champion must have a sword. Had you chosen to accept an earthly Crown, you would have been invested with this ancient and honor-able sword as a symbol of sovereignty." He glanced toward the sword in the prince's hands. "The Sobieski sword has served anointed kings over many generations and presided over great vic-tories, and presently has been sent for precisely this occasion, with the hopes and best wishes of a man who should have worn a Crown, for a man who has set aside his own wants and desires in the service of a greater good."

As he turned his glance to Washington's sword, the Master slowly unsheathed it and sank to one knee, gently laying the scab-bard on the floor as the prince likewise knelt to Simon's other side. As the Master offered Washington's sword between Simon and the General, hilt to the left, supporting it from below, the prince proffered the Sobieski sword in like manner slightly below it, hilt to hilt, blade to blade, parallel but not touching.

Drawing careful breath, Simon extended his hands above the two swords, the left hand above the hilt of the Sobieski sword, the right hand over Washington's blade. His eyes closed as he began to speak.

"Here, in the presence of The Great Architect of the Universe, I invoke the spirit of victory with which this ancient sword has been imbued, over years of honor and valor." His left hand sank to rest lightly on the hilt. "From this sword I call forth an echo of these virtues, and with them I consecrate this younger sword to valor, victory, and honor." His right hand dropped to Washington's blade, stroking lightly down it as he opened his eyes, feeling the power move beneath his hand. "May it be a potent weapon in the hands of him who shall wield it, an echo of the celestial sword of the legions of heaven."

As Lucien quietly withdrew the Sobieski sword, Simon's left hand shifted toward the hilt of Washington's weapon, both his hands now overlapping the Master's, where they supported the sword. He stiffened slightly at the new surge of power that coursed beneath his hands, but he set his focus to channeling it through the sword, feeling serenity gradually replace his own tension, feeling the power permeating every inch of shining steel and gilded hilt.

He knew when the work was finished, felt the Master's acknowledgment of the completion as he pressed the sword upward into Simon's hands and then withdrew. Drawing slow breath, Simon closed his eyes briefly and gathered his next words, praying that the General could contain the power about to be placed in his hands. Lucien had set the Sobieski sword before him with the hilt like a cross, his head bowed before it, and even the Master's head was bowed. Washington's eyes were wide with awe, staring at him in question, and at Simon's nod he slowly extended his open hands.

"Receive the sword of victory," Simon said, lifting it slightly before the General's eyes. "May you wield it in justice and honor and mercy."

With those few words did he lay the sword across Washington's hands. The General stiffened as the metal touched his flesh, bewilderment flickering in the gray-blue eyes. As his fingers closed re-

flexively around the blade and Simon released it, Washington gave a little gasp, weaving a little on his knees. Simon watched him carefully until the reaction passed, though no one touched him, then took the scabbard that the Master passed to him.

"Know when to use the sword," he said, now presenting the scabbard to the General, "but know also when to sheathe it. This is the mark of the true defender."

Pale but composed again, Washington slipped the sword into the scabbard and, at Simon's gesture, buckled it back around his waist with hands that trembled slightly. Meanwhile, a solemn and serene Ramsay had come forward with a small glass flagon, a towel laid across one forearm. As Simon stepped back, to kneel now at Washington's left side, Ramsay moved into the place he had vacated. The General straightened on his knees, setting both hands to the sides of the narrow shelf before him to steady his trembling, his eyes drawn to the flagon Ramsay held.

"In ancient days," Ramsay said, removing the flagon's stopper and handing it to the Master, "anointing was given for many things. Kings and priests were anointed, and sacrifices; but the most important anointing, by far, was the anointing with healing balm that brought relief from pain.

"As physician and healer, then, I give you anointing, not as king or priest or sacrifice, but as a bringer of healing hope to all your people: to bind up the nation's wounds and make whole the broken."

He tipped the flagon briefly against his first two fingers, then pressed them lightly to the General's forehead. At his touch, Washington's eyes closed and he reeled slightly on his knees.

"Be of good cheer, neither be afraid," Ramsay said softly, shifting his hand to the crown of the General's head, and lifting the flagon to pour a small amount of oil there as the powdered head bowed. "The Lord shall prosper thee in thy going out and thy coming in. Be thou consecrated to the healing of thy nation's wounds."

A moment he took to spread the oil slightly, handing off the flagon to the Master, laying his hand over the dampened spot as the sharp, clean smell of cedar permeated the room. Then he gently blotted away the excess with the towel from over his arm, took the flagon back from the Master, and withdrew to his previous place. As he did so, the Master rose to receive the small silver-mounted Bible that Simon now produced from an inside pocket. This the Master laid on the shelf before Washington, stepping back then, so that Washington's view of the All-Seeing Eye was unobstructed.

"Know that you kneel before The Great Architect of the Universe, to whom you have given your homage in times past," the Master said. "I ask you now to place your hands upon this Volume of Sacred Law and to pledge your oath to the cause you have chosen to uphold. The mantle you now assume is a sacred one, whose honor must never be tarnished. And because you never have and never shall take a more sacred obligation, I require you to frame this oath in your own words. Take as long as you need, for words of the heart and the soul are not always quickly summoned."

The instruction left Washington stunned, for he had not expected this. As the Master slowly moved to his right side, there to kneel facing east like the rest of them, Washington stared for a long moment at the painting on the floor cloth before him—at the All-Seeing Eye, the unfinished pyramid with its thirteen courses, at the thirteen stars and the mottoes that told of a nation aborning. When he finally moved his hands to lay them on Lafayette's Bible, the marquis dipped the flag so that it fell about the General's shoulders like the mantle the Master had described.

Washington started at that, but then his right hand lifted to catch an edge of the flag, to bring it reverently to his lips. Then, with his left hand still resting on the Bible and the right pressing a portion of the flag to his heart, enfolded in red-and-white stripes, he bowed his head in prayer. When he finally spoke, his first words were an echo of the Obligations all of them had sworn at other times and in other places, the more potent for being framed within the familiar phrases.

"I, George Washington, of my own free will and accord . . . in presence of Almighty God and this Lodge of most excellent Master Masons, who have come together to do me great service . . . do hereby and hereon . . . in addition to my former Obligations . . . most solemnly and sincerely promise and swear . . ."

He paused here to collect his thoughts as he embarked upon the

unique specifics of tonight's oath, the fingers of his left hand clenching convulsively around the silver mounts of the Bible.

"I most solemnly and sincerely promise and swear that I will keep faith with the Congress of the United States of America and the delegates thereto, from all of the thirteen colonies; that I will faithfully execute the duties of Commander in Chief of the Continental Armies of the United States, both existing now and to be created; that I do this from no desire for personal gain, but for the preservation of the nation's liberties, that we may be free to determine our own future, in what way seems to us best."

He lifted his head slightly, but tears were trickling down his face, and Simon did not think he saw as he went on.

"I further vow and declare that it is not and has never been my desire to achieve an earthly Crown; that I desire only a victor's Crown—not for my own glory, but for the saving of the nation's liberties.

"To all of this do I pledge my life, my fortune, and my sacred honor. So help me God, and keep me steadfast in the due performance of the same."

He bowed his head to kiss the Book, his cheeks wet with tears. When he looked up, he gasped to see Arabella standing directly before him, just inside the ring of candles. Even Simon had not noticed her approach, so engrossed had he been in Washington's words. She had put aside her dark cloak to reveal a flowing white gown in the Grecian style, girded at the waist with her Masonic apron, her unbound hair tumbling dark around her shoulders. The Sobieski sword was in her right hand, an olive branch in her left, and on her head was a laurel Crown. At Washington's awed intake of breath, she moved a step closer.

"I represent the Goddess of Liberty and bear both the sword and the olive branch," she said quietly. "He who would be my champion and win my Crown of victory must wield the sword to gain the blessings of peace. Are you prepared to do so?"

Releasing his handful of flag, Washington laid his right hand with the left atop Lafayette's Bible.

"I am, God aiding me."

"Then go and lay these tokens upon the altar, as further sign of your willingness to take on the burden of my Crown, and pray for strength to bear it to the end, to win the victory it betokens."

She waited while he eased stiffly to his feet, eschewing the assistance Simon or the Master would have offered, then set the tokens in his hands—the sword of battle and the olive branch of peace. He bowed to her before slowly setting off across the painted floor cloth, passing carefully between the two candles directly before the altar. His watchers could not see his face, but they could see the tension in his form as he stood before the altar, head bowed.

At length he gently placed the olive branch atop the square and compasses, then laid the sword across his two hands and set it along the front of the altar. After that he drew to attention, inclining his head stiffly in a formal bow, then turned to come back to them, moving as if in a trance. The Master had risen during his absence and bowed as Washington came back into the circle, gesturing for him to kneel once more, which Washington did.

Solemnly Arabella came to stand before him, slowly reaching to her head to remove the laurel Crown. Washington's gray-blue gaze followed her every movement, his hands once again resting on the silver-mounted Bible. He closed his eyes as she brought the Crown above his head, shuddering as it touched his hair. Before she could withdraw, he gently seized her left hand and kissed it, keeping it briefly in his as he whispered, "Thank you, Sister Wallace."

She smiled and bobbed him a minute curtsy before pulling back and to the side, for Prince Lucien now was moving before him, withdrawing a folded piece of paper from inside his uniform coat.

"Your Excellency," the prince said, bowing slightly as he unfolded the paper. "While you yet rest before this sacred altar, wearing the Crown you have chosen, I am instructed to read you these words from my royal cousin, Charles Edward Stuart.

" 'To General George Washington, Commander in Chief of the American Armies,' " he read. " 'Your Excellency: I have followed your career with great interest and have applauded your forbear-

ance, your devotion to duty, and your courage in the face of great
adversity. My respect for your bold accomplishments and my confidence in your ability are matched only by my warm affection for
the cause you have espoused. It is the vocation of a leader, whether
he be a king, dictator, or something new and not yet named, to be
the guardian of his people's liberties. This is the path you have
chosen, and America is fortunate, indeed, to have such a leader.
Had I been blessed with such service in 1745, my world might be a
far different place; indeed, even your present war might not have
had to be fought.

" 'I regret that fortune has not permitted our paths to cross
directly. Nonetheless, I send you my warmest felicitations and my
most earnest prayers for the success of the American endeavor.
May The Great Architect of the Universe prosper your work
and keep you steadfast in America's service. Yours fraternally,
Charles.' "

As the prince finished reading, hardly an eye was dry among
those who had served Charles Edward Stuart. Washington, who
had not, had buried his face in one hand, the other still clasped
around Lafayette's Bible, as much moved as the rest of them. After
a moment the Master quietly moved before him, casting a glance at
Simon and nodding as he gently set a hand on Washington's
bowed head.

"Rest now, General," he whispered. "This part of your work is
done. Rest now, and sleep."

Washington breathed out with a heavy sigh, the tension going
out of him as he slowly sank down on his hunkers. Simon's arm
around his shoulders kept him upright, steadying the lolling
head as the Master tilted it upward. The General's eyes were
closed. Smiling faintly, the Master plucked a leaf from the laurel
Crown.

"Rest now," he repeated softly, "and let the memory of this past
hour recede until it remains only as a dream. You will never speak
of this dream again, even to those who have shared it with you, but
the essence of what you have pledged tonight will remain with you
always, and will come to mind whenever you smell the scent of
laurel leaves." He crushed the leaf between his fingers and passed it

under Washington's nose. "Breathe deeply of this scent and remember it, and draw strength from the remembrance in all the
years to come."

Washington stirred slightly in Simon's arms as he inhaled deeply
of the scent of laurel, but then he subsided into deep slumber.

Epilogue

Evidence of the night's work was quickly dispersed. While
Ramsay and the prince set about dismantling the Lodge
and restoring the library room to its normal configuration,
Arabella withdrew to change clothes and lay out the cold supper
she had prepared earlier—though she, Ramsay, and Andrew would
not join them. Simon withdrew long enough to fetch Justin from
outside, and together the two carried the sleeping Washington into
the parlor, where Simon remained to keep watch while Justin lent
his assistance in the library. The Master's last act, before withdrawing from Andrew's body, was to draw Lafayette apart for a brief
exchange that left the young marquis sitting dazed and silent on a
chair in the entry hall outside.

Both Lafayette and the Commander in Chief appeared relaxed
and congenial half an hour later, by the time Simon ushered them
into the dining room to sit down to supper. Justin served at table,
as most junior among them, and the prince played on the piano-
forte after they had dined. The tone of their table talk gradually
evolved from affable discourse to good-natured banter, for Lafayette poured generous glasses of a fine vintage claret he had brought
with him from France. If a pensive note occasionally intruded on
the General's animation, it could easily be ascribed to fatigue, or

even anticipation over his young friend's imminent departure. By the time the party mounted up to ride back to headquarters, the two generals were well mellowed with wine.

Lafayette left for Philadelphia the next morning. Little more than two months later, he was to make a triumphant return, riding into Washington's headquarters camp at the head of a crack light cavalry escort.

"Mon général!" he cried, as he threw himself from his horse and ran to embrace him. "Rochambeau has landed! He has brought you the troops that were promised!"

The arrival of more than five thousand French troops marked a major turning point in the war for American independence. Little more than a year later, on October 27, 1781, Washington defeated Lord Cornwallis at the Battle of Yorktown but was denied the satisfaction of receiving the sword of a defeated British general when Cornwallis sent a mere brigadier general as deputy in his place. (Washington countered by directing one of his own brigadiers to accept the surrender.) The British troops marched out with colors cased, to a tune called, "The World Turn'd Upside Down." Yorktown essentially brought an end to the land war, though desultory fighting would continue along the coast and at sea until the official cessation of hostilities in February of 1783.

On April 30, 1789, George Washington became the first President of the new United States, though there were many who would have preferred to crown him King George I of America. Even at the time of his inauguration, differences remained over whether he should be styled "His Highness, the President of the United States of America, and Protector of their Liberties."

But he had gained his laurel wreath—which appeared on American coins as early as 1783 and persisted (as a wreath of wheat) until 1956 on the reverse of the American penny. The All-Seeing Eye in the radiant triangle and the unfinished pyramid of thirteen courses were incorporated into the reverse of the Great Seal of the United States, as were several of the mottoes proposed by "the Professor." Both sides of the Great Seal may still be seen on the reverse of the American one-dollar bill. Washington's likeness is on the face of

the bill, as are remnants of his laurel wreath. Throughout the rest of his life, he remained an active Freemason, serving as Master of his home lodge at Alexandria, Virginia, and promoting Masonic ideals.

Gilbert du Motier, the Marquis de Lafayette, returned to France and attempted to moderate some of the excesses of the French Revolution, but he was never as effective as he had been during those months when he rode at the side of his beloved general and helped change the course of the American war for independence.

Charles Edward Stuart never regained his throne, but he left a legacy of legend for Scottish patriots that endures to this day.

The treasure of Loch Arkaig is believed never to have been recovered.

Numerous sources suggest that the design of Washington's first flag and the Great Seal were inspired by a mysterious figure known only as "the Professor," here conflated with a similar figure who is said to have inspired the signers of the Declaration of Independence. The latter is mentioned by no less a source than Thomas Jefferson.

The Count of Saint-Germain remains a figure of mystery, whose influence was to extend into the French Revolution, the Napoleonic era, and perhaps beyond.

As for the Crown of America—there is little doubt that at some point it was, indeed, offered both to Charles Edward Stuart and to George Washington. The Scottish author John Buchan developed one speculation regarding Charles in his short story, "The Company of the Marjolaine." A colonel named Lewis Nicola wrote to Washington in May of 1782, outlining the grievances of the army and proposing that Washington be designated king—or perhaps some more suitable title. Washington was horrified and replied that "no occurrence in the war has given me more painful sensations than your information of there being such ideas existing in the army."

A third man may have been offered the Crown as well. An unattributed source suggests that in 1786 a committee headed by James Monroe and Alexander Hamilton approached Prince Henry of Prussia, brother of Frederick the Great; but Henry waffled for so

long about whether he wanted to live among the strange and savage Americans that the offer was withdrawn in favor of having a President.

It remains for future generations to determine whether America would have been better served by a government more akin to forms then prevalent in Western Europe or whether the great experiment of democracy will prove the better choice, and that "government of the people, by the people, and for the people shall not perish from the earth."

Historical Afterword

W hen the American colonies began to move toward separation from the Mother Country, the quarrel of the colonists was not with the King but with his ministers. Many and perhaps most Americans were staunch monarchists, loyal to the Crown, and would have been content to remain linked to England but for the growing inclination of Westminster to impose taxes over which the colonists had no say.

The seeds had been sown for a possible alternative monarchy thirty years earlier, when English Crown forces defeated the Highland army of Prince Charles Edward Stuart, son of James Francis Edward Stuart (the de jure King James III of England, called "The Old Pretender") and grandson of James II of England, who had been the last male Stuart to occupy the English throne. (Whether Charles Edward's father was, in fact, the rightful king depends upon which version of his birth one believes. If, as his supporters always maintained, James Francis was truly the son of King James II and Queen Mary of Modena, then his right to the Crown was unquestionable; if, instead, the infant James Francis was smuggled into the Queen's bed in a warming pan to replace a stillborn child, then ousting James II and his false offspring in favor of his elder daughter and her Dutch husband perhaps can be justified. Supporters of the deposed James—Jacobus in Latin—came to be called Jacobites.)

Whatever the true parentage of James Francis Stuart, the "Glorious Revolution" of 1688 expelled James II and his queen from England, along with their infant son, and in 1689 set James's elder daughter Mary and William of Orange (William III of England) on the throne. They had no heirs. Following Mary's death in 1694, William reigned alone until his own death in 1702, when he was succeeded by Mary's sister Anne. Following Anne's death in 1714, also without heir, England turned to the House of Hanover for a non-Catholic successor—which sparked a series of unsuccessful Jacobite risings in 1715, 1719, and finally in 1745, when Prince Charles Edward ("Bonnie Prince Charlie") took up his father's cause and, at Culloden, passed from the realm of historical tragedy into legend.

After Culloden, supporters of the Jacobite cause continued to keep alive the dream of a Stuart restoration for several generations, despite draconian reprisals employed by "Butcher" Cumberland, the younger son of George II, to pacify the Highlands. Hanoverian policy evolved into a systematic campaign to break the Highland chiefs and the ancient clan system and to eradicate the Highland way of life. In addition to executing more than eighty leaders of the rebellion and attainting titles and lands of participants, the government of George II forbade the wearing of the tartan or any other item of distinctive Highland dress and threatened transportation to the American colonies for anyone found continuing to support the "King over the water."

Many Jacobite supporters fled to exile in France with their Prince. Many more emigrated to the New World or were transported there under conditions hardly better than slavery. Jacobite intrigues continued to smolder in Europe, especially in France, where the Stuart cause became closely intertwined with Freemasonry, whose oaths of secrecy provided convenient camouflage. (Freemasonry was to provide a similar cover for secret plotting in the American colonies, as Hanoverian heavy-handedness provoked increasing colonial resentment.) For many years it was hoped that a Stuart restoration might begin in America, serving as a base of

operations from which Charles Edward Stuart might eventually reclaim at least his Scottish throne.

This is the story of a few of those Jacobite exiles who became inextricably intertwined in the shaping of the New Order that was to become the United States of America, and the thread of Freemasonry that bound them to the American cause, and the Unknown Master believed to have directed much of their activity from the other side of the Atlantic—toward what ultimate end, we can only guess. An independent Crown for America was a distinct possibility for many years, with at least two wearers under serious consideration. Exactly how Jacobite kings and Crowns and the thread of Freemasonry actually did figure in the eventual birth of the American Republic probably will never be known for certain, but this is how it might have been. . . .

Partial Bibliography

Background on the American War for Independence

Bernier, Oliver. *Lafayette: Hero of Two Worlds.* New York: E. P. Dutton, 1983.

Elting, John R., ed. *Military Uniforms in America: The Era of the American Revolution, 1755–1795.* San Rafael, Calif.: Presidio Press, for the Company of Military Historians, 1974.

Fleming, Thomas. *Now We Are Enemies: Bunker Hill, the Battle—and Before and After.* London: Victor Gollancz, 1960.

Forbes, Esther. *Paul Revere and the World He Lived In.* Boston: Houghton Mifflin Co., 1942.

Frothingham, Thomas G. *Washington, Commander in Chief.* Boston: Houghton Mifflin Co., 1930.

Gross, Robert A. *The Minutemen and Their World.* New York: Hill and Wang, 1976.

Harris, John. *American Rebels: A Narrative History of the Beginnings of the Revolution.* Boston: Globe Newspaper Co., 1976.

Hume, Ivor Noel. *1775: Another Part of the Field.* London: Eyre and Spottiswoode, 1966.

Ketchum, Richard M. *The Winter Soldiers: George Washington and the Way to Independence.* London: History Book Club, 1973.

———. *The World of George Washington.* New York: American Heritage Publishing Co., 1974.

Knill, Harry. *The Story of Our Flag.* Santa Barbara, Calif.: Bellerophon Books, 1992.

Langguth, A. J. *Patriots: The Men Who Started the American Revolution.* New York: Simon and Schuster, 1988.

Middlekauff, Robert. *The Glorious Cause: The American Revolution, 1763–1789.* New York: Oxford University Press, 1982.

Mollo, John, and Malcolm McGregor. *Uniforms of the American Revolution.* Poole, Dorset: Blandford Press, 1975.

Schwartz, Barry. *George Washington: The Making of an American Symbol.* New York: Macmillan, Free Press, 1987.

Simmons, R. C. *The American Colonies from Settlement to Independence.* New York: David McKay Co., 1976.

Thane, Elswyth. *Potomac Squire.* New York: Duell, Sloan and Pearce, 1963.

Thayer, William M. *George Washington: His Boyhood and Manhood*. London: Hodder and Stoughton, 1883.

Tuchman, Barbara. *The First Salute*. New York: Viking Penguin, 1988.

Wilbur, C. Keith. *The Revolutionary Soldier, 1775–1783*. Old Saybrook, Conn.: Globe Pequot Press, 1969, 1993.

Wills, Garry. *Cincinnatus: George Washington and the Enlightenment—Images of Power in Early America*. New York: Doubleday, 1984.

Jacobite Background

Aronson, Theo. *Kings Over the Water*. London: Cassell, 1979.

Blaikie, Walter Biggar. *Itinerary of Prince Charles Edward Stuart, from His Landing in Scotland July 1745 to His Departure in September 1746*. Edinburgh: Scottish Academic Press, 1975.

Buchan, John. "The Company of the Marjolaine." In *The Moon Endureth*. London: Hodder and Stoughton, 1912.

Chambers, Robert. *History of the Rebellion of 1745*. London: W. & R. Chambers, 1827. Reprint. Edinburgh, 1869.

Chidsey, Donald Barr. *Bonnie Prince Charlie: A Biography of the Young Pretender*. London: Williams and Norgate, 1928.

Daiches, David. *Charles Edward Stuart: The Life and Times of Bonnie Prince Charlie*. London: Pan Books, 1973.

Kybett, Susan Maclean. *Bonnie Prince Charlie: A Biography*. London: Unwin Hyman, 1988.

Lenman, Bruce. *The Jacobite Cause*. Glasgow: Drew Publishing, in association with the National Trust, 1986.

Linklater, Eric. *The Prince in the Heather*. London: Granada, 1986.

McLaren, Moray. *Bonnie Prince Charlie*. London: Rupert Hart-Davis, 1972.

Maclean, Fitzroy. *Bonnie Prince Charlie*. London: Weidenfeld and Nicolson, 1988.

McLynn, Frank. *Charles Edward Stuart: A Tragedy in Many Acts*. London: Routledge, 1988.

———. *The Jacobites*. London: Routledge and Keegan Paul, 1985.

Marshall, Rosalind K. *Bonnie Prince Charlie*. Edinburgh: Her Majesty's Stationery Office, 1988.

Nicholas, Donald. *The Young Adventurer: The Wanderings of Prince Charles Edward Stuart in Scotland and England in the Years 1745–6*. London: Batchworth Press, 1949.

Stevenson, William. *The Jacobite Rising of 1745*. London: Longman Group, 1968.

Tayler, Alistair and Henriette. *The Stuart Papers at Windsor*. London: John Murray, 1939.

Masonic and Esoteric

Barry, John W. *Masonry and the Flag.* After 1923. Reprint. Kila, Mt.: Kessinger
Publishing Co., no date.

Capt, E. Raymond. *The Great Seal: The Symbols of Our Heritage and Our
Destiny.* Thousand Oaks, Calif.: Artisan Sales, 1979.

Day, John. *Memoir of the Lady Freemason.* Cork: 1914, 1941.

Hall, Manly P. *America's Assignment with Destiny.* Los Angeles: Philosophical
Research Society, 1951.

———. *The Secret Destiny of America.* Los Angeles: Philosophical Research
Society, 1944.

Howard, Michael. *The Occult Conspiracy: Secret Societies—Their Influence and
Power in World History.* Rochester, Vt.: Destiny Books, 1989.

Leadbeater, C. W. *The Hidden Life in Freemasonry.* Adyar, Madras, India:
Theosophical Publishing House, 1949. Reprint. Mokelumne Hill, Calif.:
Health Research, 1973.

Morse, Sidney. *Freemasonry in the American Revolution.* 1924. Reprint. Kila,
Mont.: Kessinger Publishing Co., no date.

A Ritual and Illustrations of Freemasonry. London: W. Reeves, c. 1908.

Roberts, Allen E. *George Washington Master Mason.* Richmond, Va.: Macoy
Publishing and Masonic Supply Co., 1976.

W. O. V., *The Three Distinct Knocks, or the Door of the Most Ancient Freemasonry.* London: 1760. Reprint. Kila, Mont.: Kessinger Publishing Co.,
1992.